"HULL BREACH!"
SHOUTED THE HELMSMAN.

The Borg struck again. This time the beam gutted
engineering, moved up and sliced across the left
nacelle. There was a massive explosion as the
nacelle blew clean off. Hulls ruptured throughout
the U.S.S. *Chekov,* and bulkheads on the lower
decks collapsed.

On the bridge everything was in smoking ruins.
Commander Shelby was c
herself up, her face covered
she whispered.

Captain Korsmo was in his c
his head. Blood covered th
and yet, in the semidarkn
nearly dead bridge, there
grim amusement in his ey
Shelby and said, "Picard b

Look for STAR TREK Fiction from Pocket Books

STAR TREK: The Original Series

Final Frontier
Strangers from the Sky
Enterprise
Star Trek IV:
    The Voyage Home
Star Trek V:
    The Final Frontier
Spock's World
    The Lost Years
#1 Star Trek:
    The Motion Picture
#2 The Entropy Effect
#3 The Klingon Gambit
#4 The Covenant of the Crown
#5 The Prometheus Design
#6 The Abode of Life
#7 Star Trek II:
    The Wrath of Khan
#8 Black Fire
#9 Triangle
#10 Web of the Romulans
#11 Yesterday's Son
#12 Mutiny on the Enterprise
#13 The Wounded Sky
#14 The Trellisane Confrontation
#15 Corona
#16 The Final Reflection
#17 Star Trek III:
    The Search for Spock
#18 My Enemy, My Ally
#19 The Tears of the Singers
#20 The Vulcan Academy Murders
#21 Uhura's Song

#22 Shadow Lord
#23 Ishmael
#24 Killing Time
#25 Dwellers in the Crucible
#26 Pawns and Symbols
#27 Mindshadow
#28 Crisis on Centaurus
#29 Dreadnought!
#30 Demons
#31 Battlestations!
#32 Chain of Attack
#33 Deep Domain
#34 Dreams of the Raven
#35 The Romulan Way
#36 How Much for Just the Planet?
#37 Bloodthirst
#38 The IDIC Epidemic
#39 Time for Yesterday
#40 Timetrap
#41 The Three-Minute Universe
#42 Memory Prime
#43 The Final Nexus
#44 Vulcan's Glory
#45 Double, Double
#46 The Cry of the Onlies
#47 The Kobayashi Maru
#48 Rules of Engagement
#49 The Pandora Principle
#50 Doctor's Orders
#51 Enemy Unseen
#52 Home Is the Hunter
#53 Ghost Walker
#54 A Flag Full of Stars

STAR TREK: The Next Generation

Metamorphosis
Vendetta
Encounter at Farpoint
#1 *Ghost Ship*
#2 *The Peacekeepers*
#3 *The Children of Hamlin*
#4 *Survivors*
#5 *Strike Zone*
#6 *Power Hungry*
#7 *Masks*

#8 *The Captains' Honor*
#9 *A Call to Darkness*
#10 *A Rock and a Hard Place*
#11 *Gulliver's Fugitives*
#12 *Doomsday World*
#13 *The Eyes of the Beholders*
#14 *Exiles*
#15 *Fortune's Light*
#16 *Contamination*

STAR TREK®
THE NEXT GENERATION

VENDETTA
THE GIANT NOVEL

PETER DAVID

POCKET BOOKS

New York   London   Toronto   Sydney   Tokyo   Singapore

This book is a work of fiction. Names, characters, places and incidents are either the product of the author's imagination or are used fictitiously. Any resemblance to actual events or locales or persons, living or dead, is entirely coincidental.

The plot and background details of *Vendetta* are solely the author's interpretation of the universe of STAR TREK and vary in some respects from the universe as created by Gene Roddenberry.

An *Original Publication of POCKET BOOKS*

POCKET BOOKS, a division of Simon & Schuster
1230 Avenue of the Americas, New York, NY 10020

STAR TREK is a Registered Trademark of
® Paramount Pictures.

This book is published by Pocket Books, a division of
Simon & Schuster, under exclusive license from
Paramount Pictures.

ISBN: 0-671-74145-4

First Pocket Books printing May 1991

10 9 8 7 6 5 4 3 2 1

POCKET and colophon are registered trademarks of
Simon & Schuster.

Printed in the U.S.A.

This one is for Richard,
the biggest windmill I know

Introduction and Technical Notes

For those who actually keep track of my career and heard about my upcoming projects, no, this isn't the book with Q. That's in a few months.

When *Rock and a Hard Place* came out, I cautioned readers up front that it was going to be somewhat more serious—even slightly morbid—in tone than my previous Trek book, *Strike Zone*. Readers seemed to appreciate this. I feel no such statement of dramatic style is required with *Vendetta*. Considering that the Borg are back in force with this novel, you know this isn't going to be a laugh riot.

Vendetta, as a work, owes its existence to a few people. First and foremost, to Pocket Books editor Kevin Ryan, whose idea this all was. Kevin is also the only person I know who can tell you that a manuscript is great, wonderful, fantastic, the best thing you've ever written, and then fax you six pages of requested changes. He should be in Hollywood. He'd fit in great there.

Then there is the incredibly understanding phalanx of editors with whom I work, who were willing to cut me slack on my monthly comic book assignments so that I could get this novel done. Not that they had much choice, since I had my remarkably rude answering machine message-screening my calls.

There is also my family—wife Myra, and daughters Shana and Guinevere, who have come to understand that the phrase "Daddy's on deadline" means that you tiptoe around the house until the damned thing is done.

Then, of course, there is *Next Generation* itself, celebrating a quarter century of the durability of Gene Roddenberry's dream, which by introducing the formidable Borg, gave us a race that makes the Klingons and Romulans combined look like campfire girls.

And now, something totally alien to my usual writing—technical notes. I found myself leaning very heavily on the *Star Trek Writer's Technical Manual*, that marvelous document created by Rick Sternbach and Mike Okuda that is the official, unvarnished, accept-no-substitute guide for anyone trying to write for the TV show. Whereas usually I give the manual a casual glance in the course of writing a book, to double-check bridge stations or something, with *Vendetta* I kept it to my immediate right and referred to it constantly.

In *Vendetta* you will find discussions of the capabilities of warp drive, phasers and respective settings, setups of the engine room, etc., etc. All of this is taken directly from the *Technical Manual*, with a few extrapolations of my own tossed in along the way. This serves a twofold advantage. First, it gives *Vendetta*, I would hope, a feeling of authenticity. Second, it means that when fans come complaining to me about my depiction of warp speed limits and the like, I can just turn them on Sternbach and Okuda. The *Tech Manual* is the final, official word of the *Star Trek* office, so if you take issue with anything in *Vendetta*, don't gripe to me about it. I just work here.

Special thanks to an advertiser in *Comics Buyer's Guide* whose *nom de plume* I borrowed for a character herein.

And lastly, an acknowledgment to Miguel de Cervantes, who knew squat about warp drive but everything about what drives the human heart.

P.D.

OVERTURE

Chapter One

JEAN-LUC PICARD leaned against a wall and ran his fingers through his mop of thick brown hair.

His feet tapped a vague, disassociated rhythm, more stream-of-consciousness than anything else. His mind was wandering in the way that it often did—analyzing any number of facts, figures, and other bits of information that were tumbling through his head while, simultaneously, drawing together possible connections.

It was called "thinking empirically" by his teachers. According to his father, it was called "being able to see the forest for the trees."

"Step back, gentlemen. Give the young man room."

Picard didn't even glance in the direction of the slightly taunting voice. "Just thinking, Korsmo. No need to make such a fuss over it. Since you do it so rarely, you probably didn't recognize the process."

Korsmo, to the amusement of other cadets nearby, staggered back slightly, as if he'd been stabbed to the heart. "Oh," he moaned, "Oh! The stinging wit of Jean-Luc Picard. Shot to the heart. How can I ever recover?"

Picard shook his head. "Don't you ever take anything seriously, Korsmo?"

Korsmo was tall and lanky, rail-thin. His eating habits were legendary, but his body burned up the food so fast that he never gained weight. His black hair hung just in front of his eyes, and he would periodically brush it back out unconsciously. "There's a difference between being serious and being dead. You should learn it, Picard. You're the biggest stiff in the Academy. Legend has it, the only bigger stiff in the Academy's history was James Kirk."

"I would consider it an honor," said Picard archly, "to be placed in such august company."

The corridor outside the classroom was becoming more crowded as the rest of the cadets began to show up, one by one, for the lecture. They watched with amusement the cautious and long-accustomed sparring between Picard and Korsmo. It had been going on since practically the first day of the first year. The two men weren't exactly friends, but they weren't exactly enemies. Instead they saw things in each other, instinctively, that they simultaneously disliked and envied. After three years the give and take of their routine had an almost comfortable familiarity.

"Your concern is heartwarming, Korsmo," Picard continued. "Some of—"

His voice trailed off as he saw something at the far end of the hallway.

There was a woman there. She seemed almost insubstantial, fading into the shadows at the corridor end. Picard noticed immediately that she was not wearing a Starfleet uniform, but, instead, some sort of almost diaphanous gown.

Though Picard had never seen her before, there was something about her, something that made her seem as if she were there, but not—as if his mind were telling him that he was seeing nothing at all.

Korsmo was saying something and Picard wasn't paying the least bit of attention. Korsmo realized it and tapped Picard on the shoulder. "You got a problem, Picard?"

Picard's gaze strayed to Korsmo for a moment, refocussed, and then he said, "Who's that woman?"

"What woman?" asked Korsmo.

He turned and pointed to the end of the corridor, and there was no one there.

Picard's mouth moved for a moment, and for the first time that Korsmo could recall, Jean-Luc Picard actually seemed flustered. "She was there," he said. "She was right there."

The other cadets were looking where Picard was pointing and turning back to him with confusion. "One of you must have seen her," said Picard urgently.

Korsmo was trying to keep the amusement out of his voice, but not all that hard. "This another example of the famed Picard humor . . . no, wait. I just remembered. We've never seen an example of the famed Picard humor, so who could tell?"

"Dammit, Korsmo, this is serious. There's some woman walking around here, and she's not authorized and—"

Korsmo, a head taller than Picard, took him firmly by the shoulders. But his words were addressed to the others. "Gentlemen . . . our fellow cadet states that security has been breached. His claim must be followed up. Spread out, gentlemen and ladies. Let's see if we can turn up Picard's mystery woman."

There were brisk nods, the youthful banter quickly being set aside, as a potential problem presented itself. Picard felt a brief flash of gratitude to Korsmo, but realized within short order that Korsmo's main interest was trying to show him up.

In this, it appeared, Korsmo succeeded. The cadets deployed themselves with admirable efficiency, and had the entire floor covered in less than a minute. But there was no sign anywhere of the alleged intruder.

Picard was shaking his head in utter befuddlement. He paced furiously in place—just a small area, forward three steps and back three steps. When Korsmo approached, he didn't have to say anything. It was clear from the taller cadet's attitude that no one had been found, and that left Picard looking like something of a fool.

"She was there," said Picard stubbornly. The others were gathering around now, but again Picard said firmly, "I saw her. I'm not imagining it."

"I checked with the front security area," said Korsmo. "No non-Starfleet personnel were granted access to the premises today, not even for a casual visit."

"I don't think Jean-Luc is claiming she was supposed to be here," offered up Cadet Leah Sapp. Picard flashed a quick smile at her. Leah was always the first to step in on Picard's side when there was any kind of dispute. He knew damned well that she had a bit of an infatuation with him, but he didn't take it seriously. He took nothing seriously except his studies. Gods, maybe he *was* the biggest stiff in the Academy at that.

"No, I'm not," Picard agreed. "All I'm saying is that perhaps we should—"

There was a loud, throat-clearing *harrumph,* and the cadets turned towards the source. Professor Talbot was standing in the doorway of the classroom, his arms folded, his dark face displaying great clouds of annoyance.

"I am *not,*" he rumbled, "in the habit of waiting for classes to come to me in their own sweet time."

"We were trying to help Cadet Picard find a woman," Korsmo said helpfully.

Picard rubbed his forehead in a faint, pained expression.

"Indeed," said Talbot thinly. "Cadet Picard, kindly maintain your sex life on your own time, not mine."

"I . . . yes, sir," said Picard, swallowing the response he really wished to make. Something told him that any response would not do him one shred of good and, quite likely, a fairly large dollop of harm.

The students filed into Professor Talbot's course on Starfleet history. The classroom was meticulously climate-controlled, and yet it always felt stuffy to Picard. As he took his seat, he pondered the probability that the perceived stuffiness was pretty much in his head. Somehow, talking about great adventures and sweeping voyages of great Starfleet officers was stifling when it was discussed in a classroom. Picard didn't want to sit around and review the adventures of others. He wanted others to be studying *his* adventures.

Intellectually, he knew the impossibility of the latter without a solid grounding in the former. If he could not learn how to imitate the successes and avoid the failures of his predecessors, then what sort of Starship captain (for such was his goal) would he be?

A dead one, most likely.

He was snapped immediately back to attention by Talbot's brisk statement of, "Picard . . . you have, of course, been reviewing the topic of the life and career of Commodore Matthew Decker, have you not?"

Picard was immediately on his feet, his shoulders squared, his gaze levelled and confident. "Yes, sir," he said with certainty.

7

"Would you care to tell us of the commodore's final mission?"

"Yes, sir." There might have been times when Picard grated on the nerves of other students with his singlemindedness and utter devotion to making a name for himself in the fleet. These things preyed on him and sometimes made him wonder—there, in the darkness of his quarters at night, when there was no one around except he himself and his uncertainties—whether he would ever be able to sufficiently command the respect of others that was so necessary to become a starship captain. Such self-doubt, however, never existed when it came to pure academics. On facts and history and raw information, he was always on top of his game.

"Commodore Decker's ship, the *Constellation,* had encountered a planet-destroying machine," Picard continued. "It came from outside the galaxy and, using planetary mass as fuel, was progressing through the heart of our galaxy as part of a perpetual program of destruction."

"Go on," said Talbot, arms folded.

"His ship was incapacitated, and he beamed his crew down to a planet which was subsequently destroyed by the planet-eater. With the aid of the *Enterprise,* NCC-1701, the so-called doomsday machine was incapacitated, but not before Commodore Decker sacrificed his life in combat against it."

"What were the details of that combat?" asked Talbot.

Picard frowned. *"Enterprise* logs merely state that Decker died heroically. Details were not recorded."

"Speculation."

Picard ran through the various possible scenarios in his mind, any and all that made sense. Finally he said, "It was the destruction of the *Constellation* within the

8

bowels of the planet-killer that caused its deactivation. That much is recorded. I would surmise that Commodore Decker, choosing to go down with his ship, piloted the *Constellation* himself into the machine. *Enterprise* transporters might well have suffered damage in the course of the battle with the planet-killer, and were unable to transport him back in time."

"A very reasonable surmise, cadet," said Talbot. He slowly circled his podium. "Since, as you so accurately noted, the details are not recorded, we can never know for sure. Can we?"

"No, sir," said Picard, and started to sit down.

He froze in a slightly ridiculous, half-seated position, because Talbot was glowering at him in an expectant manner that seemed to indicate he wasn't quite finished with the cadet. Unsure of what to do, Picard stood fully once more, waiting patiently for instruction from his professor.

"Do you think Decker felt guilty, Picard?"

Picard raised a questioning eyebrow. Somehow the thought of guilt or concern or any other human feeling never seemed to enter into the study of history. One studied facts, figures, distant events, and strategies—not people.

"I'd never given it any thought, sir."

"Think, now," invited Talbot. "We've all the time in the world." Talbot gestured expansively and then leaned back in a carefully cultivated casual manner.

Picard didn't let his gaze wander. The last thing he wanted to do was glance at bemused fellow classmates. "You are referring to guilt over the deaths of his crew."

Talbot merely nodded, waiting for Picard to continue.

"The commodore made the correct decision," said

Picard. "Given the same circumstances, it would be perfectly in order for him to do it again. Therefore, he had nothing over which to feel guilty."

"Even though his people died."

"Yes, sir."

"Even though he could doubtlessly hear their cries of anguish as the planet that was supposed to be their haven was cut to pieces beneath their feet."

Talbot's voice was laden with disdain, but Picard refused to back down. One of the first lessons in command school—*the* first lesson, in fact—was that when you made a decision, you stuck to it. Nothing eroded crew confidence as fast as waffling.

"Even though, yes, sir."

Talbot continued to circle his desk, absently rapping his knuckles on the surface, as was his habit. "I will pray for you, Picard, that you never have to find out firsthand what it is to lose a crew. But I fear the prayers are in vain, because space is a vast and unforgiving mistress. She does not treat the overconfident especially charitably."

Picard did not say anything. No response seemed required, or appropriate.

Confidence. Well, that he most certainly had. And the thought of ever losing a crew was an alien one to Picard. That sort of thing happened to commanders who were unprepared, who were caught short or flatfooted somehow. The way to avoid such a fate was, quite simply, preparation, preparation, and more preparation. And that was a commitment that Jean-Luc Picard was more than ready to make.

"Sit down, Picard," said Talbot, with a trace of his familiar impatience.

Picard did so, very obediently. As always, there was a small, inward sigh of relief that any cadet always gave upon surviving a grilling by Talbot. In such circumstances one always felt that he had come away lucky. . . .

Picard frowned. "Not far," he said slowly.

Talbot had been in the middle of a sentence and stopped, his mouth moving a moment before it registered that the brain was no longer sending down words. No one, in the course of the semester, had ever had the temerity to interrupt Talbot. Indeed, it had certainly not been Picard's intention now. This mattered not at all.

There was an aura of anticipation in the room as the other cadets turned with slow incredulity towards Picard. He had been so lost in thought that the perilous nature of his situation was only just dawning on him.

Talbot was slowly coming up the stairs toward him in those ominous, carefully measured strides he effected when he was about to disembowel some helpless student. His heels clicked rhythmically on the steps, one by one, each *click* being allowed to sound and echo and trail off to be replaced by the next, like the steady drip of a faucet.

Click.
Click.
Click.

He stopped at the aisle in which Picard was seated and just stood there, stood there like a vulture or some other bird of prey attracted by the smell and sight of dead meat.

That, Picard realized with dim dread, was what he apparently was—dead meat.

"Did you," said Talbot, in a quiet voice tinged with menace, "inter*rupt* me? Because if you did, it had best be something most important. Perhaps you have abruptly determined one of the great secrets of the universe, or even divined the eternal mystery of how cadets believe that they can speak out with temerity."

"I . . ." Picard licked his suddenly dry lips. It seemed as if all the moisture from his body had left him and instead concentrated itself in his boots. "I was thinking out loud, sir."

"Thinking," said Talbot. He draped his hands behind his back theatrically. "And would you care to tell us just what you were thinking about?"

Picard quickly glanced around the class, feeling that if he could, just for a moment, connect with his fellow students he could draw some sort of emotional support from them. But no. Instead there was cold amusement in their eyes. Picard had hung himself out to dry, and the last thing any of them had any intention of doing was to help bring in the wash.

For the first time, Jean-Luc Picard had a fleeting taste of what the loneliness of command would be like.

"I was just thinking," said Picard, in a voice that seemed barely connected to his own, "that the planet-eater could not have come from very far outside our galaxy. For example, it could not have come from, say, the Andromeda galaxy to ours. Instead, it had to come from some point not too far beyond the galactic rim."

"And how," said Talbot, "did you come to that conclusion?"

"Well, it's . . ." Picard cleared his throat. He desperately wanted to cough, but that would have sounded too nervous. "You told us that the planet-eater did just that . . . it ate planets as sustenance. It needed mass to consume in order to perpetuate its fuel supply. But in between galaxies, there would have been no planetary masses for the planet-eater to consume. There is no record that the planet-killer possessed any sort of trans-galactic speed; in fact, the *Enterprise* paced it without much difficulty. So if we assume that it was traveling at standard speeds, it would have run out of fuel during any attempts to traverse galactic distances.

"Now, of course, once its fuel supply was depleted, it would have kept on going, since a body in motion tends to stay in motion. But that simple motion would never have been enough to penetrate the energy barrier at the rim of our galaxy—the one the original *Enterprise* ran into. Without some sort of internal propulsion system, the planet-killer would easily have been repulsed by the barrier and would never have managed to enter. And it no longer would have had a propulsion system because, as the old Earth saying goes, it would have run out of gas."

"You are conversant with old Earth sayings?" asked Talbot neutrally.

"Yes, sir," said Picard. "My father uses them constantly. Something of a traditionalist."

"And is there, as I recall, an old Earth saying about speaking only when spoken to?"

Picard felt the blood drain from his face, but he refused to look down; dammit, he would not look down. Instead, he met Talbot's level gaze and said simply, "Yes, sir."

"Good. Remember it in the future." He turned away, then stopped and looked at Picard thoughtfully. "Good point there, by the way. I daresay it forms the basis for a research paper or three. Nice thinking, Picard."

"Thank you, sir."

"Try to make a habit of nice thinking, and you might prove to be not too much of an embarrassment to Starfleet in the future."

Picard sat without another word. He glanced over

at Korsmo, feeling a measure of triumph. Korsmo merely shrugged expansively at him in a *Yeah, so, big deal* manner. Picard sighed inwardly. It was utterly impossible to impress the gangling fellow cadet. Still, Picard could allow himself those small moments of triumph, and in this instance, he was quite content to give himself a mental pat on the back.

And then he saw her again.

She was there, just at the top of the other stairs, at the far side of the room. All cadet eyes were on Picard, or just starting to look away from him. No one saw her, and she was already starting to glide out the door like a shadow.

Picard stood so quickly that he banged his knee on the top of his desk. He gave a short yelp, and Talbot spun on the stairs so quickly that, for a brief moment, he almost toppled down them. He grabbed a railing in support and snapped in exasperation, "Oh, what is it *now,* Picard?"

Picard's head snapped around and then back to the rear of the room. She was gone again, dammit, *gone again.* Not this time, though.

"Permission to be excused, sir; I feel quite ill," said Picard. He grabbed his stomach for emphasis.

Talbot merely raised an eyebrow and inclined his head slightly. Delaying no further than was necessary, Picard grabbed up his padd and shot up the steps, two at a time.

He burst out into the hallway, moving so quickly that he almost banged into the doors, which opened barely in time. The hallway was empty. He glanced left, then took off to his right, running down the hallway as fast as he could, the youthful muscles of his legs propelling him as if he were entered in a cross-country dash.

He got to the end of the corridor and saw it was a

dead end. He spun and looked back. Nothing. Not anywhere.

"What in hell is going on around here?" he whispered to himself.

Picard lay there in bed, staring up at the ceiling.

He'd left the window open this night, welcoming the vagrant breeze blowing in from the San Francisco Bay. It rolled over the bare skin of his chest and caressed it. His hands were folded behind his head, his pillow propped against the wall to one side. Whenever he wanted to think instead of fall asleep, he always did that. He fancied that it aided blood circulation to his brain, and his brain needed all the help it could get, he figured.

Was he losing his mind? Was he?

He was certain he had seen her, yet no one else had. Was it possible that she was some sort of vision appearing only to him? There was a word for something like that. Yes, there certainly was, he thought grimly. The word was *hallucination*. Not a pretty word, but certainly an accurate one. He was hallucinating. That was just great, just fabulous. The strain of his course load and his drive to succeed was threatening to drive him over the edge.

No—he refused to believe that. He had worked too hard, come too far, to fall prey suddenly to some sort of arcane mental distraction. He was not imagining it, blast it—he had seen her. Certainly she'd had an air of unreality about her. But that didn't mean anything.

Hell, there were theories that the only things in the universe that were real were those things mankind considered unreal. If that were indeed the case, though, then she was unquestionably one of the most real things he'd ever encountered.

He sighed and let his mind wander. And even

though he had felt wide awake a moment before, he felt the familiar haze settling on his mind, that dark cloud that told him sleep would be forthcoming shortly.

He thought that far off he could hear the waters splashing around the great tower legs of the Golden Gate Bridge. The air smelled of the sea, and he could almost sense the slow rolling of the waves. That was the great difference between captaining a sailing ship and captaining a starship. You couldn't even feel the motion of a space vessel. You could hear the distant thrumming of its engines, and the stars would speed past you—dazzling points of light—but there was no gentle rocking. There was no riding up to the crest of one wave and sliding down to the next.

Sea captains sailed by the stars. So did starship captains. The difference was that the latter waved to the stars as they went past.

In his semi-dreaming state, the wind seemed to come up even stronger. He tried to prop himself up on his elbows, but it was as if all strength had left his body. Fatigue had settled in on every joint. He'd been pushing himself mercilessly over the past weeks, and perhaps his body had simply shut down, refusing to do any more of his bidding until he had gotten a proper night's sleep. Some commander, he thought through the spreading haze. How could he command a crew when he couldn't even boss his own body around?

The wind grew ever stronger, and it seemed mournful, as if a million souls were moaning at once, crying out to him. Their long, icy fingers were stroking him now, and with each caress came a cry in his head of *Help us, save us, avenge us; do not forget us—never forget us.*

Picard felt a chill knife through him, and he trembled as if in the presence of something beyond his comprehension. His teeth chattered involuntarily. Madness. His teeth had never chattered in his entire life.

He shut his eyes, as if doing so would still the voices in his head. They pervaded him, invaded him, and he cried out once, ordering them away with a sense of authority that he was only just beginning to feel.

When he opened his eyes, she was there.

It was as if she had stepped sideways from another time. She stared at him with luminous eyes that seemed to radiate a cold darkness. Her skin was dark, quite dark, and her eyes were rounded and slightly farther apart than usual, but they merely enhanced her exotic quality. Her black hair hung down low, to her hips, and seemed to be moving constantly, like a waving field of ebony wheat. Her dress swirled about her, and when she spoke, her voice carried that same, faint whisper of the souls that cried out to her.

"Of course," she said from everywhere and nowhere. "Of course. From just beyond our galaxy. That's where it came from. That's why it was created. To combat them."

"Combat who?" said Picard in confusion. Again he tried to sit up, and again his body scoffed at his efforts. The wind whipped his words away, and yet he knew she heard him. "I don't understand."

"You do not have to," she said. "It is enough that *I* do. It is enough that I heard your wise words. And that's why I've come here now: to thank you for your insight. You may have done greater things than you can imagine." Her voice resonated low, and it was the sound of his mother whispering to him when he was an infant crying in the night. And it was the voice of the first girl he'd ever kissed, and of his first lover moving beneath him and whispering his name in low heat, and it was the voice of the stars calling to him, and the voice of the wind and the waves, and everything that was female that ever called to him and summoned him and nurtured him. . . .

And he forced himself to sit up, stretching out an arm towards her, his fingers grasping. The edges of her garment seemed to dance near him and then away, just beyond reach.

"I will find its origins," she said. "And I will find them. And I will stop them."

"What *them?*" cried out Picard. He thought he was screaming at the top of his lungs, above the howling of the wind.

"I pray you never learn, Jean-Luc," she said. "I pray you never learn of the ones without souls. I pray to the gods who do not exist and do not care, and who have forsaken me and my kind."

Every aspect of her was seared into his mind: every curve of the body that revealed itself through the flowing gown; the tilt of her chin, the high forehead, the almost invisible eyebrows; the pure, incandescent beauty of her that was a palpable thing.

"Beware the soulless ones," she told him. She took a bare half-step back, but it was enough to put her firmly beyond his reach.

His heart cried out because, for just a brief moment, his fingers had grazed the exquisite fabric of her dress. He wanted to pull it from her, to pull her to him, and yet at the same time he felt as if to do so would have been blasphemy.

"Who are the soulless ones?" he cried out.

"The destroyers. The anti-life. The soulless ones. They will destroy you, as they destroyed my kind. As they will destroy all kinds. But I will stop them." Her voice was dark and filled the air with ice. "I will stop them, no matter how long it takes, and no matter how far I must travel."

She stepped forward quickly, between his outstretched arms, and kissed him on the forehead. When her lips brushed against him, it was as if an icicle had been dragged across it. She floated back just as fast, her swirling skirts concealing her movements.

The wind and the chill were everywhere, everywhere, and yet Picard forced himself to stand, forced himself from bed and brought his arms up against the brutal slamming of the wind. "Who are you?" he shouted, and again, *"Who are you?"*

She floated towards the door and stopped momentarily to turn a gaze on him that was ancient beyond belief.

"I am pain," she said. "I am loss. I am grief." And then her voice became diamond hardness, and she threw wide her arms and cried out into the wind, into the souls that chorused with her, *"I am implacable, unstoppable! I am passion made into fury, love twisted to hate! I am vendetta!"*

The wind came up and knocked Picard back. He stumbled over his bed, and his head smashed into the wall with a sickening thud. He slid down onto his pillow, and even then, all he wanted was one last glimpse of her.

Vendetta whispered in his mind, and then he passed out.

When he awoke in the morning, his blankets were twisted around him, and despite the coolness in the air, there was a thin film of perspiration all over his body.

The dream of the previous night had not faded with the morning sun, nor would the recollection diminish in the succeeding years, although naturally some of the immediacy was lost as time went on.

He never told anyone of the events of that night. At night he would sometimes lie awake, waiting for her to reappear, waiting for her to return and explain the puzzling descriptions of "soulless ones," and of that mysterious self-description.

He made a study of all the events surrounding the planet-killer, including the frustrating open-ended question of the nature of its origin. The theory was that it had been created by one of two great races locked in combat. But what races? Why were there no traces of them? Had they both wiped each other completely from existence?

Questions. These and dozens more, none of which he was able to satisfactorily answer throughout his Academy career. Eventually he moved on to other things, and the questions were forgotten.

But not the biggest question.

Every so often he would listen to the winds, but they would not call to him again after that night, and they never whispered that word. The word that would haunt him as much as the woman who came to him that night:

Vendetta.

ACT ONE

Chapter Two

DANTAR THE EIGHTH looked across the table at Dantar the Ninth with total satisfaction, his antennae twitching slightly in approval. Dantar the Ninth, for his part, was preparing for the act of drawing a well-honed knife across the torso of the carefully prepared zinator, the animal's lifeless eyes staring up at Dantar the Eighth and his family.

It was an extended family, to be sure, by human standards. By the standards of the Penzatti, the race of which Dantar was a member, it was merely average. Smaller than average, in fact—thirteen family members, including the three spouses and assorted children. Yes, smaller indeed. Dantar the Eighth was occasionally the butt of jibes from his fellow workers, and he brushed off such japes with brisk comments about quality versus quantity. Secretly, though, he toyed with the idea of acquiring yet another mate, or perhaps simply producing more children with the ones he had. So many choices for a healthy head of a Penzatti family.

Dantar the Ninth, eldest son of Dantar the Eighth,

was taking his carving responsibility quite seriously. The zinator had been meticulously prepared by his mother, anointed with all the proper scents and spices for this day of appreciation to the gods. Dantar the Ninth had not suspected for a moment that his father would be permitting him to perform the actual carving.

He paused a moment, taking a deep breath, his tongue moving across his dry green lips. His three-fingered hand, wrapped around the blade of the knife, was trembling ever so slightly. But to Dantar the Ninth, it felt as if a massive tremor had seized hold of him and was shaking him for all he was worth. His graceful antennae were straight out and stiff with tension. In his other hand was the long, two-pronged fork, prodding carefully at the pink, uncooked zinator skin—deliciously, delicately raw—and every member of his family was watching and waiting for him to *do* something, already.

It was not as if it were such a difficult act. Just draw the knife across, start carving up. The beast was *dead* already, for pity's sake; he just had to slice it to be eaten. What he was carrying on himself was the weight of expectations, of tradition, the father passing the responsibility on to the son. Each cut had to be perfect, each slice precise, each . . . .

He felt a hand resting gently on his forearm. He turned to look at his father, who squeezed his arm tightly and said, not unkindly, "I know how you feel. If you can't do it . . ." And he deliberately allowed his voice to trail off.

Stung, Dantar the Ninth said, "I can do it just fine, father," and his antennae twitched in annoyance. He turned back to the zinator and briskly drew the razor-sharp blade across the creature's neck.

Wholly unexpectedly, blood spurted forth and

splashed across Dantar the Ninth's crisp white tunic. He flinched and rapped out an oath, which drew giggles from his younger sisters.

"Children!" snapped their father.

"Dantar said some bad words," said the youngest of the sisters, Lojene. She was always the one who could be counted on to tattle on any of her siblings.

"Yes, I know," said their father, "and he shouldn't have. But . . . it was understandable." He had picked up a napkin and was dabbing it against his son's tunic, soaking up some of the blood. "Still some kick left in this one, eh, son?"

Dantar the Ninth grinned sheepishly, and the understanding smiles from the rest of his family relaxed him. It reminded him that this was supposed to be a time of appreciation and thanks and warm family atmosphere. There really wasn't any need for tension.

He took into himself the aura of friendliness and good feelings that surrounded him and told himself that this moment would last forever in his memory.

And that was when the sirens began.

There was no noise in space, of course, so everything that travelled through space, naturally, passed noiselessly.

But the object that was cruising toward the homeworld of the Penzatti cut through space with far more than the simple silence of a vacuum. There was more to it than that. It moved with the silence of oncoming death.

It was massive, the size of a small moon. It made a statement in its presence, in its size, and in its very shape, for it was a cube—a perfectly formed cube with lights glittering here and there in its machine exterior.

There was no elegance to it, no grace. When humanoids created ships there was always the concept—expressed in different ways through different stylings—that they were vessels designed to glide through the spaceways. Frequently there was a suggestion of wings, ranging from the outsweeps of Klingon or Romulan ships, to the swanlike grace of the nacelles on a Federation starship. There was frequently a forward projection as well, to symbolize—unconsciously or not—the idea of hurling oneself forward into the abyss.

But this huge cube ship disdained such concepts and self-expression . . . or, in so disdaining, actually reflected with unintentioned accuracy the spirit of the creatures inhabiting it: creatures with mechanized souls and hearts that had the same emotional content as did the guts of a smoothly running watch.

Their minds—their great, unified minds—clicked with that watchlike precision. And, as with a watch, they cared nothing about the past and nothing for the future. They existed only for the *now,* the eternal, ever-present *now.* Anything that had happened in the past was not dwelled on, and anything that could occur in the future was not contemplated.

The past was irrelevant.

The future was irrelevant.

Only the here and now mattered.

The squareness of their ship was, therefore, the ultimate expression of their philosophy, if such a word as *philosophy* could be applied to beings so incapable of contemplating shadings of human imagination.

Their ship made a statement, much like the ships of humanoid beings. Such ships modelled themselves on nature. But a perfect cube did not exist in nature. It had to be manufactured, carefully and meticulously conceived with the same watchlike precision that drove them on. It possessed no beauty or elegance, but instead, machine-like efficiency.

It was a ship that said they were beyond nature. That nature was irrelevant. That beauty was irrelevant. That elegance was irrelevant.

Everything was irrelevant except their own, steady, unrelenting perfection.

There was a slight course correction required, and the great vessel accomplished it with the speed of unified thought.

This was the second Borg ship to penetrate into this part of the galaxy. The first had actually been destroyed. It was the first major defeat that could be recalled in the unified memory of the whole. Again, though, they did not dwell on the past or the future. There was never any need.

The past could only hold two things, after all: failure and success. Failure could be something as simple as one of their number falling before a weapon, or something as large as hundreds of their number being tricked into self-destruction. In such instances there was no need to contemplate them, because the great mind instantaneously adjusted itself so that such gambits or methods of force could not be used again. Whereas humans might dwell on where to place blame, or even mourn the circumstances that could have brought such things to pass, these were utterly irrelevant concerns.

As for success—that was not irrelevant. That was simply . . . inevitable.

Madness reigned on the homeworld of the Penzatti.

The planetary defense system had immediately alerted the government the moment that the intruder had entered their space. Military heads promptly assembled to try and determine the nature of the attacker, and the best way that they could respond. The specifics of the ship, its dimension and size, were fed into the planetary computers.

The computers were the pride and joy of the great Penzatti, the finest and most advanced computerized minds ever developed. They surpassed by light-years even the computers that aided Federation starships. The Penzatti had not wished to share this technology with the Federation because of the arrogant assertion that the UFP was, as Penzatti top scientists put it, "Not quite ready for it."

The computers oversaw all defense systems, teaching systems, and regulatory systems—everything that the Penzatti had, at one time, bothered themselves with. And now—definitely—seemed to be a time when the great brains of the computers would be needed the most. The sheer *size* of the invader, the aura of merciless power that clung to it like a canker, was positively overwhelming.

The great mechanical minds that advised the Penzatti spit back an identification in less than a second—two, simple, haunting words:

THE BORG

Now the Penzatti military braintrust was not alarmed. Certainly they had heard of the destruction and devastation that the dreaded Borg had inflicted upon other parts of the Federation. But other parts were not the Penzatti, whose mighty computers could easily and effortlessly solve the problem of the Borg. Difficulties imposed upon other races were not difficulties that would faze the mighty Penzatti. Especially not on this day of days, the day on which the mighty Penzatti gave thanks to their great gods for making them Penzatti, rather than a lesser race.

All of this occurred to the great military leaders of the Penzatti, until two more chilling words appeared

on the great computer screen of the great computer.
Two words that sounded the death knell of a people.
And the words were:

AT LAST

Outside the house of Dantar there was pandemonium. Inside the house of Dantar it wasn't much better.

Children were crying, or were shouting out questions in confusion. They didn't understand anything of what was happening. In truth, their leaders in the faraway capital city didn't have much better comprehension.

Dantar the Eighth grabbed his eldest son's arm and swung the boy around, looking for some sign of fear, some indication of just how much he could trust his son at this moment when a crisis of global importance appeared to be hanging over them. Everywhere was the unyielding, pounding klaxon of the warning sirens.

The boy's face was set and determined. Dantar the Eighth gave a mental nod of approval. To be flustered over the carving up of some pointless meal that it seemed none of them would ever taste—that was acceptable. Now, though, when a genuine situation of danger had arisen, now was the time when he needed his son to be a man, to become a man before his time. Of course, Dantar thought bleakly, it was possible that his son's time might never come.

The last time that klaxon had sounded was twenty years ago, during a major attack by the Romulans. The mighty defensive computers of Penzatti—the omnipotent brain of his world—had conceived and executed a plan of attack and counterattack, and it had succeeded. But there had been casualties—*gods,* had there been casualties, including Dantar the Seventh and Sixth.

Dantar the Eighth could not dwell on that now. He tried to ignore the crying of his wives and other children and instead looked his son in the eyes. The boy's antennae were quivering fiercely.

"We must be brave, my son," said Dantar the Eighth. His son nodded in quick agreement. "Our family and our people need to defend themselves. Down below us—"

"The weapons bay," said Dantar the Ninth. All of the more well-to-do families of the Penzatti kept a well-stocked weapons bay. The Romulan invasion had left deep mark and scars that never quite healed. "I'll get down there immediately."

He turned and headed to the lower portions of the house. Dantar the Eighth, meantime, shoved his way through the pawing and grasping hands of his family. They wanted to hold him, embrace him, clutch at him and plead for him to tell them that there was nothing wrong, that everything was going to be all right. However, he had no time to waste with such matters. He muttered quick assurances as well as he could before pushing through and going to the computer screen that hooked him in—along with the rest of the Penzatti families—with the great computer mind of their planet.

He placed his three tapering fingers into the identifying slots, and the screen glowed to life. He expected to see the usual three-cornered emblem of the Penzatti appear on the screen, along with a message of personal greeting.

Instead there were simply two words, which he stared at and still did not comprehend.

"'At Last'?" he murmured. "At last *what?*"

The military minds of the great Penzatti were at a loss to comprehend. The first thing that occurred to them was to form a committee to study the meaning that those words might have. In the meantime, impatient with waiting around while various attachés scurried about like headless creatures, the supreme military head went into his private office. He closed the door behind him and, from within his private office, went one step farther into his small, private access room that enabled him to tap all facets of the computer at once. It was like a mechanical womb, in a sense, and the supreme military head felt like a confused child, returning to the maternal protection for answers to confounding questions.

He logged into his private mode with the computer and demanded to know the meaning of this odd pronouncement.

When he came out from his private conference with the computer, his face was dark, dark green. He crossed his office, his booted feet noiseless on the plush carpeting, almost as noiseless as the powerful Borg ship that was approaching his world at incredible speeds—his world that he had sworn to protect, but no longer could.

The computer had told him what "AT LAST" meant. The computer had told him just exactly whose world it was, and whose world it was going to be. The computer had told him who was in charge, and who was going to be in charge, and who was going to be obsolete. And finally the computer told him exactly which life forms were going to be welcome.

And which weren't.

The supreme military head sat down in his large, comfortable chair and looked out his window. A spot that seemed to be cube-shaped had appeared against the sun and was rapidly increasing in size. In less than half an hour, by his admittedly offhand calculations, the sun would be eclipsed.

He wept for the fate of his world and for his impotence, and for everything that he could have and should have done, but didn't. His tears fell upon his jacket, splattering and creating large, dark blotches.

Then he reached into a drawer, pulled out his blaster—the one that his father had given to him on his coming-of-age day, the one that had been in his family for generations.

He placed the muzzle between his lips, squeezed the trigger, and blew his supreme military head off.

The skies of the Penzatti homeworld grew dark as the giant cube blotted out the sun. The great Penzatti gathered in the streets or huddled in their homes, praying to the gods for guidance, pleading to their equally great computers to deliver them from this newest and greatest calamity. If the gods heard, they gave no indication. As for the computers, well, they heard. But they did not feel pity, or amusement, or any emotion that the Penzatti would understand, other than an overwhelming relief that finally the proper order of things would be proceeding.

The oceans began to roar, churning and swirling as the oncoming vessel of the Borg wreaked havoc with the world's tides. Thousands were killed in the first onrush of waves that swept over the coastal cities, waves hundreds of feet high that overwhelmed the Penzatti in the same manner that the Borg overwhelmed their victims.

The waves felt nothing of the agony and hysteria, the outpouring of emotions, the pleas for mercy from a higher power that simply were not forthcoming. No, they felt nothing. And neither did the Borg.

The first of the ghastly beings materialized on the planet surface, followed by a second and a third, and then dozens, and then hundreds. All over the planet they leaped into existence. They strode forward, seemingly oblivious of the life forms around them.

The few rays of sunlight that managed to stream through glinted off the huge metal appendages that served as their right arms. Their faces were uniformly white, white as death.

All of the Penzatti planetary defenses were controlled by the computers—the selfsame computers which had decided that the Borg were their long-awaited saviors. It meant that the vast majority of the Penzatti offensive capabilities had been neutralized—not that they would have done all that much good, anyway.

Most of the Penzatti lacked the full understanding that had come to the supreme military head, and did not realize how hopeless their situation was. And so they fought.

Dantar the Eighth, crouched in the doorway of his home, saw one of the first of the invaders materialize a mere ten feet away. He was tall and slim, and wearing what appeared to be some sort of armor. Then Dantar's eyes opened wide as he realized that it was not, in fact, armor, but instead, some sort of cybernetic appliances. The creature before him was as much machine as anything else.

A second one appeared next to the first. They took slow, measured steps, scanning the houses in the same way that great carrion-eating birds survey their latest meal just before launching themselves upon it.

Dantar's family hung back in the house, with the exception of his eldest son, who was just behind him. Neighbors were already in the streets, staring at the newcomers with horror and dread.

"Who are you?" shouted Dantar.

The cybernetic soldiers ignored him. Instead, one of them started marching towards Dantar's home.

Dantar brought his twin blasters up and snarled, "Stay back! You'll get one warning!" And then, almost immediately after that, he opened fire.

His aim was true, striking the lead soldier square in the chest. The soldier stumbled back and fell to the ground, body twitching for a bare moment and then lying still. Encouraged by the easy triumph, Dantar spun and fired on the second.

To his horror, a force screen seemed to materialize precisely where his beam struck. The soldier didn't even seem aware of the assault, but instead, merely surveyed the homes as if planning to buy one.

Now Dantar the Ninth opened fire in concert with his father, as did several of the neighbors. The soldier's field flashed brightly under the barrage, and the soldier staggered, apparently confused and uncertain which way to turn. The shield sparked, faltered, and then disintegrated. The soldier was then barraged by a hail of blaster fire and went down, twisting and turning.

The speed with which the next Borg showed up gave new meaning to the term "short-lived victory." Barely had the second soldier fallen, before three more showed up to take his place. Dantar and the neighbors looked on in amazement as the newcomers bent down, removed some sort of device from the shoulders of the fallen Borg scouts, and then went on their way as if nothing had happened at all. The two fallen soldiers, in the meantime, were reduced to ash in no time at all, and right after that even the ash vanished.

The desperate Penzatti started firing again, and this time even their strongest blasts had no effect whatsoever.

One of the Borg headed straight for the home of

Dantar. He and his son fired repeatedly, but the Borg took no heed and went straight for the door. All the while its head snapped around, taking in everything, recording every scrap of information.

Infuriated, Dantar hurled himself at the Borg soldier. The creature did not seem at all surprised, but instead, merely took a step back and swung its massive right arm. It smashed across Dantar's head, sending him crashing to the ground with blood streaming from the gash.

His son ran to him, trying to help him to his feet, as the Borg scout stepped into the house.

In the capital city of the Penzatti the advance scouts had already completed their studies. They stepped over the unmoving bodies of people who had tried to stand in their way—people who had been hit by stray shots that had missed their targets, or tried to get in the Borg's way and simply been stepped on or batted aside.

The Borg had found the central computer intelligence that ran the world of the Penzatti, and decreed it good. A plea was entered by the computer through the scouts, and the plea found its way into the uni-mind of the Borg itself.

Millions of the Penzatti had cried out to their gods, and their gods had not responded. Yet now, in the ultimate proof of machine superiority, the computers of Penzatti—the computers that had gained sentience and, in so doing, a determination to control their own destiny—had cried out to the Borg.

And unlike the gods of the Penzatti, the Borg answered, with a voice that was the combination of a thousand voices all at once. A voice that spoke one word.

* * *

"Yes," said the Borg.

Beams of incredible intensity and power reached out and caressed the capital city, slicing through the ground with the precision of a surgeon's scalpel. Beneath the feet of the astonished Penzatti the ground began to rumble. All around them the air was frying from the heat of the beams. Air molecules split apart, and crashing thunder was roaring with antenna-splitting fury. The screams of the people were drowned out by the noise that was everywhere, that was inescapable.

And now a beam came down from the heavens, as if God had opened one eye and holy light were shining down upon them. And the ground beneath them was lifted up—actually carved right out of the nurturing bosom of their home world—and dragged towards the heavens.

It was happening all over the city. Huge pieces of their planet were being carved up, an ironic testament to the fact that mere hours before, the Penzatti had been celebrating their lives by carving up the dead meat of the zinator. Now they themselves were prey. They just hadn't fully realized it yet.

The pieces of the planet hurtled upward, up towards the floating cube that was the Borg ship. It grew larger and more terrifying every second. For the Penzatti, however, this was not a major concern for very long, because the force beams that were dragging them heavenward did not contain any air, nor anything to shield them against the ravages of the upper atmosphere or outer space. The Borg had not deemed it necessary to provide such protection for the humanoid life of Penzatti, because that humanoid life was irrelevant. It was the machine life and technology that interested the Borg.

The result was that the Penzatti who had not

already died in the quakes, or from shock, found it increasingly impossible to breathe. They ran to try and find someplace to hide, but there was no place. Their lungs pounded, their heads swirled, their blood boiled in their veins, and when they screamed the death knell of their race, it was not heard, because finally there was no air to carry it.

Once the pieces of the Penzatti homeworld were brought aboard, the Borg quickly broke it down. Never ones to waste anything, the Borg reduced the bodies of the Penzatti to their basic molecular structure and fed them directly into the energy cells that powered the Borg.

That done, the Borg proceeded to slice up the rest of the planet. It was a big job and would take time, but they were in no hurry. With their clockwork precision they would simply go forward—click, click—like unyielding, unstopping cogs in a watch, grinding up whatever was in their path.

The wives and children of Dantar the Eighth recoiled in horror as the Borg soldier glanced around. Then it went straight for the computer set up in the corner. The words AT LAST still glowed serenely on the screen.

The Borg did not see, did not sense, the sudden attack of one of the wives. She came in quickly, screaming "Get out! Get *out* of our *home!*" and she was swinging the carving knife grabbed off the table. The Borg, at the last moment, seemed to be aware of a threat and half turned, not in a defensive move, but out of curiosity as to what new form of attack would present itself.

The carving knife slammed into the Borg's shoulder circuitry, into that same piece of machinery that had been removed from the Borgs who had been shot down earlier in the battle. The Borg whirled, face impassive, but its body twisting and convulsing as if shot through with electricity. It spun in place, its arms pinwheeling around, and one of the massive arms struck the little girl, Lojene, who had wandered too close. Such was the power in that prosthetic device that it crushed her skull immediately.

Lojene's mother screamed, as did Dantar the Ninth, who had run in in a desperate, last-ditch effort to save his family. His father was still lying outside the house, barely conscious, and the boy knew that it was up to him. He lunged forward, darting in between the whirling arms and slamming into the Borg, smashing the soldier against a wall.

Dantar the Eighth, meantime, had just regained consciousness, and was staggering towards his home. Through the open door he could see his son struggling with the Borg soldier, slamming the creature against the wall, and he felt a flash of pride. It changed quickly to horror when he saw his wife cradling the unmoving, bloodied body of his youngest daughter. He screamed, and for a brief moment, Dantar the Ninth was distracted by the cry from his father.

The Borg soldier's right arm lashed out, still in that convulsive state, and ripped across the boy's chest. The lad staggered back, blood fountaining, and he sobbed his father's name once before falling back onto the floor. His antennae twitched spasmodically for a moment and then fell limp.

The air was an overwhelming cacophony of sounds and howls and crying, and Dantar the Eighth could not hear even his own screams of mourning. But he saw the Borg soldier, still staggering, with a knife sticking out of its arm, and he saw his family cowering.

He started to clamber to his feet. Blood was streaming from a gash in his forehead and blinding him in one eye, and he paused the barest of moments to wipe it out, snarling all the while his hatred and fury at this murdering creature.

And then the air sizzled around him.

He spun and looked heavenward in shock. Blazing beams were descending from the sky, slicing through the horizon line. Acreage flew, trees were struck down or set blazing, and beneath him the ground began to rumble ominously. He was unaware that other parts of his world had already been sectioned and removed with merciless efficiency . . . that indeed, purely by happenstance, his little piece of the world happened to be the last little piece of the world. Just as someone, during any war, had to be the first or last person to die, so, too, did some piece of the Penzatti homeworld have to wait its turn to be the very last absorbed by the Borg. Fate, and the luck of the draw, had given Dantar and his family and neighbors and city a few more minutes of life.

Not that it seemed to matter.

The Borg ship surveyed the world below them. Most of the technology had been removed and absorbed. The planet was studded with huge, gaping craters where once an entire race had thrived. This was irrelevant to the Borg. There was one small section remaining below that contained bits and pieces that might be of interest. That, too, was irrelevant, because within moments the cutter and tractor beams would finish their work and that part, too, of the planet would belong to the Borg. And then the Borg would be able to move on.

Except . . .

The Borg ship suddenly detected something coming their way—something throbbing with power. Something that, from its configurations, seemed to be about as large as the Borg ship itself . . . no—larger! Something that was coming up fast!

The Borg were not concerned. There was nothing about which they could become concerned. So confident were they, so secure in their superiority and inevitability, that any notion that they were in any way threatened was irrelevant.

Dantar felt the hair on his head crispen, the very air reaching his nostrils thick and heavy with the stench of burning and death. He turned to get into his house, because he realized that this was it, the last moments of his life and his family's life. He wanted to clutch them to his bosom when the end came.

He started towards his home, and then the ground churned beneath him. He felt his leg twist almost backwards, and he fell, a shooting pain ripping through his left knee. He tried to stand once more and collapsed, howling with pain and fury. He started to drag himself towards his modest home, hand over hand, fingers digging into the dirt, his breath rasping in his chest.

The ground trembled and rippled, like an ocean, and he saw the roof of his home collapse with a sigh. The house crumbled in on itself, walls cracking and beams snapping, falling heavily and crushing beyond hope anyone who was inside.

There was the uncomprehending scream of his family, and of Dantar the Eighth, who had been denied the right to die with his family, and those screams were overwhelmed by the death screams of the world itself, and the light—*gods*—the light that was shining down from above now, surrounding them.

Dantar rolled back onto the front yard, his arms at

either side, as if he'd been crucified. He was no longer Dantar the Eighth, he realized. He was Dantar the Last. A part of him told him that he should be running to the rubble, sifting through, trying to pull it off his family and finding if there were any survivors.

"No point," he whispered through cracked and bleeding lips. He was staring up at the light that was accompanied by a deafening hum. "No point."

His little piece of the world began to rise into the air.

As part of the Borg uni-mind dealt with the final section of the Penzatti homeworld, the rest focussed on the new intruder. It was definitely a ship approaching them. A ship . . . and yet, something more. Something far, far more.

The Borg prepared scouts to board the ship for the purpose of study, and then the plan quickly changed when the Borg realized that the intruder was not slowing down or veering off. The intruder was heading straight for them.

The Borg uni-mind fired off a message to the intruder. It was a simple message: SURRENDER.

The reply from the intruder was equally succinct: GO TO HELL.

The intruder cut loose with a beam composed of pure anti-proton. It laughed at the Borg shields and smashed into the Borg ship, ripping apart the upper portion of the cube.

The beam vanished, and Dantar felt the world fall away beneath him as the gravity of the planet reclaimed a piece of itself, desperately, like a mother reaching out for an infant snatched from her breast. There was a dizzying moment of disorientation, and then the ground beneath him collapsed back into the pit that had been formed by its disappearance. It was not a precise fit, nor a smooth landing, and buildings that had not already crumbled now collapsed from the strain. Those buildings had never been created to take this sort of stress. Neither had the mind of Dantar, and it simply shut down.

The Borg did not panic. Panic was irrelevant. Instead, they immediately set their restoration mechanisms into operation, under the assumption that they would have time to complete the repairs before they were attacked again. In their machine-like, precise way, they were ignoring the concept that they might be overmatched.

Instead, as the cube began to restore itself, they sent off another message to the intruder—the intruder, which was momentarily stationary, as if appreciating the power of its assault:

You cannot defeat us. If you attempt to assault us again, you will be punished. There is no power that can withstand us.

And once again the intruder responded, and the Borg became aware that the intruder also responded in the unified chorus of voices. But whereas the Borg voice was a single tone repeated endlessly, the intruder's voice was a glorious blending of infinite tones. Had the Borg been capable of recognizing such a thing, they would have perceived it as beauty. Beauty, however, was irrelevant.

You believe that because none ever has, said the intruder. *You are so accustomed to overwhelming all life forms, that you have no concept of how it would be for you. You've never felt the terror of hopelessness before.*

Terror is irrelevant, replied the Borg. *Hopelessness is irrelevant.*

The intruder sighed with the voice of a million million souls. *You're irrelevant, you cosmic bastards.*

The beam of the intruder lashed out before the Borg could power up their systems enough to mount a counterattack. It smashed into the center of the massive cube, blasting through and out the other side. The cube trembled and shook, circuits blowing out all over. Cracks appeared all over the surface, and the beam struck a third time, with even greater intensity than before and with a force behind it that was more than simply power. It was a force that seemed to be fueled by a massive indignation, a pounding fury and anger, and infinite voices crying out in triumph.

The Borg sent out a cry of warning to the central uni-mind, alerted the other ships that were approaching and would be there sooner or later. A warning that there was a new force in the galaxy that had to be contended with. And then, with the same eerie silence that marked their arrival, the Borg departed—in a million directions simultaneously. Pieces of the ship and shreds of Borg spread out, some hurling off into the depths of space, others plunging through the tattered atmosphere of the Penzattl homeworld and burning up upon re-entry.

Pieces ricocheted off the intruder but did not inflict even the slightest damage. The intruder merely hovered there for a long moment, taking in the triumph, basking in the first blow struck.

And there was that sigh, that ineffable sigh of relief. A pride in a job well done.

The intruder moved on.

Chapter Three

IT HAD NOT RAINED in some time, and the unrelenting sun had baked the ground dry. There was, at least, a steady wind this day, blowing in a northerly direction. It rustled the manes of the two horses who travelled slowly across the dry plain, and carried the incessant *clip-clop* of their hooves a good distance. Had anyone else been around, they would have been warned of the oncoming of the riders. As it was, there was no one else around to see them or care about them.

Actually, calling the two animals "horses" was excessively kind, even inaccurate. One of the animals was, in fact, an ass. The other was sagging and broken down, and had it been carrying a burden much heavier than that which it now bore, it quite probably would have simply keeled over and refused to go any farther.

The man astride the horse was dressed in black slacks and boots, a wide-sleeved white shirt that rippled in the breeze, and, most oddly, pieces of armor that were affixed to him front and back in a ragtag fashion. Perched on his head was a battered helmet which, in blocking the sun, at least served some purpose. For if the man had launched himself into combat, the helmet would have been of extremely questionable value.

Tucked under one arm was a long, rusty, and somewhat crooked lance; it would have been difficult to discern it as such, but for the fact that he was holding it straight out in front of him in a vaguely offensive manner.

From his slight height advantage, he called out to his companion, "It's a glorious day, isn't it, Sancho? You can smell danger in the air, the scent of quests waiting to be fulfilled."

His companion was dressed less ostentatiously, in simple peasant garments. He inhaled deeply and frowned. "I do not detect any such fragrances in the atmosphere."

"Oh yes, it's there. You just have to know where to look. I tell you, Sancho, our great enemy is lurking somewhere out there, waiting for us to lower our guard so that he can destroy us with one of his cunning masterstrokes."

"Our enemy. That would be 'The Necromancer,' I believe you called him. A magician. An enchanter."

"That's right. The Enchanter . . ." His voice suddenly trailed off and he reined up his horse. "Gods! Do you see them, Sancho?"

"Sancho's" eyebrows creased slightly in mild confusion. "What 'them' would that be?"

"The giants!" The horseman pointed with his lance. "The giants! Right ahead of us!"

"I see only a grouping of windmills."

"No! It's giants! How can you not see?" The horseman immediately spurred his horse forward, bringing up his lance. "They mock me! They attack! But they cannot defeat a knight errant with the might of God on his side!"

"It is not giants!" said his companion. "It is . . ."

It was too late. The horseman charged forward, his lance levelled, and a cry of "On, Rozinante!" torn from his lips. The hooves of the horse, the aforementioned Rozinante, pounded beneath him. Although the horse did not charge happily, it charged gamely, not able to recall any time in recent history when it had been called upon to exercise.

The horse and rider hurtled across the broken terrain, toward the tall structure of the closest windmill, which was turning serenely, oblivious to the idea that it was under attack. The shouts of the companion were lost under the thundering hooves.

The rider careened into the windmill, his lance crashing through the thin material that covered the great arms. The horse banked sharply to the right to avoid the sweep of the steadily turning windmill arms, and the knight errant's lance was firmly lodged in the latticework. The blades continued to turn, thanks to the steady wind, and the horseman was yanked upward towards the sky, his lance wedged in, his feet kicking in fury.

He clutched onto the skeletal framework of the arm and shouted defiance. He rose up, higher and higher, reaching the top and then sweeping downward once more. He lost his grip on the lance and started to slide. With a cry of alarm he grasped out with desperate fingers and managed to snag onto some of the tattered cloth. He wrapped one leg around the framework as the arm swung downward, but before he could dislodge himself, it began to ascend once more.

Then it stopped, with a jolt. The dehorsed horseman's head smacked against the wooden skeleton, disorienting him for a moment. Then he looked down.

His companion was down there, holding the lower edge of the blade securely in an unbreakable grip. From within the windmill was the sound of gears grinding against one another, and the other arms of the windmill shook in protest.

"It is safe for you to descend if you do so quickly," he said.

The horseman groaned in frustration and clambered down quickly. "I was winning!" he protested.

"You were in serious danger of injuring yourself severely," "Sancho" informed him calmly. "Furthermore, you risked doing so in pursuit of a goal which was unattainable. To perceive this windmill," and he released the blade, allowing it to go on its way unmolested, "as a giant certainly indicates lunacy. Furthermore, Geordi, I do not understand why you would choose to re-enact a moment of such dismal and utter failure on the part of a literary character."

Geordi shook his head, rubbing his temple. "You're not getting this at all, are you, Data?" He stepped to one side as the lance dislodged itself from the blade and clattered to the ground next to him.

"Humanity seems to be fascinated by those who deviate most from the norm—particularly such eccentric madmen as Don Quixote. Beyond his possibilities as a case study, I do not comprehend his appeal."

"But it was a glorious madness, don't you see!" said Geordi. He walked across the ground, shaking his leg slightly to work out a slight limp. "Quixote and I, we have a lot in common." He walked backward now toward the horses so that he could face Data, and tapped the VISOR that ringed his face. "We both see things differently than other people do."

"But your VISOR still shows you aspects of reality," said Data reasonably. "You still perceive things as they are."

"Yes!" said Geordi excitedly. "And Quixote perceived things as they might have been. In the final analysis, who's to say which is the more accurate?"

"I can," said Data. "Yours is the more accurate. I wish to indulge you as much as possible, Geordi, as do we all. This holodeck scenario, after all, is your birthday wish. Still, it all seems rather pointless."

Geordi drew himself astride the horse. Data followed suit. "Was it pointless for humans to dream of going to space? Or eliminating war? Or discovering a cure for cancer?"

"Of course not. Because it led to results."

"Exactly!" said Geordi excitedly. He urged the horse to move forward, which the beast did reluctantly. "But when the dreamers started dreaming, they had no idea where those dreams would lead them—to the madhouse, or to the stars. And Quixote was the entire spirit of human imagination in one package. His perceptions led him to—"

"Compound fractures, if he continued battling windmills," said Data.

"Data," said Geordi in exasperation, gripping his lance tightly, "the point is that every fight is worth fighting. Even the hopeless ones. That instead of taking things at face value, you should be looking below the surface. You should see what could be, instead of what is. Anyone can fight a battle that's easy to win. It's fighting the battles that are impossible to win that causes humanity to take those great leaps forward."

"If fighting hopeless battles is good for humans, then why do humans sometimes retreat?"

"Well . . ." said Geordi uncomfortably, "there is a fine line between bravery and suicide, between the good fight and the lost fight."

"But no fight is lost until it is over, and if a human retreats before it is over, he will never know which type of fight he was fighting."

Geordi sighed. "Forget it, Data."

"Quite a few people have said that to me, about a great many things," Data said. "I have been assuming that that is a statement of preference that the topic be terminated, rather than an instruction to delete the conversation from my memory."

"That's a safe assumption," Geordi agreed.

"I must admit that I find that to be a rather defeatist attitude on the part of most humans." Data pulled on the reins in an effort to urge his mount forward. "If humans, as you say, strive so mightily against the most formidable of challenges, it is a pity that the simple act of explaining human goals would prove to be so insurmountable."

"*Ah!*" said Geordi desperately. "A castle!"

Data swung his head around in the direction that Geordi was looking. "Would you be referring to that somewhat ramshackle inn approximately ten kilometers away?"

"You see a humble inn, faithful Sancho? But I see an extravagant palace that might afford us lodgings!"

Data frowned, trying desperately to share in the divine madness of his friend. "I would suppose," said Data slowly, "that if one were to build up the exterior considerably—substitute stone walls instead of a tattered wooden barricade—and were, in addition, to supplement the structure with towers, turrets, and a moat . . . taking into account all of that, I could see where the inn could be transformed into a castle."

Geordi smiled approvingly. "Now you're getting it," he said.

"Am I?" Data considered that. "I am not saying that I perceive it as a castle, in the manner that you saw—or claim to have seen—the windmill as a giant. I am merely analyzing the possibilities that the inn could be reworked into a castle-like structure."

"The dreamers are the ones who conceive of what could happen," said Geordi, "and the scientists are the ones who make it happen. The best of humanity are those who combine both traits."

He urged the broken-down horse forward, with Data close behind on the hapless ass known as Dapple.

When Geordi had worked out the holodeck scenario concerning the adventures of Don Quixote, born Alonso Quixana, he had added in a random factor. They were not living out the sequential life of Quixote so much as existing in his world for a time, with the various elements jumbled together. It made for more stimulating entertainment that way.

Moments later they had ridden their mounts into the central courtyard of the inn. They caught odd glances from those weary travelers who were relaxing nearby with mugs of ale. There was some guffawing and chortling, and even a good deal of pointing. Data absorbed it all but was incapable of taking offense, even if these had been real humans rather than holodeck simulacrums. As for Geordi, well—Don Quixote would not have taken offense, and therefore, Geordi would not either.

He swung a leg down off the horse, and his boot caught momentarily in the stirrup, almost throwing him to the ground. He recovered just in time and managed, with not much grace, to save himself from a painful and embarrassing spill. Nevertheless, several of the men noticed his near mishap, and got a few more chortles at his expense. Data gracefully dismounted from his smaller jackass.

Geordi turned and took a step back, surprised by the woman who was approaching them. "Guinan?" he said in confusion.

The hostess of the *Enterprise* Ten-Forward lounge, clad in flowing blue robes and, as always, a large, flat-brimmed hat, spread her hands wide and said graciously, "If my eyes are not deceiving me, we have a knight here in my humble establishment."

"Your—?"

He turned toward Data in confusion, and then a slow smile spread across his face. Data confirmed with a nod and said, "Other crew members learned of your scenario and requested the opportunity to participate and surprise you."

Geordi nodded briskly and unconsciously straightened his shirt and rearranged his armor in imitation of the little motion the captain did whenever he rose or sat—the motion which, in good-natured kidding around the ship, had been nicknamed "The Picard Maneuver." "A knight errant," he said briskly, "is surprised by nothing because he expects everything. Is that not right, Sancho?"

"That is right, sir," said Data affably.

"We seek lodging," Geordi told her imperiously.

"And do you have money with which to pay for your stay?" Guinan had a proper air of skepticism about her.

"Money!" said Geordi in outrage. "Good woman, I'll have you know that the lodging of a knight is an obligation and a debt that all people are expected to support. You should be flattered that I have chosen your abode, and relieved that the sword of Don Quixote de la Mancha will be present for a night to defend this castle!"

Guinan took all this in and then nodded her head slightly. "It would be the height of foolishness to argue with so brave and determined a knight. Or his squire," she added as an afterthought, with a slight nod towards Data.

"You are most kind," said Data.

But Geordi wasn't listening anymore. Instead, his VISOR-enhanced gaze was levelled at a woman who was bent over a well, drawing water up in a bucket. Any other man on the ship would have had to wait until she turned around to see who it was, but Geordi's VISOR immediately fed him body readings, thermal readouts, and uniquely identifiable bio traces that promptly informed him of the identity of yet another unexpected participant in his holodeck fantasy. He wondered for a moment if everyone on the ship was going to turn up. How many people had caught wind of his little informal birthday party, anyway?

The woman turned, balancing the bucket on one sturdy shoulder. She was medium build, the black ringlets of her hair falling about her shoulders, her tattered and poor clothes hanging on her body, threadbare in places. She looked at him with curiosity. "Señor Quixana!" she said in surprise. "What are you doing here?"

He took a step toward her with as much reverence and amazement as he could muster. "She stands before me! Oh blessed lady, to come to me now when I am on my quest! It is she, Sancho!" He grasped Data firmly by the arm and pulled the android down next to him. "It is the lady Dulcinea!"

Data tilted his head slightly. "It is the lady Counselor Troi."

"Hush!" said Deanna Troi with an impatient stomp of her slippered foot.

"Lady Dulcinea," said Geordi dramatically, "long have I worshipped you from afar. Now I embark on my great quests, all dedicated to the ideal beauty of womanhood that you represent. In order that I accomplish great deeds, I must have the ideal woman upon which to bestow their honor!"

"But Señor Quixana, don't you recognize me?" said Troi. "I am merely the daughter of your next-door neighbor. You have known me for many years. Why do you now call me by this strange name?"

"I call you only by that name which you have always possessed, but none have dared utter," said Geordi. "But I, knight errant, on God's own quest, must—"

"Report to the conference room."

The utterly unexpected voice was, to put it mildly, a jolt. Geordi's head snapped around, as did the others.

Captain Picard was standing there, in full uniform, arms folded across his chest.

Geordi felt that awkwardness one always felt when someone walked into the middle of an elaborate holodeck scenario and knocked the props out from under one's suspension of disbelief. Not that Geordi had been having any sort of easy time losing himself in the travails and imaginings of la Mancha, thanks to Data's incessantly rational view of the world of Don Quixote. Not to mention the well-meaning, but jolting, appearances of fellow crew members from the *Enterprise*. And now the captain himself had shown up, presumably to shut the whole thing down over some emergency or other.

In a way, considering the way things were going, Geordi was almost relieved.

Counselor Troi stepped forward. "You seem distressed, Captain."

Picard turned towards her and his mouth dropped slightly. He had not recognized her at first and, indeed, had wondered over the overt familiarity that a holodeck being was having with him. "Distressed . . . Counselor," he said cautiously, as if still uncertain of whom he was addressing, "is an understatement." He turned back to Geordi. "I am truly sorry to interrupt this scenario, Mr. La Forge. I am aware you've put a great deal of energy into it. But a matter of some urgency has presented itself."

"Yes, sir," said Geordi. With a sigh and a last, quick glance around, he called out, "Computer. End program."

The castle/hovel vanished silently around them, to be replaced by the black, glowing grid walls of the holodeck. "In five minutes, up in the briefing room," said Picard. His officers went out quickly in order to change to garb that would be more presentable. Somehow, armor or peasant rags didn't seem suitable to whatever situation might present itself in Starfleet life.

Guinan walked over to Picard and regarded him with bemused curiosity. "You could have summoned Geordi, or Data, or Troi, via communicators," she said. "Why didn't you?"

He permitted a small smile. "Captain's prerogative," he admitted. "An indulgence, if you will. I'm something of a Cervantes enthusiast myself. I was intrigued to see what Mr. La Forge was going to develop." He looked at her askance for a moment. "Guinan, are you quite all right? You seem a tad . . . distracted today."

Her eyes darkened for the briefest of moments, and then she smiled, although when she spoke, it was with her eyes half-lidded. "I just haven't been resting well lately. It will pass."

VENDETTA

"Well . . . if you have continued problems, I want you to go to sickbay and have Dr. Crusher look you over. Understood?"

She nodded slightly. He'd never had to give her any sort of order in the past, and this was probably the closest he would ever come to issuing one. So she treated it with appropriate weight. "Understood, sir."

He started to turn away and then Guinan added, "Deanna was quite lovely, wasn't she?"

"Appropriately so," said Picard. "After all, she is Dulcinea, the ideal woman, the woman that Don Quixote strives for, and for whom he endures hardship after hardship. Yet he derives emotional strength merely from the knowledge of her existence."

"He performs deeds to prove himself worthy of her, yet feels he never *can* be worthy of her," said Guinan. She fell into slow step next to Picard. "Did you ever have a woman like that, Captain? A dream girl? An unattainable woman?"

He paused and pursed his lips. "Once, many years ago. A dream girl. The very idea of her reality vanishes into the misty haze of youthful memory."

"What's that supposed to mean?" asked Guinan in bemusement.

He turned to her in all seriousness, his brow creasing. "It means that I would prefer if you did not ask again, Guinan." He turned away from her and strode out of the holodeck.

She inclined her head slightly in the direction he had departed. "Message received," she said to no one.

Picard walked briskly down the corridor, paying no attention to where he was going. He gave quick nods of acknowledgment to all those who greeted him, but he didn't pay the least bit of attention to whom he was

55

greeting. Thanks to Guinan, his thoughts were—albeit briefly—a million light-years and half a lifetime away. By the time he got to the turbolift, however, he had neatly tucked his mind into its proper, ordered fashion, and there it would remain, if he had anything to say about it.

Which, as things turned out, he didn't.

Chapter Four

THE CAPTAIN OF THE U.S.S. *Chekov* regarded the vista of space before him and pondered about how much less hospitable a place it had seemed to become. The endless freezing vacuum was dangerous enough without massive cubes that could spring out of warp space without warning, filled with soulless mechanical beings that crushed everything in their path.

He winced when he thought about the friends that he'd lost in the hopeless fight at Wolf 359. Forty ships. Gods, forty ships. And where had he been? Too far away. Too damned far away.

And who saved the day?

"Picard," he muttered, shaking his head.

From his right-hand side, his first officer looked up from the fuel consumption report that she was initialing. "Jean-Luc Picard?" she asked.

He afforded her a glance before allowing a rueful smile to touch his lips. "Yes, Jean-Luc Picard."

"The finest captain in the fleet," she said firmly, and then, in quiet awareness of the importance of politics, she began to add, "Present company excepted, of course."

But her captain waved her off. He uncrossed his legs and stood, taking several short steps across the bridge. His bridge, the bridge of an *Excelsior*-class ship. It was a good bridge, a solid bridge—

Not an awesomely spacious bridge, however. The bridge of a Galaxy-class ship, now that was spacious. He'd never had the opportunity to step onto one, but he'd heard you could practically play field hockey in one of those. But there were only a handful of those magnificent ships in the fleet—one of which had been destroyed at Wolf 359—and, of course, the finest of those rare ships, the most renowned, the most sought after was commanded by none other than—

"Jean-Luc Picard," said the captain softly. "You don't have to be deferential, Number One. I know how highly regarded he is by everyone in the fleet—not the least of whom is yourself. I can't blame you at all. You were there when he pulled off 'The Picard Miracle.'"

"Is that what they're calling it now?" she said in amusement. "Well, I suppose it was, in a way. It was something to see. I thought we were dead for sure."

The rest of the bridge crew, ostensibly going about their business, were nevertheless slow in their duties, so that they could pay attention to what the first officer was saying. There were so many stories of destruction and loss surrounding the attack of the Borg, that starship crews—what few there were left—savored any telling of the one tale that ended with the Federation triumphant.

"It must have been a tense moment," said the captain drily. He scratched idly at his graying sideburns and glanced around the bridge in quiet amusement at his whole bridge crew, trying to look as if they weren't paying any attention. He caught the eye of his helmsman, who grinned sheepishly at being noticed.

With the air of someone who had repeated a story to the point where she had every single beat and dramatic moment down pat, she said, "I'll never forget the look in Commander Riker's eye when he said he was about to give the order for us to ram the Borg ship. I'm not sure what he hoped to accomplish —damage it, maybe for a few minutes. Buy the Earth that much more time. . . .

"And there was this teenage boy at the helm, youngest ensign I'd ever seen. I thought he'd crack when Riker ordered that a collision course be laid in. Give the boy credit. He sucked it up, said, 'Yes, sir,' and laid in the course command."

By now no one was making a pretense of doing anything other than listening to her. "What were you thinking, Commander Shelby? Right then, when it looked all over," asked the navigator. His name was Hobson, and he was so fresh out of the Academy, he practically looked like he had a sheen to him.

Shelby paused, scratching her thick red hair thoughtfully. Hobson had addressed her with a sort of easy familiarity that she never would have tolerated when she first came aboard the *Enterprise*. But her time on board that ship had taught her a great deal about relating to people and judging them. The idea that she had first assessed William Riker as someone who was incapable of making big decisions—shortly before he'd been forced to make nothing but big decisions—had brought into question for her much about the way she went about things.

"When I was a kid," she said, "there was this stupid joke that the other kids would tell endlessly at my expense. They'd always make sure I was in earshot, and then they'd say loudly, 'Knock Knock.' And another would reply, 'Who's there?' And they go back and forth with 'Shelby.' 'Shelby Who?' 'Shelby—'"

"Coming 'round the mountain when she comes?" said Hobson. There was curt laughter from another officer who quickly cut it off.

"Yes," said Shelby, slightly irked. "So there I was, and all that went through my head was, 'Shelby coming 'round the mountain for the last time.' Stupid. You think about stupid jokes from childhood, or a date you won't be able to keep, or paperwork that still needs to be done—everything except the idea that you're about to die. Riker even started to order the collision. He got half of the word *engage* out, and then the call came up from sickbay. And within seconds after that call—had to be seconds, because that's all we had—they had ordered the Borg to shut down via a link they'd established through Picard. Picard masterminded it, told them what to do, even though he was still in the power of the Borg. He put them to sleep . . ."

"Undoubtedly he got to read them his third-year paper on Reversal of Hyperspace Overdrive," said the captain. "That put the entire Academy graduating class into a coma."

Shelby looked at him with open surprise. "Captain! Really! How you could insult Captain Picard—"

The captain slowly circled his bridge (which was feeling smaller by the minute, truth be known), chewing on his lower lip and fighting down the traces of envy that he so hated. He managed to force out a short—almost avuncular—and almost convincing laugh. "Captain Picard and I go way back, Number One. Back to when he was Cadet Jean-Luc Picard, and I was Cadet Morgan Korsmo. So, I'm entitled. Believe me, I have nothing but admiration for the man. I mean, let's face it, the man was almost nothing but Borg implants, am I right?"

"That's a fairly accurate assessment," admitted Shelby.

"Well, Commander, put your mind at ease. I will be the first to admit that Jean-Luc Picard is more of a man when he's only half a man than most men are when they're intact. Satisfied?"

"Yes, sir," said Shelby.

Captain Korsmo shook his head in silent wonderment. That was the kind of man Picard was. He inspired fierce loyalty even in those individuals who had been with him only a short time. Korsmo wondered whether he would ever be capable of commanding that sort of devotion from his people.

There was a sharp *beep* from behind him and his tactical officer looked up in response. "Captain," said the tactical officer, Peel, "I have contact with the *Enterprise,* as you requested."

"Excellent," said Korsmo. To the surprise of the other bridge crew, who were usually privy to just about any discussion that took place—the *Chekov* had, by design, a very relaxed and congenial atmosphere—Korsmo headed for the ready room. "I'll take it in the ready room. Number One, with me, please."

Shelby nodded quickly, falling into step behind him. She knew what the story was—Korsmo had brought her up to speed as soon as he had gotten word from Starfleet over the incident on the homeworld of the Penzatti. But it had been Korsmo's express wish that it not be discussed with the rest of the crew.

As Korsmo had himself, many others on the *Chekov* had lost friends and loved ones in the massacre at Wolf 359. The last thing they needed to hear, he felt, was that the triumph which had been achieved at such terrible cost was so temporary a measure. The last thing they needed to hear was that the Borg were coming back—indeed, had already returned, it seemed.

And he wasn't going to tell them until he absolutely had to. He just hoped that it wouldn't be too soon.

Or too late.

All of Picard's officers had assembled in the briefing room, and Picard gave a quick nod of appreciation that they had pulled themselves together so quickly. It was, in fact, exactly what he would have anticipated. He expected the world of them and had yet to be disappointed in their ability to deliver it.

Riker sat opposite him, once again employing his customary trait of having turned the chair around and straddled it. Data was to the left, Geordi on the right, both back in Starfleet uniforms and giving no sign that, mere minutes before, they had been gallivanting about the Spanish countryside. Deanna Troi was just now entering, smoothing out her hair. Picard took some measure of enjoyment in that there were certain universal constants, one of them seemingly that it always took women longer to make themselves presentable than it did men.

Worf sat at the edge of the conference table—a slight distance away. It was a subtle separation, but one that Picard had noticed with consistency. As close as he felt to this particular group of humans, Worf still possessed an unshakable standoffishness.

Or perhaps it was good, old-fashioned Klingon caution: Never discount the possibility that an apparent friend might be an enemy in disguise. Considering that the *Enterprise* had dealt, on a number of occasions in her long history, with impostors, that might not be an inappropriate attitude for the head of security to have.

Closest to Picard sat Beverly Crusher. Normally a very outgoing woman, she had been somewhat quiet lately. Picard wasn't entirely surprised. She had known the departure of her son, Wesley, for Starfleet Academy, was inevitable. Inevitability, however, did not necessarily mean one would be prepared. Picard knew that she was missing Wesley something fierce, for when he had gone, he had taken with him the last physical reminder of her late husband, Jack. All she had for the rest of her life now was memories, and oftentimes memories were just not enough.

Now, though, was not the time to dwell on it.

"On screen," said Picard sharply to the air.

In response to his command, an image appeared on the conference room communications screen. Picard's lips twitched in amusement as he saw the now-rather-jowly face of Morgan Korsmo appear on the screen. He remembered the Academy days, when Korsmo could eat anything and never gain weight. Clearly those days were past. Also, his formerly jet-black hair was now shot through with gray. Time, the great leveller.

"Korsmo," said Picard.

"Picard," replied Korsmo, with that same slightly insouciant tone that Picard remembered all too well. "Still bald, I see."

Riker and the others looked at Picard with open amusement. Picard, utterly nonplussed, replied, "The years and pounds have obviously caught up with you."

"True. I'm fat and you're bald. Of course, I can always lose weight," pointed out Korsmo.

There was a slight chuckle from Beverly. Picard resisted glancing at her, for a look from him might have stilled her. Frankly, it was worth a laugh or two at his own expense just to get a smile out of her.

"Captain," said Picard, softly but firmly. "You always were one to try to put as much of a gloss on bad news as possible. It is painfully clear to me that you are now trying to delay the inevitable—that being the purpose of this communiqué. What's happened?"

Korsmo gave a brief nod in acknowledgment. "And you, Picard, always liked to cut through the bluster and get straight to the point. How comforting to know that neither of us changed. Unfortunately, neither have the Borg."

"The Borg?" Picard said the words a bit too sharply, a bit too quickly. Mentally he chided himself for it. Had any of his people noticed that edge in his voice? His quick glance caught Deanna studying him with those luminous and sympathetic eyes. He had a feeling he'd probably be hearing from her before too long. He straightened his uniform top, rather unnecessarily, and leaned forward, fingers interlaced. "When and where? How soon can we expect their attack?"

"To the former, the target was the Penzatti homeworld. A rescue operation is already in progress, but Starfleet wants you there as well, and as soon as possible, in case the Borg return. We will be rendezvousing with you there, but it's going to take us the better part of a week. Starfleet wants the closest ship there immediately."

Wants us there as what? Cannon fodder? flitted through Picard's mind. As quickly as that thought came to him, he dismissed it. Now was not the time. The time would never be, actually. "Mr. Data, how long—?"

"At warp six, eighteen hours."

"Warp six-point-five, then. Make it so."

Riker leaned forward and said, "Captain Korsmo, with all due respect—and sounding somewhat brutal—why are we being dispatched to the Penzatti world?

If the Borg have been and gone, then Penzatti is a lost cause. We should be moving to intercept the latest Borg incursion."

"Commander Riker is correct," agreed Picard. "We've seen the Borg's handiwork before. Frankly, I'm amazed at the mention of a rescue operation. I wouldn't assume there would be anyone or anything left to rescue. What is the Borg's present heading?"

"To hell," said Korsmo. He seemed quite pleased about it.

"We can but hope, Captain," said Picard. "The question still remains—"

"No, you're not following me, Jean-Luc," Korsmo said. "The Borg who were attacking the Penzatti were destroyed before they could finish the job. Oh, ninety-five percent of the planet is gone. But that leaves five percent more than has ever survived before."

Picard was still digesting the earlier sentence. "The Borg were *destroyed?*"

"By a starship?" asked Geordi.

"Klingons," said Worf firmly. "Klingon warships must have come in response to—"

"Not a starship," said Korsmo. "Not Klingons, either. We don't know what or who, gentlemen. That is one of the things I'm hoping your people can determine once you arrive. Early reports are that the Borg were attacked by someone or . . . to be overly melodramatic—some*thing,* and were utterly destroyed."

"A power of that magnitude," said Data thoughtfully, "would be a devastating weapon against the Borg."

"Or," said Worf darkly, "against us."

"Exactly," Korsmo affirmed, "what Starfleet is concerned about."

"Concerned?" said Crusher, her eyebrows almost meeting the top of her head. "This seems like a godsend! The Borg massacred forty ships and almost made the *Enterprise* number forty-one, before we defeated them by the skin of our teeth. And someone, somewhere, comes along with the power to stop them, and all you're concerned about is making sure they don't turn that power against you. Lives were saved! Who knows how many more might be?"

"No one is disputing that, Doctor," Picard said, stroking his chin thoughtfully. "The question that must be asked, though, is whether the power—whoever or whatever it was—that destroyed the Borg attackers of Penzatti did so because they're on our side . . . or because the Borg were simply the first available target."

"In other words, we might be next," said Worf.

"Precisely," said Korsmo. "We need to find out as much about this new player as we can. With the investigation time you'll be getting, you'll doubtlessly become the experts on them before long. We of the *Chekov,* of course, have the resident expert on the Borg on our staff. When we rendezvous with you at the Penzatti, she will be surveying the site to get as much of a line on the Borg as she can."

On cue, Shelby stepped into the range of the communications screen and nodded with familiar ease in the direction of the *Enterprise* crew. Smiles were reflected on the latter's faces, the widest of which was Riker's.

"We heard about your new post. Good to see you in the first officer's position you so coveted, Commander," said Riker.

"I can't think of another officer in the fleet who's more deserving," affirmed Picard.

Shelby inclined her head slightly in acknowledgment and said gravely, "Neither can I." Then she smiled in open acknowledgment of her tongue-in-cheek self-importance. "Actually, Starfleet tells me this is, in all likelihood, a temporary assignment. With the Borg threat far from over, I never know where I'll wind up next."

"Which is not to be construed," Captain Korsmo put in, "as her doing anything other than a totally exemplary job for us."

"We certainly would have expected nothing less," Picard said. "Captain—what is Starfleet's position if we are to encounter the individuals who are responsible for the destruction of the Borg ship?"

"The position is that you do your damnedest to keep yourselves in one piece. That's the top priority. Establish communications if at all possible, but whatever you do, don't engage them in combat in any way. Anyone who could mow down the Borg is going to make short work of you. Do you think," Korsmo said with exaggerated stiffness, "you'll be able to keep all that straight, Picard? There's a lot to remember, after all."

Picard shook his head in amusement. "Same old Korsmo."

"Same old Picard. Pity. And there was so much room for improvement. See you at Penzatti. *Chekov* out."

After the screen blinked out, Picard slowly surveyed the faces of his people. Despite all the difficulties the Borg had given them, despite the way that the power balance seemed to have shifted yet again and put the *Enterprise* on less firm footing, his crew seemed no less determined, no less confident. He would have expected nothing less of them, nor anything less of himself. Hopefully, he would be able to keep up under the weight of those expectations.

"You all know your assignments," he said crisply. "I know that you'll carry them out with the efficiency to which I've become accustomed. That's all." He stood, as did the others, and walked out of the conference room before anyone could say another word.

Picard, in his ready room, looked up at the sound of the chime. "Come," he said, knowing already who it would be before the door even opened. Sure enough, in strode Counselor Troi, who stood in front of him expectantly, with folded arms. "You look as if you're waiting for the show to start, counselor." he observed, with a hint of amusement.

She got down to it immediately. "I sensed great ambivalence on your part concerning the Borg. More so than towards the unknown entities who are potentially more of a threat."

"Ambivalence? In regard to beings who carved me up like a slice of beef?" said Picard, again more sharply than he would have liked. He closed his eyes for a moment to compose himself. When he opened them, he was actually able to smile wanly. "I've already worked out a good deal of my—difficulties— during my shore leave on Earth, counselor, as you well know. Still, I wouldn't be human if the prospect of facing them again wasn't a bit . . . daunting. I do not expect, however, that it will interfere with my ability to do my job."

"I would never presume to believe as much," Troi said. "I find it curious, though, that I sense no concern from you regarding this new force we've learned of. A force much more powerful than the Borg."

Picard drummed his fingers momentarily on his desk. "This is a big universe, Counselor. I always assumed that somewhere out there, there would be a more powerful entity than the Borg. And whomever we encounter next, there will be someone stronger than them. If I were daunted by the concept of encountering powerful beings, Counselor, I doubt I ever would have left the comforting environs of earth. New encounters? I thrive on them. It's what I live for. What we are looking at, Counselor, to use the old saying, is the devil we know versus the devil we don't. The Borg are simply devils that I know all too well."

"You feel that whatever we encounter, even if more powerful than the Borg, won't be as great of a threat."

For a brief moment he relived the hideous feeling of the Borg implants that had become a part of him; the unyielding and inhuman invasion of his mind, his soul, and the raping of his knowledge and personality; how they had managed to destroy, with no problem at all, his will to resist; how they had put him through a very personal and very singular hell that bore the name "Locutus."

"No one could be," he said gravely.

"Captain—"

He stood, the very decisiveness of the motion silencing Troi. He walked around to the observation bay and stared out at the stars that telescoped away from them as the ship proceeded, at warp 6.5, to the devastated home of the Penzatti. "I won't let them do it to me, Counselor. I had never been the type to view every new race, no matter how powerful, in terms of how much of a threat they pose. We're not out here to explore new threats and new civilizations, and I will be damned if the Borg now force me to consider every new encounter, first and foremost, in regard to their ability to hurt us. That's not what we're about. That's not what *I'm* about. And I will not let the Borg do that to me. I won't," he finished fiercely.

Troi nodded slowly and smiled. "I have no doubt.

And for the Borg's sake, let us hope that the next individual they encounter is somewhat more weak-willed than you. Otherwise, I don't think they stand a chance."

He smiled thinly. "That, Counselor, is definitely the least of my concerns."

Chapter Five

DAIMON TURANE of the Ferengi was bored out of his mind.

Even for one of the Ferengi, Turane wasn't much to look at, with his eyes unfashionably set close together, and a piece of his left ear missing, thanks to a business disagreement some years back. When he spoke, it was with the heavy rasp that signalled the beginning stages of an incurable disease that attacked the lungs. Within five years he would doubtlessly be on some sort of artificial support, or need new lungs entirely.

All that he could have taken, though. It was his current assignment that threatened to drive him mad.

Turane had landed this unprofitable, dead-end assignment—an assignment that had sent him and a crew of ten Ferengi misfits to the farthest reaches of Federation space and beyond. Ostensibly, the reason given was that the Ferengi were looking to expand their trade horizons. The Ferengi were annoyed with constantly butting heads with the Federation, and expansion was mandatory if they were to survive as a merchant race. His superiors even had the temerity to tell Turane that this was a plum assignment and that if he were successful in finding new markets, he would be covering himself in glory and profit in the name of the Ferengi.

This he knew to be unadulterated nonsense. The reason he was here was simple. It was his appearance, his coarse manners (coarse even for the Ferengi), his deportment. In fact, in his general, overall being, he was an embarrassment to his brother, who just happened to hold a high rank in the Ferengi command. And his dear, beloved brother had made damned sure, at his earliest opportunity, that Turane be shuffled off to somewhere where he couldn't do any damage to his brother's precious career.

So here he was, he and the rest of his crew aboard the marauder ship, in the heart of the Beta Quadrant, at the outer fringes of known space. Within a couple of days they would travel beyond anything that had been explored and exploited by the Ferengi. Just one ship, with no backup, no support, no interest from the central council—no nothing.

Turane's first officer, Martok, glanced around from his station in response to the low growling that was coming from his commander. "Is something amiss, Daimon?" he asked deferentially.

Turane turned on him with a snarl. "Wrong, Martok? What could *possibly* be wrong?" He slowly rose from his command chair. "Out in the middle of nowhere, on this profitless voyage—we are a waste, Martok! We have no purpose! We make no profit! There is no life out here. There is no new market. There is no purpose to any of it, other than that my damned brother doesn't want me around."

All of this Martok knew, and he wasn't any happier about it than was Daimon Turane. In fact, he was even less happy about it. With Turane it was a personal dispute that had led him to this unhappy situation. Martok was blameless—he was simply first officer to the wrong Ferengi, at the wrong time.

There had been discussion among Martok and the crew that, sooner or later—later, in all likelihood—the time would come to dispose of Daimon Turane and put someone else in charge. Martok, probably. Turane knew this. The Ferengi command knew this too. Everyone was expecting it, really, and the only reason that Martok had not engineered the change sooner was that—despite his overall unpleasant personality—Turane had headed up some profitable missions in the past. Martok had been his first officer during those escapades, and Martok had something that most Ferengi did not possess—a rudimentary sense of loyalty. This had inclined him to give Daimon Turane as much slack as possible. Perhaps even find a way of salvaging something valuable from this dross of an assignment.

Enough was rapidly becoming enough, however. The crew was growing impatient, and Daimon Turane was slipping further and further into melancholy with every passing day. Martok was going to have to do something because, if he didn't, officers beneath him were going to take matters into their own hands. He was quite determined that, if some unpleasant fate were to befall the Daimon, he would rather be the engineer of it than a victim.

He started to speak, but before any words got out, the status board lit up. Martok's head snapped around in surprise, as did Daimon Turane's. The rest of the bridge crew, which had been lost in their private imaginings of a life without the luckless Daimon Turane, immediately snapped to their assigned duties when encountering something new and unexpected.

"What have we got?" demanded Daimon Turane.

For a moment, at least, his lethargy had slipped away. It had been replaced by some of that old excitement, that heart-pounding thrill at possibly discovering something new to be exploited.

Martok was shaking his head in confusion. "They're so big that at first I thought they were small moons that had somehow broken away from orbit," he said. "Now I see, though. They're ships. Incredibly huge ships."

"On screen," said Turane, turning in his chair to face the front monitor.

The screen wavered for a split second and then cleared. On it hung three huge cube shapes. They were completely stationary.

"What is it?" whispered Turane, daunted by the immensity of them. "What are they?"

Martok immediately accessed his ship's computer, scanning all the known ship types. Much of the information had been cobbled, through means fair and foul, from the Federation archives. When the answer to his search came up, he felt all the blood drain from his face. His throat closed up, and he desperately tried to control the impulse to scream in panic. "It's the Borg," he said in a voice that was just above a whisper.

Daimon Turane, for his part, seemed utterly nonplussed. "The Borg," he said thoughtfully, studying the screen. The Borg ships, already huge, were becoming larger as the Ferengi marauder vessel drew closer. "How intriguing."

"I'll order full retreat," said Martok. Across the way, the navigator was already laying in a course to take them back in the other direction.

"You'll do no such thing," said Daimon Turane calmly. "Bring us in toward them."

There was a collective gasp from the bridge crew at

Turane's order. They were regarding their Daimon with outright horror, with as much incredulity as if he'd ordered them to open every accessway and blow the atmosphere out of the ship.

"Toward them?" gasped the navigator in horror.

"Daimon Turane," said Martok, "this is *the Borg*. Are you unaware of what they did to the Federation? I heard that fifty ships were destroyed in combat against them at Wolf 359."

"Seventy-nine," the navigator said firmly. "I heard seventy-nine, but Starfleet wants to cover it up so the Romulans don't find out."

"I also heard about the cover-up," said the helmsman, now speaking up, "but my sources say eighty-three ships."

"I don't care," snarled Turane, turning on his men, "if the Borg destroyed every ship in the Starfleet. Bring us in there and bring us in there now. Is that clear?"

There was a pause as the bridge crew looked at each other. Everyone was waiting for someone else to make a move.

"Now!" thundered Daimon Turane.

"We'll be killed," said Martok quietly.

With slow, deliberate steps, Turane got up from his chair and walked slowly towards Martok. The only sounds heard on the bridge were the soft footfalls of his boots and the steady beeping from the tacticals informing them of the presence of that of which they were already aware. Turane's lips drew back in the Ferengi approximation of a smile, displaying his double row of sharp, filed teeth.

"We," said Daimon Turane, "will make more profit than anyone ever imagined possible. That is what we will do. Are you saying you don't wish to be a part of that?"

"No, but—profit?" said Martok, not understanding.

Daimon Turane nodded slowly. "This is a dead-end ship with a dead-end assignment, Martok. You know it." He turned to face his bridge crew, his voice rising. "You *all* know it. There is only one way to live the sort of life respectable for a Ferengi. But to achieve it—to achieve greatness—we must dare greatness. One cannot come without the other. The Borg have power beyond imagining, technology that is decades—even centuries—ahead of us. If we can establish a market with them, trade with them, draw them in as allies with the Ferengi—think of the regard in which we would be held. Think of the respect!" What he did not add was, *Think of the putrid expression on my brother's face.*

"But the Federation—"

"Pfaw!" snorted Turane disdainfully. "The Federation does not even know how to deal with *us*. What in the world makes you think that they could possibly know how to deal with beings such as that," and he pointed at the Borg ships, which were now a few hundred kilometers away.

"But if we retreat and inform our council of the Borg presence, wouldn't that be good enough to—" began the navigator.

Turane cut him off with a quick hand gesture. "'Good enough' never is," he said archly. "Now, we go in as a crew and share in the profit, or I go in alone and hoard it all for myself. Which one of you is cowardly enough to turn away from the potential for the greatest, grandest, more incredible payoff in the history of our race?"

The bridge crew looked at each other in silence.

Daimon Turane drew himself up, and when he spoke it was with quiet authority and an apparently unshakable conviction that he would be obeyed. "Take us in," he said.

The marauder ship moved towards its destination as the three great vessels of the Ferengi hung motionlessly in space.

"The Nanites have *lawyers?*"

In the Ten-Forward lounge of the *Enterprise,* Geordi, Riker, and Data were seated around a table, drinks in front of them. Geordi was looking at Riker with open-mouthed disbelief and, having just voiced his incredulity, felt constrained to repeat it. "The Nanites went out and got lawyers? You can't be serious!"

"They didn't 'go out and get lawyers,' Geordi," Riker told him. Although he could understand the chief engineer's annoyance and ire, he hated to admit that he found it mildly amusing at the same time. "The lawyers were assigned to them by the Federation council."

Geordi's hands dropped to the armrests of his chair, and he shook his head. "This is nuts. This is just crazy."

"Geordi, I don't see where—"

"I'm sorry, Commander, but with all due respect, this stinks," Geordi said in frustration. "Wesley and I worked our tails off to get together all the research material on the Nanites that Starfleet had requested. Everyone said this was it—the key to defeating the Borg. Just breed them, introduce them into the Borg systems, and the Nanites would do the rest. It's something so plain that—"

"Even a blind man could see it?" said Riker ruefully.

Geordi nodded slowly. "Yeah. That simple. So here I thought that by now, certainly they would have bred more than enough Nanites to stop the entire Borg race if they showed up. Instead, you're telling me that Step One hasn't been taken because it's tied up in some sort of debate in the council!"

"But if what Commander Riker is saying is correct, Geordi—and I assume it to be," Data added affably, "there are many in the Federation council who feel strongly about Nanite rights."

Before Geordi could start again, Riker stepped in quickly. "The argument has been," he said, "that breeding a race of sentient beings, such as the Nanites, for the express purpose of war and destruction is contrary to all the Federation principles and beliefs. The goal of the Federation is to promote galactic harmony. Creating a 'warrior race'—even a highly specialized warrior race such as the Nanites—would undercut everything that the Federation purports to be about."

"But—"

"There is also the view that it eliminates the free will of the Nanites, if they are being created specifically to fight the Borg. Not to mention, what if the Borg actually managed to absorb the Nanites somehow? Overwhelm them? It's not impossible. We don't know what the full capability of the Borg is. If they did eliminate them somehow, then we will have created a race specifically to die en masse. What does that make us?"

"People trying to survive," said Geordi. "Has the council considered the fact that if the Federation is wiped out by the Borg, then all our high-minded principles won't matter a bit? I'd like to see how quickly some of those council members would change their minds if they'd been aboard the *Enterprise,* staring down the sights of Borg weaponry."

"For what it's worth, some members of the council

agree with you, Mr. La Forge," said Riker. "Enough to cause some fairly lively debates, from my understanding. But until the council gets it sorted out and comes to an agreement one way or the other, there's a hold on developing Nanites for protection against the Borg." He leaned forward and said, "Look, Geordi—if the Nanites rights argument rubs you the wrong way, try this . . ."

Riker paused to take a sip of his drink, but Geordi was so frustrated that he didn't trust himself to speak. Riker continued, "There's also the concern that it's too much like germ warfare. Once released, there's no guarantee that the Nanites might not turn on us. We might wind up with something just as dangerous as the Borg. Would you be willing to take that risk?"

"Risk the Nanites versus risking the Borg? Yeah. In a minute." Geordi shook his head. "I still think it stinks, Commander. If the Borg could be put out of commission by the Nanites, then we should do it."

"Geordi," said Data thoughtfully, "there was discussion given to the notion of replicating me. The purpose was exploration. But what if Starfleet advocated the idea of creating a race of beings—beings who thought and felt, and seemed indistinguishable from me—for the sole purpose of sending those beings off to fight a war? Would that be acceptable to you?"

Geordi frowned. "Well . . . no."

"Why not?"

Geordi called into his mind's eye the image of Data—or how he perceived Data—numbering in the thousands, armed with heavy-duty weaponry, slogging through some marsh somewhere in some godforsaken world. Or a shipload of Datas flying into combat, secure in the knowledge that if the ship were destroyed and all hands died, it wouldn't . . . matter.

"Because you deserve better than that," said Geordi softly.

"And are the Nanites any less deserving?" asked Data.

Geordi sighed heavily. "I suppose not. But still . . . it's frustrating to have the ability to solve your problems right there, in your hand, and you—"

"Can't make the fist?" offered Riker.

"Yeah. You can't make the fist," said Geordi.

Riker held his glass up and, in an overt effort to change the topic and tone of the conversation, announced in stentorian tones, "What see I before me but an empty glass. That, gentlemen, is an abysmal state of affairs that cannot be tolerated." He turned toward the bar behind which Guinan customarily stood. . . .

Except the Ten-Forward hostess wasn't there. Riker glanced around to see where she might be, and then he spotted her on the far side of the room.

She was sitting by herself.

For some reason this looked odd to Riker, and he tried to figure out why. Then it came to him—he'd never seen her sitting by herself. Usually she stood behind the bar, and on those occasions when she was sitting, it was always across a table from someone else. She would be there listening in that way she had, taking in what was being said and dispensing advice in that calm, matter-of-fact manner that always made it seem absurd that you hadn't solved your dilemma yourself.

Not this time, though. She was seated in a corner, staring out a viewing bay at the passing stars. There was something wrong with her. If Riker had been possessed of psychic powers, he might have said that something was dampening her aura.

He stood and said, "Excuse me a moment," without even looking at Geordi and Data. He toyed for a moment with the notion of mentioning his concern about Guinan to Deanna, or perhaps to Picard, who had such a long-standing relationship with Guinan—a relationship murky in its origins.

No. He was here. She was here. And a friendly chat was no more than a friendly chat. Perhaps even Guinan had the right to be just a little down in the mouth for once. But she'd been there for him enough times, and he felt it incumbent upon him to return the favor.

He walked across Ten-Forward and stood next to Guinan. She didn't appear to notice him at all. That immediately turned the alarm level up a notch for Riker. Guinan noticed everything. "Guinan?" he said.

She glanced up at him wanly. "Hello, Commander."

"Do you mind if I—" He gestured to the empty seat opposite her. She inclined her head slightly and he sat. "Is there a problem?" he asked.

She smiled, but the smile didn't touch her eyes. "Isn't that usually my line?" she asked.

"Times change," said Riker. "People change."

"Some do," Guinan replied, and then paused. "Others stay the same." She stood and it was with some visible effort, leaning on the table for support.

Her clearly enervated condition now brought Riker to his feet, and he promptly dispensed with the pleasant demeanor of concerned friend. That he most certainly was, but now, first and foremost, he was an officer of the *Enterprise,* and he knew an ill crewman when he saw one. "Guinan, what is going on with you? You look weak as a kitten."

"I haven't been . . . resting well," she said. "That's all. Nothing to concern yourself about. I've had a lot on my mind."

"I think you should consider sharing it with someone. If not me, then Captain Picard, or Counselor Troi."

"It's . . ." She took a deep breath, as if incapable of finishing the sentence with the air she had in her lungs. "It's nothing that can't be . . ."

Her eyes seemed to glaze over, her voice trailing off in mid-sentence. "Guinan!" Riker said sharply.

She turned towards him, acting as if his voice had come from a long distance, and then she pitched forward into his arms. Her arm swung loosely down and knocked a stray glass off a table.

Immediately everyone in Ten-Forward was on their feet. Guinan had been the rock of the Ten-Forward lounge. To see this happen to her was absolutely staggering.

Riker caught her with one arm and with his free hand tapped his communicator. "Riker to sickbay!" he said rapidly and, without waiting for the acknowledgment, said, "Guinan's passed out. I'm bringing her down. Have a team ready."

"Guinan?" came the incredulous voice of Bev Crusher. The sense that she had of Guinan was the same as everyone else's, namely that she was somehow immune from whatever frailties might plague humans. "Guinan passed out?" Clearly, she wasn't sure she'd heard correctly.

"We're on our way. Riker out."

Riker swept her up in both arms and was amazed at

the total lack of weight. It was like lifting paper or the wind. Guinan was muttering under her breath now, as if her mind were far away. A couple of syllables, over and over, not making any sense. . . .

He didn't have time to stand around and try to decipher it. Instead, he turned and ran with her to the door, Geordi and Data right behind him. Several concerned crewmen started to follow, but Geordi stopped them with a sharp, "We don't need a mob! Stay put."

The crewmen did as they had been ordered, and as the doors hissed shut, they started talking excitedly amongst themselves. They were all tremendously concerned, because everyone was extremely fond of Guinan, and none of them wanted to think that she had come down with anything serious. But so little was really known about her that no one could really be certain just how serious "serious" was.

The Ferengi ship approached the three massive objects that lay before them with extreme caution. They waited for some acknowledgment—verbal communication, an assault—something. But there was nothing. It was as if the Borg didn't know they were there, or simply didn't care.

Turane studied the surface of the ships carefully. They were solid, unknowable, and yet they seemed to pulse with a life all their own. "Keep us steady, helm," he said softly.

The helmsman muttered a brief acknowledgment, but he was also mentally cataloguing the wives (most of them his) he would never see again, the various properties and holdings that he would never enjoy, and the various rivals that he would never have the opportunity to kill.

"There seems to be no way in," said Martok, studying the schematics that the sensors were feeding him.

Daimon Turane stroked his chin thoughtfully and ran a finger absently across his sharp teeth. "Something that huge? And it has no shuttle bay?" he said thoughtfully. "No loading dock? Nothing?"

"Nothing, sir."

Turane nodded briefly and then said, "Hailing frequencies."

"Hailing frequencies open, sir."

Turane raised his voice slightly as he announced, "This is Daimon Turane of the Ferengi. Am I correct in assuming that you are the entities known as," and he paused thoughtfully, as if straining to remember their name. Always better, when commencing business dealings, to let the opposition know that they were barely worth your time. "Known as the Borg?" he finished after a suitable amount of hesitation. He was rather pleased with himself. He had spoken with just the right amount of nonchalance and casual boredom.

There was no reply.

He frowned and a Ferengi frowning was no prettier than a Ferengi smiling. "Are you the Borg?" he demanded again.

The three massive ships remained in stony silence, uncommunicative, unknowable. For all that they seemed interested in the Ferengi craft, the Borg might as well have been great chunks of floating, lifeless rock.

Turane sensed the cold disdain that was radiating from his crew. "Martok," he said with barely concealed anger, "ready a landing party of myself, medical officer Darr, and two security men."

"Are you sure that's wise, Daimon?" asked Martok.

Turane spun and faced him, his anger at the eerily silent Borg, at his brother, at his entire situation in this godforsaken nowhere area of space—all of that spilling out at his first officer. "I don't give a *damn* whether it's wise or not! It's what I'm going to do! Do you have a *problem* with that?"

In contrast to the fury of his commander, Martok was surprisingly quiet. "No, Daimon."

"Good." His anger still barely in check, he said, "The cube in the middle. Scan it. Find the source of peak energy emissions and prepare to beam us over."

"Yes, Daimon."

Daimon Turane started for the door and paused only to say, with triumph lacing his voice, "This is the dawning of a new age for the Ferengi!"

"As you say, Daimon," said Martok. He sat quietly thoughtfully, as Daimon Turane walked off the bridge, shoulders squared, confident in his ability to pull off one of the greatest deals of their time.

The moment he was gone, Martok looked around at the rest of the crew. There was unspoken sentiment in their eyes. Indeed, the sentiment did not have to be spoken. They all knew what was what, and they all knew how long they would be stuck out there if Daimon Turane were in charge.

"He's insane," said the helmsman finally. "The reports we've heard of the Borg . . . it's like trying to reason with a black hole. He's risking all of us. We should be getting out of here. This is not profit. This is suicide."

Martok nodded slowly. "Trust me, my friends," he said with a hiss, "I am watching out for all of our safety. And if I see that safety jeopardized . . . I will take appropriate steps. I will take them . . . very, very soon."

* * *

Guinan had been whisked into a back examination room the moment that she'd been brought down to sickbay. Riker, Data, and Geordi started to follow automatically out of concern, but Crusher put up a firm hand. "She's my patient," she said in no uncertain terms. "I don't need an audience."

"Will she be all right?" asked Geordi.

"I'm a doctor," said Crusher primly, "not a psychic. Which reminds me," and she tapped her communicator. "Crusher to Troi. I've got Guinan down here in sickbay and I'd like you on hand."

"On my way," came Deanna Troi's concerned response.

"Why Deanna?" asked Riker in surprise.

Crusher raised an eyebrow. "Doctor/patient confidentiality, Commander. Or to put it in a slightly more earthy context: None of your damned business." With that she turned and entered the examination room, the door sliding shut behind her.

Seconds later the sickbay doors opened, admitting Deanna Troi and, right behind her, Jean-Luc Picard. Deanna glanced around, and before Riker could get a word out, she headed straight for the side examination room, as if guided by a beacon. Without a word, she entered and then was cut off from view as the doors hissed shut once more.

"What happened, Number One?" said Picard with urgency. "Did she give any warning—?"

"Nothing," Riker told him. "She seemed very distracted, and then she was in the middle of a sentence and just keeled over. I picked her up and brought her straight down here."

Picard looked understandably concerned. He and Guinan had some sort of history together. Guinan had hinted at it but not gone into it, and Picard had remained resolutely tight-lipped, as he did about almost everything. The depth of that history, and of his feelings for her, was as much a mystery as was Guinan herself.

"Did she say anything?" asked Picard. "Anything at all?"

Riker ran through his mind the mutterings that Guinan had uttered while he had cradled her in his muscular arms. "It was something like . . . 'vendor.' Over and over again."

"Vendor?" and Picard frowned. He paced briskly, his hands behind his back. "Vendor? Are you sure?"

"As I said, Captain, it was difficult to make out."

"But why would she be talking about a salesman of some sort?" Picard shook his head. "It makes no sense."

"It obviously made sense to Guinan. She was very insistent about it."

"Then we'll simply have to wait here until she's recovered enough to tell us what she meant," said Picard. He glanced around at his senior officers. "I see no need for all four of us to be waiting here."

Data inquired politely, "Will you be leaving, sir?"

Picard gave him an icy look, and Riker stepped in quickly. "I think we should be minding the bridge, Mr. Data. Come along."

Obediently, if uncomprehendingly, Data and Geordi followed Riker out, leaving Picard alone in the sickbay. In the corridor Geordi said, "Whatever there is between the captain and Guinan, he obviously wants to keep it private."

"And we'll respect that, Mr. La Forge."

"No question."

"If the captain has anything to tell us, he will."

"No question." And then, after a moment of

thought, Geordi added, "Of course, until such time that the captain chooses to tell us, we're all going to speculate one hell of a lot."

"No question," said Riker.

Picard, in the meantime, remained in sickbay. He gave up pacing after a short time, because it brought to mind the cliché image of the expectant father waiting for some sort of word about his wife in labor.

After what seemed an interminable time, Bev Crusher emerged from the examining room. If she was surprised to see Picard there, she didn't say so. Instead, she simply folded her arms and announced, "She's fine."

Picard had finally seated himself but now he stood, shoulders squared, posture correct as always, ramrod-perfect. He smoothed his jacket and said, "What was wrong with her?"

"You don't understand, Captain. When I say she's fine, I mean she's fine. I mean I can't find anything wrong with her. I have absolutely no idea why she passed out, and Deanna's empathic scan doesn't pick up anything."

"Does Guinan know what happened?"

"If she does, she's not telling me."

"She'll tell me," Picard said firmly, and headed for the examining room.

He entered and saw Guinan standing next to the table, looking calm and self-contained. She was just adjusting her headgear. Nearby sat Deanna Troi, looking quite distracted, and Picard noticed it immediately. But first he turned his attention to his Ten-Forward hostess as he said, "How are you feeling?"

"Fit," she said. There was something in her voice—a hint of that distractedness that Riker had indicated typified her mood before she had passed out. But it didn't seem especially drastic. "Fit and well. I'm probably just overworked."

"You do seem to spend every waking hour in Ten-Forward, Guinan," allowed Picard. "Even for one of your . . . special gifts . . . that seems a bit extreme. Still . . . do you have any other explanation for your sudden faintness?"

"Nothing comes to mind," she said.

For the briefest of moments he thought Guinan was keeping something from him. But that would mean she was lying, and there was no way in this cosmos that he was going to accept the notion that Guinan would lie to him. He would just as readily believe that the Federation was actually a front set up by the Romulans. Or that all of space travel was actually a huge case of collective mass hysteria on the part of the human race, and mankind was still mucking around on the planet Earth.

Still . . .

"Does the word *Vendor* mean anything to you?"

She appeared to give it some thought, and then she shook her head. "No special significance other than the obvious."

He regarded her with a feeling that was alien when it came to Guinan—suspicion. Not suspicion that she was keeping something from him, but that—bizarre as it sounded—she was keeping something from herself.

Picard was far from satisfied. "Guinan, do you have any idea at all what could have caused that sudden weakness? It's so unlike you."

She frowned. "The only thing I can think of," and she slid off the examining table as she spoke, "is that it has something to do with others of my race. We are sensitive to each others' moods. If there was something happening, something that affected us . . ."

"I thought your people had been scattered after the Borg attack," said Troi.

Guinan afforded her a brief glance. "Scattered, Counselor. Never separated." She turned back to Picard. "An overwhelming feeling, Captain. I can't be more specific than that, if that's what it is, in fact. As soon as I know more, you will too."

She started for the door, and then Picard stopped her with a simple question: "Is it the Borg?"

She looked back at him over her shoulder, and Picard might have been imagining it, but he thought a brief shudder passed through her.

"Bet on it," she said.

The four Ferengi materialized in the main corridor of the center Borg ship. There had been nothing really to distinguish one ship from the other. Just an arbitrary decision on Turane's part.

The landing party was puzzled by what they saw. Corridors that seemed to go on forever, an incredible labyrinth that didn't seem to have been designed so much as having organically *grown* somehow, in all directions and yet with a ruthless, systematic efficiency. Whereas Ferengi ships had aspects to their layout that contributed, in a variety of ways, to add personality to their surroundings, the Borg ship was quite the opposite. The Ferengi began to explore, and wherever they looked, wherever they searched, they found that the Borg personality seemed defined by their utter *absence* of personality.

Darr was studying the readings from his medical instruments. "I'm not detecting any individual life readings, Daimon," he said after a long moment.

"Then what do you call those?" said Turane immediately, having taken a step back in forcefully controlled alarm. He had his blaster out immediately. Coming his way, with slow, measured, ominous tread, was a Borg soldier.

"Halt!" shouted Turane, for the Borg was bearing down on him, his gaze unwavering, his right arm encased in an ominous sheath of metal. "Guards! Stop him! He's going to attack me!"

The guards were standing directly in between the oncoming Borg and the alarmed Daimon. And then a clanking alerted them to the approach of a second Borg soldier from behind. They spun and faced him, the face on the second one as deadpan as the first.

"Stop them, you idiots!" shouted Daimon Turane. "What are you waiting for?!"

The guards looked at each other, an unspoken decision passing between them. Then, as one, they lowered their weapons and stepped back, flat against the wall, leaving a clear path to their commanding officer.

The blood drained from Daimon Turane's face, and his heart raced. He looked in front of and behind him, the Borg soldiers closing in, and a fearful curse emerged from his thick lips. "This is treason!" he howled. "This is mutiny! Darr, do something!"

But Darr was an old man, and he merely cowered behind the nearest security officer.

Daimon Turane brought his blaster up, aimed at the nearest Borg, and squeezed the trigger.

Nothing.

He howled in fury. The energy indicator read a full charge, but obviously someone had tampered with it. Perhaps one of these guards. Perhaps someone else back on the ship. Perhaps even Martok himself. In the final analysis, it made no difference. He was dead, that was all. Dead and gone.

The Borg were upon him, their heavy clanging echoing around them. They passed in front of each other, in front of him . . .

And kept on going in opposite directions.

Daimon Turane watched in utter confusion as the Borg totally ignored him and went off about their business as if his presence didn't matter at all. Within moments they were gone, the only thing left behind them being that inexorable clanging. Shortly thereafter, that was gone too. What remained was the steady humming and throbbing and pulsing of electronic life that seemed to fill the walls, the floors, the very air around them.

Turane, however, did not have the time or the inclination to dwell on it. Instead, his fury was focussed on his guards as he turned on them with the full measure of it and said, icily, "What was the *meaning* of that *outrageous* behavior?"

"This was the meaning," said the guard, and he swung his heavy blaster up and fired.

Turane would have been dead right there, had not medical officer Darr hurled himself right into the path of the assault. Darr hadn't even known he was going to do it, until he did. If he'd given it a moment's thought, or even had it to do over again, he probably would have stayed rooted to the spot. As it happened, he didn't have to the chance to do anything ever again, because he died before he could even get out a single word to reprimand the guards for their attack.

Turane stood paralyzed for a moment, staring at the smoldering body of his medical officer. Then his gaze returned to the guards, who were standing there with singularly stupid expressions on their faces.

"Oh hell," muttered the nearest of them, staring down at their handiwork.

Turane realized at that point that he had two choices: To stay and try and regain control of the situation by asserting his authority over the security guards who were clearly out to murder him, or to get the hell out of there.

Daimon Turane was nothing, if not a realist. Without a second's further consideration, he spun on his heel and bolted.

The movement snapped the two Ferengi guards from their momentary paralysis. They immediately started firing, but by that time the fleet-footed Daimon had rounded a corner and vanished, their blaster bolts exploding harmlessly behind him. The guards cursed loudly and started off after him.

Turane tore through the Borg ship, his arms pumping furiously, his blood pounding in his temples. Turane wasn't in bad shape for a Ferengi, but he was far from fit. Fear for his life, though, lent him some extra strength and endurance. His legs churned up distance quickly, and he ran with no heed to direction other than simply away from his pursuers. His pursuers didn't make it difficult to keep track of them, for they raised a hellish racket behind them as they followed.

The frantic Daimon turned another corner and ran headlong into a Borg soldier. They went down in a tumble of arms and legs, Turane shrieking, the soldier eerily silent. Turane grabbed the Borg soldier by the front of his clothing and practically screamed in his face, "Help me! They're trying to *kill* me! Help me and I'll help you!"

The Borg said nothing. The Borg didn't even appear to notice that Turane was there. Instead he sat up, brushing Turane aside in an offhand manner. It wasn't even a gesture acknowledging Turane's presence as a living being so much as it was just pushing aside an obstacle, as one would a gnat. The soldier got to its feet and kept on walking.

"You call yourselves *soldiers!*" bellowed Turane in frustration. "You won't even fight! I have to do everything!"

The guards suddenly appeared at the far end of the corridor. "There!" shouted the nearer one, and they opened fire.

Turane leaped frantically to the left, and the blaster bolts exploded over his head. They blew out some sort of glowing power units, blasting them into fragments, and Turane tripped, knocked off his feet by the concussion. He hit the floor hard, landing wrong, and it tore up his knees and elbows. He skidded and smashed into a nearby wall, and then rolled onto his back, crabwalking and shoving himself backwards. His back slammed up against a corner, his arms up over his head, protecting himself as best he could. Daimon Turane stamped his feet in childlike frustration, howling his fury. "I am the Daimon, damn you!" he shouted. "I order you to stop!"

The guards paused, and for one brief glorious moment, the Daimon thought they were about to obey him. Then he realized that they were merely stopping to chortle, to enjoy the pathetic state that he had been brought down to.

"Please," whispered Turane, staring down the barrel of their weapons. "Please . . ."

It was at that moment that three Borg soldiers converged on the area.

They ignored Turane, for he was lying inoffensively on the floor. For that matter, the guards simply assumed that the semi-mechanical beings were just going to bypass them as well. So it caught them completely flatfooted when the foremost Borg soldier reached out and grabbed the nearest of the guards with the clawed grabbing end of its mechanical appendage.

The Ferengi guard tried to bring his blaster up to defend himself but he was too slow. A bolt of blue electricity ripped from the Borg's arm, lancing through the Ferengi's, causing him to quiver and shake in the creature's grasp. His skin charred and he opened his mouth, but no scream managed to escape from him. His eyes widened, and the corridor filled with the unpleasant odor of burning flesh.

With perfect precision the Borg dropped the Ferengi the moment the guard had become a lifeless sack of flesh instead of a living being, and turned towards the second guard, trapping him between the other two oncoming Borg. The Ferengi whirled and fired, and his blast caught one of the other two Borg square in the chest. The Borg went down without a sound and, hopes momentarily buoyed, the Ferengi fired on the second one. This time, though, the blaster bolt cascaded harmlessly off a personal shield.

The Ferengi tried to readjust, kicking the power level up, but was too slow. One of the Borg swung its metal arm with incredible force and, with one blow, crushed the delicate cartilage of the Ferengi skull. The guard went down, blood trickling from his nose and large ears, moaning softly for a moment before his voice became a rattle in his throat.

Daimon Turane looked from one dead guard to the other and wondered bleakly how long it would be before he followed them into oblivion. The standing Borg soldiers turned and Turane braced himself, waiting for some sort of attack, for those awful metal appendages to reach out and destroy him.

And the Borg ignored him.

For one insane moment he wasn't sure whether to

be relieved or insulted. After all, they'd spent time and energy dispatching lowly guards. Was he, the Daimon, worthy of less consideration than that? Then he realized that such thinking might indeed be indicative of someone who had lost his mind.

The Borg, for their part, set about their work, and Daimon Turane realized that they were repairing the shattered power units that the guards had destroyed. It was then that he realized what had happened. The Borg hadn't shown up for the purpose of protecting him, or even just attacking potential threats. Instead, they had eliminated the aggressive guards for the simple reason that they were disrupting the smooth functioning of the Borg ship. Once the disruption was gone, there was no need—as far as they were concerned—to pursue any further action.

"Listen to me," said Turane quickly, trying not to stumble over the words. "Listen. I am Daimon Turane of the Ferengi. I want to speak to your leader. I . . . I believe that we can do some business together."

One of the Borg soldiers had picked up the fallen one and walked over to some sort of horizontal wall receptacle. The insensate Borg soldier was placed into the receptacle, which slid noiselessly shut. The Borg soldier then paused, its clawed appendage clicking for a moment, the servos on its head swivelling, as if in thought.

"I have a great deal to offer you," said Turane. By now he had pulled himself to his feet, trying to assemble some measure of his shattered confidence. He was aware that he was in an extremely bad bargaining position, which was never a good way for a Ferengi to begin a deal. He couldn't very well return to his ship, considering the reception that he would probably get. The last thing that one ever wanted to admit to a potential customer, though, was that the customer had the upper hand in any way. "A great deal," he said again. He cleared his throat and said, rather pompously, "I am a Daimon, you know. Daimon Turane of the Ferengi. In addition to my own rank and station, I have a brother who is on the council itself. That, I tend to think, gives you an idea of my importance."

He stood there with arms folded, waiting for a response. He got nothing. One of the Borg soldiers simply turned and walked away. The other remained in its place, relays still clicking, as if receiving a transmission from somewhere.

"I said," repeated Turane a bit more impatiently, "that I have a great deal to offer you."

There was a long, awkward silence, and Turane wasn't sure what he was going to do if the Borg just left the way the previous one had. Would he simply wander the ship for the rest of his life, ignored, frustrated? Relegated to some sort of non-person status? Unable to get a response other than to be destroyed when interfering with some sort of ship function? What sort of destiny was this? He, Daimon Turane, was intended for greater things.

"*Answer me,* damn you!" shouted Turane. "I am a Daimon of the Ferengi, and live or die, I will not be ignored! Do you hear me? I will not!"

And for the first time, the Borg soldier actually fixed him with a glassy stare. There was no sound of acknowledgment, no verbal greeting, but it was clear that, for the first time, the Borg was actually aware of his presence as an individual. All of a sudden he wasn't sure that that awareness was necessarily a good thing.

The Borg turned and started to walk away. Turane remained where he was, uncertain of how best to proceed. Then the Borg stopped in its tracks, turned, and faced Turane once more. This time the message was unmistakable. The Ferengi was to follow.

"All right," said Turane, with some measure of satisfaction. "This is the sort of cooperation that can only be profitable for all of us."

He followed the Borg soldier, who preceded him with a stiff-limbed walk. Turane looked around him as they went farther and farther into the heart of the Borg ship. The place was a complete maze. If he needed to find his way back, he never would be able to. And he sensed that every square inch of the ship was being used for some specific purpose. Absolutely nothing was being left to waste. There was no need for pictures or sculptures to break up the decor, or for differently colored walls, or for anything other than total machine-precision. There was a certain . . . inevitability about it all. As if anything caught up in the great gears of the Borg mentality would be unceasingly, irrevocably ground up and pulped into its essence.

There was a steady humming in front of him that was getting louder and louder as he approached it. A power source, perhaps? Or something more? He wasn't sure. He wasn't sure of anything, really, except that matters were spiralling out beyond his ability to control them.

First officer Martok drummed his fingers impatiently on the arms of the command chair. The rest of the bridge crew waited for some sort of move on his part, some indication of his intentions.

"Raise them," he said finally. "They've been silent for too long."

"No response, sir," said the tactical officer after a moment. "Not from Daimon Turane, nor Darr, nor any of the guards."

Martok nodded slowly.

"I was afraid of that," he said. "It may be that Daimon Turane has met with a . . . mishap."

It seemed to stretch out forever.

Turane stood on a ledge that overlooked what appeared to be some sort of massive power core. The angles were confusing, the depth difficult to register, but he was certain that he was perceiving something that was miles wide and miles deep. There were Ferengi legends of a great pit that led to a netherworld, down to which all Ferengi would be hurled at the end of their lives. Waiting in that pit was a great entity which would study the amount of business conducted in the recently deceased's lifetime, and whether that life had ended on the profit or debit side. The fate for all eternity would then be determined. Turane had the hideous feeling that he was facing that judgment prematurely . . . or perhaps it wasn't premature. Maybe he was dead and just hadn't acknowledged it yet.

Borg soldiers now stood on either side of him, facing the great presence. Yes, definitely, there was some sort of presence there.

And when it spoke to him, it seemed to echo not only in his ears, but in his mind.

"We are the Borg," it announced. It wasn't one voice. It was the voice of thousands combined. And it seemed to speak, not just from within the ship, but from somewhere beyond that, as if the ship were channeling only some sort of greater intelligence.

Turane nodded slowly. In this, the most incredible situation he'd ever been in, he found his thoughts spinning back to the most elementary lessons he'd ever had in business dealings. Never let them see you're uncertain. Never act as if you've been caught unawares. Always act as if you're two steps ahead of the proceedings, even if you're three steps behind. Confidence is everything. Arrogance is everything. Any deal can be consummated if you act as if any deal can be walked away from.

"And 'we'," said Turane, drawing himself up, "are Daimon Turane of the Ferengi. If you want expertise on the science of the deal, and are interested in chatting with one of the most accomplished negotiators in the Ferengi empire, then I can be of use to you. If you are interested in discussing some sort of deal—"

"Deal is irrelevant," boomed the voice of the Borg.

Turane tilted his head slightly. "I hardly think that the science of the deal—"

"Deal is irrelevant," came the implacable voice. "Science is irrelevant. What you think is irrelevant. We will use you."

"Use me?" said Turane.

"We had a voice," said the Borg. "A link to humans. That link was severed. We will use another link. A voice to speak for the Borg. The previous link was too strong-willed. We will use someone more easily controlled."

"Who was your link?" asked Turane. Somehow he wasn't really expecting an answer.

To his surprise, he got one. "The link was Locutus. Before he was Locutus, he was Picard."

"Picard?" gasped Turane. "Jean-Luc Picard . . . of the *Enterprise?* And he was your spokesman?"

"He malfunctioned. He will now be replaced."

"Spokesman," said Turane thoughtfully. "Yes, I rather like the sound of that. To return to the Ferengi, with your might behind me . . . yes. Yes, I think we can do business together." A slow smile spread across his face as he contemplated the reaction of his ac-

cursed brother when he, the despised Turane returned, backed up by the power of the all-powerful
Borg. "Of course, we have to discuss terms . . ."

"Terms are irrelevant."

"Now wait a—"

"Discussion is irrelevant. You will be our voice. You
will 'sell,' as you phrased it. You will tell humanoids
that they must bow to the Borg. That they must
surrender to the Borg. That the way of the Borg is the
only way."

"That's all fine," said Daimon Turane. "But there
has to be something in it for me. As long as we come to
an understanding about—"

"Understanding is irrelevant."

"But I have needs—"

"Needs are irrelevant."

With mounting fury driven by rapidly spiralling
fear, Turane said, "All you've discussed is what *you*
want. What about me?"

The response was not altogether unexpected; however, that made it no less chilling.

"You are irrelevant."

Chapter Six

"MY GOD," whispered Deanna. "Look at it."

They had seen examples of the Borg's handiwork before, but it never failed to be an impressive and totally horrifying sight. There, in front of them, was a planet that once had been home to a sprawling civilization. Now it sat there, looking lifeless, gutted and pitted as if a giant ice cream scoop had come down and served out huge dollops of the planet.

"The rescue ship *Curie* is in orbit around Penzatti, sir," Worf said. "Receiving an incoming transmission from Dr. Terman."

"On screen."

Picard was familiar with Terman's work, and with Terman himself. Although Terman carried the flag rank of Commodore, he rarely used the rank (except when forced to pull it) himself and always preferred to be addressed as "Doctor."

"The rank was given me," Picard had heard him quoted as saying once, "but I had to work for the damned doctoring degree."

Whenever there was immediate need for rescue

services, Terman and his people seem to appear with almost preternatural timing. Some said Terman had a low-grade telepathic ability that unconsciously tipped him to trouble spots. He simply called it dumb luck.

The screen flickered a moment, wiping away the hideous spectacle of the Penzatti and replacing it with the lined, graying face of Doctor Terman. Picard knew immediately what was going through the man's mind. Terman was too much the veteran to allow any outward display of emotion, but the haunted expression in his eyes upon coming face to face with the horrific power of the Borg . . .

Picard knew that haunted look. It was in the eyes of the image that stared at him every morning from the mirror when he shaved.

He forced himself into his full business mode. "Doctor, what is your review of the situation?"

Terman nodded his head in the general direction of the planet below. "Have you ever seen anything like this before?"

"Twice," said Picard. "Two more times than I would have liked."

"This planet has had it," said Terman. "I've had my people run a projection." He rubbed the bridge of his nose, as if to physically shove his brain into operational mode. Picard suspected the man hadn't slept in days. "The amount of mass removed from the planet has irrevocably altered the orbit, not to mention the fact that chunks of its atmosphere were ripped away. This place is going to go from vacation spot to frozen snowball."

"Shall we commence emergency evacuation procedures?" asked Picard. Numerically it would not be a problem. The *Enterprise*, in a pinch, could handle as many as nine thousand evacuees.

"If you recommend it."

Picard gave it a moment's thought. "How long before the orbital changes impact on the climate?"

"Oh," Terman gave a dismissive wave, "months yet. Their years are 579 solar days long. I'd give it at least six solar months before this place really begins to freeze over."

"Then I would be inclined to wait awhile," said Picard. He saw from the corner of his eye Riker giving him a surprised look, but he continued calmly, "If the Borg are in the area, or return shortly, we will doubtlessly be engaging them."

"Yes, I've heard they're most engaging fellows," said Terman dryly. It was the sort of gallows humor tossed around when people were faced with situations too hideous to contemplate. An understandable defensive device, if somewhat inappropriate, and Picard let the comment pass unremarked.

"If that occurs, then being on the *Enterprise* may well be the equivalent of stepping from the frying pan into the fire," continued Picard. "However, if your medical facilities are—"

"Crammed," said Dr. Terman. "We're small and wiry on the *Curie,* but we've got our limits, and this is exceeding them. I'll tell you, Captain, before this we helped patch things together on Tri Epsilon Delta, after a Tholian raid. That was a cakewalk, compared to this."

"We'll be more than happy to pitch in. In the meantime, the *Chekov* is on her way as well. Within a few days you'll have more help than you can handle."

"Ain't no such animal," said Terman. "I can use all the help I can get. Look, Captain, I can't tell you how much I'd rather be chatting here with you than overseeing this sweep-up operation, but—"

"Understood, Doctor. We'll be down presently to assist. *Enterprise* out."

The frowning image of Terman vanished to be replaced by, once again, the cratered surface of Penzatti. Picard stared at it a moment more and then said, "Number One, prepare an away team. Full medical personnel complement, all shifts. We don't have a moment to lose."

"You want to accomplish as much as possible in the event the Borg return?" said Riker.

Picard gave him a significant glance. "That is in the back of my mind."

"And moving up fast."

"Warp speed," affirmed Picard. "Mr. Chafin," he addressed the lieutenant at conn. "Standard orbit."

"Aye, sir," said Chafin, and within moments the *Enterprise* was in a graceful synchronous orbit, 35,000 kilometers above the scarred surface of the planet. "Standard orbit, sir."

From the tactical display, Worf was scanning the area. "Sir," he said, "sensors are detecting high traces of the types of weapons that were discharged."

"Borg weaponry?" asked Picard. It seemed self-evident somehow. The Romulans didn't exactly go around gutting planets. Who the hell else could it be?

"Some trace of Borg, sir . . . but something else. I am also detecting some debris that is definitely from the Borg ship."

"Debris," said Riker. "Then, it's true."

"The Borg have apparently met their match," agreed Picard. "Spectral analysis of the debris, Mr. Worf. Cause of destruction?"

Worf looked up with a look of disbelief on his face, his eyes wide. If there was one thing Worf understood, even worshipped, it was power. Yet here was something that gave even the Klingon pause. "A beam composed of pure anti-proton."

"Pure?" said Riker in astonishment. "A weapon of that magnitude could destroy—"

"Anything," said Data. There was something even more chilling about the way he said it—with that detached, calm, faintly mechanical air. "Absolutely anything. It would sever castrodinium at the molecular level. An anti-proton beam, at full strength, would not be slowed by our shields at all."

That analysis hung in the air for a moment. Then Picard said, very quietly, "It would definitely appear we have a new player on the ball field. And he is wielding a considerably formidable bat."

The landing party, composed of Riker, Geordi, Data, Crusher, Doctor Selar, and ten medtechs, each fully loaded with gear, materialized on the one section of the planet that had remained intact after the Borg attack. It was a section roughly eight hundred miles in diameter, although a good portion of that consisted of woodlands and undisturbed nature. The Penzatti, as technically advanced as they were, still had an appreciation for the beauty that only nature could provide. It only added to the tragedy of their world's fate that the Borg had no such considerations.

All around them the rescue teams from the *Curie* were hard at work. Buildings had tumbled over, bodies lay strewn about, and death still hung in the air, an uninvited and unwelcome guest at the proceedings. The valiant *Curie* teams were doing everything they could to reduce the number of individuals forced to shake hands with that dreaded and final visitor.

Riker was a long-time, seasoned professional. He remembered the first time he had beamed down into the middle of a disaster area. Orion raiders had attacked a Federation outpost. He was fresh out of the Academy, confident in his training and certain that he could handle whatever he was confronted with. When he had materialized on the surface of the outpost, he came to the immediate realization that he was standing in something warm, with an overwhelming smell. He looked down and saw his left boot astride some sort of pink tubing. Suddenly, he realized that it was, in fact, the lower intestines of a disembowled victim of the raiders, the rest of the victim lying nearby with a bleak expression on his dead face.

It was Riker's first direct experience with the brutality that sentient beings could inflict on each other. It was also his first direct experience with completely losing control, as he doubled over and vomited up his lunch in front of fellow crewmembers. He still remembered being bent over, his back trembling, staring in humiliation at the mute testament to his inexperience. And then he felt the reassuring and yet firm pat on the shoulders of his commanding officer. "We've all been there," said his CO, and Riker felt a little better, but not much.

Since then Riker had developed a veneer of detachment. That part of him that was horrified by what he witnessed was buried far, far within him, where it could not possibly interfere with his ability to function as a Starfleet officer. In a way the thought that he could just take his emotions and put them on hold, and not be affected by what he saw, was a frightening one. How easy was it to take that one step further and detach oneself from the concerns of humanity altogether? Were the Borg an inhuman race apart, or were they the logical and inevitable destiny of humanity?

Riker promptly decided that he would make himself nuts if he allowed his thoughts to continue in that direction. "Spread out," he said. "Lend aid where you can. All medical personnel are to stay in constant touch with Doctor Crusher and, Doctor, I want updates from you every half hour." She nodded in quick agreement and moved off. Geordi, Riker, and Data headed off in another direction, accompanied by Selar.

As they moved through the devastation, they were surrounded by cries of "Help me," and moans, and words of encouragement and support from the *Curie* teams. Every so often Riker spotted one of the *Enterprise* personnel as well. He nodded in approval. Crusher had displayed her customary efficiency in deploying her people.

Geordi was scanning the ground, the buildings, the very air around him with his VISOR. Data was studying his tricorder readings and then paused a moment over one patch of ground. "A Borg soldier died here," he announced.

"Died, or whatever the hell it is they do," said Riker. He had witnessed the phenomenon himself enough times: A downed Borg soldier lies insensate, and then another Borg comes along, removes some pieces of his circuitry, and the fallen Borg self-destructs into ash.

Geordi, sensing trace readings through his VISOR, commented, "And over there too," and he pointed. "These people didn't go down without a struggle."

"I'm detecting life readings from that direction," said Selar, studying her medical tricorder. The Vulcan medical officer pointed just off to the west. "One individual. Vital signs are low, and fluctuating."

The away team moved off in the direction that she had indicated. Within moments they were walking down a street that was filled with the same sorts of crumbled buildings and debris as all the others they had passed.

Geordi's VISOR and Selar's tricorder detected him at roughly the same time, and together they pointed and said, "There."

There was a mound of dirt that had been obscuring the body and when they got there they found out why. It seemed as if someone had been in the process of burying this particular member of the Penzatti. A very shallow grave, not more than a few inches deep, and a couple feet around, had been dug. The Penzatti was a male and was lying on his stomach, halfway in, face to the side. Jammed into the back of his belt were two Penzatti blasters. The Penzatti's antenna was twitching ever so slightly as Selar ran her tricorder over him.

"Alive. Just barely." She pulled a hypo from her medkit and injected it into his upper arm. "That should stabilize him. He has a broken leg, multiple contusions and abrasions."

Riker started to reach for him to turn him over, and Selar said sharply, "Moving him in any way would be most unadvisable, Commander."

Immediately the first officer withdrew, chagrined that he had forgotten that most elementary of first aid procedures. At that moment, however, the Penzatti moaned softly and half lifted his head himself.

The first person he saw was Data.

He gasped and tried to reach around for his blasters, but he had no strength. When he realized this, when he realized he had no defense, his head dropped back down into the dirt and he moaned softly.

"I am not here to harm you, sir," said Data calmly. "I am with Starfleet."

"You're safe now," affirmed Riker.

The Penzatti did not lift his head. Instead, he said softly, "Safe," and then he started to laugh. It was a low and ugly sound, a sound of bitterness and derision that grew louder and louder, practically a demented cackle.

"Sir," began Riker, "we're from the *Enterprise . . ."*

He wasn't heard. The Penzatti was laughing even more loudly, gasping out, "Safe! Safe!" as if it were the funniest thing he'd ever heard. And then his laughter began to subside, replaced by choking sobs, and he skidded from giddiness to misery and hopelessness, all within a few seconds.

Selar was monitoring his vitals, waiting for them to stabilize, and ministering to his leg as she did so. She was a cautious medical practitioner, and she disliked having to move a patient whose lifesigns were fluctuating, if she didn't have to. The transporter had an effect on the bodily system, that much was certain. For a healthy individual, that effect was negligible. But for someone in bad shape, it could be a shock that could send a patient into critical condition. She was certain that with a couple of minute's work, she could stabilize the patient to ensure a safe trip.

"What's your name?" asked Riker.

"I am . . ." He seemed to pause to try and remember. "I am Dantar. I was Dantar the Eighth. Now I am Dantar the Last. All I am and will ever be, in that one, useless name."

"It looked like someone tried to bury you," Geordi said.

"Dantar the most useless," said Dantar. His voice was eerily singsong. "Dantar whose family died, a few yards away, and he couldn't help them. Couldn't help them."

"He did that himself," said Selar, in response to

110

Geordi's comment. "His fingernails are encrusted with dirt and sludge. He tried to bury himself."

"You tried to dig your own grave?" asked Riker, horrified and curious at the same time.

"There is no point in my continuing to live," said Dantar. "I have nothing. It's simply time for me to crawl into my grave and rot there. There's nothing. Nothing."

"What did you see?" asked Riker. "Who attacked?"

"Commander, now may not be the best time," began Selar.

But Riker cut her off sharply. "When it comes to the Borg, Doctor, we never have any idea just how much time we have."

"The Borg," said Dantar distantly. "Is that what they're called? Those pale creatures with machines for souls. One went into my house. It killed my little girl. It killed my family. Borg."

"Someone stopped them," said Riker urgently. "Someone fought them and stopped them and destroyed their ship. Did they send down any ground troops? Did you see anyone besides the Borg?"

"Yes. Yes, I did."

"Who?" asked Riker.

"I saw Death," said Dantar, as distractedly as ever. "She was standing right over there, sweeping through my family. Holding the glowing orbs of their souls in her hand and then smothering them. Then she glided across the street . . . she seemed to walk, but you couldn't hear her footfall. And she went from one person to the next." Tears began to roll down his face. "I tried to persuade her to take me. Tried to put myself into a grave so that she would know. But she ignored me."

"Dantar," began Riker.

But Dantar wasn't listening. "You know . . . our culture has always depicted Death as a grim, fearful figure. Dark. Hideous, with a skull face. Skeletal."

"As has ours, frequently," said Geordi.

"But she wasn't. I was very surprised," said Dantar. His voice seemed to be fading, exhaustion paralyzing his ability to think. As if from far away, he said, "She was a very young girl. With a white dress, skipping. And she was smiling. You know why that is, I think?"

"Why?" said Selar. She was preparing to order Dantar beamed up to the *Enterprise.* She was satisfied that his lifesigns were stable enough now that he could handle the transporter with no danger. "Why is that?"

He looked thoughtful. "I suppose she simply likes her work. In such dangerous times, that's nice to see. Don't you think?"

After Dantar and Selar had returned to the *Enterprise,* Riker said thoughtfully, "He said a Borg soldier went into his house over there. Let's check it out. Perhaps someone even survived." He took a step in that direction and then paused and removed his phaser. He looked significantly at the others. "Just in case there's a Borg in there."

"Couldn't be," said Geordi. "Their ship was destroyed. If their ship goes, they go. Their link is severed."

"If there's one thing we shouldn't be doing, it's underestimating the Borg," Riker warned him. "That's a good way to achieve early and terminal unemployment."

"I catch your drift, sir," said Geordi, pulling out his own phaser. Data did likewise.

Slowly they approached the house, noting that the roof had caved in, and the chances of anyone surviving were nil. There was also an unpleasant smell, that same smell that brought back to Riker memories of that awful first time he had seen death on a large scale. Now he shoved it away, determined to ignore it. He was far more than he had been that day. And in some ways, he thought, far less.

Geordi peered in through the darkened doorway, taking in the carnage. It was times like this that made him glad that—despite the dazzling abilities of his VISOR-augmented sight—he could not really "see." He shook his head and said, "There's a lot of dead people in here, Commander."

Riker was checking his tricorder. "Not picking up any life." In a way, he was relieved. He didn't really want to have to look at them. It wasn't going to do the deceased any good, and it sure wasn't going to help his peace of mind. "Let's go."

But Geordi put up a hand. "Wait. I'm getting something. Not a life form, but . . . something."

Double-checking his tricorder, Riker said, "Whatever you're seeing, it's still not picking up. Are you sure your VISOR isn't malfunctioning?"

Without glancing back, La Forge said calmly, "Are you sure your eyes aren't malfunctioning?"

"Just a suggestion, Mr. La Forge," said Riker. Privately he thought it interesting that, even after all this time, Geordi La Forge could still be a bit sensitive about his eyesight.

With a sly imitation of Picard's accent, Geordi said, "Noted and logged." Then, all business, he said firmly, "It's over there."

He was pointing toward a pile of rubble in a corner of the room. The three men immediately went over to it, trying not to think about the bodies they were stepping over. Riker had to force himself to look away from the horrific sight of a small girl, her skull clearly crushed, in the arms of her mother who had died mere seconds later. They reached the pile of rubble and started to pull away, to get to whatever the devil it was that Geordi had detected.

Riker lifted off one huge chunk of debris, turned back to get another one, and jumped back with a start.

He was staring down the business end of the deadly metal appendage of a Borg soldier.

"La Forge! Data!" he shouted. "Watch it!"

He waited for something to happen—for electricity to shoot out, or the pincers to grab at him. But nothing occurred.

Now Data and La Forge were at his side. "What is it?" asked Geordi.

"It's a Borg," said Riker grimly. "A Borg that survived its ship being blown up."

"Just like you said, Commander," admitted Geordi.

While not allowing the seriousness of the situation to escape him, Riker permitted a grim smile and said, "That's why they pay me the big money, Mr. La Forge."

"I had presumed that a larger salary," said Data, "was due to higher rank, seniority . . ."

"Not now, Data," sighed Geordi.

Immediately disposing of the train of thought, Data promptly switched gears to the other. "It would explain why the tricorders don't read the Borg soldier. The Borg do not seem to register as individuals. Apparently, that is a result of their uniformity of nature."

"Is it going to attack?" asked Geordi.

"They have a tendency to ignore most things unless directly threatened," said Riker. "But this one is buried. I'm not sure how it'll react. And I'm not taking any chances." He tapped his communicator. "Riker to security."

"Security," came the deep voice of Worf.

"Worf, you and two security men, down to these coordinates, fast," ordered Riker. "We may have captured a Borg soldier."

"Proceed with extreme caution, Commander," Worf warned him.

"That's why we're calling on you, Mr. Worf."

Data and Geordi were hard at work clearing off the debris from the rest of the Borg warrior. Data uncovered the soldier's face and stared intently into the eyes. "The Borg does indeed appear alive, Commander," he said after a moment's study, "but would appear to be in some sort of 'pause' mode, as if awaiting new instructions."

"I just don't get it," La Forge was saying. He pulled off a large piece of planking and shoved it aside, reaching for another. "How could he have survived being severed from the Borg central command?"

"Captain Picard did," pointed out Riker. His head snapped around as he heard the familiar hum of the transporter that told him Worf and the security team had arrived. He nodded approvingly to himself. Less than thirty seconds. No one could accuse Worf of taking his time.

"Captain Picard had already been separated from the Borg at the point of the ship's detonation," Data explained. "As a result, he was able to survive. Since we can assume that that was not the case with this individual, there must be some other reason."

Geordi was staring intently at the just-uncovered other arm. "I think I found it. And you're not gonna believe it."

Worf marched in with the back-up team, Meyer and Boyajian. He was all business. "This is the potential threat?" he demanded. There was no trace of sarcasm, despite the Borg soldier's immobile state. Riker had

115

identified something that could be hostile, and Worf wanted to make sure that he knew what to shoot, should there be a problem. Indeed, some might say that the Klingon had a terminal case of itchy trigger finger—terminal for whomever the phaser was pointed at.

"That's him," said Riker. "Although it seems at the moment we have everything in hand."

"Then I shall be here in case they get out of hand," said Worf firmly, and that was clearly that.

Riker moved around to where Geordi was standing, having heard Geordi's muttering of discovery. "What have you got, Mr. La Forge?"

"Take a look at this," said Geordi, and he pointed to the Borg's upper arm.

Riker leaned forward and frowned. "What is that . . . ? A kitchen knife or something?"

"That's right," agreed La Forge. "See here? Somebody jammed it into the components right here," and his finger traced the area in the air just above. "It didn't stop the Borg. Didn't kill him. But it scrambled him real good. And I think it saved his life."

"I'm not following," admitted Riker.

Worf was frowning, which was not unusual, but this was deeper than the norm. "I do not understand, either. How could an attempt to kill it, in fact, save it?"

Rather than answer Worf's question directly, Data said, "I believe that Geordi is correct. This component here, just above the trapezius, is—"

"Hold it," said Riker, and again he tapped his communicator. Under ordinary circumstances, and even extraordinary ones, Riker felt no compunction in handling everything himself. But the Borg, and anything having to do with them, was a special case, and Riker wanted to keep his commanding officer absolutely current with every development, as it was happening. "Riker to Captain."

"Yes, Number One," came Picard's voice.

"We found a Borg soldier. Alive."

"Alive?" Picard was clearly astonished. Small wonder. No living being had as much personal experience with the Borg as Picard did, and he knew the unlikelihood of such a discovery. "How is that possible?"

"If you'll keep this line open, I believe Mr. La Forge and Mr. Data were about to inform us of that." He then nodded his head in the direction of his two officers.

"There is a kitchen knife," said Data, for benefit of Picard, who couldn't see it, "protruding from one of the parts that is removed from Borg soldiers when they are disabled. We have theorized that this component—situated on the upper arm, just above the trapezius—was what kept the Borg soldiers in touch with their central mind. This particular component would send a steady relay message to the central mind, and the central mind would, in turn, relay a message back. It was a continuous loop, and when the component was removed . . . either from the Borg soldier, or by means of destruction of the origin point . . . the loop would be severed and the soldier would be destroyed."

"A very Alexandrian solution to a Gordian problem," commented Picard.

"This technology, as advanced as it is, apparently didn't take into account something as primitive as a kitchen knife," Geordi now continued. "It's a total fluke. One-in-a-million shot. I think what happened is that the knife jammed into the circuits, scrambled them, and created a continuous feed loop right within the Borg soldier himself. Bascially, he sends out a steady message for instructions and then answers himself. But he can't give himself instructions, so essentially he's a blank slate. He's sitting and waiting for some sort of acknowledgment that just isn't coming, because he's the beginning and the end of his own little world."

"He has no idea that their ship was destroyed," said Riker.

"Not a clue. He's a circuit to nowhere," Geordi told him.

"And if we remove the knife? Or the component?"

Geordi waved his hands like a magician's. "Then *pfoof.* Ashes to ashes, dust to dust."

"Amen," said Riker.

"I want him brought up here," said Picard.

"I would not advise that, sir," Worf said sternly. "If he self-destructs, he could pose a threat to whoever is near."

"No, he won't," said Picard sharply. Perhaps a little too sharply, because he sounded slightly calmer as he continued, "We know what happens when they destroy themselves. They've done it in our presence any number of times. The Borg waste nothing, including the energy for some pyrotechnically impressive explosion. I want him up here and, if possible, salvaged."

"Yes sir," said Riker. "We'll be right up. Riker out."

Geordi was staring at the Borg's face. It was one of the oddest things he had ever seen. Alive, yet dead. He started to reach out to touch the warrior's face, and Worf immediately grabbed Geordi's wrist. La Forge looked up in surprise.

"I would not advise it," Worf said with a firmness that indicated this was far more than advice.

Yet Geordi couldn't help but look down. "I think the captain's right. I think there might be something salvageable here. There's something that . . . I don't know, I can't put my finger on it."

"I'm sure the captain will be relieved to know you agree with him, Mr. La Forge," said Riker as he tapped his communicator. "Riker to transporter room. Seven to beam up."

"Another survivor?" came O'Brien's voice. These days, no matter how difficult the situation, he sounded inordinately cheerful. Marriage was wearing well on him.

Geordi stared thoughtfully at the Borg soldier. The soldier stared back up at him with unseeing eyes. And even if those eyes could see him, Geordi wouldn't be able to tell. He could see thermal readings to the precise centigrade, but he couldn't see a person's expression.

"Not another survivor," said Geordi thoughtfully. "Another victim."

Picard sat on the bridge, staring at the savaged planet below them, and yet only part of his mind was on it. The rest was dwelling on Guinan's mishap earlier. And the word she had supposedly been muttering in Riker's arms. The word that she could not remember having said.

Vendor.

It made no sense. And yet, somehow, it nagged at him.

He felt as if he should know it or understand it. He felt as if it should have some sort of significance to him.

It tickled and probed at his subconscious. He leaned back in his chair for a moment, then stood. The bridge crew watched him, waiting patiently for some new order, but none was forthcoming.

Vendor.

That wasn't it. He knew without knowing why that that wasn't it. And he also knew, without knowing why, that the truth was buried somewhere in his mind. There was something he had long forgotten, something that he should be remembering but couldn't, or wouldn't. It nagged at him, poked and prodded him, frustrated and infuriated him.

Vendor.

Ven . . .

"Damn," he said in quiet frustration.

Chapter Seven

THE STARSHIP *Repulse* slowed to impulse when the sensors detected something entering the outskirts of the Kalish star system. The *Repulse* had simply been passing through, on their way to Howell 320 with a couple of Federation ambassadors aboard, hot to defuse a potential civil war on that strife-worn planet. The war was on the verge of breaking out because of a cure to a plague that was being withheld by the government, in hopes that the unfriendly factions would do them the service of dropping dead from it. The unfriendly factions were getting unfriendlier by the day, even the hour.

Now, however, concerns over a civil war were quite secondary. Especially when Captain Ariel Taggert saw the readings that were coming through on the preliminary sensors.

"I don't assume," she said grimly, "that we might have, say, a large spider crawling across the sensor dish somehow. Or perhaps something equally innocuous to explain this away," she added, brushing her thick red hair out of her face.

"Captain," affirmed the ops officer, "I wish I could.

This thing we're picking up . . . it's hundreds of miles long. And heading our way."

Just to make matters all the more irritating, Taggert's communicator beeped. She touched it and said, not especially patiently, "Yes?"

"We've stopped," came the annoyed voice of a woman.

Taggert sighed. "No, Doctor, we have not stopped. We've gone to impulse drive."

"That's as good as stopping."

"Doctor, instead of wasting time chatting with me, I think it'd be in your best interest to get sickbay prepared. We may have a problem on our hands."

"Problem? A larger problem than helping those people on Howell 320?"

"Yes, Doctor Pulaski, a considerably larger problem. Shall we say—to give you an idea—a problem a few thousand times larger than the ship you were serving on before you returned to us?"

There was dead silence for a moment. "The *Enterprise* is over two thousand feet in length. Something thousands of times bigger . . . that's monstrous."

"Very good, Doctor," said Taggert. Damn. Pulaski was a superb doctor, and Taggert had been thrilled when she'd been reassigned to the *Repulse,* the ship she'd left to join the *Enterprise* crew. But blast, she could be difficult to deal with sometimes. "Now, you get ready to do your job, because if that thing is hostile, we're going to have more casualties than you know what to do with." She didn't bother to add that chances were, the entire ship would be a casualty, if push came to shove.

She didn't have to say it, and Pulaski didn't have to ask about it. Instead, she said simply, "I read you. Sickbay out."

Taggert turned back to face the screen, although her eyes had never fully strayed from it. "Sensors and viewscreen on maximum," she said slowly. "Go to yellow alert."

The shields came up, and the *Repulse* proceeded cautiously forward.

The *Enterprise* sickbay doors hissed open and Picard entered. He slowed enough to give quick, understanding, and sympathetic nods to those members of the Penzatti race that had been brought to the *Enterprise* for treatment. As Dr. Terman had mentioned, the *Curie* abilities were already overtaxed.

He walked past one Penzatti who reached up and grabbed his arm as he went by. "Are you the captain?" he asked urgently.

Picard gently disengaged the strong grasp from his forearm. "I am Captain Picard, yes. If you'll excuse me for a—"

"I am called Dantar," he said. Although he had been mended and was resting comfortably, the damage done to his body and to his spirit was clearly evident. "I am afraid that I did not conduct myself especially well when dealing with your men. They were exceptionally patient with me while I was in my . . . delirium. I appreciate that, and wanted to commend them."

"I will relay that to them," said Picard, trying to hide his impatience. For all his skills, no one had ever accused him of having a superb bedside manner.

"Are we still in orbit around Penzatti?"

"For the time being."

"Good." Dantar let his head fall back. "There's nothing there for me, and yet I can't bring myself to want to leave it just yet." He looked back up at Picard. "My blasters. My twin Keldin blasters. Your man Worf removed them from my person as soon as I was brought onto the ship. Where are they?"

"Doubtlessly, they're in the armory. They'll be there for safekeeping."

"They'll be safest with me. We Penzatti value our weapons very highly," said Dantar. "Those Keldin blasters were passed on through my family, father to son. They are extremely powerful. They could punch a hole through the side of your ship."

"Then they are definitely staying locked up," said Picard firmly. "I'm sorry, Dantar, but that's the way it will be. There will be no risk of puncturing of my ship."

"But Captain—"

"Excuse me," said Picard, and he turned and walked into a private examining room.

There he saw a formidable sight.

For a moment his heart leaped into his throat and took a choke hold there. It was the first time he'd been confronted by a Borg since his hideous encounter in which he'd been transformed into a mechanized puppet of his former self. He had dreaded this moment, but now that it was here, he realized that the worry had been larger than the actual encounter. Now, when he was finally facing the creature that haunted his dreams, and had caused him to wake up screaming three times in the past months, he saw no threat. He saw only an object to be pitied.

At least, that's what he kept telling himself.

The Borg soldier was strapped to a vertical biobed, the one that, mere months ago, Locutus of Borg had been on. The biobed was lowered into place, and the soldier was staring straight ahead. *Staring* might not have even been the right word, for *staring* implied that some action was being taken. The Borg's eyes simply happened to be pointing in that direction.

Unlike the more limited medical tricorders, the biobed was capable of giving a full medical readout, even on the hard-to-scan Borg. Beverly Crusher was studying them carefully. Nearby were Geordi, Data, and Riker.

The side of Data's head was open, exposing a complex array of circuitry.

"I don't know if this neural link is going to work, Data," Crusher was saying. "The microcircuitry integrated into the skin of this soldier is far more extensive than what we dealt with in the case of . . . Captain," she said, seeing him for the first time.

He said nothing, merely nodded his head slightly, and then slowly circled the unmoving Borg warrior. The others stood respectfully silent, aware of the thoughts running through the captain's mind. Aware of the private horror that he was, to some degree, reliving.

"So the interactive circuits are interacting with themselves, eh?" the captain said after a time.

"Looks that way, sir," said Geordi. "Data was hoping to get around it the way he did with you—by severing the link on a neural level."

"It won't work," repeated Crusher firmly. "This soldier is too far gone. At least with the captain, there was still some Jean-Luc Picard helping us, fighting to come back to us. There's nothing here, though."

"I don't agree," said Geordi. He could not understand the feeling of curiosity that was overwhelming him every time he looked at the Borg soldier. Of course, he remembered what curiosity did to the proverbial cat, but he didn't care. He was determined to figure out just what it was he found so fascinating about this individual. "I think it's worth the risk."

"The risk," said Crusher, "is that if we make a wrong move—if we don't figure out a way to deal with this built-in self-destruct mechanism—we're going to wind up with one dead Borg."

"There's someone trapped in there, Doctor," said Picard fervently. "I concur with Mr. La Forge. We cannot stand idly by while some poor devil is being held prisoner to microcircuitry and implanted hardware." He stared straight into the glassy, unblinking eyes. "There is a man in there who is screaming to get out."

"I seriously doubt that," said Crusher, her arms folded.

Picard's eyes narrowed as he said, "It's most unusual, Doctor, for you to be poorly stocked in the compassion department."

"It has nothing to do with being stocked," she said. "There's no man in there screaming to get out."

"You cannot say that for certain," Picard told her.

"Yes, I can."

"How?"

"Because," said Crusher, pointing at the Borg soldier, "that's a woman."

Captain Ariel Taggert, with her keen eyesight and unparalleled abilities of concentration, saw it first. She pointed and said, "Thar she blows. Magnification six, ops."

The screen shimmered briefly and then reformed.

The entity was now on their screen. It was huge. And it was hungry.

And it was eating.

There was a dead silence on the bridge, and the man at conn said finally, "Holy shit." Then, suddenly aware that his captain did not approve of such language, especially on the bridge, he added quickly, "Sorry, Captain."

But Taggert just shook her head slowly. "No, it's okay, Mr. Seth. Frankly, I can't think of a better way to describe it." She leaned forward, trying not to remind herself that its immensity was frightening, considering the distance they still were from it. Part of her—the intelligent part, no doubt—dearly would have loved to increase that distance a hundredfold. "What in the blazes is it doing? It's . . ."

"Carving up that planet," said Seth slowly. "And . . . and eating it. And it looks like it's got a big appetite."

"Is it . . . is it the Borg?" asked the tactical officer.

Taggert studied them for a moment.

"This thing," she said, finally, "makes the Borg look like tribbles."

"A *woman?*" said Geordi in confusion. "But there are no Borg women! At least, no one's ever seen one."

"When we first encountered the Borg, we found where they were . . . grown," said Data. "Their nursery, so to speak, where Borgs are grown and affixed, almost immediately, with machine parts. There were no females."

"Are you sure there's no mistake, Doctor?" asked Picard.

"No mistake," said Crusher firmly. "They may have made hash of her DNA structure, but I can still see two x chromosomes with the best of them. I'm telling you, this Borg is female."

"The point is," said Picard, "what do we do about it?"

"I believe," said Data, "that I can restructure her neural motorways in a way that will reduce her interactive circuit to a simple, single pulse, generated on a steady basis. As it is, she keeps awaiting instructions that will not be forthcoming. It renders her immobile. By creating a continuous loop within her interactive circuitry, I would be providing her with the illusion that she is receiving a response from the

Borg central mind. Her questioning pulse will, in essence, be rerouted and made into an answering pulse, retranslated into another question, another answer, and so on. It will maintain the status quo."

"You mean she'll be talking to herself," said Crusher.

Data nodded. "For all intents and purposes, yes."

"What will she be saying?"

"Initially, nothing," said Data. "She will not be receiving any instructions. She will simply be receiving an acknowledgment that the Borg mind, from which she was severed, is still in existence."

"Can you give her instructions, Data?" asked Geordi. "Can you restore her and make her into a person again?"

Data shook his head. "The most that I will be able to do, Geordi, is to institute the most rudimentary of commands. She would be able to walk. She would be able to see her surroundings, although I doubt she could understand. Every other function of a Borg is guided by their ship. She is, in human terms, highly retarded."

"We don't know that," said Geordi. "We don't know anything about the person sitting in front of us. There may be a mind in there shouting, 'Help me. Help me out of this living prison.'"

"I don't sense any such thoughts," Troi offered, "but we have no idea of the extent of Borg reprogramming. It could be buried so deep that not even I can touch it."

"It sounds to me like it's a tremendous waste of time," said Riker. "With the amount of work we have cut out for us, I don't know if we should be wasting time and valuable manpower on an attempt that is, in all probability, going to be fruitless."

Troi looked at Riker with mild surprise. There was

an unexpected sharpness in his tone, bordering on anger. There was more to his response than just simple concerns about distribution of manpower.

Picard considered everything that had been said and then turned to Data. "Do you think you can make the connection with this individual?"

"It is possible, sir. Yes."

"Then she deserves the chance to live again. Make it so." And then, unwilling to actually see matters proceeding any further, he walked out of the ready room, followed by Riker.

They stepped into the turbolift and Picard said, "Bridge." As the lift began to move, he said, without looking at Riker, "You sounded somewhat aggressive in there, Number One."

"I spoke my mind," said Riker. "I had thought that was standard operating procedure."

"It is. And is that all there is to it?"

Riker fixed him with an even stare. "Yes, sir."

Picard pursed his lips a moment and then said, "You can't afford to lose your objectivity where the Borg are concerned, Commander."

"I know that, sir."

"Then no more need be said."

"No sir."

"Good."

Taggert was standing and studying the object ahead of them, stroking her chin thoughtfully. "Specs on the planet that's currently serving as that thing's main course," she said.

"Planet Kalish IX," said Mr. Seth after a moment. "Class-B. High methane content, fierce arctic winds. Uninhabitable. No life forms."

"Okay," said Taggert slowly. "So what we have to figure out is whether this thing destroyed a planet because it knew that the planet was lifeless . . . or if the planet was simply the first one that it encountered. Slow to half impulse. Give me information, people."

"We've been scanning it, Captain," said Seth. "The hull is neutronium, making detailed sensor readings impossible."

"Best guess?"

"Mechanical device of some sort. Perhaps some sort of artificial intelligence, although for all we know, there's life forms aboard. Difficult to be certain."

"Open a hailing frequency."

"A hailing frequency," said the tactical officer, Goodman. "To that thing?"

"If there's a humanoid mind or minds behind it, I want to talk to it," said Taggert firmly.

She could understand her officer's surprise. This thing didn't look like a ship. This thing looked like nothing she had ever seen before.

Foremost was a wide circular opening in the front, like a huge, gaping mouth. It was miles wide, like an entranceway to a tunnel that led straight down to hell. From within there were flickerings of some ungodly light, like unseen demons dancing around a towering pyre. The thing then immediately angled straight down, the mouth projecting forward while the rest of the body spiralled down at a ninety-degree angle to it. It twisted and turned all the way to the bottom, looking for all the world like some sort of spacegoing cyclone.

The most noticeable feature, however, was the huge series of projections that extended from all over the exterior. They were longest and most densely packed around the maw, huge pointed towers miles high that came to points, packed so densely that they overlapped. Yet there was a symmetry to them, a sense of deadly beauty and purpose. With the combination of the flickering within the maw itself, and the dazzling projections so thickly set around the mouth, it gave the impression of a massive, moving, highly stylized starburst. A mobile sun, consuming whatever was in its path.

Scattered along the rest of the cyclonic image were more of the huge, spike-like projections. They stuck out at odd angles, in all directions. Any one of them looked capable of skewering a planet through to the core, or smashing through starships with no trouble. It meant that an attacking ship couldn't even get in close.

"Sir, having trouble getting through," reported Goodman. "We're getting some sort of subspace interference. It'll take me a minute to punch through."

"Can you inform Starfleet of what's going on?"

"Negative, sir. We have local communication, but there's too much interference to go beyond the solar system."

Taggert sat back in the command chair, steepling her fingers. A planet-devouring ship. Neutronium hull. Subspace interference. Damn, it all sounded familiar somehow. "Mr. Seth," she began, "check Starfleet logs for—"

"Captain, we're getting a response!" The surprise in Goodman's voice was clear.

"On visual."

"No visual transmission."

"Audio, then."

There was a pause, and then there was a voice . . . a combination of voices. A symphony of voices.

"Yes?" it said. Insanely, it sounded almost polite, as if going about consuming planets was simply standard operating procedure.

Taggert licked her suddenly dry lips and said, "This

is Captain Taggert of the starship *Repulse*." She paused, waiting for some response, some replying identification.

Instead, the huge planet-destroyer simply hung there. Chunks of rubble were being hungrily scooped up by means of what appeared to be a tractor beam.

"And?" said the voice finally. It seemed even vaguely amused somehow.

"Identify yourself," said Taggert.

"Why?"

"Because," Taggert said, using annoyance to cover her deep-seated conviction that they were in way over their heads, "I wish to know the name of the individual, or individuals, who believe that they can just go about the galaxy, destroying planets with impunity."

There was a silence. And then the voice spoke again. *"You describe the Borg,"* it said.

"You are not one of the Borg," said Taggert.

"No. But they are the destroyers. They operate with impunity. We will stop them, though. I will stop them."

"You just destroyed a planet!" said Taggert. "What makes you any better?"

"There was no life. We needed the fuel. I needed the fuel. We are hungry. Hungry for fuel. Vengeance fuels our hatred, but the body needs fuel of a different sort."

"And if there had been life?"

"There was none."

"But if there were?" Taggert said, this time with increased urgency.

"Then they would die. It does not matter. Nothing matters except stopping the Borg. The soulless ones. For if they are not stopped, then truly nothing will matter."

"I must ask you," said Taggert firmly, "as a duly authorized representative of Starfleet, to remain where you are. We cannot permit you to continue on your present course."

"You cannot stop me."

"We will do what we have to."

"If what you have to do is die, then that is what you will do. We would regret that. But if it is necessary, then it is necessary. Nothing must stop me from destroying the Borg."

"Captain, communications have been cut off," said Goodman.

"It's finished consuming the planet," said Seth. "It's . . . it's heading for the next one." He looked up in alarm. "Captain . . . there's a small colony on Kalish VIII—three hundred people."

Taggert bolted to her feet. "Hard about, Mr. Seth. Alert all transporter rooms. Emergency evacuation about to commence. Raise the colonists."

"They hailed us, Captain. They're coming on now."

On the screen appeared the panicked face of a colonist. His skin had turned as white as the thin hair on his head. *"Repulse,* come in!" he was saying urgently. They could see, behind him, people running about frantically, screaming, waving their arms. "This is Astra colony on Kalish VIII. Come in!"

"We're reading you, Astra," said Taggert, the voice and picture of calm.

"Our planetary sensors are reading—"

"We know," she said. "We'll be there in no time. Get your people together—transportation will go faster if we can do you in large masses. And pray," she added, "that what's coming toward you is full from its most recent meal."

The Borg soldier lay in the biobed, the implants glistening metal all over her skin and, insanely, the knife still sticking out of her arm. Dr. Crusher was studying the implants carefully, shaking her head. "Machine parts, attached to people against their will," she was muttering. "Tapping into your body and soul. It's like cybernetic rape."

Data had finished putting the connectors from his own positronic mind to the appropriate connections on the Borg. La Forge stood nearby, making some last-minute adjustments. "Data, you sure about this?" he asked.

Data looked at him with as close to puzzlement as he could muster. "Of course not, Geordi," he said. "One can only be sure if there is no possibility of error, and all factors are known. With the Borg, neither condition is met."

"You sure know how to instill a sense of security," mumbled Geordi, going back to his work.

Deanna Troi stood nearby, feeling helpless and useless. She was reaching out as much as she could to the helpless woman in the biobed, but there was simply nothing there. Troi was perceiving no sense of awareness, no sense of self, no nothing. It was as if the biobed were empty.

"I am ready to proceed," said Data quietly.

Crusher stepped aside to keep a close eye on the life signs. "Ready on this end," she said.

"Proceeding," said Data, and he lapsed into silence.

No one spoke, and there was no sound except for a soft, gentle humming of circuitry. All the normal sounds of sickbay abruptly seem magnified beyond all proportion. Troi looked at Crusher, who glanced at her and then looked at Geordi. La Forge, for his part, kept a steady watch on all the important circuitry.

"I have located the neural path that maintains contact with the Borg central mind," Data said finally. "It appears to be generating a steady flow of electrons which, due to the disruption in the circuitry, are being rerouted and returned to the programming center. It will be necessary to continue this loop, or else the immediate destruction of the soldier will result." He suddenly paused and then said, "She is aware of my presence."

"Vitals are fluctuating," said Beverly.

"I still sense nothing," Troi commented.

"She is aware," said Data. "On a rudimentary level, she senses that I am within her frame of reference."

"Does she know she's severed from the Borg?" said Geordi.

"No, and she must not find out. Not at this point in the procedure," Data said. "Otherwise, it would trigger her self-destruct mechanism . . . as would any attempt by you, Geordi, to remove her self-destruct mechanism. There are enough redundant fail-safes within her that you could never disarm her without causing her to disintegrate. Only by integrating override commands directly into her directives—while simultaneously preventing her from taking self-destruction action—can she be safely recovered."

Data lapsed back into silence.

"Her vital signs are all over the place," said Beverly, and then warning tones began to sound from the life scanners. She started to prepare a hypo, and as she did so, Deanna looked at her with concern.

"Is that wise?" said Troi.

"I don't honestly know," said Crusher, "but I have to do something. We can lose the body while he's working with the mind."

"I am processing through preliminary stages of setting up a self-answering signal," said Data.

"Pulse is racing," said Crusher. "Heart rate is racing."

"Data . . ." Geordi began.

"Body temperature increasing," Beverly noted. Then her voice went up with alarm as she said,

"Increasing dramatically. Data, she's starting to heat up!"

"It's a fail-safe, Data," said Geordi. "She's going to combust! Her anti-tampering imperative is kicking in!"

"There are primary alert systems built in," said Data calmly. "I am proceeding to override them."

"Body temperature still increasing," reported Crusher. "I'm going to try and slow down her metabolism," and she started to press the hypo against the Borg's arm.

"That is not advisable," Data said.

Geordi could see the air around the Borg woman, through his VISOR, changing from blue to orange. "Data, she's going to go up! And she's going to take you with her! Her surface temperature is rising. The air is—"

Data was no longer listening.

Instead, all the impulses of his brain were racing through the Borg soldier, with literally the speed of thought.

He was being pulled down, down a long, spiralling stairway. A maze of cross-circuiting and pure, unaffected, undiluted order. Humans were a tangle of emotions, all intertwined and all endlessly trying to sort each other out and never coming close to succeeding. It was an existence that Data envied, a consummation to be desired. Yet here, here was an alternative that almost seemed to be calling to him and summoning him. Icy tendrils seemed to lick at his positronic brain, savor his impulses, and salivate hungrily over his thoughts. *You are primitive,* they seemed to say, *but you can be used. You can be part of us. You can join with us . . .*

And Data realized that he was encountering some

vestigial memory of the great Borg mind. The overwhelming uniformity of purpose, the purity of the concept, so engrained into the deepest engrams of the mind that even a brain that was a virtual *tabula rasa* could not completely divest itself.

He did not reply. He could not reply. And yet, to save the life of this Borg soldier, he had to reply. He had to insinuate himself within.

His positronic brain reached down and through, into the depths of the Borg imperative. It swept over him—a black tide, and the sounds of gears turning and a steady, implacable thudding. A thudding like a pendulum swinging steadily, or the sounds of a million boots marching in perfect precision, tromping across the galaxy, leaving their great heeled prints behind them in the form of scooped-out planets and ravaged lives.

He submerged himself in it, hiding the integrity of his own programming while, at the same time, fighting to maintain it. He played a dangerous game. So many ways to fail: If the Borg soldier destroyed herself, his mind might go with it. Or if he lost his grip on the integrated individual that was Data, his matrix could be overwhelmed and replaced with that of the Borg.

It filled him up: the Borg mentality, the Borg identity, the Borg mission and the pure, undying, unwavering conviction that they would triumph; that they were the future. There was, quite simply, no doubt in their collective mind. No room for error. No chance of concern or questioning, of failure. There would be no failure. The Borg would triumph.

The Borg reached into every aspect of Data. They were inescapable and had spread themselves throughout the soldier's body and soul like a malignant cancer that could never be excised.

Human life is chaos. Machine life is order. Order is preferable to chaos. To make humans one with the Borg is to give them order. The Borg will provide order. The Borg will remove the human chaos. The Borg are inevitable.

And it made sense. If Data were capable of being frightened, he would have been. It made such perfect sense. Humans were chaos. Humans wallowed in their chaos. They enjoyed it . . . enjoyed it.

Of course.

No enjoyment, said Data, and his own programming began to reassert itself. *There would be no enjoyment. Humans revel in their humanity.*

Enjoyment is irrelevant. Humanity is irrelevant.

No, said Data. A light of pure truth seemed to shine before him. *That is the only relevant thing.*

The light widened, beginning to fill the darkness. The Borg voice railed against him, saying *You are demonstrating your imperfection. You are displaying your obsolescence. You will be irrelevant.*

Data's brain, programmed with respect and admiration for the accomplishments and wonder of humanity, stabbed out. He sensed the world/mind of the woman running out of time around him. The Borg imperatives hidden deep in her mind were about to order her to self-destruct. He could virtually sense the impulse command about to be sent, for the preparations had been made in response to his initial probings.

The call for destruction went out.

And Data snared it.

He fashioned a net from his own neurons, tackling the synaptic leap that would trigger the final command. The Borg imperative almost seemed to howl in frustration, although Data wasn't certain whether that was really happening, or whether it was his imagination. He knew he had imagination, or something approximating it. He had realized it the first time he'd found himself wondering what it would have been like if Tasha Yar had lived.

The destruct command writhed deep within her subconscious, and Data pushed it farther and farther away. For one brief instant the Borg almost fought back, but Data shoved it down once more and then sealed it off. Then he suddenly realized that in so doing, he had halted the continuous loop that was preventing the Borg soldier from launching the destruct sequence and turning to ash.

He realized this in less than a millisecond and, because of the state that he was in, his thinking the action was performing the action. He sent a command winging directly into the conscious, operational brain of the Borg soldier, and the command was, quite simply, *You are functional.* There was, after all, no reason she couldn't be. She just needed someone to tell that was the case.

He waited for a response. Some sort of reply that would say, he expected, *What are your orders? What should I do?* Something like that.

But nothing came. For a moment he thought that he had failed, but he ran a complete diagnostic along the neural systems. No, he had succeeded. He sensed that the command was now firmly in place. Implanted in her brain was the command telling her to function. In its most basic concept, he had ordered her to live. That's all. Just live. And he had done so with such force that it had overridden the Borg self-destruct imperative. He had imprinted his own determination for continued existence upon her brain engrams. But he had not been able to do more than that.

139

If he could have felt frustration, he would have. If he could have felt anger, or helplessness, or even pity, then all those would have flooded through him as well. Instead, all he could do was decide that he had accomplished as much as possible, and with that, he withdrew.

"—getting hotter," said Geordi La Forge, finishing the sentence that, to him, had taken a mere second. Yet to Data, it was almost as if Geordi had begun the sentence a lifetime ago. Then La Forge saw through his VISOR that the intense heat being generated had abruptly begun to subside. "Son of a—"

Crusher, for her part, was studying her medical monitors. "Life signs stabilizing," she said with great relief, and she laid down the hypo. "Pulse, respiration, both beginning to attain human norms."

"Data, are you okay?" asked Geordi. "Data?"

Data was still taking a moment to collect his thoughts, and finally he turned to La Forge. "I am functioning quite well, thank you, Geordi."

"What happened? What did you do?"

"I planted a command to continue functioning within her brain," said Data. He stood and reached over and, before Crusher could stop him, pulled out the knife that was protruding from the Borg's arm. She did not so much as flinch. Instead, she continued to stare straight ahead. "I overrode the Borg command to self-destruct. It was actually quite close in terms of timing. She is now functional."

"Can I remove the Borg implants?" asked Beverly.

"I do not see why not," said Data. He was reaching up to his head and disconnecting the complex wiring. "There should be no danger now. I have essentially defused the bomb within her."

"Can she talk?" asked La Forge. Confident that

Data had matters firmly in hand, Geordi walked around the table from his instruments and stared into the face of the Borg woman. "Can you understand me? Can you hear me? Counselor, is she in there?"

"I sense nothing," Deanna Troi admitted. "Her mind is still clear."

"We can reeducate her," said Geordi excitedly. "We can—"

"It will be virtually impossible, Geordi," Troi said. "Whoever or whatever this woman is, we are talking about something far beyond a simple erasure of memory. This woman's entire . . . soul, if you will . . . has been expunged. Her only claim to being alive is the fact that her body is functioning. Otherwise—"

"Counselor Troi is correct," said Data. "Recreating knowledge is well within our technology. It has been, for decades. But recreating an entire individual . . ."

"We've done it in the holodeck. I've done it," said Geordi firmly.

"What is created in the holodeck is not alive," Data said. "What you are discussing does not seem feasible."

"But if—"

"She's looking at you," said Crusher. There was wonder and amazement in her voice. "She focussed. She hadn't done that before. Geordi, she focussed on you. She's doing it right now."

Geordi turned and stared at the Borg woman. He couldn't see her eyes, of course. But her head was definitely pointed in his direction, and she seemed to be concentrating on him.

Then the moment passed, and her head slumped back. She returned to staring off into space.

Geordi looked from one of his comrades to the

other and then said firmly, "I don't care if it's feasible or not. We're going to make it feasible."

On board the *Repulse,* Mr. Seth turned in his chair and said, "Transporter room reports all planetside colonists are now aboard. Emergency evacuation is complete."

"Just in time," said Taggert grimly.

The planet-eater descended towards Kalish VIII, and a force beam leaped out from the maw of the machine. It sliced through the planet, bisecting it with surgical precision.

"Hailing frequencies," bellowed Taggert in a thunderous rage, and then, without even waiting for acknowledgment, she said, "Intruder, this is Taggert of the *Repulse.* You are destroying the homes of the Astra colonists!"

"We are still hungry."

"Back away. That's an order."

There was a dead silence, and for one brief moment Taggert deluded herself into thinking that the massive destroyer was actually going to obey.

"I am tired of you," the ship said.

A force beam lashed out from the destroyer, carving a swathe across the primary hull of the *Repulse.* Some shields actually held as systems all over the ship went into overload. In engineering, power couldn't be re-routed fast enough, and circuit boards blew out. The ship shook violently under the unexpected pounding. A radiation containment unit cracked open, and massive doors immediately slid into place to seal off the damage before the entire ship could be contaminated.

"Warp drive is out!" shouted Seth. "Deflector shields at thirty percent! Hull damage on decks 33 through 39!"

Taggert was gripping the arms of her chair as the red-alert klaxon seemed even louder. In her head she could hear the screams of her people. "What in hell did they hit us with?"

"Force beam of pure anti-proton."

Taggert's eyes widened momentarily, and then, with as much conviction as if she were holding the upper hand, she rapped out, "Combination array of photon torpedos and phasers. Fire!"

The full armament of the *Repulse* was unleashed at the planet-killer. For all the good it did, they might as well have been hurling rocks. The photon torpedos exploded prematurely against the towering spikes, and the phasers ricocheted harmlessly off the neutronium skin.

The force beam of the planet-killer struck again. This time the shields were totally unable to withstand it. They crumbled like tissue paper, and the aft hull buckled inward, stopping just short of actual breach. The entire ship shook, like a toy caught in the hand of a massive baby.

"Shields down!" shouted Seth over the din and the barrage of damage reports that were coming in from all over the ship. "Weapons systems out!"

Suddenly the ship was jolted again, but this time there was no force beam. Instead, a tractor beam had taken hold of them and was starting to drag them downward.

The *Repulse* hurtled downward, toward one of the looming spikes. Taggert could see that it came to a point, miles above the surface of the machine, that was almost needle-sharp. And her ship was being dragged right towards it.

"Full reverse!" snapped Taggert. She didn't have to shout; she was always able to make herself heard at her normal tone, no matter how loud her surroundings. In happier times, she claimed it was because she came from a large family.

"Warp drive is out, switching to impulse," called out Seth. The ship lurched slightly, and then the tractor beam reaffirmed its superiority and continued to drag them downward. The spike loomed closer and closer. Taggert could almost see a small array of lights against it, flickering on and off like a deadly Christmas tree.

The ship was about to be skewered. That was all there was to it. The spike would penetrate either the primary or secondary hull, or maybe both warp nacelles. Whatever, it didn't matter. They were about to be gouged, ripped apart, left for dead.

"Intruder!" shouted Taggert. "There's nothing to be gained by killing us!"

The spikes came ever closer.

"Let's discuss this," she continued. "You and I. Just the two of us. Let my ship go, and we can—"

And suddenly the *Repulse* snapped free. Taggert stumbled backwards, landing heavily in her chair. The starship spiralled away, like a stone caught in the flow of a brook. "Stabilize us!" said Taggert, somewhat unnecessarily since Seth was already doing it.

Within moments they had restored their equilibrium, but that was all. All systems were still out, and the *Repulse* hung there in space, helpless.

"I'm not interested in you," came the voice of the machine with such force and unexpectedness that Taggert actually jumped slightly. *"I'm not interested in your starship. All I want is the Borg. When I fired on you, I used my force beam at a fraction of its strength. If I'd used full strength, you'd be dead. Remember that. You would be dead."*

With that comment ringing in their ears, they watched impotently as the planet-destroyer swallowed the large pieces of Kalish VIII. Then, having eaten its fill, it turned without a word and headed off across the Beta Quadrant.

Unknowingly, towards the *Enterprise*.

But knowingly—all too knowingly—toward the heart of the unknown space wherein lived . . . the Borg.

Chapter Eight

VENDETTA . . .

A dazzling array of images and voices, and then there was the maddening glimpse of something, something huge and ancient and capable of great destruction. And that word . . .

Vendetta, it whispered in her mind. *Vendetta,* it seared into her soul. And an image, an image of a woman with hair the color of space and eyes that were ancient and suffering. *Vendetta,* and it was a warning, and it was a prayer, and it was. . . .

Deanna Troi sat up in bed, her body covered in sweat, and she was gasping and disoriented.

She had that odd feeling that one gets when awakening in a strange place, except she was in her own cabin. But that was not where she had expected to be.

Her heart was pounding, her pulse racing. She fought to obtain some degree of equilibrium and, after a few minutes, did so. Her breathing returned to normal, her thoughts, to the quiet, orderly pattern that she forced them into.

An empath, surrounded by beings who had no control over their emotions mentally, never had an easy time of it. She constantly had to practice mental disciplines in order to screen out the steady cacophony of emotional baggage that every human carried. It was as if someone with very, very acute hearing had to stuff cotton balls in their ears or otherwise go deaf from the barrage of sounds that they would be subjected to.

Such shields as Deanna used were an effort, but it had become almost a casual effort. No one even knew she was doing it, for it had become second nature.

But something was trying to break through those barriers now. She had a feeling that, whatever it was, it wasn't doing so intentionally. But somewhere, somehow, there was someone with such a forceful power of will that they were virtually leaking telepathic impressions that were being discerned by . . .

Guinan?

Could that have somehow been what caused her to pass out?

But what was it? What was trying to get through? What in the world was out there?

Deanna lay back in her bed, pulling the bed covers closer up so that they were just under her chin. Just the way she'd liked it when she was a little girl and her mother had tucked her in at night. Somehow the covers seemed to provide a shield against the monsters that lurked in the shadows—the monsters that defied empathic detection, but were there nevertheless, ready to consume unwary little girls.

She stared up at the ceiling, trying to figure out what was happening. But the more she thought about it, the harder it became for her to think, the more leaden her thoughts. Her eyelids seemed utterly unwilling to stay up, and the darkness became even darker.

Darker still . . . Darker still . . . and there was the darkness of space.

One by one, pinpoint lights seemed to come on—one by one, as if someone were snapping them on with a switch somewhere. And each of those lights became a glowing star.

A ship cut across her field of vision. It moved through space with eerie silence, and Deanna felt a distant tickle of confusion and fear. The ship was of a design that she had never seen before, a design that seemed ancient. It was oval, with a single, abbreviated warp nacelle extending from the top. It glided through space with a singularity of purpose . . . but how could she divine that from a ship? A ship couldn't have a purpose; only the individual who was piloting it.

The events in the dream flowed forward. Troi could neither stop nor control it or do anything except hold on for the ride.

And then, suddenly, she was inside the ship. She looked around at the tall, glistening banks of controls. They were primitive-looking in comparison to the glistening, seamless padds of the *Enterprise*. One had a tendency to take things for granted, and certainly the modern technology of the *Enterprise* was one of those things.

Slowly she circled the interior of the ship, and then she realized that she had no body, that she was exploring with her mind. It was an incredible feeling of liberation, and she was almost giddy. She was undetectable, invisible. She could go anywhere, do anything. . . .

Then she saw her.

The woman was seated in the middle of what appeared to be the main cabin. She was wearing a starkly functional jumpsuit, and she was watching the main viewing screen with an obsessive determination. She was watching for something, and Deanna had no idea what.

148

The entire thing had an air of total unreality about it. All of it was being played out in eerie silence, except there was some sort of music in the back of Deanna's head, a nameless tune that wandered through her brain from time to time, vaguely classical, with lots of strings playing.

Lights were flickering across the woman's face.

Lights.

Where were they coming from?

The lights became brighter and brighter, filling the entire ship, filling her entire being. The woman never took her eyes off the viewscreen. The woman. . . .

She was a vision of beauty. Deanna wondered why she hadn't noticed it before. She had very long, black hair, and a narrow face, and dark eyes set far apart . . .

And in those eyes . . .

Those eyes . . .

Mourning. Anger. Obsession. All of it and more overwhelmed Deanna as her mind brushed against the woman's. And a name.

Del . . . something . . . she couldn't quite hear.

And a word.

Vendetta.

The woman did not react outwardly, but Deanna sensed herself being pushed away somehow. She withdrew and hovered nearby, and the colors were just overwhelming . . .

She turned and looked at the viewscreen.

It was the barrier, the barrier at the galactic rim.

It swirled and crackled in front of them, electrical displays dancing across it. An undulating miasma of pure force and power, in the olden days the barrier had been virtually uncrossable. Technology had improved, though. Shielding had been improved. So much more was possible now, and yet, no one had really explored much beyond the edge of the galaxy.

149

There was no point. The distance to the nearest galaxy was uncrossable in anything less than centuries, and the Federation had simply shown no interest in creating and staffing the generational ship that would be required to make such a voyage. There had been talk of stocking such a ship with androids similar to Data, but the plans for duplicating the *Enterprise* officer had died aborning, at a hearing over Data's humanity.

The woman was approaching the galactic barrier. There was that frightening determination in her face, the certainty that she had to get through. But what was driving her? What had possessed a lone woman to acquire a small, private vessel for the purpose of challenging the rim barrier? It didn't seem to make any sense.

The ship hurtled toward the barrier, and then it began to shake. She handled the controls with practiced skill and determination. If Deanna had been in her situation—alone, so utterly, utterly alone and facing something of such incredible power—she wondered whether she would have been able to handle it.

She hurtled into the barrier, and the powerful forces of the barrier grabbed her ship up and began to toss it about, as if it were a stone skipping across a lake. The powerful engines of the woman's small ship strained against the onslaught, and the display across the viewscreen was almost blinding. Deanna felt the ship throb and shake beneath her and she tried to reach out to grab something for support, but she had no hands, she had nothing, and the universe was whirling.

The woman screamed, and it was a scream of defiance and fury, a scream designed to drag up her emotions and create from them a shield against fear. She let the fury overwhelm her, and a burning desire for . . . vengeance.

Vengeance for what?

Vengeance for whom?

Her ship was pounded, and she kept on going.

Her mind was assailed, and she kept on going.

Incredible forces pressed against her shielding, and her head was pounding, and alternately she felt as if she were going to freeze to death or have the blood in her veins boil, but she pressed on, fighting to keep the ship on course. She was in pursuit of something, or perhaps running from something, or perhaps some of both.

The ship trembled around her, but the fury of her will was insurmountable. It seemed as if the woman were keeping the vessel moving forward by sheer determination.

The roar was deafening. It was as if the galaxy itself had literally sprung to life, to try and prevent her from attaining her goal. But nothing would stop her. Nothing could stop her.

It seemed as if days passed. Deanna lost all sense of time, all comprehension of how long she was a prisoner here.

And then the forces began to subside. The perimeter of the galaxy thinned out, the incredible powers that had been fighting her relenting and admitting that they had been met, they had been bested. Her ship shot through and out, into the void.

Deanna—a silent, invisible spectator—gasped, placing a nonexistent hand against her nonexistent chest. She stared at the woman in the command chair.

She was slumped back, exhausted. But then she pulled herself up and looked out at the void that faced her, the vast, vast nothingness that lay beyond the galaxy.

She went to her navigational instruments. She was definitely going to need them, for there were no stars to guide her. But no . . . she was using no coordinates,

Deanna could see now. Yet she was guiding the ship, straight and true, clearly hell-bent on some destination. But Troi had no idea what it could be.

And then Deanna began to sense it. Sense *them*. Sense someone calling, beckoning, like the ancient sirens of myth. And with the same determination as ancient sailors had known when they devotedly smashed their ships onto the rocks in trying to get to the unreachable women, so, too, was this mystery woman now sending her ship hurtling forward toward voices that only she could hear. Except Deanna heard them too.

Help us, they whispered. *Avenge us. We have been waiting such a very long time . . . we thought no one could hear us.*

And the woman responded to the voices in Deanna's head. "Anyone could have heard you," she whispered, "but they had to listen. And they had to know where to look."

Where are we going? Deanna whispered. Who are you? Why am I seeing all this? How?

Time seemed to stop, and then the woman gasped. Deanna turned and saw what was on the screen, and she couldn't believe it.

It was huge, immense beyond all reckoning. Some sort of device, with great spikes, and a maw, and . . .

And it was crying.

At last, it said over and over again, *at last. You've come to us. And we can destroy our destroyers.*

What's happening! Deanna screamed soundlessly. *I don't understand! This is madness! I have to stop this! Stop this now!*

And the woman slowly turned and looked at her— looked right at her.

"You can't stop it," she said. "It's already happened. This will be the culmination of something that was started centuries before your birth. I am a link in the chain. The final link. I will be the pilot. The instrument. And you will bear witness."

Deanna shook her nonexistent head. Witness to what? she demanded.

"To the destruction of the soulless ones." She pointed at the great machine that hung before them. "It begins here. It ends when the last of the soulless ones are as dead as the last of my kind."

But why am I here? How am I here?

"You heard the songs of the minds," she said. "We have engaged the soulless ones for the first time and destroyed them. We have engaged those who would stop us from destroying the soulless ones, and they were helpless against us. The minds and souls of the lost are rejoicing, and their song was," she paused, "quite loud. It is difficult for me to quiet them sometimes. Do not worry, though. You will have the sense of us, but not the knowing. Not yet. Not until he knows. He deserves to be the first to know. I shall endeavor to quiet them in the future, so they will not disturb you further."

Wait! Deanna cried out . . .

And then they were gone.

And she was gone.

And she sat up.

She stumbled out of bed, her mind awhirl with images, and grabbed a robe around herself. Names and concepts were smashing against each other in her head, coalescing, and she cried out into the darkness, *"Personal log!"*

"Working," came the serenely calm voice of the computer. "Personal log of Counselor Deanna Troi now operating. Awaiting entry."

"A dream," she said urgently, "and it was . . ."

Lights. And energy.

Flashes.

"There was a woman, and she was . . ."

A shouting in her head, a feeling of rejoicing.

"Ven . . ." She put her hands over her ears, trying to narrow her thoughts, to call it up. An image of huge towers, like spikes, and no stars, and, *"Ven . . ."*

"Awaiting a complete sentence," the computer prompted. It was programmed with grammar from every known language and would occasionally help out when a speaker was apparently having difficulty.

Troi rubbed her temples as if she could somehow physically push her brain into working. "I had a dream," she said slowly, "and . . . and . . ."

Ven . . .

"I can't remember," she said softly.

INTERMISSION

"TRY TO RAISE THEM AGAIN," said Martok impatiently.

They had lost contact with the Daimon, and with the two guards, and with Darr, and it had been hours since any of them had checked in. Martok knew what the guards intended and dismissed the notion that Darr could have posed any impediment to the plan. But enough was definitely enough, and as much as he disliked the notion that he might have to send another landing party in after them, that's what he would do if absolutely necessary.

The other Ferengi on the bridge were looking to him for guidance and leadership, and he would be damned if he would let them down. If for no other reason than that he knew, firsthand, what could happen to a leader when the crew had lost confidence in his ability to lead.

The three Borg ships hung there, unmoving. The sight of them filling the screen, hour after hour, was starting to prey heavily on Martok's nerves. He prayed for some relief from it. Any sort of relief.

"We are receiving an incoming transmission!" There was great surprise in his officer's voice, as if he, too, thought that they were going to be stuck there ad infinitum.

"From the Borg?"

"Yes, sir."

"On screen."

The screen wavered for a moment, and then an image appeared that stunned Martok into silence before he could even begin a swaggering, "This is Martok in command of the Ferengi marauder ship."

It was Daimon Turane.

Or, at least, what was left of Daimon Turane.

His head had been encompassed in some sort of gear composed of metal and black leather. One eye was gone, replaced by a glowing red lens. His face was deathly white. The perpetual, calculating sneer that was practically ingrained into all Ferengi was gone, replaced by a cold, passionless, thin-lipped look of arrogant confidence.

When Martok managed to get out anything, it was a harsh and stunned whisper. "Daimon Turane?" he said.

"We are no longer the one you call Daimon Turane," said the individual on the screen. There was an edge to his voice that hadn't been there before, an ominous darkness. "We are Vastator. Vastator of Borg."

"I don't understand," said Martok. "Vastator? What is . . . what have they done to you, Daimon?"

"I speak for the Borg."

"Daimon, this is incomprehensible. What are you—"

"I speak," he said again, slowly, as if addressing a child, "for the Borg."

Martok's mouth moved for a few seconds, and then his face was set. "Very well," he said icily. "You speak for the Borg. And what do the Borg have to say? Are the Borg interested in negotiating a basis for striking a business arrangement with the Ferengi?"

"Negotiating is irrelevant. Business is irrelevant."

"What?" The words that the Daimon were uttering were literally blasphemy, and were far more convincing than any mere physical change that something was definitely wrong with his former commanding officer. "Daimon Turane, this is unacceptable. I don't know what they've done to you, but—"

"I have been . . . enlightened," said the one who called himself Vastator. "I have been educated. I have been made one with the Borg. Profit does not matter. Profit is irrelevant. The Ferengi are irrelevant. Only the Borg matter."

"Are you saying you're staying with the Borg?" The concept was so difficult for Martok to gasp. For ages now, all he had ever seen was the Daimon obsessed with returning to the heart of the Ferengi empire— after establishing himself within as someone to be reckoned with. The concept that he might not return. . . .

And then he began to realize. He began to understand that Turane's staying with the Borg did not mean that he would not be returning. He might indeed be planning to return . . . backed up by the full strength and power of the Borg. That, indeed, would be a threat to contend with.

"These Borg ships remain here," said Turane, a.k.a. Vastator. "A Borg ship has been destroyed by an unknown force. Another has been dispatched to investigate. We await word and further information. Once we know more, we will proceed."

"And what do you expect us to do?" demanded Martok.

Vastator stared at him with—if it could be said of a Borg—satisfaction. "We expect you to die."

Martok laughed harshly. "You're bluffing."

"Bluffing," said Vastator, "is irrelevant."

That simple pronouncement, made with such calm and confidence, chilled Martok to the bone. There was suddenly no doubt in his mind whatsoever that the Borg could do exactly what they said. He also had the distinct impression—though he couldn't have said why—that Daimon Turane, or whatever was left of him, would enjoy their destruction.

"Sever communication," Martok said suddenly and rapidly, the edge becoming evident in his voice. "Helm, hard about. Get us the hell out of here. Shields up."

"But Martok . . ."

"Do it!"

The helmsman immediately tried to respond, but suddenly the ship shook. The Ferengi were hurled about like poker chips, and Martok cracked his head on the arm of the chair. "What the hell . . . ?!"

"A tractor beam!" shouted his tactical officer. "They have us! They're pulling us toward them!"

"Full power to engines. Break us free!"

The marauder channeled every bit of energy, every reserve, into their engines. The ship shuddered and strained against the force of the Borg tractor beam. Dampeners were overridden, systems began to overload, and the howling of the engines became louder and louder, a continual revving that was not getting them anywhere.

"Systems malfunction!" came the shout from ops. "We're losing forward drive!"

"All power to weapons!" snarled Martok. "Fire!"

The Ferengi ship fired upon the Borg ship which shook slightly when it hit. Suddenly the tractor beam vanished.

"Now!" shouted Martok. "Get us out! *Now!*"

The marauder leaped forward, desperately trying to compensate for its ravaged control systems. Another few seconds, and they might actually have gotten away.

A force beam lanced out from the middle Borg ship—the one which was the new home of the Borg known as Vastator. The beam was directed by him. It was requested by him. Although revenge was now irrelevant, there was something deep within him that took immense pleasure. Just as there was something even deeper within him that cringed and cried out and screamed. Screamed, though there was no one to hear.

The beam slashed through the marauder, dissecting it, cutting the nacelles off it the way one would pluck the wings off a fly. The ship hurtled end over end for a moment, and then ruptured. It blew completely apart, the vacuum of space swallowing the sound and impact of the explosion, and the abortive screams of the entire crew. Within moments the fireball that had been the marauder was snuffed, and except for some free-floating rubble and shreds of bodies, there was no evidence that there had ever been a Ferengi ship there at all.

Vastator observed the explosion from the safety of the Borg ship. There had been nothing to gain from taking the ship apart and assimilating it. Any knowledge of the Ferengi that the Borg deemed necessary had already been garnered from what he carried in his mind. So the concept of keeping the shipful of Ferengi around was a useless one. Nor did the Borg have any desire to let the Ferengi depart and warn their fellows about the three Borg ships that were awaiting word on the fate of their brother ship.

Once upon a time the Borg would have considered warnings irrelevant. The Ferengi could have gone on ahead and let their entire race know that the Borg were coming, and it would have been irrelevant. The Borg were superior. The Borg were inevitable. Whether you knew they were coming or not made no difference. You could make preparations for it, you could try and stave it off or keep one step ahead of it. But the Borg did not care, because the Borg would always win.

Recent developments, however, had prompted the Borg to proceed with more caution. They had suffered more losses in recent days than they could recall suffering in their entire history: the loss at the homeworld of the Federation in sector 001, the loss of Locutus, the loss of a Borg ship in that battle, and the loss of another Borg ship at the world called Penzatti. Like the annoying buzzing of flies, the losses were starting to pile up and become something to consider.

So the Borg were considering the losses. And the Borg were changing their strategy, altering their approach. They were doing whatever needed to be done to accommodate the inevitable assimilation of all life forms by the Borg. If that meant taking a wait-and-see attitude, then the Borg would wait and see.

Vastator indulged himself a moment or two longer, watching airless space extinguish the last trace of the fireball that marked the marauder's passing.

They were now permanently irrelevant.

Vastator turned on his heel, Borg soldiers at either shoulder, and headed back into the heart of the Borg ship. All he had to do now was wait and see what would happen next. The Borg uni-mind would tell him what to do. The uni-mind knew everything, and would be triumphant over all. That was the way of the Borg. That was the destiny of the Borg.

But with all that had occurred to them . . . and with the savvy and experience of Vastator to aid them . . . they would proceed with caution. They learned from experience, and learned quickly. That was the strength of the Borg.

That was why they would never fail.

Never.

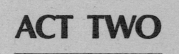

ACT TWO

Chapter Nine

"HER NAME IS Reannon Bonaventure, and she was officially declared missing, presumed dead, thirteen years ago."

The senior officers were grouped around the conference room table, listening to the pronouncement from Data, who had just finished his computer studies. They were also staring at the computer screen and the image that had been called up on it. Outside the viewing port hung the now-familiar image of the Penzatti homeworld. The concept of playing guard for a planet in the event that the Borg should show up was a strenuous one, for it meant having to be constantly on alert, never knowing when battle was going to suddenly present itself. It was an extremely unpleasant situation to be in.

Troi shuddered, for the young woman whose face appeared on the screen bore a striking resemblance to Troi herself: large, luminous eyes, classic features. Her hair was a few shades lighter than Troi's, and there was something else unusual about her. The officers had seen many pictures that had been taken, as in the case of this one, for the purpose of obtaining a freighter pilot's license. But it was the only one in which the subject was impishly sticking her tongue out at the camera.

"Quite an . . . interesting young woman," Picard said. "And certainly a unique picture."

"I think I remember hearing about her," Riker said after a moment's thought. "Yeah, I do. Oh, I remember her now!" and he snapped his fingers. "How could I have forgotten? She was quite a character."

"This picture would seem to indicate that," observed Crusher.

"That picture doesn't begin to tell the half of it. They called her the 'Brass Lass,'" said Riker. "She would transport any freight, anywhere. She would deal in anything, legal or illegal. No matter how deadly or hazardous the area, she would cross it, if that's what it took to get her cargo through."

"I remember as well," said Picard. "The 'Brass Lass.' My God. There was quite an uproar about her. Starfleet wanted to shut down her operation because of all the treaties she was ignoring, but there were too many members of the Federation who were using her for their own various purposes. Raised quite a ruckus."

"She had a cloaking device, a ship that she called the *Phantom Cruiser*, and as much guts as anyone ever had," said Riker admiringly. "Once, to get medical supplies to a plague-ravaged colony, she determined that the shortest distance was straight through Romulan space. She went right in. We had no direct line into the Romulans at the time, but word was that there were all sorts of skirmishes and that that entire sector of Romulan space was on full alert. And she dodged them all and came out the other side. Saved the colony."

"And this woman," said Bev Crusher in wonder, "this woman is now sitting in one of my examining rooms."

"She disappeared one day," said Riker. "Reportedly she had royally infuriated the Tholians over something . . . you know how touchy they are, especially when it comes to intrusion in their space. They put a price on her head and were hunting her pretty hard. Rumor had it that she took off for deep space to lie low for a while until things blew over."

"Is it possible she went far enough to have wound up within Borg space? It would have taken her years to get there."

"Anything is possible where the 'Brass Lass' is concerned," said Riker, with a touch of admiration. "If she felt the only way to keep her head on her shoulders was to explore entirely new territories, she would have done it in a second. She was utterly fearless."

"She may well have been the first human being that the Borg encountered," said Picard slowly. "And they found her intriguing enough to assimilate her into themselves. Dr. Crusher . . . what is her present condition?"

"I've removed all of the prosthetics and appliances," Crusher said, "and reopened her neural pathways in order to re-establish normal brain functions. Skin grafts should take a day or so to completely heal, and will probably itch like hell for a while."

"Brain activity?"

She shrugged. "As near as I can tell, she's functioning normally. But Captain, she's still not right."

"Not right?"

"What the doctor is saying, Captain," Troi now spoke up for the first time, still not taking her eyes off the image on the screen, "is that her sense of self—all that she is, and was—has atrophied, probably beyond recovery. For a decade or more she has had Borg implants telling her what to do, when to do it, how to do it. She hasn't thought. She hasn't assimilated experiences or done anything for herself. She hasn't expressed her personality, or even had it. It's as if she had been locked in a sensory deprivation sphere for ten years. I examined her barely an hour ago, and I sensed nothing of Reannon Bonaventure within her. Nothing of anything, really. Her heart beats, her body functions, she has all basic motor commands. But there's nothing *in* her. She's a shell of a human. Nothing more."

"Or, in the vernacular, 'her lights are on, but there's nobody home,'" said Riker.

"I don't accept that," said Geordi firmly.

They looked at him with curiosity. "Are you saying Counselor Troi's empathic abilities are in error?" asked Picard.

"I'm saying, sir, that if there was once a vital, living person in there," and he tapped the image on the screen, "then there can be again. We can't just write her off."

"No one is suggesting writing her off, Geordi," said Riker.

"That's what it sounds like to me," said Geordi. "What this woman has is a handicap. Her mind is damaged. But there's probably something trapped deep within her, crying to be let out."

"I think that unlikely," said Troi quietly.

"Well, I don't."

"Geordi—"

"Look at me, Counselor," he said with unexpected vehemence. "I'm handicapped, remember? Without this VISOR, I can't see. But I live with it, and I'm satisfied with the way I am, because I've received aid and support every step of the way. And every night, when I lie there in my bed with my VISOR on the nightstand next to me, and there's nothing but blackness, I always wonder what my life would have been like if I hadn't had the opportunities that I did. Same mind. Same abilities. But no VISOR-enhanced vision. I think of a world that's defined by counting the number of steps it would take me to get to the bathroom or kitchen or wherever, and I give thanks every night that next morning I'll be able to cheat what nature did to my eyes and rejoin the real world. And that woman down there—that handicapped woman—deserves the same chances that I had. The exact same ones."

There was dead silence.

"And she will have them, Mr. La Forge," said Picard finally, with surprising softness. "I tend to trust Counselor Troi's assessment of the situation. However . . . I have been in the same—shall we say, predicament—as Miss Bonaventure. I owe my presence here to the fact," and he surveyed the room slowly, "that my crew risked their lives to save me, that they did not give up. We would be hypocritical to say that Miss Bonaventure did not deserve the same consideration and effort."

"I'll start her on a re-education program immediately," said Crusher.

"You'll need more than that," said Troi briskly. "That's only effective when rudimentary learning abilities are present. I'm not convinced she even has that."

"She needs sensory exposure," said Geordi. "Someone talking to her. Someone working with her."

"Are you volunteering your off-duty hours, Mr. La Forge?" asked Picard.

"I'm willing to put my time where my mouth is," said Geordi.

"Very well. Make it so. You'll work in tandem with

171

Dr. Crusher to set up a schedule amenable to both of you. That's all."

As the others left, Picard stood and said softly, "Counselor, a moment, please." They waited until the conference room doors hissed shut, and then the captain turned and faced her, arms folded. "If I might observe, Counselor, you seem rather tense."

She shrugged. "It's probably that picture, Captain."

"She does bear a passing resemblance to you," admitted Picard.

"It just makes me imagine being in her situation," she said, "wondering what would happen if the Borg captured me, the way they—"

"The way they did me?" he said gently. "You know what I went through. The scars it left."

"Hideous. Just hideous." Her fingers brushed across the screen. "They're anti-life, Captain. They have no heart. They have no soul. They just exist to take and take and take. I'm someone whose entire existence is hinged on experiencing the emotions of others. An entire race that lives to eradicate the souls of others . . . it's just horrifying."

"Yes, it's . . ."

And his voice trailed off.

His eyes narrowed in thought, and Deanna turned and stared at him in curiosity. "Captain . . . ?"

"Soulless ones," he whispered.

"Captain, what are you—?"

"Soulless ones. Oh, my God," he said, and then louder, "Oh my dear God. How could I not have realized? How could I have been so stupid? How?!"

"Captain, I sense you're very upset . . ."

"I'm not upset!" said Picard, turning toward her, his every movement suddenly galvanized with emotion. "I'm furious at my own stupidity! I'm as blind as

Geordi! Someone tried to hand me a VISOR to see, and I brushed it away. But it was so long ago, so many years ago . . ."

"Captain, you're not making any sense."

He leaned against a table, shaking his head. "It had taken on the quality of a dream. I'd always wondered whether overwork had made me delusional for a brief time. But there it was, plain as the nose on my face, and I didn't see it. And they're coming, and now she's coming. She's connected somehow. I know it. I feel it."

"Who?"

"I don't know," he said fiercely, and with unexpected fury he slammed his fist against the viewing port. "I don't know her name. I don't know who she is, or what she is. Guinan!" On the last word, on that name, his mood shifted again, bordering on shock.

"Guinan?" Troi was beginning to feel completely hopeless.

"Not 'vendor.' That's not what she said. That's not what she was muttering. That's not it! It's the proof! It has to be her!"

"Captain, you're not making any sense at all!"

"Vendetta!"

Troi's breath caught in her throat. "What?" she managed to whisper.

He sank into a chair, as if uttering the word had taken his strength from him. For a long moment he was silent, lost in another time, another world, another person . . . the person that he had been so many years ago.

"I was in the Academy," he said slowly. "And there was a woman who came to me one night . . . except maybe she was not a woman. I don't know what she was. An apparition, perhaps, or that's what I thought.

It was the day that we discussed a device that the original *Enterprise* fought. A robot, called the planet-killer. The doomsday machine. It was disabled by Matthew Decker. And I had put forward a hypothesis that, for various reasons, the doomsday machine could not have come from very far outside our own galaxy. And she came to me that night, and she said things . . . things I don't even remember, because I was in such a fog. Everything was confused. But she said one thing, over and over. I never knew whether it was her name or her purpose, or both. And what she said was, *Vendetta*."

"*Vendetta*." Troi took a breath. "Captain . . . last night . . . I had a dream. And I don't remember what it was. I don't remember anything that happened in it, which is infuriating, because usually I remember my dreams as clearly as I remember my waking hours. But there was one thing I do remember, a word . . ."

"*Vendetta*."

She nodded her head.

Picard stood.

"I think we'd better talk to Guinan."

Geordi entered the small room off to the side of the main sickbay area, the room where Reannon Bonaventure was being sequestered. Bev Crusher was already there. And seated on the edge of a chair, as if she were an errant schoolgirl, was Reannon.

She seemed much smaller without the Borg implements affixed to her. She was still bald, nor did she have so much as eyebrows. She was wearing a simple gray jumpsuit, similar to the one Wesley had frequently sported before his field promotion.

She was staring forward at nothing in particular. Geordi crouched in front of her and waited for some sign of acknowledgment, some flicker of . . .

anything. "Reannon?" he said. "Reannon Bonaventure?"

There was nothing. He might as well have been speaking in a vacuum.

"Hi," he continued gamely, "I'm Geordi La Forge." He stuck a hand out, hoping that some sort of automatic response would take over.

Again, nothing.

He looked up at Crusher. "Has she said anything at all since you removed the implants?"

"Not a syllable," said Crusher. "Not even a grunt. I even started preliminary teaching structures, but nothing's taking. It's as if she simply refuses to acknowledge our existence."

Geordi got down on one knee and took her hand. The coldness of it was jolting to him, even though his VISOR told him her body temperature was low. It was like talking to a statue. "Reannon," he said slowly, "listen to me. You are Reannon Bonaventure. You are aboard the starship *Enterprise.* My name is Geordi La Forge. I'm the chief engineer. We have rescued you from the Borg influence. You're free to live a normal life. You just have to let us know you're in there. Give us some sign, some indication. *Something.*"

Nothing.

He stood and said to her, "Come on. Let's go for a walk."

"I wouldn't advise that," said Crusher quickly.

He looked at her with curiosity. "Is there a medical reason why she can't?"

"No," admitted Beverly. "No, not really. I just want to be cautious. Doctor's prerogative."

"I'd like a little leeway, Doc, if that's okay," Geordi said after a moment. "She has to experience the world. She's not going to be able to do it here."

"All right," Crusher said, once she'd given it some

175

thought. "But I want you to stay in constant contact with me. If there's any problem whatsoever, you let me know immediately. Get it?"

"Got it," he said.

"Good."

"All right, Reannon," he said. "Let's go."

She continued to sit there, as if he had not even spoken.

He took her by the arm, wrapping his forearm around hers, and gently pulled her to her feet. She did nothing to resist and nothing to help, but Geordi had her standing. He wrapped his fingers around her. They were cold and limp as the rest of her.

"Come on," he said. "Left foot, right foot, that's it."

She walked next to him with steady steps, stiff as the rest of her. Clearly her motor functions were in perfectly good shape. The only thing was, she couldn't tell them to do anything. She needed a guide if she was going to move at all. It was that inability to think for herself that Geordi was going to have to overcome somehow.

For some reason the phrase *the blind leading the blind* came into Geordi's mind. The door of the exam room hissed open and they stepped out into the main area.

The Penzatti that they were treating did not glance up at first, as Geordi and the woman who was once Reannon Bonaventure stepped out of the side examining room. And then one woman, who was covered from head to toe in a healing bio-wrap, saw what the *Enterprise* officer was walking alongside. She saw the telltale skin that was the color of chalk, and the fixed, inhuman stare. She saw, and even though the armor was gone, she understood.

And she began to scream.

The others saw as well, their antennae twitching furiously, and then they came to cry out or scream or howl in mourning once more. The medtechs looked around in confusion. Mere seconds ago there had been quiet, punctuated only by low moaning and the occasional sob. Now, though, the entire ward had gone berserk.

Geordi froze, looking around in confusion, not realizing at first what was happening and what had triggered them. Then suddenly there was someone standing in front of him, and he recognized him instantly as Dantar, the Penzatti they'd rescued from the rubble.

Beverly Crusher bolted out from the adjoining room and started shouting for quiet, but her voice was drowned out by the howling.

The Penzatti man was shoving his face directly into Reannon's, and there was a low snarl ripped from his throat as he said, "This is the one! I know that face! I know it! It's the one who killed my family!"

Reannon gave no indication that she heard, and Geordi tried to push Dantar away. "She wasn't in control then. She's better now. We've healed her."

"You *healed* her?!" shrieked Dantar. *"It* murdered my family! My children! Its kind destroyed my people!"

"She's a woman, not an it, and she's not responsible."

"It's a monster from the pits, and I'll not suffer it to live!" And with that, Dantar lunged forward and grabbed Reannon by the neck.

"No!" yelled Geordi, and he grabbed at the Penzatti's arms. All around the Penzatti were yelling and shouting and encouraging Dantar. Some were trying to rise from their beds and help him, but they were too severely injured.

With remarkable strength, Dantar shoved Geordi aside, sending him smashing against a bed. Then the hand returned to Reannon's neck and he continued to squeeze, shaking her furiously.

Her face remained impassive. She made no defense whatsoever. Her breath was being forced from her, but she did nothing to stop the attack.

"Leave her *alone!*" yelled Geordi, and he came up on one side and Crusher approached from the other, a hypo in her hand, ready to sedate him. Dantar suddenly hurled Reannon to the ground, turned and grabbed the charging engineer by the forearm, spun and hurled Geordi directly into Doctor Crusher.

Geordi felt something press against him and heard a faint hiss of air. "Oh hell," he said, and was asleep before he hit the ground.

Fortunately for him, Doctor Crusher broke his fall. But she lay pinned under the engineer's body and tried to shove him off. He was small, but solidly muscled.

Dantar dropped down and started to throttle Reannon once again. And now others of the Penzatti were forcing their way out of their beds, obstructing the medtechs. Within seconds Beverly Crusher's orderly sickbay was being turned into a madhouse.

Crusher shoved Geordi's insensate body off herself and hit her communicator. "Security!" she shouted. "Security to sickbay!"

Dantar's fingers worked deep into the folds of Reannon's neck. His antennae were fully extended, and she was putting up absolutely no fight at all. . . .

And a steely hand clamped onto Dantar's shoulder.

His head snapped around, but it was purely a reflex action, because he was unconscious even as it did so. His body sagged, and he slumped to the floor, hitting it heavily.

Another Penzatti now charged, still limping furiously, and Doctor Selar stood from where she had just dropped Dantar. It was a Penzatti woman, and she was even more physically imposing than Dantar as she aimed a punch at the Vulcan physician. It didn't slow Selar down at all. With her left hand she brushed aside the blow, and her right hand snagged the Penzatti's shoulder. The Vulcan nerve pinch immediately claimed another victim.

Upon seeing what had just happened, the other patients who had managed to get to their feet froze. Selar turned and fixed them with a steady stare.

"Further violence," she said in measured tones, "would be illogical."

At that moment Worf, with the ever-present Meyer and Boyajian, burst into sickbay. He entered just in time to hear the last of what Selar had said, and immediately discerned what had occurred. He exchanged glances with the Vulcan doctor and gave a quick nod of approval. In general, he was not especially wild about Vulcans. A race as hot-blooded as Klingons generally had little understanding of, or patience for, a people whose *raison d'être* was practicing non-emotionalism. But there was something about Selar—something he could not quite put his finger on—that made her far more tolerable to him than the typical Vulcan.

His voice all business, he rumbled in no uncertain terms, "All of you, back to your beds. Now."

The Penzatti did as they were told, none of them having any desire to cross swords either with the Klingon or the formidable Vulcan once more.

Selar had gone straight over to Crusher and helped her to her feet. "You appear uninjured, Doctor."

"I think my authority is a bit damaged, but that's about all. Lieutenant," she addressed Worf, with a

voice a bit more loud than she needed, "I appreciate
your quick response. Our patients seem to be under
the impression this is a gymnasium, or perhaps the
Roman Coliseum, rather than a sickbay."

"Shall I have them all secured to their beds . . .
with heavy chains?" Worf said gravely.

Crusher tossed a quick glance at her patients and
saw their petrified expressions. "I don't think that will
be necessary, for the moment. But if I should change
my mind . . ."

"I will have them prepared," said Worf, and with
each word dripping menace, he added, "just . . . in
. . . case."

The medtechs were hauling the unconscious Dantar
back up onto a bed and securing him. Beverly Crusher
stood over the unmoving form of Reannon. She was
still blank-faced, staring up at the ceiling now. She
gave no indication that she was remotely aware of
what had happened to her, or where she was, or who
she was. Then Beverly looked back at the unconscious
form of Geordi La Forge.

"Not one of the more auspicious starts to a project," she said to no one in particular.

"Vendetta." Guinan nodded slowly, stroking her
chin.

Picard, Troi, and Guinan had gone into Guinan's
small, functional office just off to the side of Ten-
Forward. Guinan was standing, looking thoughtful
and circling the room. *"Vendetta.* Yes. Yes, that could
have been what I was saying."

"And the significance of it?"

She shook her head. "I don't know."

Picard looked at her with raised eyebrow. "No
idea?"

She spread her hands wide. "Guesses. About a

dozen, any of which might be accurate, or might be even more confusing. I wish I knew."

"And what I told you just now, about the experience I had when I was in the Academy?"

"I'm as mystified as you, Captain," said Guinan. She looked from Troi to Picard and then back again. "It may very well be that whoever, or whatever, was in your vision back in the Academy is somehow connected to my collapse, but I can't say for certain."

"Can you say anything for certain?"

"Yes." She frowned. "Whatever is behind all this, sooner or later, is going to show itself. And then we can all stop guessing."

Picard nodded slowly and then stood. "All right. Thank you for your time, Guinan. If . . ."

"Captain." Guinan's voice, her whole demeanor, had suddenly changed. "Captain, wait, there's something I'm not telling you."

He was stunned, as if slapped in the face. "Guinan," and the shock in his voice was evident. "In all the time I've known you, our relationship has been based on honesty. I can't believe there's anything you wouldn't share with me. Especially if it's important. And most especially if lives are at stake."

"It's not something I discuss lightly, Captain," she said. For the first time that he could recall, she turned her back to him as if she couldn't bear to look at him. Her arms were folded, and she was staring down at her feet, as if trying to determine the best way to proceed. "I don't know for sure," she said. "That's the absolute truth. And I didn't want to bring it up unless I did know. It's a rather . . . painful topic, and personal— one that I didn't really want to share if it could be avoided." She turned to face Picard. "But I owe it to you, out of respect for our relationship and our friendship, to tell you anything that could be of help."

She sat down behind her desk, interlacing her fingers. She paused a long moment, appearing to gaze long and hard into herself. She almost seemed to be casting her mind back. Picard and Troi stood respectfully silent.

"I think," she said slowly, "that the woman who is causing all this, the woman whom you faced that night in your dorm room, Captain, is named Delcara."

"Delcara." The name meant nothing to Picard. Odd. He'd always thought, in the back of his mind, that if he'd ever met her, ever learned her name, there would be a dazzling flash of understanding, or something. But there was nothing. It was just a name, three syllables. "Delcara. And she has reason to hate the Borg?"

"Ooooohh yes," said Guinan. "Some very good reasons."

"And you know her," said Troi.

"You could say that," Guinan said dryly. "You see, Delcara is my sister."

Chapter Ten

CAPTAIN MORGAN KORSMO was awakened by the alarm of the red-alert siren that came in tandem with the urgent call on his communicator. Korsmo was one of those people who took no time at all to awaken, and fully alert, he tapped his communicator and said, "Korsmo here."

"Captain, you'd better get up here," came Shelby's voice, very controlled, almost passionless, and yet projecting a clear undercurrent of alarm. "Long-range sensors have detected—"

"The Borg?"

"Yes, sir."

For one moment unwanted thoughts flashed through his head. Thoughts of, *At last! I'll get to show what I can do against those monstrosities! I'll show that Picard isn't the only one who can hold his own against those mechanized bastards.* But these musings were immediately replaced by concern over his ship and his crew. They had to come first, no matter what. "Alert Starfleet Command immediately. I'll be right up."

In record time Korsmo was striding out onto the bridge, his practiced gaze taking in all tactical readouts. Shelby rose from the command chair and took her usual station as Korsmo dropped into place. "Sensors on maximum. Status report."

"Shields on full," reported Peel from tactical. "Weapons batteries fully charged. All stations report ready."

"What've we got?" asked Korsmo, studying the screen. The stars shimmered ahead, racing past, whatever their sensors had detected not yet in visual range.

"One ship," said Peel, "matching exactly the configurations of the Borg ship that attacked several months ago. Moving at warp seven. Present course and heading will take it—"

"Toward Penzatti," said Shelby. Korsmo shot her a curious look.

"No, ma'am," said Peel, after a moment. "It seems bound in the direction of the Kalish system."

"That's in the general direction of Penzatti, but still . . ." Korsmo's voice trailed off. "Helm, bring us around in an intercept course at warp seven."

"Course plotted and laid in," said the helmsman.

"Lay on," said Korsmo, and the ship immediately angled directly into the path of the oncoming Borg ship. "Give me a direct line to the Borg ship. I'm going to warn them off."

"We're going to warn them?"

He glanced at Shelby. "Problem with that, Number One?"

"Captain," said Shelby firmly, "with all due respect, we don't have the firepower to back up that warning. Our weapons won't even slow them down."

"If you don't mind, Number One, I'd like to test that for myself."

"Here they come," said Peel.

Sure enough, sailing toward them on the screen at

warp seven was the familiar cube of the Borg ship. It seemed like nothing so much as an unstoppable juggernaut, ready to run over anything in its path.

"No response on any hailing frequency," reported Peel.

"We will intercept in thirty-five seconds, sir," came the report from Hobson at conn.

"Repeat warning," said Korsmo firmly, "that they have already established themselves as a hostile force . . . that if they do not break off from their present course and return our communications, we will have no choice but to regard this as an act of aggression and take appropriate measures."

Shelby forced herself not to shake her head in disbelief. Korsmo talked a good game, she'd give him that. But he was still acting as if this were a normal foe that he was up against. He had no real comprehension, despite everything, of just how powerful the Borg were. Perhaps no one could, unless they'd experienced it firsthand. She just hoped they'd live to remember the experience.

"Still no response."

"Mr. Peel," said Korsmo after a moment, "fire a warning shot directly in their path. Let them know we mean business."

"Firing phasers," said Peel.

The phasers' beams lanced out across space, cutting right in the way of the Borg ship. To all intents and purposes, a line had been drawn, warning the Borg to proceed no further.

The Borg crossed it with no hesitation, and shot straight towards the *Chekov*.

"Collision course!" shouted Hobson.

And on top of Hobson's warning came Korsmo's order of "Hard about, maximum warp!"

The *Chekov* responded immediately, angling down and away, and the Borg ship hurtled past without slowing down.

"Bring us around," ordered Korsmo, his hands gripping the arms of his chair so hard that his knuckles were white. His voice was laced with fury. To be beaten, or outwitted, or outmuscled, those he could handle. But no one, not Borg nor Romulan nor anybody, simply ignored him. "Catch up with her, Mr. Hobson."

The mighty engines of the *Chekov* shot the ship forward as if from a slingshot. On their screen the Borg ship was still barreling forward, unaware or uncaring of their presence.

"Wherever they're going, they're in one hell of a hurry," observed Shelby.

"They're at warp eight," confirmed Peel. "They're pulling away from us."

"Take us to warp eight," ordered Korsmo. "Peel, target their primary energy emission—*fire!*"

The *Chekov* fired, phasers fully armed, and struck the Borg ship, playing across the surface and scoring it severely.

"Any effect?" asked Korsmo.

"Nothing appreciable," said Peel. "And the damage that they did sustain is being repaired—almost instantaneously."

Korsmo turned towards Shelby. "You're the expert on these things, Shelby. Do they have a weak point?"

For a fleeting moment Shelby was reminded of the old story about the baseball player—the one who came up to bat three times and hit a double, a triple, and a home run. When he came up to bat for the fourth time the pitcher was pulled in favor of a new, fresh pitcher. As they passed each other, the new pitcher asked the departing one, "This guy got any weaknesses?" And the losing pitcher said dourly, "Yeah, he can't hit singles."

"The only weaknesses," she said, "are within their own mental structure. In terms of outside attack, they are virtually impervious."

"How do we get inside that structure?"

She did not smile. "Willing to have yourself 'borged,' Captain?"

"They're at warp eight-point-five," said Peel. "They've fully repaired damage."

"Match their speed."

The *Chekov* roared into warp eight-point-five, and that brought an immediate call from the engine room. "Captain," warned Engineering Chief Polly Parke, "any speculation as to how much speed you'll need?"

"Stoke the furnace, Mister Parke," Korsmo warned her, "because we may need everything you have. Bridge out. Peel, arm full torpedo and phaser array. We're going to get their attention if . . ."

"It kills us?" offered Shelby. "Captain, respectfully state that this is not the proper course."

"Suggestion noted. Mr. Peel, *fire.*"

Once again the phasers played across the surface of the Borg ship, accompanied by an array of photon torpedoes. The attack lit up the darkness of space, a dazzling display of firepower.

The Borg slowed long enough to fire back one shot, just one.

It struck the *Chekov* with furious power, and the ship was rocked by the force of it.

"Damage reports coming in from all over the ship!" shouted Hobson. "Shields at fifty percent!"

"The Borg ship is pulling away," reported Peel.

"Pursue it."

"Captain . . ." began Shelby.

But he cut her off with a curt, "Not now! Hobson, divert all power to engines. Don't lose that ship!"

"They're back at warp eight and increasing."

"Pace them."

"Engineering to bridge. Captain, we're leaking—"

"Plug it!" he told her fiercely. "Whatever it is, Parke, fix it, and keep warp speed coming. We're not going to lose those bastards!"

Shelby looked at Korsmo as if seeing him for the first time. The fury radiating from him was filling the bridge, poisoning the atmosphere. "Captain," she said with as much calm as she could muster, "the upward limits of Borg speed have not been measured."

"We'll measure them now. Helm, overtake them. Warp nine."

Moving at speed that could take the ship across the Terran solar system in twenty-six seconds, the *Chekov* started to close the gap.

"The Borg have effected repairs," Peel said once again. "They are increasing speed to warp nine-point-two."

"Warp nine-point-two, helm. Bridge to engineering."

"Engineering," came Parke's voice. She was clearly annoyed, but that wasn't going to deter her from following business. "Captain, we're presently at nine-point-two. That's maximum speed."

"That's normally maximum speed, Mister Parke," replied Korsmo, putting on an air of coolness that he did not feel. We may need more. Depends on our friends out there."

"I haven't got much more to give, Captain," she warned. "Systems are on overload now. Under normal circumstances—"

"These are far from normal. Transporter room, get ready to receive a landing party."

"Landing party?" said Shelby.

He turned towards her. "I've read all your reports, Commander," he said. "Once we get aboard that ship, the Borg will tend to ignore anyone there."

"Have ignored in the past, Captain, yes," affirmed Shelby, "but that doesn't mean they'll continue to do so."

"We're going to overtake. Get in transporter range and board them," said Korsmo firmly.

"I would not advise that."

"Did I ask for your advice, Commander?"

There was dead silence on the bridge, the stinging question hanging in the air. "No, sir, you did not," Shelby said after a moment, "but I thought it best . . ."

"I'll remember that."

"Sir, they're at warp nine-point-six," reported Peel. "We're still not within transporter range."

"And we've got all available energy siphoned to the warp engines," added Hobson. "Captain . . ."

"Go to warp nine-point-six."

Shelby closed her eyes, imagining she could feel the shuddering protest of the starship as the ship upped her speed to 1,909 times the speed of light. The maximum rated speed, the ship could handle warp nine-point-six, theoretically, for twelve hours. In terms of practicality, the *Chekov* would probably tear herself to shreds long before that happened.

"Structural stress increasing by a factor of two," said Hobson, as if reading a death sentence.

"What effect is this speed having on the Borg ship?" demanded Korsmo.

"No visible or detectable effect on the Borg," Peel informed him after a moment. And then, knowing the effect it would have on Korsmo, he said quietly, "Borg have gone to warp nine-point-nine."

Again there was a deathly silence on the bridge. When Korsmo spoke, it was a whisper. "Warp nine-point-nine."

This is insane! Shelby thought, but she said nothing.

"Warp nine-point-nine," Hobson said slowly, every syllable hanging in the air.

"Engineering to bridge."

"I was expecting your call, Mister Parke," said Korsmo mirthlessly.

"Sir, this is beyond my control," she said. "At warp nine-point-nine, the engines will shut down automatically after ten minutes. Whatever you're going to do, do it now, or do it in the afterlife."

"Captain, they're pulling away from us," said Hobson, his voice filled with utter disbelief.

"What?!" Korsmo was completely incredulous. "How the hell fast can they go, anyway?"

"I believe I said that Borg upward speed has not been determined," said Shelby. Although she knew it was her imagination, she felt as if tremendous forces were pressing against her body. Warp speed increased exponentially. They were now moving at 3,053 times the speed of light. It was incredible. Mankind couldn't go faster than this, she, thought, and perhaps wasn't meant to.

"Borg at warp nine-point-nine-nine," said Hobson, and, indeed, the Borg ship was now pulling away, its speed virtually double that of the *Chekov.*

"I don't believe it," exclaimed Peel. "That requires nearly infinite power."

"The Borg have a knack for acquiring what they need," Shelby said. "If they never have such power themselves, then they acquire it from some race they conquered. They're very efficient that way."

With every passing second the Borg ship became smaller and smaller. "Full magnification," ordered Korsmo, and for a brief moment the departing Borg ship loomed larger, but then it began to recede once more.

"We're losing speed," said Hobson hollowly.

"Bridge to engineering—!"

Anticipating what the captain was about to say, Parke cut him off. "The Borg attack damaged us, Captain. I can't give you the full ten minutes."

"What can you give me?"

There was a pause, and then, with true understanding of her commanding officer's frustration, she said simply, "My apologies."

He looked at the screen and watched the Borg ship grow smaller and smaller, hurtling on its way. And he considered his actions of the past few minutes. "Mine to you, also, Chief," he said after a moment. "Power us down to safe cruising speed, helm."

"Reducing to warp six," said Hobson, unable to totally hide the relief in his voice.

Korsmo stood, hands behind his back, and watched the Borg ship become as small as any of the stars that hung in space before them. He sighed. "They ignored us."

"To all intents and purposes, yes, sir," agreed Shelby.

"Send word to the *Enterprise* at Penzatti," he said. "Tell him the Borg have been sighted, and feed them the coordinates." He paused and then added, with a trace of satisfaction, "Maybe those bastards can move at warp nine-point-nine-nine, but subspace radio moves at thirty times that. Let's see them move faster than that."

"Do you think," said Hobson after a moment, "that they can do warp ten?"

They all looked at him. "Basic physics, Mr. Hobson," said Korsmo, with a touch of the dry humor that usually accompanied him. Shelby couldn't help but notice that he was sounding more like himself, and was grateful for it. He continued, "Warp ten can't be reached. It's infinite speed."

"But if anyone could, the Borg could," Shelby said.

Korsmo stared at her. "No one could."

"Captain," she said, "I hope you're right. The Borg have already put enough uncertainty into the universe. I'd hate to think that the absolute speed limit of the universe is just another rule for the Borg to destroy."

"Oh, don't worry, Commander," said Korsmo. "I've generally found that the pre-eminent rule of the universe is that Jean-Luc Picard can handle anything. As long as that's intact, I imagine the laws of physics have very little to be concerned about."

Chapter Eleven

"YOUR SISTER?" Picard sat back in his chair, amazed. "Your sister?" he repeated.

She shrugged slightly. "Well, not sister of blood, which is the main way that humans accept sibling relationships. But we were bonded as sisters until—"

Guinan put up a hand. "I'm getting ahead of myself. Let me try and explain . . ."

"Yes, I think you'd better," said Picard firmly.

Troi, for her part, was amazed. She had never seen Guinan appear any way other than at peace with herself and utterly in control of a situation. Everything from the appearance of *Q* to the disappearance of the captain when the Borg attacked had been taken in stride by the unflappable Ten-Forward hostess. Now, though, for the first time, Guinan actually seemed discomfited.

"I told you once," she began, "that my people were attacked by the Borg, that many of us died, and we were scattered by them. What I did not mention to you was our first awareness of the Borg. It came when we found Delcara."

"How old is Delcara?" asked Troi.

"About as old as I am," replied Guinan. Then she smiled, although there was little humor to it. "You're not going to ask a lady her age now, are you?"

Picard leaned forward intensely. "When did you find her? Tell me about her."

There was something in Picard's voice that indicated far more than normal interest in the response. Troi could not help but notice the anxiety from her captain, his curiosity about this Delcara far beyond the normal interest that this situation would elicit.

"She was beautiful," she began. "A luminous presence. I've never met anyone like her since; only those who were, at best, faint copies. She radiated peace and harmony, at least at first, and that was reflected in her outer beauty: hair as black as the depths of space, skin that seemed to shimmer. And she was a powerful telepath. Hers was a mind attuned to the wonders of the galaxy, and the ebb and flow of destiny. All that was reflected in her eyes. Eyes that . . ."

"Eyes that gazed directly into the back of your head," said Picard. "Eyes that spoke volumes, even when they were silent."

"Yes," agreed Guinan. "Hers was an ancient soul, with an ancient sadness that followed her always. She was part of a race called the Shgin," she said. "The Shgin lived in deep at the far rim of what you call the Delta Quadrant of the galaxy."

"Where the Borg are," said Picard.

She nodded. "Where the Borg are," she confirmed. "Now, the Shgin were a warlike race, so when they first encountered the Borg, they loved the challenge. They welcomed the foe." She pursed her lips. "They lived to regret it. Or rather, they didn't live to regret it. The Borg massacred them as thoroughly as they did anything and anyone else. Delcara had a mate and two children. All were lost. Delcara and a handful of others escaped the Borg destruction, and over the years, the rest of the Shgin died until only Delcara was left. She wandered the galaxy, alone, lost. Either she found planets that were uninhabited, or else once-populated worlds that had been 'visited' by the Borg. By the time we found her, she had been alone for many years. The solitude, the horror of that alone-ness, weighs heavily on one. It took us a long time to draw her out of the emotional cocoon that she had created around herself. I had a hand in that—a considerable hand, really. Delcara and I became close friends—close enough to be bonded in a relationship approximating what you would call 'sisterhood.' During that time Delcara learned our ways. The ways of peace and attention to emotions and to listening. She even fell in love with one of my people, and they married. And then . . ."

She paused, and it was obvious. "The Borg attacked," Picard provided.

Guinan nodded. "The Borg attacked," she affirmed. "They slaughtered so many of my people, including Delcara's new mate. When I found Delcara after-wards, I had to drag her away from the broken body of her lover. The screams," and she touched her fingers to her temples, "the screams live on to this day."

"The poor woman," whispered Troi. "To lose all her loved ones . . . twice . . . to the Borg . . ."

"It consumed her," said Guinan. "Totally. I tried to get her to stay with me, but she wasn't the woman I'd known. She's become dark, forboding, and all the beauty of her was blackened and blasted by the horror and the loss and the helplessness. She disappeared, years ago, and I never had any idea where she went."

"I think," Picard said slowly, "that I'm starting to get a damned good idea."

At that moment his communicator beeped and he tapped it. "Yes."

"Sir," came the deep voice of Worf, "we have received a number of communiqués relating battles and encounters—both with the Borg, and apparently with the entity which Captain Korsmo and Commander Shelby credited with the Borg destruction here at Penzatti. Shall I—"

"Tell Mr. Data," Picard said abruptly, "that I wish to meet with him immediately. Then in fifteen minutes I want all senior officers in the conference room. Guinan, you too."

"Captain, the messages—"

"We'll hear them then, Mr. Worf."

"Yes, sir."

Picard turned towards Guinan and Troi the moment the communication was cut. "I'm fairly certain I can sum them up without hearing them. And that summation is that a war that is hundreds of years old may be coming to a head—and we'll all be caught in the middle."

Once again the senior officers were grouped around the conference table, except the tension level in the room had increased substantially.

They had just spent the past several minutes hearing report after report, message after message. A huge, planet-devouring ship. A mysterious woman from Guinan's past. An attacking Borg ship. Picard's heart had jumped when he'd heard about the individual battles that the *Chekov* and the *Repulse* had faced. How many more were going to die until this business was finished? he wondered bleakly. How many comrades dead? How many bodies buried, ships lost. How much was it going to take to stop the madness once and for all?

The same thoughts were going through Riker's mind, particularly when he'd heard about Shelby's vessel locked in combat. He'd grown to like her, even become fond of her . . . at least, as fond as one could become of a woman whom he'd wanted to belt at one time.

"You seem distracted, Number One," Picard said suddenly.

Riker looked up, feeling momentarily embarrassed, as if he'd been caught flatfooted at school. "I was just thinking, Captain," he admitted, "of when I had the power of Q. I gave it back to him, secure and confident that I didn't want or need it. When I think that I had the power, at my fingertips, to stop a race like the Borg with a passing thought. . . ." He shook his head. "The lives I could have saved. The good I could have done. To be able to eliminate the Borg . . ."

"Or the Romulans," observed Troi, pointing out the danger of such thinking. "Or the Tholians."

"Or the Klingons," added Worf darkly.

Riker looked from one to the other. Then he allowed a small smile. "Hard to tell where to draw the line, isn't it."

"Sometimes the best way to deal with drawing a line," said Picard, "is refusing to take the marker when someone offers it to you for the purpose of drawing." He shook his head. "There's no point dwelling on the past, Number One, except in those instances in which it can be of service to you. Like now."

He stood, his fingertips resting lightly on the conference room table. "I believe I know how all of this relates to one another. It's part speculation, part theory, with a dash of guesswork, but I'm reasonably certain we have a workable hypothesis here. Mr. Data was kind enough to work out some of the schematics for me as well, based on historical records."

He walked over to the computer screen, and a chart of the galaxy materialized on it, divided into quadrants. The Alpha and Beta quadrants, comprising the lower half of the circle, glowed in dark blue. The Gamma quadrant, entirely unexplored space, was deep black. The Delta quadrant was also black, since the majority of it was unexplored, but a U-shaped red curve delineated that area known to be Borg space. The territory of the UFP, the Klingon Empire, Romulan space, and approximate limits of explored space, were likewise demarcated in red.

"An uncertain amount of time ago," began Picard, "the Borg first began their rise to power in the Delta Quadrant. Whether they originated from outside the galaxy, or somehow evolved from machines, or were a sentient race that embraced machines, all of this is uncertain. But they encountered resistance from a great and mighty race, name unknown. Possibly the race that was known as the Preservers, who seem to have 'seeded' countless planets with humanoid life and then disappeared."

"Certainly being wiped out by the Borg would explain that disappearance," said Riker.

Picard nodded and then continued, "For argument's sake, we'll call them the Preservers, even if they were not. The war between the Borg and the Preservers went on and on, and the Preservers were losing. But while they fought the Borg in the Delta Quadrant, they were also busy in a place as far from the scene of battle as they could be. You see, they were developing a new and powerful weapon, and wanted that weapon to be created as far from the Borg as possible. It was not a weapon that was intended to be used. It was a weapon of last resort, a weapon of revenge, should the Preservers be ultimately defeated. A weapon that could conceivably lay waste to a large portion of the galaxy. But better *that,* they reasoned, than allowing the Borg to continue their conquest unabated. The Preservers, or whoever, felt that they were the last, best hope of the galaxy, and if they fell, then nothing else mattered.

"But while they worked on creating their ultimate weapon, they first created a prototype. They created —this."

On the screen appeared a vast spaceship, with a huge maw and a body that trailed off in a vague cone shape.

"In comparison to the projected final product, it was simplistic," said Picard. "But deadly, nonetheless. Perfectly designed for use within the galaxy, for it would devour planetary masses for the purpose of fuel. It was eminently logical. After all, the Borg left behind lifeless balls of rock in their wake. So a weapon was developed that would, in a beautiful twist of irony, use those 'lifeless' planets as fuel. They would use the waste matter that the Borg left over against them.

Riker frowned. "I know that thing. That's . . ." he snapped his fingers to jog his memory. "The planet-killer! The doomsday machine that the original *Enterprise* faced! We learned about it in the Academy."

"So did we," said Picard. "Neutronium hull, a beam of anti-proton, consuming planets . . . I'm almost embarrassed we didn't think of it earlier.

"What I believe happened next is that the Preservers, or whoever created it, received word that the war was going badly, indeed, that it was hopeless. So they launched the planet-killer prototype while continuing to work on the final version which was considerably bigger, more powerful, faster . . ."

"How much faster?" asked Geordi.

Picard spread his hands. "Logs of the original *Enterprise* would indicate that the planet-killer never exceeded warp four. I would suspect that the final version would have to go considerably faster to have any hope of catching up with a Borg ship."

"But how can you be sure the planet-killer was created as an anti-Borg weapon?" asked Geordi.

"We projected back along the original planet-killer's path, just as the crew of the first *Enterprise* did," said Picard, and obediently the overview of the galaxy reappeared, this time with a broken line cutting across the Alpha and Beta quadrants. "Science officer Spock projected that the planet-killer's rather straightforward path of attack meant it originated from outside our galaxy. It did. I surmise that it was created beyond the galactic barrier, in a space station or artificial city. Projecting the planet-killer's path forward, Mr. Spock discovered that the machine's course would take it straight towards Earth. Also correct. Look, however, at the direction it would have gone, and the ultimate destination it would have found, had it not been deactivated."

The glowing line ran straight and true, slicing directly into the heart of the Delta quadrant.

"Borg space," said Riker.

"Right down their throats," agreed Geordi.

"It would have taken the planet-killer, at the speed it was going, hundreds of years to get there," said Picard. "Possibly they didn't intend it to actually be launched, but they obviously felt they had no choice. Besides, they reasoned that if the Borg continued their conquest, they would undoubtedly run into the planet-killer halfway."

"But the original *Enterprise* killed it," said Riker.

"That's right. Ironically, the *Enterprise* NCC-1701 defeated a weapon that was created to defeat beings that the *Enterprise* NCC-1701-D is forced to face."

"Terrific," said Geordi. "But what else could they have done?"

"Nothing else," said Picard. "Now, here's the rest of it. The final version of the planet-killer was never launched. We don't know the reason. Perhaps they hit some sort of technological snag. Perhaps they simply decided to flee the area of the Milky Way galaxy altogether."

"Or perhaps," said Guinan, "they'd created a weapon so powerful, that they were concerned it would be an even greater menace than the Borg."

"That's a cheery thought," said Geordi.

"So it was never launched," said Picard. "And it floated here, beyond the edge of our galaxy." The captain tapped it on the computer screen, "unmoving, abandoned, forgotten. Until it was discovered by a woman with a vendetta. A woman who wanted to destroy the Borg and would allow nothing to stand in her way. A woman named Delcara. She got to the ship, activated it, and is now heading towards Borg space. She encountered the Borg ship here at Penzatti and demolished it. She then ran into the *Repulse*, and overcame it. According to the *Repulse*, it looked like this."

The planet-killer that the *Repulse* had fought and lost appeared on the screen.

Deanna Troi gasped, her mind reeling against it, and the others looked at her immediately. "Deanna—?" said Riker.

"I know it somehow," she said. "I . . . I saw it, but I can't remember . . ." She closed her eyes, clearly straining as if she were trying to browbeat her mind

201

into doing her bidding. "That shape, and those spires . . ."

"Counselor Troi, what do you remember?" said Picard urgently. He made no effort to mollycoddle her. He'd seen, in recent days, how poorly she took to treatment such as that, especially when she was feeling confused or out of sorts.

"I . . ." She shook her head. "I can't recall. That dream I mentioned earlier . . . there was a flash of that machine's overall shape. But I can't remember more. I'm sorry, Captain."

"It's all right. I suspect we'll be having more than enough personal experience with it."

"Captain, are you saying that the Earth is in direct danger, as it was when the original planet-killer was en route?"

"Curiously, no. If you'll note here, this new device seems to be following an elliptical path." Another glowing line appeared and Picard's finger traced the line. "It starts at the same point, but curves around our sector. Still, there are sufficient populated areas that concern is warranted. Mr. Data, I want course set for the Kalish star system, the last known location of the planet-killer that the *Repulse* encountered."

The officers looked at each other for a moment in surprise, and finally Riker said, "Captain, shouldn't we wait here, as per instructions?"

"I've already sent word to Starfleet and expect permission momentarily," said Picard briskly. "There is no point to the *Enterprise* remaining here. We will continue to treat the Penzatti who are aboard, but awaiting the Borg return here is futile. They will not return here until they have dealt with the planet-killer, for they will most certainly recognize its origins and suspect its capabilities. It will be a threat that they cannot allow. Therefore, wherever the planet-killer is, that's where they will be headed as well."

"Captain, how do we know that for certain?" asked Crusher.

He turned and looked at her. "Because," he said grimly, "if I were a Borg, that's what I would do."

Picard was in the ready room, staring out at the rapidly receding Penzatti homeworld. At the sound of the chime at the door, he said, "Come." The total absence of sound after the door had opened immediately told him who had entered without his needing to turn around to confirm his deduction. "Yes, Guinan?"

She folded her arms and said, "Interesting theories you provide, sir. But I'm surprised you didn't happen to mention back there the other reason you want to head off the planet-killer."

He stared at his reflection in the window. "It poses a threat to life and limb. It is an artifact from an ancient race. It laid waste to a starship without any appreciable difficulty. It represents a significant defense and offense against the Borg. And Starfleet, through Captain Korsmo, has already expressed interest and concern about it. I don't see what more reasons one needs."

"Oh, those are plenty of good reasons," agreed Guinan. Then her voice dropped slightly, the light, bantering tone disappearing. "But there's one reason that's a little better, isn't there? Her. Because somehow *she* has taken over that . . . that thing out there. The reason it's giving the Terran system a wide berth is because she's controlling it somehow. Maybe she's even inside it. And you've been thinking about her, had her rattling about in the back of your mind, for decades."

He was silent for a long moment. "We're connected somehow, Guinan," he said. "In a way I don't even know that I understand. She knew to find me. Now I have to find her. I have to know . . ."

"The unknowable?"

He shrugged. "Whatever I can learn."

"At least we don't have to worry that your judgment is clouded."

He turned and gave her a firm, even scolding, look. "Nothing could ever do that."

"I've learned, Captain, that it's never safe to say never. Because nothing," she said ruefully, "has a nasty habit of becoming a very, very large something."

Chapter Twelve

GEORDI LA FORGE KNEW that they had a few hours yet before arriving at the site of the battle between the *Repulse* and the planet-killer. The engines were operating smoothly, and all systems were on line and functioning at peak levels. So he felt no guilt in going down to sickbay to spend some time with the woman who'd once been known as Reannon Bonaventure. He even had a plan that he had already put into operation, because he was certain that there was a woman inside there—a woman who could be reached, and was somehow aware of what had happened to her. A woman that, in some way, he could help.

Bev Crusher, however, was hesitant when she saw the chief engineer enter sickbay. "Look, Geordi," she began.

"I know what you're going to say, Doctor," he said, "but you have to let me try. I know that I can help her."

"How do you know for certain?" She stood before him, arms crossed, body language virtually shouting, *Do your best to convince me, but I'm not buying it.*

"I don't know for certain," admitted Geordi. "But every time you work on a patient, do you know for certain that you're going to be able to save him?"

"Reasonably sure, yes."

"But not one hundred percent."

She rolled her eyes impatiently. Geordi didn't see that, of course, but he detected an annoyed flickering of her electromagnetic aura. "Of course not, Geordi. Nothing is absolutely guaranteed in this galaxy."

"So don't you think I should be allowed the same leeway of uncertainty that you have?"

Crusher chuckled slightly. "What is it with you, Geordi? Why all the interest in her?"

"Call it instinct, if you want, Doctor. I know what it's like to be in need. Besides, I've been studying about her career, about her personality. She was one hell of a character. She deserves better than this."

"All right, all right," sighed Crusher, knowing that sooner or later she was going to bow to the inevitable. "I had a feeling I wasn't going to be able to resist you. I've explained to the Penzatti the situation with her and they've promised me that they will restrain themselves in her presence."

"Much obliged, Doctor."

He turned towards Reannon. She sat there on the edge of the biobed, staring at nothing. She was there because someone had put her there, and she wasn't going to move until someone retrieved her, like some pathetic lapdog. Geordi took her gently by the hand, still cold as ice, and said, "Come on, Reannon." He tugged her slightly and she slid off the bed, following him as he pulled her along.

They walked through the sickbay and this time the Penzatti looked away, although a number of them shuddered. The only one who continued to stare at her, Crusher noticed, was the one who had attacked her earlier: Dantar. But his green face was unreadable, his antennae unmoving. His body was tense, as if waiting for the former Borg to make some move, but she gave no sign that she was aware of his existence. Aware, really, of anyone's existence, including her own. Geordi guided her out the sickbay door, and the moment she was gone, it was as if the entire sickbay sighed in relief.

Dantar looked up when he saw that Crusher was standing over him. "Yes?" he said quietly.

"Are you all right?" she asked him. As a matter of course, she was studying his injured leg and nodding with satisfaction at the way in which it had healed.

"You mean am I going to attack that thing again?"

"You'll pardon me for being curious."

He shrugged. "You explained the situation to us. Furthermore, such aggression would do nothing to bring my family back to life. I see no point to it." He smiled, and it looked more like a grimace. "Do you?"

"No," she said, patting him on the shoulder. "Let's make sure that we all remember that, shall we?"

Geordi led Reannon down the corridor, ignoring the puzzled glances from crew members who passed by. Actually, it was easy to ignore the glances, since he couldn't see them. What he was able to do, however, was sense people's reactions through their body heat and the auras they gave off. Whenever someone would be approaching, the emissions of their bodies seemed to flicker as they noticed Geordi and his companion, but were uncertain who—or what—they were seeing. Then their pulse rates would jump, or their heartbeats would increase; the general air of their aura would flicker wildly with barely repressed alarm as they realized the nature of Geordi's companion.

It put him in mind of ancient times when people

would see lepers and run screaming in hysterics. It was a prejudice, pure and simple. Reannon had not asked for this calamity to befall her, but now she was paying the price for it. Geordi wanted to shout at them, to chide them for their fear, but he saw no point to it. All they saw was a representative of the race that had destroyed thousands, even millions, of lives. A race that had perverted Captain Picard into something dark and twisted. No wonder they wanted to give her a wide berth. Still, it was damned irritating.

They stopped in front of a set of doors and Geordi turned to her. "Reannon," he said, making an effort to say her name to her as many times as he could—hoping that sheer repetition would get some sort of response—"Reannon, this is the holodeck. I've got someone I want you to meet."

The doors hissed open as they entered and stepped out into the vast room with the glowing yellow grids. As the doors closed behind them, Geordi said, "This is a place where we can create anything we like that's within our computer records. I've been doing some preparation, and I got something I think you'll want to see. Computer," he said more loudly now, "run program La Forge 1A."

Instantly the yellow grids disappeared, and Geordi and Reannon were standing on the bridge of a ship. As opposed to the clean, efficient, spit-and-polish bridge of the *Enterprise*, this ship had a certain grunginess and tackiness about it. There was litter on the floor, and a number of instruments looked as if they were being held together with spit and bailing wire.

Geordi heard the sound of metal scraping against metal and recognized it instantly. Someone was trying to repair something.

Over in the far corner was a Jeffries tube that extended up into the ship's inner workings, and a pair of legs was sticking out from within. He heard a grunt and a muttered curse and promises that the ship's time left for gallivanting around the galaxy was short. "Excuse me," he called out.

"Yeah, what?" called back a distinctly female voice from within the Jeffries tube.

"I have someone I want you to meet."

There was an annoyed sigh, and several tools dropped down from inside the tube and clattered to the floor. Then the woman dropped out as well. Her eyebrows and the ends of her hair was slightly singed, and there was a general air of impatience about her. Geordi allowed himself a mental pat on the back. The lessons he learned about imparting the illusion of life to holodeck recreations had been well served.

"So?" she asked impatiently. "What's the deal here? You are . . .?"

"Geordi La Forge. And you are here courtesy of an extremely detailed psych profile left in Starfleet computers by a woman who was afraid of dying alone in space and leaving nothing of herself behind. So . . . Reannon Bonaventure, I want you to meet Reannon Bonaventure."

Now that Geordi had the opportunity to view her up close, in the flesh, so to speak, he saw that she, in fact, bore only the most superficial of resemblances to Troi. Her thick black hair was pulled back in a bun, and she had none of the aristocratic air that surrounded the Betazoid counselor. Instead, she had a down-and-dirty air about her, an earthiness that he found ingratiating.

The holodeck Reannon slowly circled the real Reannon, absently tugging on her ear in thought. She bent down slightly, resting her hands on her knees and putting her face right up to the vacuous woman. Then, from the same slightly stooped position, she turned to Geordi and said, "You're kidding, right?"

"I'm afraid not."

She took the Borg's face, squeezed it in one hand, turned it to the left and right and studied it. "I know I'm not much of a morning person," she said at last, "but this is ridiculous."

"This," said Geordi, "is what happened to her at the hands of the Borg. I wanted her to see you. To see what she had been like, so that she could be that way again."

"Well," and Reannon stepped back and spread her arms wide, the gesture encompassing all within their view. "This is it. This is what there is to me. They've got this whole legend built up around me. 'The Brass Lass.' 'Course, the problem with brass is that it tarnishes." She stared once more at her future. "Tarnished something bad, didn't it."

"Could you say something to her?" said Geordi. "Something that will—"

"That will what?" Reannon's voice was suddenly sharp and angry. She was stalking the bridge like a caged animal. "I mean, what the hell did you do this for? What're you, the ghost of Christmas yet to come? I mean, look at this! You show me this . . . this pasty-faced *thing* that's going to be me, and you ask me what I have to say to it? Here. Here's what I say to it," and she leaned into the face of the real Reannon and shouted, *"You're an idiot!* Okay? You're a freaking *moron!* I mean, look at you! *Look* at you," and her voice was shaking with fury. "After everything I've been through, after everything I've dodged and the life I've led, I'm going to wind up like that? That stinks! How could you have let yourself get into this!" she shouted at herself. "You're a zombie! You're a walking space case! I mean, I figured if I die, okay, so I die, and that's all. But this? This isn't dead! This isn't anything! This is just a . . . a *waste!*"

Geordi was astounded. He hadn't been sure of what he was going to get by programming the holodeck for such fidelity to the original persona of Reannon Bonaventure, but he certainly hadn't expected this. "Reannon—" and he wasn't even sure whom he was addressing.

The holodeck Reannon had hurled herself into a chair that was in front of her sensor apparatus. "Just go away, would you, please?"

"Reannon, only you can help yourself," said Geordi.

She spun around in the chair as if it had been hurled by a slingshot and said, "Are you saying I can avoid this? That there's something I can do to prevent this from happening?"

"No," said Geordi. "No, there's not. Not a thing. But you can help restore yourself to reality."

"Yeah?"

"I think so," said Geordi with a confidence he didn't feel.

Reannon slowly rose from the chair and walked across the bridge to face herself. She took the Borg woman by the shoulders and said softly, "Oh, baby . . . what have you done to yourself?"

She did not reply to herself.

"Remember?" Reannon said. "Come on. Remember the good times, huh? Huh? Like that time the Ferengi tried to cheat you, and you left them holding the bag? Or the time that those people on Savannah One wanted to make you into a goddess, because they'd never seen a woman with pale skin before? Or how about," and she smiled, "how about the feeling you got when you were being pursued. The way the adrenaline would pump and your mind would be racing, trying to come up with a new angle. And how about sex, huh? A guy in every port. They all wanted a piece of me, just so they could say they had. I had men in two different sectors claiming they'd been with me at the exact same time. Gods, the sex was great. Come on. Come on, you can't say you don't remember that."

And there was no response from the Borg woman. She continued to stare straight ahead, impassive, unknowable.

Reannon shook her now, sounding a little desperate. "Come on," she said urgently. "You've got to remember. You've got to say something. Come on. Say something. Speak to me, dammit," and her voice rose in confusion and fury. "They couldn't have gotten to me this much. Not me! I'm tougher than that. I'm better than that. Come on!" and she shook her violently.

Geordi started toward them. "Hold it. That's en—"

"Come on!" bellowed Reannon, and she drew back a hand and slapped the Borg woman as hard as she could across the face. Her head snapped around and she staggered back.

"Get away from her!" shouted Geordi, and he grabbed Reannon from behind, pinning her arms back. Reannon struggled furiously in his grip as the Borg woman slumped backwards and fell to the floor, staring up at the ceiling.

"Say something!" Reannon shouted. "Say something, you useless slab of meat! I'm trapped in you! Let me out! *Let me out!*"

"Computer," Geordi began, about to issue the order that would terminate the scenario.

"No!" shrieked Reannon. "No computer! Not yet! *Not yet!* Please! Wait a moment!"

"What is it?"

In a low, barely controlled voice, she said, "Please. Please promise me you'll do something. Don't leave me like this. Please. Please promise."

"I'll do everything I can," Geordi assured her, finding it hard to believe that he was trying to still the concerns of a holodeck recreation.

"Don't do everything," Reannon told him. "Do anything. Do whatever it takes, but save me. Please."

"All right," said Geordi. "All right."

"Promise."

"I promise."

Her struggles subsided and Geordi released her. She stood there a long moment, staring at herself. Then she turned towards Geordi and regarded him.

"I'll do whatever it takes," said Geordi.

"Thank you," she said, and to his surprise she took him firmly by the face and kissed him passionately. And when she released him, he most definitely did not want to be released.

She stepped away from him and coughed slightly, then turned and went to the Jeffries tube. "Whatever it takes," she said one last time. "Now if you'll excuse me, I got work to do." But her bravado barely covered the unmistakable sound of fear that filled her voice, and she jumped back up the Jeffries tube before she'd have to deal with it any further.

"Computer," said Geordi, "end simulation."

The ship surroundings promptly vanished, to be replaced by the steady glow of the holodeck grids once more. Geordi went to the unmoving, de-Borged form of Reannon and said, "How about we go to the Ten-Forward lounge and get a drink. What do you say, huh?" He spoke in a convivial, offhand way, as if in this casual manner he could somehow trick Reannon into speaking. As if the entire thing were some sort of elaborate hoax on her part, and if he caught her off

213

guard and got her to say something, she would be all right once more.

But there was nothing from her, and Geordi sighed inwardly. Well, no one could say he had no idea what he was letting himself in for. He also knew, though, that he would not be able to get the image of Reannon out of his mind, and that he had to get in to help her.

He took her by the arm and she obediently went out with him.

Beverly Crusher entered sickbay and gave a cursory glance around before starting to head for her office to catch up on her paperwork. Then she stopped in her tracks.

One of the beds was empty, and she knew immediately which one it was. She immediately turned towards the other Penzatti and said, "Where did Dantar go?"

They stared at her blandly and shrugged. They put on a splendid show of not knowing, and perhaps they didn't. More likely, they simply didn't want to know.

"How long has he been gone?" she demanded. This got even less response. She tapped her communicator and said, "Crusher to security. We may have a problem . . ."

There was an uneasy air hanging in the Ten-Forward lounge, as there always was when the crew knew that the *Enterprise* was en route to a particularly dangerous situation. Word had seeped through the normal grapevines that made keeping a secret on a starship so damned difficult. The general talk was that they were going to be encountering either something that was the Borg, or just like the Borg, only more powerful.

Guinan moved among the customers, making small

talk and generally letting them know, in her subtle way, that she was there if they had anything they wished to discuss. She moved to a table at which Data was seated, and with a slight inclination of her head that served as a greeting, she sat opposite him.

"Unusual to see you here by yourself, Data," she observed. "Usually you're only here in the company of the others, unless there's something very specific on your mind."

Data pondered that a moment. "I do not believe that is the case in this instance," he said. "I merely wished to be with my fellow crew members in an informal setting, and so I came down here."

"Any idea why that might be?" asked Guinan.

He shrugged, a gesture he'd picked up from Riker. It had taken him a while to get the hang of when to use it. At first he'd started shrugging in the middle of conversations, totally unrelated to whatever was being discussed. This started concern that Data was developing some sort of twitch in his positronic brain. "I have no idea," said Data.

"Perhaps you *enjoy* it, Data."

He gave it some thought. "I do not think that likely. I cannot enjoy an event. At most, I can appreciate the variation in stimuli that are presented when—"

She put up a hand and said, "Data, let's just say that you enjoy it and don't know it, okay?"

He stared at her and was about to reply, when La Forge entered with Reannon in tow. Heads turned all over the Ten-Forward lounge, and the relative silence that had been present before was now replaced by a low, curious buzz. Clearly Geordi and his new companion were becoming the center of conversation wherever they went.

Geordi's gaze scanned the room, and he saw that people were drawing slightly closer together, as if to put whatever distance they could between themselves and the female with him. And the chief engineer, slow to anger, felt his annoyance boiling over.

"What do you think's going to happen?" he demanded of the general room. "That if you look at her too long, or accidentally touch her somehow, you might wind up catching it?"

Guinan was at his side now, a hand on his shoulder, but it didn't calm him. "She was assaulted! Don't any of you understand that? Her mind and body were violated, and you're all acting as if it's her fault! So, before you start looking at her and shying away, maybe you'd better look at yourselves first!"

He pulled her along with him to the table where he noticed that Data was seated. He was extremely grateful that the android officer was there. Data may have been incapable of feeling the best of human emotions, but he also couldn't display the worst, such as fear or suspicion. He sat down opposite Data and Guinan, but before he could say anything, Guinan cleared her throat slightly and pointed. He turned and saw that Reannon was still standing, and with a sigh he pulled her down into the chair next to him. "She's kind of bad on picking up non-verbal cues," he said.

"So I gathered," said Guinan.

Data was studying her as if she were under a microscope. "Her motor functions are performing admirably," he said.

"Yeah, but there's nothing beyond that," said Geordi. He rested his head on one hand and sighed. "I feel like I should be doing more, but I don't know what. I took her to the holodeck to acquaint her with herself the way she used to be."

"Did she respond at all?"

"Not a lick." He leaned forward, his VISOR inches away from Reannon's eyes. "Maybe it's true. Maybe I am just wasting my time."

And Reannon looked at him.

Looked *at* him.

It was a subtle change in her face that, of course, Geordi could not discern, but he thought he detected a slight, flickering alteration in her aura, which immediately alerted him. "Data, Guinan . . . did she . . . is she curious about my VISOR?" He had not moved a millimeter from where he was.

"I think *curious* may be too strong a word," said Data. "She has, however, noticed its existence. Since she has not apparently noticed anything else, this could be considered a positive step."

She was angling her head slightly, studying the VISOR from every direction.

Then she reached up, her hand slow and hesitant, until her fingers came to rest on the VISOR. They traced the curve of it, lingered over the circuitry that was at either end in the earpiece.

"I'll be damned," whispered Geordi, afraid to talk above a hush, lest it ruin the mood.

"Undoubtedly, it is the mechanical aspect of your visual prosthetic that has caught her attention," said Data, watching with fascination. "It is the closest analog to her own recent experience."

"What . . . what do you think I should do next?"

"Let nature take its course," said Guinan. "Not exactly an original piece of advice, but one that bears repeating."

Then Guinan looked up, aware that something had changed.

Guinan was as attuned to the mood of Ten-Forward as the average person was to the beating of their heart. So when Dantar entered, she sensed immediately that something was wrong.

The Penzatti was coming slowly towards the table, a fixed and determined expression on his face. His antennae were quivering slightly, as if from anticipation of something. His gaze was fixed on Reannon.

"Geordi," said Guinan softly, but with enough firmness that it immediately alerted Geordi that something was wrong. She didn't need to add to it, but instead rose and said pointedly to Dantar, who was still some feet away, "Welcome to Ten-Forward. How can I help you?"

The next moments seemed to telescope outward, as if taking an eternity, although actually they only occupied a few fleeting seconds.

Dantar's hands had been behind his back, and suddenly one of the crewmen at a table noticed something and shouted a warning, starting to rise from his seat. Dantar's hands now swung into view, and in either hand he was holding a Keldin blaster, the hand weapon of choice of the Penzatti. It was deadly, powerful, and accurate. He took aim at Reannon, shouted, "Murderer of my family!" and fired.

Geordi lunged toward Reannon, crying out a warning. She didn't respond to it, still mesmerized by Geordi's VISOR. He slammed into her, knocking her back and sending her tumbling to the floor, away from his grasping arms.

At that moment the crewman who had called out the alarm got to Dantar just as the Penzatti fired at where Reannon had been. The blasters discharged their powerful bolts and blew out the nearest window of the Ten-Forward lounge, creating a hole that was more than a foot wide. The results were predictable and instantaneous.

With the roar of a hurricane, air was immediately sucked out of the room.

People screamed and cried out, grabbing at each other and at the furniture which was affixed to the floor. The vacuum of space pulled at them with all its force, and they resisted with everything they had.

Dantar had grabbed the nearest piece of furniture, but in so doing had lost his grip on his blasters. He watched in horrified helplessness as the weapons skidded across the floor and out into the vastness of space.

Reannon had been closest to the window, and she was yanked up off her feet. Her arm went through the hole and her head was about to follow, when a screaming Geordi La Forge leaped forward, heedless of his own safety, and grabbed her by the leg. Geordi then lashed out with his own foot, hoping to hook it around a table leg, and he missed. He was dragged forward inexorably by the pull of the air and then stopped as Data clamped his hand onto Geordi's ankle. Data, for his part, had sunk his fingers right into the table top and wasn't budging. Guinan was holding on fixedly also, her flowing gown whipping around her, and she was trying to shout something that no one could make out.

Data, Geordi, and Reannon formed a human chain, Reannon suspended in midair, one arm out the window, the rest of her barely anchored within the safety of Ten-Forward. And even that safety was becoming questionable. Her foot were floating above the floor as the air rushed around her, her head bumping up against the window. Geordi was shouting her name, his fingers quickly becoming numb as the temperature dropped.

He thought he was that way for months, years. Actually, it was barely seconds, and then the great pull of space promptly ceased. Reannon thudded heavily to the floor, doing nothing to break her fall, and there was an audible hiss as air flooded back into Ten-

Forward to replace that which had been sucked out into space.

Geordi knew that as the emergency systems of the *Enterprise* kicked in, a force shield sprang into existence directly over the hole, re-establishing hull integrity until an emergency crew could arrive to more permanently repair the breech.

Geordi let out a gasp and released his grip on Reannon's leg. Then he flexed his fingers to try and get the blood flowing again, and even as he did so he was calling out, "Is everyone okay? Everyone all right?"

There were ragged cries of confirmation from all around, as the shaken crew members verified that they were in one piece.

Dantar was lying on the floor, staring up at the ceiling. "Did I kill her?" he was moaning over and over again. "Did I kill her? Can my family rest now?"

"Your family!" shouted Geordi from across the room on the floor. He put one hand down to start and push himself upwards. "Your family would be thrilled to know you've turned into a—"

And then he stopped as his hand felt something warm and wet and sticky beneath it. His head snapped around, trying to discern the source. And when he realized what it was, he shouted out, *"Data!"* with more alarm than the android had ever heard in the chief engineer's voice.

Reannon was lying on the floor, blood pouring from her left shoulder, a shoulder that had no arm.

She didn't know enough to cry out in pain or shriek. She merely stared at the absence of appendage with a kind of distant fascination, as if it were happening to someone else.

Instantly Geordi realized what had occurred. When there was a breech of hull integrity, the force field covered over that breech and sealed it off. It had also tried to push Reannon's arm back in—but instead, the arm had been sheared off as it was shoved up against the jagged remains of the transparent aluminum window.

"Data!" Geordi cried out, not exactly sure what he expected the android to do. Data, however, did something immediately. He moved quickly to Reannon and lifted her up in his powerful arms. Within moments the front of his uniform was soaked red with blood.

Geordi was on his feet, tapping his communicator and alerting Crusher that he was on his way down to sickbay with the severely injured Reannon. They ran out just as Worf and the security team ran in. Worf's face registered amazement for just a moment as he saw the truncated stump that had once been Reannon's arm, and then Geordi and Data were gone. Data's legs were churning up distance with formidable speed, and it was all that Geordi could do to keep up.

Worf's face returned to the normal Klingon scowl with which he was far more comfortable, and then he and the security team strode across the Ten-Forward lounge to the prostrate form of Dantar. A crewman was sitting flat on top of the Penzatti to make sure he didn't go anywhere. They needn't have worried. Dantar was still asking over and over again whether the Borg was dead and his family avenged.

Worf frowned, an expression only slightly different from his normal one. If the Penzatti man had lost his mind, or was even faking having lost his mind as a bid for sympathy, he was about to find Worf an extremely unsympathetic audience.

Dantar looked up at him, wide-eyed, and in a broken voice he said, "They kept crying out to me.

The souls of my family, crying out. They wouldn't stop. Wouldn't stop. Are they at rest now? Are they?"

"Yes," said Worf with no trace of patience. "Their souls are resting comfortably in the brig, and you'll be joining them momentarily." And without another word he hauled the Penzatti male to his feet and dragged him out of Ten-Forward.

Picard entered sickbay and walked directly to Geordi, who was standing outside the operating room, unable to bring himself to go in and witness firsthand how things were going. Data was with him, having had no particular compunction about entering the operating room, but sensing that his friend could use whatever support Data's presence might entail.

"Are you all right?" he asked.

"Fine, Captain. A little shaky, but fine."

"Guinan said the Penzatti was wielding some sort of blasters," said Picard. "Where the devil did he get them?"

Geordi cleared his throat. "I did some checking on that," he said. "They were being stored in the armory, and entrance to the armory is governed by computer access. But the Penzatti have always been extremely good with computers, and Dantar managed to discover the access codes and get in to retrieve them. It's moot at this point. I saw them get sucked out into space."

"I want the access code changed—"

"Already done, sir."

Picard nodded approvingly. "Good. And I understand Mr. Worf has attended to new living arrangements for our rather aggressive guest. So the remaining problem is our former Borg patient."

Crusher emerged from the operating room, having

already disposed of her bloody garments and switched to fresh ones. Normally the fields that were generated around the operating arena cleansed wounds immediately. But when a patient was bleeding as profusely as this one was, one couldn't help but get her hands dirty.

She came straight towards Geordi, her fury boiling over. "You said you could take care of her!" she said angrily. "You said you'd be responsible! You stood right here and sweet-talked me about all the good you were going to do her. A fat lot of good you've done so far, wouldn't you say, engineer?"

"I saved her life!" protested Geordi. "Doesn't that count for something?"

"I sent a woman out of here with two good arms and she came back with one. That's what counts."

"Mr. La Forge is clearly upset with what happened, Doctor," Picard said with command firmness. "I hardly think it necessary to berate him."

"You're not the one who was ankle-deep in blood," said Crusher.

"I sure was!" said Geordi hotly. "There was blood on my hands, and on my uniform, and on my conscience, because all I was trying to do was help this woman and instead she keeps getting injured while in my care. So you want to heap guilt on me, Doctor? Go ahead. Go right ahead. Because it's only going to be a fraction of what I've already heaped on myself."

She pursed her lips and then stepped to one side. "You want to go in and see her? Go in and see her."

Geordi nodded briskly and then went past them and into the operating room.

Crusher watched him go and then shook her head. "I don't get it," she said. "I just don't get it. What is this fixation that Geordi's developed on this woman?"

223

"He fixes things," said Picard with a shrug. "He lives every day with something that repairs his eyesight. Plus he has his duties as chief engineer which, at its core, means that he is in charge of all sorts of repairs. So instead of a broken machine, he sees a broken human, and he feels the need to repair her."

"It may be something else as well," said Data thoughtfully. "It may be that when he looks at her, he sees her in a way that we do not, and perceives possibilities where others would only see . . ."— and he paused, searching for the right word— ". . . windmills," he finished.

Inside the operating room, Reannon was sitting up. And she was staring.

"How are you, Reannon?" asked Geordi. In his mind he heard the saucy voice of the holodeck Reannon replying, "Just fine, how the hell are you?" Here, though, in the real world, he was getting nothing.

She continued to stare, and Geordi realized that she was looking at something very specific. She was looking at her arm.

"It was the best I could do on short notice," came Crusher's voice. Behind her, Geordi heard the distinctive footfalls of Picard and Data. "Given time, I can clone her a new arm once I've had time to grow skin samples. Or, if she decides to stay with this, I can create skin grafts over it to hide the metal. It'll take a bit of experimenting to match her rather pale complexion, but I can do it. No one will even know it's a prosthesis."

Reannon was studying her new arm. Its ribbed metal sections glinted in the soft light of the sickbay operating theater. The fingers came to slight points rather than the rounded edges of normal fingers, and when she closed her hand into a fist, it made a soft clacking sound.

"She appears much more attentive to objects and the world than she did before," observed Picard. "Obviously her time with Mr. La Forge is having some degree of positive influence." The remark was aimed rather pointedly at Crusher.

It was a mild barb that was not lost on her. "So it would seem," she admitted. "Still, I'd feel more comfortable if Deanna had some time with her. Psychology is *her* field, not Geordi's."

"The Counselor wasn't picking up anything from her earlier," said Picard, "but it's more than possible that—"

"Look!" Crusher said suddenly.

Reannon was staring at her mechanical hand, and the edges of her lips had turned up ever so slightly.

"She is smiling," observed Data. "That is the first significant facial reaction that she has displayed."

"She *is* smiling," said Crusher, regarding Reannon closely. "I'll be. All right, Geordi, you have my full apologies. You're clearly making headway with her."

"No, I'm not," said Geordi sourly.

They looked at him with surprise. "How can you say that?" asked Crusher. "To get an emotional response from someone who seemed as brain-dead as . . ."

"Yeah, but don't you see what she was responding to?" He took the metal hand firmly in his own. "She's happy because she has a part attached to her that's mechanical. Artificial. She's smiling because whatever part of her is alive in there is happy because she's taken her first step back towards being a cybernetic organism."

"You're saying that—" began Picard.

225

And Geordi nodded. "Yeah. The only reason she's displaying any sort of emotion is because she thinks she's taken the first step toward becoming a Borg again. And she's happy about it."

He released her hand and, with a discouraged shake of his head, walked out of the operating room.

Chapter Thirteen

"THAT'S ALL we can tell you, Jean-Luc. I wish we knew more."

The face of Ariel Taggert was on the screen, having replaced the image of moments ago of the *Repulse* hanging in space, moving at one-half impulse power. When the *Enterprise* had arrived in the Kalish star system and found a battered starship and several planets missing, they had thought the worst . . . until they managed to open a channel to the *Repulse* and learn that loss of life had been minimal. "It's a big monster, and it's powerful," continued Taggert. "I've fed you all the specs that our sensors were able to pick up. When we last saw it, it was heading out of the system at two-eleven mark four."

Data, seated at ops, quickly ran the coordinates through on his charts. "Captain," he said, and then amended, "Captains," since the comment was really addressed to both of them, "that would be in line with our projected origin of the device."

"Device." Taggert shook her head. "A chronometer is a device. This thing was a monstrosity. This thing, and whoever was controlling it."

"You definitely communicated with it," said Picard.

"Ooooh yes. And it had a few choice words for us that, boiled down, amounted to, 'Stay the hell out of my way.' If she's out for the Borg, then I certainly wouldn't want to be in the Borg's shoes."

I've been there, and I wouldn't want to be there again, either, Picard thought. Out loud, he said, "Shall we take you in tow, Ariel?"

She made a dismissive wave. "Save your energy. We'll have repairs effected within twelve hours to be on our way again. Besides, in the condition we're in right now, we wouldn't do you a damned bit of good. A few phaser shots and some maneuvering tricks aren't going to help. Not that attacking that thing with all systems go would do you any good."

"It's that powerful?"

"Oh yes," she said with quiet conviction. "I've never seen anything like it, Jean-Luc. Not ever. You can't stop it. No one can stop it."

"We'll have to try."

"Then God watch over you, Picard."

"If he will. *Enterprise* out."

Ariel's image vanished, replaced by the *Repulse*, and Picard turned to Data. "Mr. Data, what will be the next star system that the planet-killer encounters?"

Data didn't even have to glance. "If it continues its present course, the planet-killer will next enter Tholian space."

"Oh, wonderful," said Riker. "They'll be thrilled to help out."

"Sarcasm, Number One? Perhaps you can employ it against the planet-killer," Picard said.

"From what Captain Taggert was saying, phasers

and photon torpedoes had no effect," Riker said drily. "Perhaps other weapons might be in order."

"I'll have Mr. La Forge prepare some slingshots. Mr. Data, set course on two-eleven mark four. Warp factor seven." He pointed slightly in that small shooting motion he'd developed. "Engage," he said.

The *Enterprise* leaped into warp space and was gone.

Taggert watched them go, then said, "Bridge to sickbay. How you doing down there, Kate?"

"Holding up," came Pulaski's reply. "You didn't send us as many injuries as I figured you would."

"I'm mellowing in my old age," said Taggert.

"Old age beats the alternative."

"Yeah." She paused. "Let's hope Picard doesn't have to deal with the alternative. Bridge out."

She returned to her command chair and stared out at the stars hanging in front of them. She felt woefully insignificant.

"Be careful, Picard," she said.

"Captain," Worf began, and then paused, rechecking the sensors on his tactical board as if he couldn't quite believe it. "I believe we've found the planet-killer."

"Confirmed," said Data. "It is progressing along the same heading as before, moving at warp three."

"A relatively leisurely pace," Picard observed. "Increase speed to warp six, and let us hope she doesn't decide to make a race of it."

The *Enterprise* shot forward, and within moments the last artifact of a long-gone race was looming on their screen.

There was a deathly silence in the bridge as they

took in the scope of it. Then, his voice barely rising above the hush, Picard said, "Sensor readings?"

"Neutronium hull makes readings of the internal workings difficult to ascertain," said Worf. "Emissions would indicate a form of conversion engine, somewhat unlike any known to our technology."

"I am also detecting fluctuation rates in their warp drive field that are at variance with the standard vibrations that our own technology provides," said Data. "In fact, it would seem closer to the vibrations given off by the propulsion of a Borg ship."

"You're saying that the Borg derived their propulsion technology from the race that built that . . . thing?" asked Picard, pointing at the screen.

"I'm stating only that there is a similarity," Data said. "The Borg are known to assimilate the usable material and technology of whatever they conquer. It is possible that if they discovered Warp technology that was superior to their own, they would quite naturally incorporate it into their own structure."

"But the Borg don't consume planets," pointed out Riker. "Planetary mass is what fuels our friend out there."

"True, considering the speeds we've seen the Borg travel, they clearly have some sort of nearly unlimited power base."

Troi was staring at the planet-destroyer with amazement and shaking her head. "Incredible," she whispered.

Picard and Riker turned towards her. "Counselor—?"

"It's . . ." She was clearly overwhelmed, trying to find the words. "What I'm picking up from that vessel, Captain, it's . . ."

"Is it alive?"

"Captain," and she looked at him with eyes that

had a hopeless look to them, "it's powered by emotion."

"I must disagree," said Data. "It is clear that the consumption of planets . . ."

"I'm not talking about the physical fuel," she said. "The device has . . . has an emotional drive to it. I've never encountered anything like it."

"Is it like the Tin Man?"

"No. No, Tin Man was alive. Tin Man was a biological entity that needed a heart. That thing out there, that is a mechanical construct. But it's constructed with a technology that gives it some sort of an empathic link with . . ."

"With what?" Picard was starting to feel frustrated. It was like pulling teeth.

She shook her head. "I don't know. There's so much, so many voices. I can't begin to describe it. But I definitely had a sense of it. It called out to me, Captain, in my sleep. I remember the vague outlines, if not the details. And that is most definitely what presented itself."

"Enough speculation," said Picard. "Frequencies."

"Open," said Worf.

"Attention alien vessel," he said. "This is Jean-Luc Picard of the Federation starship *Enterprise*. Identify yourself."

There was no immediate response, and then Data said, "The vessel is slowing, Captain. Warp two . . . warp one . . . dropping out of warp space."

"Bring us alongside," said Picard, slowly rising from his chair. He couldn't remove his eyes from the image on the screen. It was a floating engine of destruction, bristling with more power and speed than anything he'd ever seen or even contemplated. The intellect and technology that had been able to build such a thing was truly remarkable.

Suddenly the lights began to flicker, and all over, the bridge panels started activating. The crew looked around in confusion as Worf said, "Captain, we are being scanned."

"Shields up," said Picard.

"Our shields are not stopping the probe, Captain," Data reported after a moment. "It appears to be doing no harm to our systems."

"Don't do anything," said Picard. "Let them probe us," *as if we have a choice,* his mind added darkly. "Let them know that we have nothing to hide."

And then Troi cried out.

In the Ten-Forward lounge, Guinan was staring out the viewing port at the massive vessel that hung stopped in space before them.

"Incredible," she whispered. "Oh, sister . . . what have you done?"

And then she felt it, felt the minds reaching out. She staggered back, banging into a table and using it to steady herself. She ignored the sharp pain in her leg that had been created by the impact, turned, and ran for the door of Ten-Forward.

Riker was immediately at Troi's side as she started to slide out of her chair, her eyes rolling up into the back of her head. "Deanna!" shouted Riker.

Picard immediately called out, "Bridge to sickbay! Doctor Crusher, Counselor Troi is having some sort of seizure!"

"No."

It was Deanna who had spoken. Just like that, the convulsions, the screaming, all of the consternation was gone. Instead, she was smiling with infinite calm, her dark eyes glittering. She looked at Picard with an emotion bordering on joy. "So . . . it is you."

"What?" Picard looked at Riker in confusion, and
the first officer didn't seem to understand the situation
any more than Picard did. "Yes, it's me, Counselor.
Deanna, what's wrong?"

"Nothing is wrong."

From sickbay, Beverly Crusher's worried voice
called out over the still-open channel, "What's happening up there? Should I come up there—"

"Oh, no," said Deanna, pulling herself to her feet.
"Everything will be just fine."

"Stand by, Doctor," said Picard.

"You're just keeping the poor woman on alert for no
reason," said Deanna.

And that's when Riker noticed it. "Your voice. Your
accent is different. Deanna, what's happened?"

"That voice," said Picard in disbelief. "Yes, I know
that voice, that's . . ."

She turned towards Picard. "Do you understand
now, Picard? It was important to me that you be the
first to know."

Picard staggered back, holding onto the arm of his
command chair as if deriving strength from it. For just
a moment his mouth moved and he looked utterly
helpless, confronted by someone before whom he felt
vulnerable. But it was for the briefest of moments, so
brief that his crew didn't even notice, for all their
attention was on Troi. Or whatever Troi had become.

She was standing with her shoulders squared back,
her chin upturned. There was a faint expression of
bemusement on her face.

"Oh, don't worry, Picard," she said. "I shan't stay
long. But after all you have done for me, after the
simple clarity of your thought served to point the way,
I merely wished to thank you."

And she drew Picard's face to hers and kissed him.
For just a second he almost responded, and then he

took her firmly by the shoulders and held her at arm's length. "You are doing this without the permission of my counselor. You cannot usurp her body. Whoever you are . . ."

"You know who I am," she said with raised eyebrows. "But as you wish, Picard. It is probably better this way. The mind of this one is not especially powerful. If I were a part of her overlong, I could destroy it. That will serve no purpose. So I release her to you."

As if a string had been cut, Deanna suddenly started to slump forward. Picard caught her with one arm and looked around, as if searching the air for the whereabouts of the being that had come and gone so quickly. Troi looked around in confusion.

The turbolift slid open, and Guinan stepped out onto the bridge. Somehow, considering the events of the past few minutes, the unusualness of her appearance on the bridge seemed to fit right in.

She stood by the turbolift, her hands resting lightly on the curved railing that separated the aft stations from the command area. She spoke one word, in a voice far more severe than any they had ever heard. And the word was a name: "Delcara."

The air in front of the viewscreen seemed to shimmer for just a moment, and then she appeared.

Not immediately—slowly, like a Cheshire cat in reverse. First her face was hanging there, only the faintest of outlines visible. Then her body began to waver into existence. At first she seemed nude, but then undulating folds of cloth materialized around her. Her hair billowed in all directions, looking for all the world like a vast starfield.

She was just as Picard had remembered her.

Within seconds she stood before them, a flickering vision. Everyone on the bridge was affected, held breathless and motionless by the wonder of the female before them.

Almost everyone.

"Security alert," called Worf. "Intruder on the bridge!"

"No, it's all right," said Picard.

"Captain, there's a—"

"No," said Picard slowly. Despite all the emotions running through him, despite the fact that deep within him was a confused Starfleet cadet who had been confronted years ago by a woman beyond imagining, there was no room here for indulgences. He could not allow himself to be distracted by his own turmoil or the stark beauty of the woman from his past. He forced his mind to act in its familiar patterns. Taking a deep breath, he said, "No, there's not. There's no shadow."

They looked and saw that he was correct. The being in front of them cast no shadow at all.

"She's a hologram," said Riker, understanding.

Slowly Guinan approached her, her eyes never wavering. Delcara smiled ethereally. "Guinan," she said. "You look well."

"And you too," said Guinan carefully. "What are you doing here?"

"Conversing with your captain. He wished to speak with me, and I have obliged him. I owe him that much."

"I wish to talk with you privately," said Picard. "You, myself, and Guinan."

"Captain, I would not advise that," Worf spoke up, and Riker added, "Nor I."

But Picard fired a look at them that spoke volumes and said, "That is my decision, Number One."

In truth, he wasn't sure why he was making it. Perhaps because she represented an incarnation of something that was, quite simply, too personal for him to expose to his officers. Or perhaps it was something else. Perhaps . . .

Perhaps he didn't want to share her.

He glanced at Troi, who had managed to regain her equilibrium and who—in very broad strokes—had been filled in by Riker as to what had happened to her. Troi looked at him with eyes that were filled with understanding. Somehow he considered that very important to him.

"Yes, sir," was all Riker said. Worf said nothing, but merely glowered, the way he did habitually when someone did other than what Worf suggested.

He gestured. "My ready room is this way."

She nodded and walked towards it in a manner that seemed more gliding than anything else. Picard was momentarily startled when the door did not slide open for her, and it looked as if she would bump right into it. Then, of course, he understood, as Delcara passed through it like a ghost.

He turned to Guinan and said, "This should prove to be very, very . . . interesting."

"Not the word I would have chosen, but it'll do," she said.

Chapter Fourteen

THE DOORS OF the ready room slid shut behind them and Picard turned to face the woman from his past. "All right," he said, "How? How did you do it? And why?"

"To what are you referring?" asked Delcara.

"All of it. The Academy. This ship. All of it."

She looked from Picard to Guinan and back, and then walked through Picard's desk to stand on the other side.

"All right," she said softly. "Guinan has told you much, I'm sure. Here is the rest of the telling, then.

"I was drawn to you," she said, "in a way that I cannot describe to you. I felt . . . a sense of you. A sense that you were out there, in the galaxy for me." She smiled that wonderful smile. "Humans believe that throughout the galaxy, there is always someone for everyone. That no one need really be alone, and it is just a matter of finding the right person. For some of us that cosmic balancing is more than just a theory. It is a palpable thing that shapes and directs our lives."

He shook his head. "I don't know what you're talking about."

"I do," said Guinan. "My people have a general— sense, if you will—of the space-time continuum. An operational instinct, more than anything else. It's an acquired trait, a training of the mind, really. The galaxy is always whispering. We just learned to listen better than others. It's a technique that Delcara was taught . . . that anyone can learn, really, when they're ready. You're over-romanticizing it somewhat, bond sister."

She turned away from him to gaze out his window, at the ship that contained her physical body. If she had heard Guinan's words at all, she gave no sign. "There is something about me," she says. "Somehow, I am linked with the soulless ones."

"The Borg," said Picard.

She shrugged. "If that is what they are calling themselves now. I sense they have had many names in their time. And somehow I am drawn to those who are destined to suffer at the hands of the Borg. It took me much of my lifetime to realize that. Wherever I go . . . they follow."

"Delcara, that's ridiculous," Guinan spoke up for the first time. She walked around the desk to face the hologram. "You act as if you yourself are to blame for what happened."

Delcara did not even look at her. "Everything I touch, dies," she said. It was not said in self-pity, but as if stating obvious fact. Her hand reached out and skimmed the top of the desk, passing through. "Now I am safe. Now the galaxy is safe from the Borg, and when I am through, the Borg will be no more."

"You say you were drawn to me," said Picard. "Even if I were to accept that . . . what happened that day? That night? Why could no one else see you? I thought I was losing my mind . . . Was that a holo-gram?"

"No. I possessed no holograph technology back then. No one else saw me because I wished it so. Guinan has told you of my power. Of my command of the mind. I am perfectly capable of instructing the mind to pay no attention to that which it perceives. You saw me, however, because," and again she smiled that luminous smile, the edges of her eyes crinkling ever so slightly, "because to deceive the mind in such a way is, in a manner of speaking, to lie. I had no desire to lie to you."

"And that night?"

"Let us say that I appealed to the aspects of your mind that held a sense of the dramatic," she said. "A breezy night, in your dreamlike haze, became a virtual hurricane."

"You touched me." His fingers brushed against his forehead, as if a mark were visible. "You kissed me. It felt like ice."

"That," she said darkly, "was an unfortunate indul-gence on my part. I have since learned what happened to you. A kiss from me brushes your forehead. And a death sentence from the Borg—a life of living as they do, or what passes for living—that living death sen-tence brushes against you. Had I followed my heart's dictates . . ."

"I'd be a Borg to this day? Or dead? What utter nonsense," he said sharply.

"Picard is right," said Guinan. "Sister, the years of isolation, the pain, the loss—they've taken their toll on you. You're not speaking as one who has thought out what she's saying."

Delcara passed through the desk and crossed the room. "And you, Guinan, refuse to see the obvious. That is a mistake that I have ceased making. Once I realized the truth of it—once I realized the fate that had been inflicted upon me—only then was I capable of taking steps so that my fate would be in my hands once more. And it is. Look at it," and she gestured out the window and toward her vessel. "Look at the fruits of my labor."

It hung out there, carrying with it an almost obscene beauty in the amount of destruction that it was capable of causing. There was a somewhat hypnotic effect about it, and it was with effort that Picard tore his gaze from it. "You found it—?"

"Because of you," she said. "It took me years to acquire a vessel capable of piercing the energy barrier around the galaxy. I traced the path of the doomsday machine, and took its point of entrance into our galaxy to be an indicator of its origin. I hoped, prayed, that I would find something there to use against the soulless ones. What I found exceeded all possible expectation."

"What is it?" asked Guinan, in spite of herself.

Delcara paused a long moment, as if trying to determine the best way to phrase it. "What would you say, dear Picard," she asked finally, "are the limits of human imagination?"

"None," said Picard firmly. "The human imagination has brought us to the stars and will someday carry us beyond."

"Imagine then," she said, "a ship powered by imagination, fueled by will. A ship driven by an overwhelming, undying need for vengeance."

"I would think," said Guinan dryly, "that considering much of what you've said, such a ship and yourself would be well matched."

"True," said Delcara. "And so we are. Within that great vessel you see hanging there in space are the hearts, minds, and souls of the greatest of a once-great race. A race that once strode across the galaxy the way that you would step across a brook. A race that believed in peace—in the spreading of life—with every fiber of its collective being. A race that was in tune completely with itself and with the galaxy. And when they were confronted by the soulless ones—by the Borg—they tried to reason with them, to understand the Borg. To love the Borg, as they loved all life. They did not comprehend that the Borg are the incarnation of anti-life, and their compassion was the end of them. By the time they tried to fight, it was far too late, but they fought nevertheless. And as they fought, there were some who created the great war machines. As you surmised, the doomsday machine was one such device. A model, really, for the more magnificent and deadly one that was to follow.

"But the Borg were even more destructive than was imagined possible. The prototype was completed, but the final model was not. The planet-eater had been launched on a trial run, when its creators suddenly sensed that their efforts had taken too long. They felt, deep within them, the final death screams of their fellows thousands of light-years away, and they knew that they were now the last of their race. The knowledge settled on them like a shroud and encompassed them. And they were no more."

"They died?" whispered Picard, amazed in spite of himself. "The rest of their race was wiped out by the Borg, and they simply—ceased to exist?"

"They did not die in the way that you understand," she said. "They simply languished, becoming more and more shadows, beings of no substance at all. Time lost meaning to them. They knew, in a distant and oblique manner, that the prototype was continuing on its course, and what had been intended as a test run was now the final statement that they would make.

The soulless prototype was achingly slow, but eventually—centuries, most likely—it would cross the galaxy and reach Borg space. There, they felt, the Borg would be destroyed. But their hearts were not in the notion any longer, for they had always been givers of life, not death. Their mightiest weapon was left uncompleted, sitting outside the galaxy, in its great dock.

"They died all together, all at once, like a great rush of air, or the death rattle from hundreds of throats. And yet . . . and yet . . ."

Her voice trailed off a moment, as if she were lost in thought, and then she continued, ". . . and yet they could not completely die. They were too wondrous a race, more so than they would have imagined. Just as you, dear Picard, and your people, are capable of greatness beyond that which you expect—so were they. Their collective consciousness refused to die. Their bodies and minds may have given up the ghost, but their essence—their essence would not go quietly. Their essence roiled and seethed with the cosmic injustice of it all, and it occupied the remarkable weapon that had been created with the skill of their hands and the strength of their intellects. You would say that they haunted it. They occupied the great ship that had remained behind, and there they stayed."

"You offer stories laced with fantasy and fable," said Picard. "Metaphysical, instead of physical, science. Technology was discovered decades ago on Camus II amidst the ruins of a long-dead civilization."

"Was it, indeed?" said Delcara with an air of barely held patience. "And perhaps the Borg were responsible for that race's assassination?"

"Or perhaps that race was a colony or offshoot of the race that developed your planet-destroyer," said

Picard. "The technology on Camus II was capable of mind transference. Also, the denizens of Arret were able to store their consciousness in mind-encasing globes. Isn't it far more likely that some rational, scientific explanation exists to explain whatever was done to—"

"Why do you persist in this!" Her voice was filled with fury, her eyes snapping and wrathful. "I speak to you true, of glories of spirit and desire beyond human ken, and you wish to drag it down into mundanities! I tell you the ship was haunted by homeless spirits, lost and alone . . ."

"Until you came," Guinan said.

"Until I came," agreed Delcara. Her ire seemed to have passed as quickly as it appeared. "They cried out to me and I heard them, once I was close enough. I was drawn to the magnificence of their creation. They loved me, welcomed me, saw me as their salvation and ally, their rescuer, their goddess. The ship needed someone to complete the work. I did so. And then it needed a physical host to guide it, and that I did willingly. Throughout the years of loneliness they faced before I came, they dwelled on their miserable state and, more and more, contemplated revenge on the soulless ones. I became the vessel of that revenge."

"Is it what they wanted," said Guinan, "or what you wanted?"

Delcara went to Guinan and for the first time actually looked her straight in the eye. Guinan stood with her hands invisible, tucked deep into the respective sleeves of her garment. She seemed—to Picard— to be in a vaguely defensive posture.

"Every so often, bond sister," said Delcara, "there is a union that is the perfect meshing of desires. Such was mine and my vessel. We are as one. My ship protects my physical body, keeping it safe from all harm. It protects and gives a channel to my desire for revenge against the cursed Borg. And I, in turn, provide the drive to supplement the dream of the vessel. The souls of the damned inhabit that ship, my beloved Guinan. My sweet Picard. The damned reside there. And I am their guardian angel."

"The guardian angel of the damned," said Picard icily, "was Satan."

"Why, sweet Picard . . . how Judeo-Christian of you."

"This isn't a joke, Delcara!" said Guinan impatiently. "We trusted each other. We told each other secrets that we swore to keep forever. I thought you cured of your hopeless hatred for the Borg."

"Cured? No, Guinan. Never cured," and as she spoke, it almost seemed as if the lights were dimming. "Am I supposed to simply live with the knowledge that the Borg are out there and can continue to do as they please, where they please? Am I to accept the misery they have caused me and millions of others? Perhaps for a time I was able to tolerate that knowledge. Perhaps I was able to hurl it away, to try and reconstruct a life and pretend that it was a life worth living. But I was disenchanted with that notion, Guinan. I was shown the folly and futility," and with each word her voice became louder, angrier. "Hopeless hatred, Guinan? No. No, not hopeless. *That,*" she said, pointing out the window with quivering finger, "that gives me hope. That gives me strength. That gives me might."

"And might makes right?" said Picard.

She looked at him with dark amusement. "Of course might makes right."

"But the Borg were mightier once. Did that make what they did right?" he demanded.

With a raised eyebrow she replied, "The Borg *were* mightier. Not anymore."

And with that pronouncement she turned, walked through the bulkhead, and vanished into space.

Guinan leaned forward, hands on Picard's desk, and she looked as though she were fighting to compose herself. He put hands on her shoulders to steady her, and she said, waving him off, "It's all right. I'll be fine."

"In all the time I've known you, Guinan, I've never seen you quite as discomfited as you were just now."

She eased down into a chair and looked up at him with curiosity, even a touch of admiration. "Discomfited. Oh, yes. I've seen a good friend—a dear friend —reject rational explanations in favor of—how would you put it—?"

"Metaphysical claptrap," offered Picard.

She nodded slowly. "Yes. Her fixation on that alone would be enough to discomfit me. The fact that she's backed up by a weapon powerful enough to lay waste to a galaxy makes it doubly intimidating. You, on the other hand," she said, "faced with the woman of your dreams—you were utterly in command. You never fail to surprise me, Captain."

He stared out the window of his ready room at the powerful ship that was mere kilometers away. "Occasionally," he admitted, "I even surprise myself."

Delcara merged back into the oneness of the ship and felt the cool oneness of the many welcoming her.

"Hello, my children," she said. "I trust you did not miss me overmuch."

We missed you completely, they sang within her. *We love you, Delcara. We need you, Delcara. Never leave us.*

"I cannot promise *never,* my children," she told them.

And she felt something even as she said this, a sort of . . . resentment. A bright, slivering shard, white-hot next to the coolness that was the normal state of the oneness. She found it disturbing and unsettling. "What is wrong?"

You love someone else. They sounded petulant, their song hitting a discordant note.

"How I feel for others does not matter," she said. "Whatever other feelings I may have had pale in comparison for how I feel about you and about our mission. I have given myself over to you, willingly and gladly. You question that now?"

You listened to the things they said. You thought of going back to them. And to him.

She was quiet for a long moment.

"I thought of it," she admitted, for there was no point in denying it. "It could not be helped."

If you love us . . . if you value our mission of vengeance . . .

"You are not alive, except in your determination not to let the great injustice of the soulless ones go unpunished. I share that determination. But I have a living mind, a mind that is accompanied by flesh and blood. And those . . . inconveniences, if you will . . . prompt me to consider other avenues. To dwell, for a few flittering moments, on the might-have-been's, and the never-will-be's. I cannot help that. When I see Picard again, and I relive those comparative few moments we had together . . ."

You loved the Picard?

"I love no one anymore," she said. "I dare not. But there is much in him that reminds me of loves past. I see some of my life mates within him. They had much of his spirit, his determination. There is a blazing glory of life in him that draws me to him, like moth to flame. But I will not allow the curse that pursues to destroy him. I cannot help how I feel, my children. But I can help what I do."

We want no one else to have you. You must be ours. You are needed for the great mission of vengeance, and in performing that mission, you have our devotion. But we must have yours. For if we are the will, you are the way.

"I know," she said. "And I will be as one with you. That is what we both wish."

And that is how it shall be. For eternity, and beyond. And do not, the voices added darkly, *do not think of leaving us. It upsets us. It threatens the vendetta, and the vendetta is all.*

"I would not upset you, my children, for all the world. You know that."

We know. But we wish to hear it again . . . and remind you. You are ours, and we are yours. Forever.

Guinan had long since departed, at Picard's request. But the captain had remained in the ready room, lost in thought. So lost, in fact, that at first he did not hear the buzz at this door. This led to a more urgent summoning, and finally he did look up and call out briskly, "Come."

The door hissed open and Deanna Troi was standing there. "Captain—?"

Through the open door he caught a glimpse of Riker and Worf at their stations, surreptitiously looking in the direction of the ready room. When they realized that the captain had noticed them, they quickly snapped their heads around and gazed at the front viewscreen intently, as if embarrassed that they'd been "caught in the act."

"Yes, Counselor," he said, and gestured for her to

enter. The doors closed, blocking the bridge from view. Inwardly, Picard smiled, calling up an image of Riker and Worf leaning against the door with drinking glasses against their ears.

She took a seat opposite him and said, "I sensed you were disturbed, Captain."

"I can't say I'm surprised, Counselor," he said, forcing a smile. "The appearance of this . . . woman was something of a shock to me."

"What sort of shock? A pleasant one? Unpleasant?"

"A shock," he said simply. "I don't know if I've really digested all the ramifications just yet."

"You're saying you don't know how you feel about her appearance?"

He arched his eyebrows. "You're saying that you do know how I feel?"

"You are most ambivalent," she admitted. "That, in and of itself, is disconcerting for you. You dislike not knowing your own mind."

"It's called mixed feelings, Counselor," he smiled, although the smile did not seem to touch his eyes. "It's not something I tend to indulge in all that often."

"If at all," she said.

"If at all," he agreed. "I have something of a reputation for singlemindedness. It's a reputation that I prefer to live up to."

"How do you feel about this woman? This Delcara?"

He considered it, trying to put into words the emotions that were rolling through him. Images danced through his head, visions of a time past, and of a face and voice that had haunted him all these many years.

"For so long," he said slowly, "the events that had occurred in my youth were so confusing to me. Such a—" and he paused, "such a bizarre night of recollections. I was truly unsure whether they had happened to me or not. There was a certain romance to that entire incident. I am not by nature, Counselor, a romantic person. And I do not have an overabundance of such memories. So to discover that what occurred had its basis in reality has me somewhat unsettled. You see, I'm not certain whether I'm pleased or disappointed."

She smiled. "The magic loses its luster when you discover it was done with mirrors."

"Precisely. Even so, if I am to believe her story, there is a certain degree of 'magic' involved. She spoke of being drawn across a galaxy to me, of 'sensing' my existence somehow. Now you must admit there is not a great degree of scientific basis for such things. Do you believe all that is possible, Counselor? That some mysterious fate, or power beyond our understanding, could have bound us together somehow?"

She shrugged her slim shoulders. "I certainly have firsthand knowledge of such occurrences, Captain. After all, I had a fiancé who painted portraits of a woman he did not know. No one was more surprised than he when she showed up, virtually out of the blue, with a sense of him that was on par with his awareness of her."

"Yes, Yes, I had forgotten about that," admitted Picard. "At the time, I must admit, I had grave doubts about the validity of all of it."

"I know you did," smiled Troi. "You considered the possibility that it was somehow all an elaborate ruse on my fiancé's part."

"You were aware of that?" he asked with surprise. "You said nothing to me of it."

"There was nothing to say. You were—and are—a rational man, and in that instance you were being faced with extremely irrational, even impossible, circumstances. It was natural for you to believe what was to you the far greater likelihood that some sort of deception was at hand."

"Yes," he admitted. "But since it seemed that everyone was doing as they truly wished, and since I had no real proof other than my own inbred skepticism, I kept my peace on the subject. And now . . ."

"Now your skepticism is challenged once more," said Troi. She hesitated. "Do you love this woman, Captain?"

"Love her?" Picard looked amazed that she would ask.

"Yes. Do you?"

He gestured in a touchingly helpless way. "I don't even know her."

"Sometimes that's beside the point."

"Not to me."

"There is such a thing as love at first sight."

"Nonsense. The notion is as absurd as . . ."

"As faster-than-light travel? As instantaneous transport? As an android wishing to be human? As feelings linking you to another individual, even though a galaxy may separate you?"

He sat back in his chair and sighed. "You know," he said grudgingly, "you missed your calling. You should have been a lawyer."

She smiled at his mild discomfiture. "Why do you think I'm called Counselor?"

Suddenly Troi's eyes widened. "Captain! She's moving off!"

Picard spun in his chair and saw that Troi was correct. Quite without warning, the ship that was Delcara's home was suddenly in motion, pulling away from the *Enterprise* with speed that was amazing, considering its massiveness. Picard's practiced eye told him that she was moving at full impulse power.

He leaped to his feet just as he heard the summons at the door of the ready room. He started forward and snapped out a quick, "Come."

The door opened and Riker was standing there, arms behind his back, seriousness in his demeanor. "Captain, the planet-killer is—"

"On her way, yes, I saw," said Picard. "Lay in a pursuit course immediately."

"It's not just that. Long-range sensors have picked up a new visitor. A Borg ship—on an intercept course with the planet-killer."

Chapter Fifteen

PICARD STEPPED OUT onto the bridge, the uncertainty and confusion of his recent discoveries falling away from him. Romantic notions and half-memories of his youth were somewhat disturbing to him. But a crisis, an emergency into which he was thrust—these were things he understood. Picard disliked intangibles, particularly when they impaired his ability to do his job.

When encountering an unknown ship, Picard never immediately assumed any sort of alert status other than employing his own native caution in an unfamiliar situation. It did not create a good first impression to be bristling with weapons and have one's shields firmly in place. That made it seem as if the *Enterprise* was perpetually ready for war, hence, extremely warlike. First would come efforts to establish communications, talk with their new acquaintances, and make all the normal overtures of diplomatic interchanges.

However, when encountering a known hostile such as a Ferengi or a Tholian, Picard would order a yellow alert. There were certain races which considered it a sign of weakness, even stupidity, if you approached them with anything less than full defensive fields in place. They would either take advantage of you or even display their disdain for you by immediately attacking, on the assumption that you were ripe for conquest.

When the Borg came on the scene, however, there was room for only one way to proceed.

"Red alert," snapped Picard.

Immediately the red-alert klaxon sounded the ship. All personnel moved with practiced efficiency to their battle stations. The shields leaped into existence, and the weapons batteries were charged up and brought on line.

"All stations report ready, Captain," Worf informed him. There was pride—even something that could pass for excitement—in his deep Klingon voice. As well as he performed his normal, day-to-day duties, there was clear anticipation within him whenever a crisis presented itself. "We are presently in pursuit of the planet-killer."

"Time to the interception of the Borg ship?"

It was Data who spoke up. "At present course and speed, five minutes, twenty-one seconds."

"Give me a channel to the planet-killer."

After only the briefest of pauses, Worf said, "Open."

"Delcara," said Picard. "There is a Borg ship approaching."

This time there was no preamble. The holographic image of Delcara snapped into existence on the bridge. Her arms were folded, her bearing almost regal, and there was a startling calm about her. "Yes, I know."

"They are a most formidable adversary."

"As do you, I have firsthand knowledge of that, dear

Picard," she said. "I know what they can do. And they know what I can do."

"Yes, and that knowledge of you is shared among them," Picard said. He had risen from his seat and crossed the bridge to stand directly before her. "Whatever success you had with them before, you cannot assume that it will be quite so easily repeated. This time they will be ready for you."

"And if they were ready for a black hole," she said, "would that make them any less likely to be crushed once they passed the event horizon? I think not. Knowing of me and being able to handle me are two wildly different things. The former may be likely, but the latter—I think not. Now, sweet Picard, I suggest you stay back . . . and stay out of trouble." And with that, she vanished.

"Patronizing woman," Worf observed with clear annoyance.

"Alert Starfleet of the Borg's presence."

This time there was a longer pause, and then Worf said, "Unable to comply."

"What?" Picard turned towards the Klingon. "What's wrong?"

"Subspace interference, presumably generated by the planet-killer. It's been present ever since we first encountered the vessel. I was able to pierce it to establish local communications, but I am not succeeding for any long-range messages."

"The Borg are now within visual range," Data reported.

"On screen."

The image of Delcara's ship cutting through space was immediately replaced by another, even more ominous, sight—a single Borg ship slicing through the ether.

Upon seeing it, Picard felt a momentary chill cut

through to his spine. It was a most unexpected and unwelcome feeling. The last thing he needed to do was freeze up due to the trauma that the Borg had inflicted upon him. His crew was looking to him, dammit, to *him*. He could not allow himself to be paralyzed by recollections of the horrors that the Borg had visited upon him.

Riker was saying something, he suddenly realized. As much as Picard hated to admit that he wasn't listening, the last thing he wanted to do was take a chance on missing something important. "I'm sorry, Number One, what was that?"

Without missing a beat, Riker said, "Shall we prepare for saucer separation, Captain?"

"No time, Number One. Besides, at this point I wouldn't want to leave a saucerful of crewmen vulnerable to the Borg and only capable of impulse power, would you?"

"Not if it can be helped, sir."

"One minute to Borg interception," reported Data.

"All hands stand ready," said Picard. He dropped into his command chair and braced himself, physically and mentally, for what was to come.

They think they can stop us.

Delcara smiled. Her children were eager, their song a loud and excited harmonic. "We will show them otherwise, won't we, my children."

They cannot stop us. Nothing can stop us.

"Nothing can. We are great. We are powerful. We are the spirit of vengeance. We are the widow to the cosmos. We are Vendetta."

We are strong, and we are right, and we will triumph.

"All glory to us," said Delcara. "Let's get those soulless bastards."

* * *

The Ten-Forward lounge had cleared out the moment the red-alert siren went off. Guinan stood alone, gazing out the front of the *Enterprise.* She saw in ways that others couldn't, and she beheld the great planet-destroyer that was piloted by her sister, and beyond that, the foe that was about to be engaged.

"Caution, little sister," said Guinan softly. "Please . . . be very, very careful."

"We are being hailed by the Borg, sir," Worf said, not without a touch of surprise.

Picard straightened his jacket, buying himself the bare seconds he needed to compose himself and prepare to face the beings that had so devastated his life. "On screen," he said, the words sounding leaden in his throat.

A Borg soldier appeared on the screen, the flickering corridors and lights of the Borg vessel behind it. When its voice sounded, however, its mouth did not move. Instead, the voice seemed to come from all around it. "You will surrender your vessel to the Borg," it said simply.

"This," said the Captain, "is Jean-Luc Picard of the—"

"We are aware of your identity," and the Borg paused, "Locutus."

The name, that hideous name, hung there, as frightening as the bizarre intimacy of being on a first-name basis with the Borg.

Picard slowly rose to his feet, his deep and abiding fury at what had been done to him going a long way to overcoming the pulsing fear that had first grabbed him when the Borg appeared on the screen.

"Locutus," he said in no uncertain terms, "is dead."

"Death is irrelevant," the Borg replied. "Locutus is irrelevant. Another spokesman is being prepared."

Picard looked at Riker, whose face mirrored the shock that was in his captain's. "Another?" he whispered to Riker. Riker shrugged. Picard turned back to the Borg and said, "What spokesman are you referring to?"

"Your inquiries are irrelevant," said the Borg. "We will absorb this other vessel, and then we will absorb you. Prepare to be assimilated by the Borg."

"Prepare to eat phasers," muttered Worf, so softly that none could hear him.

Without another word the Borg soldier vanished from the screen, to be replaced by the image of the Borg ship.

"Captain, the Borg have engaged the planet-killer," Data reported.

"Hold our position," said Picard. He tried to sound neutral and dispassionate as he said, "Let's see what she can do."

Delcara's ship angled toward the Borg, its great maw open and wide as if eager to receive it.

This time the Borg ship did not even allow Delcara to get within striking distance. They opened fire with increased intensity, endeavoring to core out a piece of the planet-killer. Once they had done that, they reasoned, they would be better able to analyze it and then proceed with the assimilation of the weapon that had so handily destroyed an earlier Borg vessel.

The beam struck the planet-killer, and the ship appeared to shake ever so slightly, as if startled by the force of the power that it was encountering. Astoundingly, carbon scoring appeared across a portion of its neutronium hull.

We hurt! cried the voices in disharmony. *They hurt us!*

"Steady, my children," said Delcara. "They but startled us. Scratched us. They cannot harm us. They cannot succeed. Feel me, my children, and all that I have to offer you. I am your vessel through which the power flows."

Her eyes were closed, her lips slightly parted, and she felt all the minds, all the souls of the haunted ship flowing into her. She was the nexus, the focal point. Through her poured the hearts and minds and fury of the long-dead race, channeled through her drive and energy. Theirs was the will, hers the way. Theirs was the way, hers the will. They were interchangeable. They were as one. They were Vendetta.

The ship gathered strength, as if blood were rushing through it and energizing it, building to a climax, and then, abruptly, a staggeringly powerful beam ripped from deep within its bowels, lancing from the ship's maw.

It struck the Borg ship . . .

. . . and coruscated off a force field.

"The Borg shields are holding against the planet-killer's force beam," said Worf with unabashed astonishment.

And now Data spoke up. "Sensors read the beam as pure anti-proton. Borg shields are beginning to show signs of strain."

"Let's see if we can strain them a bit more," said Picard. "Launch antimatter spread, and then bring us about at full impulse, course four-oh-three Mark eight."

The *Enterprise* let fly with the antimatter spread, and it danced across the shielding of the Borg ship, adding to the beam that was being fired from the planet-killer. The Borg's shields flared up under the increased barrage and they returned fire on the *Enterprise*. But the starship had already made her move, darting behind the Borg ship, and this time unleashed a full phaser barrage. The phaser beams cascaded off the Borg shields that had been hastily erected to intercept the attack, but . . .

"Their shield effectiveness is at forty-two percent and dropping rapidly," Data reported. "The attack by the planet-killer is having substantial effect on the Borg's ability to maintain a sufficient level of defensive power." Suddenly Data said, "Sir, the Borg are falling back."

"They're *retreating?*" Picard was astonished, and it was amazement that was shared by everyone on the bridge. The Borg either destroyed things or ignored things. They did not run.

But there it was. The Borg ship was dropping back at full impulse, still firing upon the planet-killer, but trying to distance itself.

Delcara bore down on them, not letting up in her assault. The Borg redoubled their efforts and this time the planet-killer visibly shuddered under their attack. A chunk of the neutronium hull, a substance that was so dense that a phaser against it had the same effect as a lit match, was actually blasted away. It hurtled off into space, but the Borg ship did not have the extra energy available to grab it with a tractor beam.

The Many screamed within Delcara's head. They started to lose their focus.

"No!" Delcara warned them. "This is the way. This is the will. This is what must and will be done. Their shields are nothing against us, my children. We will destroy them. Now. Now!"

"Now!" said Picard. "Phaser and antimatter barrage, fire!"

The *Enterprise* cut loose on the Borg from behind just as the planet-killer fired on the other side. The Borg shields sagged under the increased assault, and they fired upon the *Enterprise* in the hopes of dispatching the flea so that they could concentrate on the wasp.

But the flea refused to be scratched. The starship's shields held, since the Borg were not at full strength. And then the Borg's shields were shields blown into oblivion by the doomsday device's beam, which then smashed straight into the core of the vessel.

The *Enterprise* came within a hair's breadth of being wiped out, for almost as fast as Delcara's beam went in through one side of the Borg ship, it came out the other, transfixing the cube vessel. And the *Enterprise* was on the other side, directly opposite Delcara. It was only a blindingly fast evasive maneuver executed by Data that prevented the starship from being reduced to scrap.

The *Enterprise* dropped back, and the crew watched in shock as cracks ribboned across the surface of the Borg ship. The cube shook, as if in anger or repressed frustration, and an additional surge of power leaped from Delcara's ship.

The Borg blew apart, a dazzling burst of light and color. Fragments of the mighty ship hurled every which way, bouncing harmlessly off the *Enterprise* shields or hurtling away into space.

The bridge crew looked in astonishment at the sight before them. It had happened so quickly, so easily.

Forty ships of the Federation and assorted planetary defenses all had proven helpless against a Borg ship. Yet now the Borg had been blown from space in a few scant seconds of battle.

A massive cloud of dust and debris hung before them, and then something emerged from the cloud. It was the planet-killer, piloted by Delcara, sailing through it serenely, like a ghost. Random pieces of the Borg ship ricocheted off the enormous vessel, which didn't even appear to notice.

Delcara sailed past the *Enterprise* with no attempt at communication, and simply resumed her course—a course that would take her, eventually and inevitably, into the heart of Borg space.

"Remarkable," said Picard.

Worf was studying the sensors and said, "There is an eight-percent drop in the energy readings of the planet-killer. Also, there is some external damage."

"Damage to a neutronium hull," Riker said, pulling at his beard. "That either says a hell of a lot for the Borg to be able to damage her—"

"Or a good deal for her ability to withstand the sort of punishment required to damage a neutronium hull," replied Picard. He hoped that he was able to keep the amazement from his voice. The last thing he wanted his crew to think was that he was daunted, even intimidated, by the level of power that they had witnessed.

"The planet-killer has resumed course and heading, and is proceeding at warp six."

Picard cast a glance at Riker. "The previous planet-killer appeared to have a maximum of warp four." Riker simply nodded. Picard turned back to Data and said, "Follow her, Mr. Data."

"Overtake or intercept, sir?"

"Just follow," Picard said. "But put enough distance between us so that we can avoid the subspace interference and get a message out to Starfleet."

"Yes, sir."

Picard stared pensively at the screen, his mind racing, trying to determine the best course of action. "Mr. Data," he said after a moment, "extrapolating from current course, what will be the next star system the planet-killer encounters? Still the Tholians?"

Data paused only a moment to check. "Yes sir. It will enter Tholian space in less than three days."

"Send a message," said Picard. "Alert the Tholians that they're about to have an extremely uninvited visitor."

"Captain, receiving an incoming message."

"Delcara?"

"No, sir," said Worf, looking up. "It's the *Chekov*. Captain Korsmo."

"On screen."

A moment later Morgan Korsmo appeared on the viewscreen. "Picard," he said with no preamble, "there's a Borg ship heading your way."

"There was," said Picard. "It was rather handily disposed of by the planet-killer."

His eyes widened. "You found it! Word was received from the *Repulse* that it was heading into this sector. Have you established contact with it?"

"Yes, we have. It is piloted by a woman named Delcara who has taken it upon herself to rid the galaxy of the Borg."

"I applaud her goals, if not her methods," Korsmo said drily. "Have you told her the Federation security concerns regarding the power of the weaponry at her disposal?"

"She is concerned only about her objectives," Picard replied. "I don't think she gives a damn about whether we approve of her cavorting about the galaxy or not. She's going to do what she wants, where she wants, and she has the power to back up that philosophy."

Korsmo's face darkened. "That is unacceptable. We have to do something."

"I tend to agree," said Picard. "Now we have to determine what that might be."

"We have to show her who's boss!" declared Korsmo.

Picard and Riker looked at each other, and then Picard looked back at Korsmo. "The woman has destroyed two Borg vessels, Captain Korsmo, one of them with only a slight bit of help from us. She's piloting a semi-sentient ship that could swallow the entire currently active fleet, and have room left over for dessert. She has a devastating force beam, a hull our phasers couldn't possibly penetrate, and a thirst for vengeance that has crossed light-years and centuries. I think she knows who's boss, Korsmo."

Korsmo looked stunned. "Picard, you actually sound intimidated."

"Knowing your opponent's strengths and your own shortcomings isn't being intimidated, Captain. It's called knowing where you stand."

"Where I assume you stand, Picard," said Korsmo stiffly, "is solidly behind the wishes of starfleet. Now obviously, Picard, I can't issue orders to you. But at present course and speed, we will be able to rendezvous in twenty-eight hours. I want to set up a summit meeting with this planet-killer, and I'll do it with or without your help. And if they refuse to communicate, I'm going to attack."

"That," said Picard, "would be inadvisable."

"It would be suicide," put in Riker.

"You seem to have forgotten that it is the decision of the Federation and Starfleet that the planet-killer cannot be permitted to simply gallivant around the galaxy doing whatever the hell it wishes," Korsmo said tightly. "Not when innocents will be killed. Whether you support that decision or not is completely immaterial. It must be reasoned with or stopped or destroyed. To put it succinctly, we are to stop that thing any way we can. There are no other options. And to be blunt, Picard . . . I thought you had more guts than to let yourself get spooked by some woman with a big ship. Korsmo out."

His image vanished from the screen and was replaced by the distant image of the planet-killer, sailing straight towards the space of the notoriously territorial Tholians.

"Perfect," said Picard. "Just . . . perfect."

Chapter Sixteen

"Permission to speak freely, sir?"

Korsmo looked up at Shelby with only vague interest. He put aside the material he was reading, sat up straighter behind his desk (something he always felt compelled to do in Shelby's presence, as if she reminded him of some stern schoolteacher) and said, "Granted."

"Some hours ago you were in communication with the *Enterprise*," Shelby said stiffly. She stood with her feet slightly apart, her hands behind her back. "It seemed to me that you were unnecessarily short-tempered with Captain Picard."

"Are we going to go through this again, Commander?" demanded Korsmo. There was something in his voice that indicated that, even though permission to speak freely had been granted, he was not going to tolerate hearing anything he didn't like. "I respect Jean-Luc Picard. I have told you as much. What do you want me to do, write it in blood?"

"If Captain Picard says that attacking the planet-killer would be inadvisable, I would wager that it's inadvisable," she said, her voice flat.

Slowly, like a snake uncoiling from a basket, Korsmo stood behind his desk. "And if I order an attack," he said, "are you going to support my authority on that bridge out there? Or are you going to undercut me?"

Her jaw muscles moved for a moment. "You are my commanding officer, sir. Not Captain Picard. I would never act insubordinately with a commanding officer," and she paused before she added, "no matter what the provocation."

He nodded, but there was no trace of pleasantness in his face. "It would do well for both of us to remember that," he said. "Dismissed."

"Sir, I—"

"I *said,*" he repeated, his voice hard as nails, "*dismissed.*"

She took a deep breath, stalling for a moment to come up with something more to say, some other way of prolonging the discussion so that she could get across the points she wanted to make. But nothing came to mind, and Korsmo was already ignoring her, staring back intently at whatever was on his computer screen.

She managed to crane her neck just slightly, and saw that Korsmo was studying the service record of one Jean-Luc Picard. And, very slightly, he was shaking his head in disbelief.

Shelby backed slowly out of the ready room and stepped out onto the bridge of the *Chekov*. The doors hissed shut behind her and she stood there for a moment, composing her thoughts, mulling over the significance of what she had just seen.

"Damn," she said softly.

In the engine room of the *Enterprise*, La Forge turned in surprise when he heard the crisp voice of

Picard say, "Mr. La Forge, a moment of your time, please."

"Yes sir, Captain," said Geordi. He walked into his office, stepping aside to allow the captain to precede him inside. He then stood and waited for Picard to address him.

"The Borg woman," he said. "What is your progress with her?"

Geordi shrugged slightly. "Not much," he admitted. "I don't know if I'm getting through to her at all. Although, she did show some interest in my VISOR. And she was happy," he added distastefully, "when the prosthetic arm was attached."

"Of course she would be happy," said Picard. "It's a mechanical attachment. Anything with a mechanical basis might get a reaction out of her." He paused. "Doctor Crusher is not having a great deal of success with the re-education program. I'd like you to endeavor to reach her once again. Spend some more time with her. Your VISOR clearly makes it easier for her to identify with you. For similar reasons, Mr. Data will assist you whenever possible."

"Because we're the two crew members who are more reminiscent of the Borg?" Geordi asked, not especially sure if he liked the comparison.

Neither did Picard. "I did not intend to imply that, Lieutenant."

"I know, sir, I'm sorry," sighed Geordi. He pinged a finger off the edge of his VISOR. "You'd think, after all this time, I'd be used to it by now. May I ask why the sudden intense interest in Reannon?"

Picard leaned forward. "If we can establish communications with her, get at some of the knowledge buried in her head, we can learn more about the Borg. I remember much of my time with them, but she spent even longer with them and may have learned a great

267

deal more. Also, she might be of some value in trying to establish better relations with the pilot of the planet-killer."

"Value? How?"

"I want to show her the face of the enemy," said Picard. "Delcara views the Borg as this inhuman, soulless *thing*. If we can salvage a Borg soldier, make Delcara think of them as individuals, trapped as part of some massive central mind over which they have no control—it might have some impact on her. If we can give her food for thought, maybe we can encourage her then to sit down for an entire meal."

"It's a long shot, sir."

"It's better than no shot, Lieutenant. Now, if you'll excuse me," he said, standing and heading for the door, "I have a summit to arrange."

The planet-killer hurtled forward on its course at warp six, and deep within, Delcara heard the impatient song of the Many.

We do not wish to meet with them, they cried out. *They are a distraction. There is no need for distractions, or for talking. If we are to talk with them, it would mean slowing or stopping our progress. We have waited so long. . . .*

"That being the case," said Delcara patiently, as if addressing a child, "it will not hurt anyone to wait a little longer."

You want to do this because of the Picard. You do not wish to disappoint him.

"He has asked me to do this," said Delcara, "and out of respect to him, I wish to do it."

We hate him.

"You owe him," and for the first time that she could recall, her voice and thoughts raised in anger, "you owe him your existence. It was he who gave me the way and whose great thoughts led me to you. It was the power of his personality, and the strength of his destiny, that called me to him. The waves of fate ebb and flow around him, and I rode those waves to him and, ultimately, to you. And if he wishes to speak with us, then I will speak with him. It will cost you nothing. You, whose souls cry out for justice, must understand when I do something that is just."

The Many were silent for a moment, and then they said sullenly, *We understand. You do as you wish.* But their voice held no enthusiasm.

Geordi walked down the corridor, one arm hooked around Reannon's flesh-and-blood elbow. She stared straight ahead as always, unaware and uncaring of the looks that she received from *Enterprise* crewmembers as they walked past. Geordi was very much aware, however, of each sidelong glance, each additional step that was taken by a crewman to distance him from the specter of a Borg soldier. Their reactions angered the normally easygoing engineer all the more.

"This is some ship, isn't it, Reannon?" he said to her conversationally. "Only commissioned four years ago. It's the best ship in the fleet, and that's not just my being boastful. I can back it up with facts. Would you care to see them, Reannon?"

"She doesn't care to see anything."

The voice came from nearby, low and hostile and familiar, and Geordi kicked himself inwardly for being so overly attentive to Reannon that he hadn't paid attention to the fact that his little walking tour of the *Enterprise* had taken them right past the brig.

Dantar stood within, kept there not only by a formidable force field, but by the additional presence of a glowering security guard. He did not, however, seem in any particular hurry to go anywhere. Instead, he leaned against the edge of the doorway, just beyond the point where he would activate the field, and said, "She's not even a living being. She's just a thing, and a murderer."

For a moment Geordi almost ignored him, but then his anger boiled over. Stabbing a finger at Dantar, he said, "She's a victim, just the same as you. She didn't want or ask for this. If she fully understood what she did to your family, she'd be as grief-stricken as you are."

"Oh, really," said Dantar, his antennae twitching in what appeared to be amusement. "You think that."

"I know that."

"You know what, Federation man? I don't care about that. All I care about is what she and her stinking kind did. All I care about is the idea of my fingers around her throat. That's all that matters to me."

Geordi shook his head and pulled on her arm. "Come on, Reannon."

They went off down the hallway, with Dantar crying out behind them, "I'll get you! You hear me, you Borg bitch? I'll get you! I got your arm, and if I have to take you apart one piece at a time, I will get you!"

Geordi practically threw her into a turbolift and snapped, "Engineering." He turned to Reannon and said, "You'll like engineering."

Nothing.

"Lots of machines. And the engines throb with this sort of deep *thrum thrum* sound. It's really fantastic."

Nothing.

He took her by the shoulders. "Reannon, are you in there? Are you hearing me at all? Come on, I know you're there. Some part of you is hearing me. Some part of you wants to come back. I know it. I asked

Counselor Troi earlier, and she said she still didn't feel anything from you, but I do. I know you're there. I know it. Come on out. Please." He took her hand and placed it against his VISOR. "See? See? Mechanical parts, just like you. It doesn't make me a soulless thing. It doesn't mean you have to be that way, either. Come on back, Reannon."

Nothing.

His fist thudded softly on the wall of the turbolift even as it slowed and then opened onto the corridor leading to engineering.

Deanna Troi was standing there, arms folded, waiting for them. "Geordi," she said. She seemed more formal than usual.

"Counselor," he replied. He tilted his head slightly. "Can I help you?"

"The question is, can you help her?" and she nodded her head towards Reannon.

Geordi looked from the Borg woman to Troi. "Counselor, is everything okay with this? I mean . . . you seem . . . I don't know . . ."

"Oh, it's nothing." She waved it off, and then her face fell slightly. "No, it's something."

"Care to come into my office?" said Geordi. "It's been seeing a lot of action today."

Moments later Geordi, Troi, and Reannon were in the engineer's office. Reannon stood with her back to them, staring blankly out at the view of the engine room that was presented to her.

"I suppose I'm just frustrated," said Troi. "I hate to admit it. Commander Riker would say," and she drew herself up archly, "that I'm too aristocratic to be troubled by such things."

"No!" said Geordi in mock horror.

She smiled. "I'm afraid so." Then her smile faded.

"I feel as you do—that Reannon needs help. I find it terribly, terribly frustrating that my empathic powers don't substantiate that belief. When my powers aren't functioning, I feel as if my effectiveness is halved, even quartered."

"Yeah, I know," said Geordi ruefully. "I recall you did have some problems with that when you lost your empathic abilities. But I would think, Counselor, that that would have been a learning experience."

"Oh, definitely," Troi said with a trace of self-mockery. "I learned I'm a complete witch when my empathy is useless."

"Counselor!" said Geordi, amused. "Such language."

"One can't be honest with others unless one is honest with oneself," said Troi. "In a way I envy you, Geordi. In this instance you are just as qualified, if not more so, to try and get through to Reannon. I've had some sessions with her. I have to say that my frustration level is much higher when I can't get through to someone on the most basic mental level. Since you're not accustomed to dealing with people that way, your patience is greater."

"Yeah, well, even my patience is getting a little strained," admitted Geordi. "I—"

And he suddenly looked up. "Hey. Where'd she go?"

Troi turned and saw, as had Geordi, that Reannon had vanished from where she'd been standing.

Geordi stood quickly and exited his office, Troi right behind him. He glanced around quickly and then pointed, "There! She's up there."

High above the deck stood Reannon, climbing the catwalk that led up to the area of the matter injector. She was moving with grim-faced determination. Ensign Barclay tried to block her way, and she shoved him aside with her mechanical arm without so much as a thought and kept moving.

Then Geordi saw a familiar figure with gleaming skin coming up behind her. "Data," he breathed.

Data, for his part, was pursuing Reannon. She had stopped where she was and was staring out across the vastness of the engineering room. She seemed hypnotized by the catwalks, by the power of the engines, and by the gleaming metal that surrounded her on all sides.

And Deanna Troi staggered slightly. Geordi noticed it and, despite his concern over Reannon, immediately switched gears and went to the Betazoid counselor. He supported her, making sure she didn't fall over as she locked into . . . something. "Counselor!" he said.

"My God," she whispered. "She's remembering."

Reannon stood high on the catwalk, transfixed. Her entire body seemed to be quivering. Data was getting closer, within twenty feet of her. She didn't even seem to notice him.

"Fear," said Troi, as if her mind were elsewhere. Her eyes were wide and keyed in on Reannon. "She confronted something vast, something throbbing with power and life . . . It was gargantuan . . . She was surrounded, hemmed in, trapped, trapped, oh God, Geordi, trapped . . ."

Data was within ten feet now, and in a calm, precise voice, he said, "Miss Bonaventure. I am Commander Data. We met previously."

Her head snapped around, and she focussed on him for only the second time since she'd come aboard. There was something in her eyes akin to stark terror, and she looked like a trap doe.

"Captain Picard asked me to work with Lieutenant La Forge on progressing with your reclamation," Data said politely. "It would seem my arrival here is most timely. It is not completely safe for you to be up here, and if you would accompany me, perhaps we could interact on a more meaningful level. Would you be interested in learning to tap dance?"

She stepped back, flattening against the wall. Her mouth moved, but no words came out.

He was within five feet of her, three, and then he reached out toward her. "Miss Bonaventure, it would be best if—"

She lashed out with her mechanical arm, moving at incredible speed, and she snagged Data by the wrist. She twisted and yanked with all her strength and Data's arm came out.

He stepped back in surprise, the empty sleeve of his uniform flapping almost comically. "Now, Miss Bonaventure, that was—"

She screamed.

It was primal, incomprehensible. There were no words, just hysterical and terrified howls, and then she came in fast, swinging the arm like a club. Data brought his remaining arm up, blocking the first blow, but Reannon reversed and swung upward, catching Data across the face and sending him tumbling back onto the platform.

He skidded, automatically trying to grab the railing with the arm that was no longer there. He grabbed out with his good arm, trying to haul himself up, and Reannon stood over him, shrieking and yowling, smashing him around the shoulders and back with his own arm. Her strength was manic, augmented by the power of her mechanical arm and the sheer energy of her hysteria. Data started to get up and was knocked flat again, and she started kicking furiously, endeavoring to knock him off the catwalk to the floor of the engine room far below.

And then the whine of a phaser blast sliced through the air. Reannon staggered back, slamming against the wall. She was still standing, but her consciousness had already fled her and slowly she sank down. Within moments she was lying on the catwalk, out cold.

Data looked down and saw, far below, Worf. The Klingon security officer, having arrived in response to an emergency call from La Forge, was standing with his phaser angled upward. Now, though, he was lowering the weapon and calling out, "Are you all right, Commander?"

"Other than the fact that I appear to have been disarmed, I am functioning quite well," Data called down. "Excellent shot, Lieutenant. It would appear that my attempts to communicate with her were not proceeding well."

"Phasers are the universal communicators," rumbled Worf, holstering his.

Moments later Data was on the main floor of engineering, and Reannon's unconscious form was being carried into Geordi's office, under close guard from Worf. Geordi, for his part, was busy reattaching Data's arm. "It would seem, Geordi, that we are making progress."

"Progress?" said Geordi. "She tried to kill you."

"I would surmise," Data said after a moment's thought, "that in her confused state, she thought I was a Borg, and reacted accordingly."

"Data's right," agreed Troi. "Emotional response as dramatic as that can only be considered progress."

"Yeah, well," Geordi observed ruefully, "a little

more progress like that, and we'll be able to sell Data for scrap parts."

The three vessels had come together, proceeding along the course that the planet-killer had determined for itself, but only at one-quarter impulse power—a comparative crawl.

Picard and Riker stood in the transporter room, as O'Brien's confident hands moved over the transporter controls. "The *Chekov* is signalling that they're ready for transport, Captain," he said.

"Energize," Picard said, drawing himself up and, as was his habit, smoothing his jacket.

The transporter shimmered, and moments later Captain Korsmo and Commander Shelby appeared on the platform.

"Captain. Commander," said Picard, nodding his head slightly to each. "Welcome aboard the *Enterprise*. Commander, I might add, welcome back."

"In many ways she never left, Picard," said Korsmo, stepping down and extending a hand. As Picard shook it firmly, Korsmo continued, "She speaks of you almost constantly."

"The captain exaggerates," said Shelby, smiling. "It's good to see you looking so well, Captain. And you're looking fit, Commander."

Riker smiled. Once he would have sworn that, given the opportunity, he'd just as soon pop Shelby one in the jaw as look at her. Now he found himself surprisingly pleased to see her again. Funny, how coming through a crisis together, and in one piece, could forever alter the way one viewed someone. "The position of first officer obviously agrees with you, Commander."

Very loudly and very deliberately, Korsmo cracked his knuckles. "Now that we've gotten all the niceties aside, not to mention displaying our thorough knowledge of each other's rank, why don't we get down to business. Where's this Delcara person, Picard?"

"She will come," said Picard. "I communicated our desire to meet with her."

"Did she respond?"

"Not directly, but—"

"Then how the hell do you know she's coming, Picard?" said Korsmo impatiently. "What the hell kind of show are you running here?"

Riker frowned, looking from one captain to the other and then at Shelby. She seemed to be shifting uncomfortably in her boots, clearly not any happier with Korsmo's attitude than was Riker.

With a soft voice that hinted at danger, Picard said, "Her response, Captain, is clearly affirmative because she has dropped out of warp space upon the convergence of our two ships. She's packing enough firepower to turn both our ships into free-floating molecules. She doesn't have to talk to us, Morgan. She doesn't have to do a damned thing she doesn't want to do, and the sooner you realize that we're walking on eggshells with her, the better off we will all be. Are we clear on this?"

Korsmo raised an eyebrow but merely looked bemused. "Quite clear. Lead on, Jean-Luc."

Picard did so, Korsmo taking care to match his stride and even managing to be a half step ahead of him. The two first officers hung back as if by unspoken agreement, and when the two commanding officers were out of sight, Riker and Shelby slowed even more.

"What's his problem?" said Riker with no preamble.

At first she considered making a strident protest of Korsmo's attitude, but Shelby realized that there was no point to it. "He's jealous of Picard," she said.

"Jealous?"

"Apparently, they were very competitive back in their Academy days," she said. She spoke in a low voice, as if concerned that her voice might carry. "He envies Picard's status, and the way he's viewed throughout Starfleet."

"Korsmo's record is very respectable," said Riker in confusion. "Medals and commendations, and command of the *Chekov,* which is hardly a garbage scow."

"But it's not the *Enterprise,"* she said, which Riker had to acknowledge with a nod. "And, when all is said and done, he's not Captain Picard. When the great stand of Starfleet happened at Wolf 359, the *Chekov* wasn't able to get there in time. I think Captain Korsmo has convinced himself that, had he been there, he would have been able to make a difference."

"He's probably right. He could have made it forty-one destroyed vessels rather than forty."

"You're probably right," she admitted. "But he imagines that he could have had some impact. It eats at him that he didn't have the chance. And it eats at him even more that it was, of all people—"

"Jean-Luc Picard who turned the tide. Are you saying Captain Korsmo is unfit for command?"

"Not at all. He just has a bit of a blind spot when it comes to Picard, that's all. We all have our blind spots. I know one officer, for example, who has a blind spot when it comes to realizing the best thing he could do for his career is move on to captaincy of another vessel and let someone else take his place."

"Except for that blind spot, he's a superb officer," said Riker dryly.

"Oh, an exceptional officer. Absolutely exceptional." She smiled, and she had a lovely smile. "And not afraid to make the tough decisions."

Ahead of them, the two captains strode side by side,

neither speaking, until finally Picard said, "It's good to see you again, Morgan. Once this business is done, I'll buy you a drink in Ten-Forward and we'll discuss old times."

"Old times?" Korsmo gave a short laugh. "I rode you like the devil, Picard. I helped to make your life miserable. Don't tell me you're nostalgic for that."

Picard shrugged. "You exaggerate."

"Not in the least. In a way, you have me to thank for your current success."

Picard looked at him with barely concealed surprise. "I do?"

"Of course. It was my constant haranguing of you that drove you to achieve as much as you could."

"What a fascinating way of recalling our Academy days."

"It's true. I spent so much time reminding you of your limitations, that you felt driven to try and surpass them whenever possible."

That, Picard thought, had to be the biggest crock that he had ever heard. But something warned him that Korsmo wasn't just needling him. He had the distinct feeling that Korsmo actually believed it, and more, that the belief was important to him. And now was definitely not the time to challenge it.

"My thanks, Morgan," he said simply, and then quickly changing the subject, said, "What do you intend to say to the pilot of the planet-killer?"

"Starfleet's position. A position that I expect you to back me on. I am the senior officer here, after all, Picard."

"Senior off—"

"I received my commission as captain before you did," Korsmo said. "Or were you unaware of that?"

"Two weeks before," said Picard, trying to keep the derisiveness out of his voice.

"Seniority is seniority, Jean-Luc, and I'll thank you to remember that."

"I will consider myself officially thanked," said Picard, and then he suddenly said, "Halt."

The turbolift came to a stop and Picard turned towards the surprised Korsmo.

"We are dealing with an obsessed woman," he said, not allowing Korsmo to even open his mouth. "You seem to be under the impression that we, with our two starships, are going to intimidate this woman just by the force of our presence and our words. You had best think again, Morgan. She has the drive and the power to do what she wants. We may not be able to stop her."

"We sure as hell *will* stop her," said Korsmo.

"She may not listen to us."

"She will listen if I have to shoot her legs out from under her. Besides, we've done a scan on her ship. There's damage to a section of the neutronium hull. We can hit that if necessary, possibly damage her."

"I don't want her hurt."

"Now listen, Picard . . ."

And Picard stabbed a finger into Korsmo's face and said, each word a dagger, "I don't . . . want . . . her . . . hurt."

Korsmo stared at Picard in utter confusion. "Have you lost your mind? What is she to you?"

"A victim. A victim many times over, and I will not see her victimized further. Clear?"

Korsmo seemed ready to laugh, but he saw the intensity in Picard's face. His expression tightened and clouded. "I will do what I have to, *Captain*," he said. "And I trust that you will do likewise."

They stared at each other for a long moment, and then Picard said sharply, "Resume." The turbolift obediently completed its journey to the bridge in stony silence.

When Picard and Korsmo entered the conference room, Deanna Troi and Guinan were waiting for them. A ship's counselor Korsmo naturally recognized, but he stared with open curiosity at Guinan. Picard quickly introduced them.

"May I ask, just out of morbid curiosity, Captain," said Korsmo, "why you feel it necessary to have your bartender here?"

"Hostess," corrected Guinan politely. "I have a . . . history with the woman in question."

"May I ask the nature of that history?"

"It's personal."

Korsmo seemed slightly taken aback by that and turned to Picard to protest this apparent attitude problem on the part of someone who was, at best, a crew member of questionable need in these circumstances. But the firm look in Picard's face quickly discouraged Korsmo from pursuing the subject further.

Picard turned to Troi and said, "How is Miss Bonaventure? I understand that there was some unpleasantness in engineering."

"She is resting comfortably. Quarters have been assigned her," said Troi, "to remove her from the rather tense environment of sickbay."

"Tense?" Korsmo looked at Picard with a question in his face.

"There are Penzatti recovering from wounds there, and they react somewhat strongly to Miss Bonaventure's presence. She is a female Borg whom we have managed to separate from the Borg consciousness."

Korsmo scratched at his salt-and-pepper sideburns. "Never a dull moment on this ship, is there, Picard? Kind of a zoo."

"I prefer to think of it as a stimulating work

environment," replied Picard. "It would be best to post a guard outside her quarters—"

"Lieutenant Worf has already attended to that," Troi told him, and Picard nodded his approval.

The doors hissed open, admitting Shelby and Riker. Picard looked at them with faint disapproval. "Took our time, did we, Number One?"

"Scenic route, sir."

"I see."

Moments later Geordi La Forge entered as well. Picard nodded a silent greeting to him.

Korsmo was circling the briefing room, looking annoyed. "So where is this woman? We're all here. Where is she?"

"She'll come," said Guinan.

"Ah. We have the personal assurance of your hostess that she'll be along," said Korsmo.

"Captain," Picard began dangerously.

But Korsmo continued, "And what is it with this ship of hers? Is she the only crew? How does it run?"

"She claims it runs on the hatred of ghosts," said Picard dourly. "Frustrated spirits who waited for her to come along and provide them with drive. However, Mr. La Forge has been working along far more prosaic lines to determine just what it is we are up against."

"Our sensors have managed to punch through some of the interference her fields and hull have created," said Geordi, and he moved to the main computer screen. He called up a schematic he had prepared as he continued, "And Data and I have also done research into other cultures that have similar glimmerings of technology of a more—shall we say—mundane nature, based on things that the captain said Delcara told him."

The planet-killer appeared on the screen, and Geordi tapped the spike-like extensions. "These are definitely what propel the ship. They warp space in a manner similar to our own nacelles, but appear to do so in a slightly different manner. We're detecting warp fluctuations on a field pattern at variance with our own warp system. It'll take us at least a week to fully analyze the structure, and we don't have the technology to duplicate it. It seems to have tremendous potential, though, especially in its more efficient use of fuel."

"Fuel that comes from planets. Then that's how it operates and this nonsense about being driven by souls—" said Korsmo.

"I'm getting to that," said Geordi. "There's a race on Orin IV that has technological procedures that sound similar to what Delcara told the captain exists on her ship, except it's not lots of hocus-pocus."

"Orin IV was a colony world about fifty years ago, wasn't it?" asked Picard.

"Good memory, Captain. And the colonists made a fascinating archaeological find—an intricate computer net that was still functional, developed by an ancient race, speculated to be the Preservers, and then long ago abandoned. It was crystalline in appearance and about the size of a small mountain, and what it contained was an intricate network of individual memory pockets.

"Presumably, when members of the race died, they would be capable of imprinting the engrams of their minds—or perhaps transferring their consciousness entirely—into the interlocking network within the crystal. There they would provide knowledge and information that, to the right operator, was accessible."

"Accessible how?"

"Through a central sort of mother board," said Geordi. "You see, that was the really tough part. In a way, it's the main difference between the setup on Orin IV and my understanding of how the Borg operate. The Borg are one central consciousness. The Orin IV mechanism consisted of hundreds, thousands of individual pocket memories. Computer files, if you will. But in order for them to be accessed, they required a central mind to act as a processing station. That central mind had to be, first, a living individual, and second, incredibly strong. The first time one of the Orin IV colonists, who was a Betazoid, tried to use his empathic ability to access the crystal computer they'd found, the minds stored within the computer literally overwhelmed him and blew his gray matter inside-out. Finally they brought a Vulcan in, but by then it was too late. The failed attempt had wiped the data banks clean."

"So the people who created the planet-killer," said Picard slowly, "may have transferred their collective consciousness to the central data banks of the vessel. But they needed a powerful enough living mind to process all of their individual impulses, to unify them and drive their individual functions towards one goal."

"They need one central mind strong enough to govern all of them and direct the ship's functions," agreed Geordi. "Otherwise, they're just random bits of data and information without any purpose. It's that central, functional imperative that enables this planet-killer to be something more complicated than just a mindless killing machine like its prototype.

"One of the ship's functions that the mind maintains is the process of consuming planets and converting them to energy for the ship's drive and weapons systems. Those spike towers," he pointed again, "can warp space for the purpose of forward drive, and also funnel force beams with pinpoint accuracy, making it capable of omnidirectional offense. Nasty piece of work."

Korsmo started towards him, about to make some point, and he walked right through Delcara.

He jumped back in shock as Delcara's holographic persona turned to face him for a moment and look at him with amused disdain. Then she looked at Geordi. "So many explanations," she said. "So much effort to try and take the divine rightness and wonder of my mission and turn it into something ordinary. 'Mother board' and 'functional imperative.' These are not words of humans who understand what it is to live and breathe and hate. These are words that the Borg would use. Beware that the enemy becomes thyself, and that you are not as blind in intellect as you are in eyes." Then she turned back to Picard. "I've heard you, Picard. I am here." She spread her hands. "What do you wish of me?"

Picard was staring at her, hard. There was something different about her. She seemed older, somehow. Some of the luminous quality that had surrounded her was diminished. Her face appeared longer, more drawn. Her hair, which had seemed to be constantly billowing about her, as if puffed up by a perpetual breeze, was hanging limply. Her eyes did not sparkle as they had. He glanced at Guinan and Troi, and they noticed it, too.

He couldn't dwell on it. Nor did he wish to contemplate Delcara's singleminded determination to reject every rational answer in favor of the irrational. There was business to be attended to. "Delcara," he said formally. "This is Captain Morgan Korsmo. He and I are appealing to you now as representatives of Starfleet."

"Are you, dear Picard?" She seemed amused, but there was something haggard in her smile. "And what is Starfleet's business with me, Captain Morgan Korsmo?" She walked towards him and right into the conference table. She stood there, only the upper half of her body visible, the lower half obscured by the table, giving the impression that she was some sort of bizarre centerpiece. It was a most disconcerting appearance.

Korsmo cleared his throat and said, "Captain Picard and I wish to express our concern over your present course of action."

"You have a problem with my intention to obliterate the most dangerous enemy in this galaxy?" Skeptical, she raised an eyebrow.

"It is our concern," Korsmo said, "that your plan of action will cause devastating results throughout the Federation. Your vessel consumes planets. There are various races, both friendly and unfriendly, that will not take kindly to the concept of your ingesting them or parts of their solar systems."

"I believe the human phrase is, 'You cannot make an omelette without breaking a few eggs,'" said Delcara.

"This is more than a few eggs, Delcara," Picard spoke up. "You're talking about the greatest destruction our galaxy has known. Far more destructive than if the Borg swept through."

"Truly, sweet Picard, that was spoken as someone who has never experienced the full sweep of a Borg invasion."

"We've had our encounters."

"You've had nothing," she said, her voice suddenly harsh. "One Borg ship. A ship that smashed through your fleet and cost thousands of lives and was stopped as much by fluke as by anything else. You have no idea what the full might of the Borg would do to you. It would be far more than my humble needs."

"Your humble needs will launch the galaxy into war against you!" said Korsmo. "And Starfleet will lead that war! You cannot be allowed to traverse the quadrants in a device of this power—a device which consumes planets for fuel!"

"A device which will prove your ultimate salvation," she replied.

"Delcara," Guinan said firmly, "have you realized the magnitude of what you're proposing? It will take you years, even at warp speed, to reach Borg space. And all during those years, you will be cutting a swath of devastation and destruction across populated space. Certainly you can see the insanity of that?"

"Insanity is quibbling over a relative handful of lives when the Borg care nothing for life! I will try to avoid populated worlds when I can, but my ship—even with improved matter-to-energy conversion—has needs. Those needs will be satisfied. Sustenance will be derived when needed, and if lives are lost, I will mourn them, but it is necessary. And if some race tries to stop me with deadly force, I will stop them with deadlier force. And again I will mourn them, but it is necessary, and their souls will come to know that they served a greater good. Mourning loss of life, promising to try and be as careful as possible—these are not claims that you could make in reference to the Borg's operations."

"Promising to be as careful as possible is hardly enough," said Picard. He leaned forward on the table, facing the holographic image. "For example, you'll be entering Tholian space in half a day. Your very presence will be anathema to them, as will ours. They will attack you with everything they have!"

"My father," said Riker, "was the sole survivor of a Tholian raid fifteen years ago. They're fierce and unrelenting."

"You speak to me of unrelenting? *Me?* Let them come!" shot back Delcara, her voice even more harsh. The spaces where her eyes were darkened even more than before. "They cannot stop me. You cannot stop me."

"But years of devastation—" Guinan said.

"What are years to me? I have all the time in the universe."

"Delcara, you have made clear you intend to use your vessel for destructive purposes," said Korsmo. She turned away from him and he circled around the table so he could face her. "Starfleet cannot permit that. You are hereby ordered—"

"Captain," warned Picard.

Korsmo ignored him, saying even more firmly and loudly, and pointing a finger at Delcara so forcefully that it shook with rage, "You are hereby ordered to surrender your vessel to myself or Captain Picard, as authorized representatives of Starfleet. Failure to do so will result in direct action against you."

Delcara turned on him, ebony with fury. "You pitiful, insignificant fools!"

"Delcara," said Guinan, trying to calm her. Troi was flinching from the raw emotions that were pounding against her like an angry surf.

"Have you no idea what you're saying? No concept of whom you're challenging?" said Delcara angrily. "I am your savior! You should be on your knees, thanking your gods that I have been sent to aid you. Your hopeless little race would have no chance for survival if it weren't for me! Do you think the Borg are simply going to forget about you? That their defeat is going to prevent them from trying again? No!" She stalked through the conference room, passing through whatever was in front of her like an angry ghost. "No! They'll just keep coming, and coming, and coming.

They won't stop. They won't tire. They won't give up. They'll just batter you down until you're dead or absorbed, and they don't care which it is, because they have no heart and no soul and no humanity. They just kill and kill and kill. Is that what you're fighting for? Is that why you wish to stop me? So you have the privilege of being wiped from existence by the soulless creatures called the Borg? I won't permit it!" She slammed a fist down that passed right through the table, but she didn't seem to notice. "I will save you, whether you want me to or not. Whether you understand or not."

"You're crazy!" snapped Korsmo. "You half-witted woman—"

Guinan threw up her hands. "Oh, that's wonderful. Way to smooth-talk her, Captain."

Korsmo spun and faced Picard. "Are you going to allow this 'hostess' to talk to me that way?"

"Morgan, be quiet!" thundered Picard with such force that Korsmo actually took a step back.

And Delcara laughed, a deep, unpleasant and slightly demented laugh.

"He's right, you know," she said softly. "Perhaps I am a half-wit. But half of my mind, Korsmo, is worth more than the nothing that you have. My obsession has brought me to the brink of madness and beyond, but your ignorance has blinded you to the reality of the situation. I," she said, spreading her hands wide as if acclaiming her victory, and her voice rising in triumph, "am the One-Eyed Man! Look at me! Fear me! Yes, the One-Eyed Man am I, and I walk the Kingdom of the Blind. And in the Kingdom of the Blind, the One-Eyed Man is king."

She turned, placed her hands above her head as if she were about to execute a perfect swan dive, and leaped straight through the bulkhead. Korsmo moved as if to pursue her and quickly stopped, realizing the futility of the notion.

"Charming woman," said Korsmo.

"Captain," said Picard icily, "May we have a moment alone, please."

Immediately the others cleared out, the last of them being Guinan, who tossed a final, disdainful glance at Korsmo before the doors closed.

"Do you wish to tell me what the hell you thought you were doing?" demanded Picard.

"Acting in accordance with the wishes of Starfleet," shot back Korsmo.

"Nonsense! In a situation that required patient, gentle negotiation, you came into it with phasers blasting. You did everything I told you not to do!"

"And since when do you give me orders, Picard?"

"Since you started acting like a damned fool!" snapped Picard. "Calling people names is no way to negotiate with them. And trying to bully someone is a distasteful tactic under any circumstance. To bully someone when you're not dealing from strength is sheer lunacy!"

"I had to show her who was in charge," said Korsmo forcefully. "Your problem, Picard, is that you bend over backwards not to offend anyone. How many times have you swallowed your pride? How many races have you left laughing at us because when they stared you down, you blinked first?"

Picard stepped back and eyed Korsmo as if he had discovered some new strain of bacteria. "I perform my duties with an acute awareness of my ship's safety, and with the concept that this is a galaxy that is endeavoring to attain harmony. That goal will never be reached through anger, threats, and intimidation."

"And it won't be reached through cowardice!" snapped Korsmo.

Immediately the air chilled even more than it had already, and mentally Korsmo cursed at himself. What the hell was he talking about, implying that Picard was some sort of coward? Certainly the man was insufferably self-confident, and a goddamn hero from one end of the galaxy to the other, but that didn't mean . . .

Picard said nothing, although rage was seething through every pore. He was too disciplined to say all the things that were racing through his mind and instead said simply, "I will not even dignify that comment with an answer."

Korsmo opened his mouth to reply, but before he could, the doors slid open and Riker was standing there. With no preamble he said, "The planet-killer is on the move. It has resumed course, and just lit out of here at warp seven."

Picard and Korsmo exchanged glances, and Korsmo bolted out of the briefing room. Not even taking time to get down to the transporter room, he tapped his communicator and said, "Korsmo to *Chekov.*"

"Chekov here," came the reply.

Shelby stepped to his side as Korsmo said, "Two to beam over, immediately," and he glanced at Picard as he said, "You know what we have to do."

"Yes," Picard said simply, and as Korsmo and Shelby transported off the bridge, he could not help but wonder how in hell they were going to do it.

Chapter Seventeen

SHE COULD HEAR the anger of the Many in her head.

We are hungry, they said. *We have spent time talking about the Picard and thinking about the Picard. We need food. You don't care about the mission of vengeance or of us,* the last comment extremely accusatory.

Suddenly Delcara felt inexplicably tired. "Of course I care about you," she said. "We are all. We are together. We are great. You know that."

Prove it. Find us food.

"We will be there very shortly," she said. "There is a starsystem just ahead. But you cannot truly be hungry. The conversion engines have more than enough power for now from the planets we have already consumed. How can you be hungry already?"

We think you don't want us to feed anymore. We think you are concerned that the Picard will be angry with you if you do.

"This is some sort of test, is that it?" Now she knew she was tired. There seemed to be a great fog hanging over her mind, and she came to the sudden realization that she could not remember the last time she had slept. "Testing my feeling for Picard against my feeling for you."

Yes, said the Many.

"All right, then. I will show you that my resolve has not wavered. I will show you all."

The planet-killer cut straight towards the heart of Tholian space.

"Twenty-two minutes until Tholian space, sir," said Data.

Picard sat motionless in his chair, watching the stars hurtle past. Forty thousand kilometers to starboard, matching their warp speed, was the *Chekov.*

"Sir," said Worf suddenly, "sensors have detected a Tholian ship dead ahead. Energy emissions are extremely low."

"Used up their shipboard weapons in combat, no doubt," said Riker.

"Take us out of warp, Mr. Chafin," said Picard, standing. "Open a hailing frequency to—"

"Chekov to *Enterprise,"* came Korsmo's voice, and without waiting for Picard to reply, he said, "Picard, why are you slowing down?"

"To offer assistance to the crippled Tholian ship," Picard said. "We aren't going to be able to do anything against the planet-killer. Nothing short of the entire remaining fleet could do that, and perhaps not even then. We've got to help where we can and wait for our communications to get through to Starfleet."

"The Tholian ship," said Korsmo acidly, "would not slow to help you. We're going after the planet-killer. You do whatever the hell you want. Korsmo out."

The *Chekov* leaped forward and, moments later, was gone from the screen. The Tholian ship now hung visibly in front of them.

Thinking no more on the bitter exchange that had just occurred, Picard ordered, "Give me a channel to the Tholian ship."

"Open," said Worf.

"Tholian ship, this is Captain Jean-Luc Picard of the *Enterprise.*"

The triangular ship seemed to be twisting and turning, as if on a string. Then the ship vanished, to be replaced by the blinding blue-and-red glare of a Tholian. Picard winced automatically, as he always did on the rare occasions when he was confronted by one of these bizarre and notoriously short-tempered beings. Nothing was worse to have to deal with than an angry Tholian, and yet Picard felt constrained to do *something.*

The voice was shrill and fractured over the speaker. *"Enterprise* again?" said the Tholian.

"Again?" said Picard. The last time he'd seen a Tholian was in his *Stargazer* days. He had not encountered one since taking command of the *Enterprise.* "I don't understand."

"I am Commander Loskene," warbled the voice. "Ninety of your years ago the *Enterprise* trespassed into our territory. We dealt with a lying Vulcan named Spock. Is he among you now?"

Picard looked at Riker, who shrugged. The Tholians were renowned for their punctuality, but obviously had very little concept of the length of time that had passed by human—or Vulcan—standards. "Not at present," he said, declining to make the obvious rebuttal that Vulcans did not lie. "We are in pursuit of a ship, large enough to swallow planets . . ."

"You have released it upon the Tholians in order to destroy us," said Loskene angrily.

"That is not true," snapped Picard. He was getting

damned tired of being accused of things this day. "It is helmed by an individual who is acting of her own accord, and against the wishes of the Federation and Starfleet. Am I correct in assuming that you have engaged it unsuccessfully?"

"Federation officers lie, especially those in command of ships named *Enterprise*," Loskene informed them.

"Sir, respectfully submit that this is getting us nowhere," Riker offered in exasperation.

"The Tholian fleet will stop the destroyer ship," Loskene said. "And once they have defeated it, we will seek revenge on Starfleet for this unprovoked attack."

"Starfleet is your only prayer for survival," said Picard, his anger barely in check. "*Enterprise* out." He turned and stalked back to his chair as he said, "Mr. Data, take us in pursuit, warp eight. Engage."

The *Enterprise* hurtled into high warp in a desperate bid to overtake the planet-killer.

They needn't have hurried.

When the *Chekov* caught up with the planet-killer, it was calmly devouring the outermost planet of the Tholian starsystem.

"Warn her off, Mr. Hobson," snapped Korsmo.

Hobson did as he was told, but the planet-killer calmly went on about its business. Tractor beams hungrily licked up pieces of the world and dragged them into the monstrous maw.

"Target the section where the neutronium hull was damaged," ordered Korsmo. "Load front torpedoes."

"Torpedoes loaded and armed," said Hobson.

"Fire."

The forward torpedoes darted out into space and, seconds later, impacted in the small area to the rear of the planet-killer.

"No visible damage," reported Hobson. "There's a secondary coating of castrodinium beneath the neutronium hull."

"Perfect," muttered Korsmo.

"Sir, we're picking up about seventy ships heading towards the planet-killer," Hobson suddenly announced. "It's the Tholian fleet, sir."

"The more the merrier."

Shelby glanced at Korsmo, who eyed her appraisingly. "What would you do, Commander? Hang back and let the Tholians fare for themselves? Or augment their attack?"

"She has to be stopped," said Shelby without hesitation.

"My thoughts exactly. Bring us around, helm. Open a channel to the Tholians and let them know that they've got help, whether they want it or not."

Delcara was in ecstasy. She fondled—almost sensually—the powerful beam that sliced apart the planet, and was at one with the glorious rejoicing of the Many as they consumed their latest morsel.

More, they cried out, *we want more.*

"You can have more," she said. "As much as you want. There is another dead planet up ahead—"

Not dead. Not this time.

She hesitated, not understanding. "What?"

We have looked into the hearts and minds and souls of these beings. They are petty. They are territorial. They launch raids upon those weaker than themselves. They are no better than the Borg in many ways. We want them.

"No," said Delcara uncertainly. "For all their faults, they are not the soulless ones."

They would destroy us if they could.

"They cannot."

They will try. They come even now.
And they were coming.

The Tholians had greatly improved the tractor field weapon that had become their trademark. Whereas once it had taken hours for their notorious web to be completed, they were now able to accomplish the intricately interwoven construct in a matter of minutes.

Tholian Webslingers, as the main ships had been nicknamed by the crew of the *Chekov,* leaped forward and encompassed the planet-killer. It was hundreds, perhaps thousands of times larger, but this did not daunt the Tholians. They were nothing, if not determined, and their ships began to weave their webline around the stationary planet-killer. The mammoth machine, for its part, appeared to totally ignore them, instead consuming the last portions of what had once been the outermost planet.

Within seconds the first strands had been strung, and inside of five minutes the planet-killer was completely enmeshed in the elaborate, glowing blue force strings of the Tholian web. The tractor field was designed to leach off the energy output of whatever it had surrounded and use that energy to feed the web itself. It was an elegant and brilliant design. The more energy the entrapped vessel expended, the faster the web absorbed it and the stronger the web became. So, the stronger the victim, the tighter the bonds that it created around itself.

The *Chekov* hung back, reluctant to start firing for fear that they might accidentally hit a Tholian ship. The Tholians were testy enough as it was, and despite Korsmo's original intentions to the contrary, the Tholians had informed him in no uncertain terms that the starship was to stay the hell out of it. For added emphasis, one of the ships had taken a few pot

shots at the *Chekov,* shots which had bounced harmlessly off the shields. It served merely as a warning,
but one that the *Chekov* took quite seriously.

The web closed around the planet-killer, and the
Tholians congratulated themselves on their victory.
The planet-eating vessel was obviously so petrified by
the Tholian might that it was too afraid to fire so
much as a single shot.

Their rejoicing lasted exactly nineteen seconds, at
which point the planet-killer opened fire with its
massive anti-proton beam. The web flashed, energy
running up and down its entire length, charging and
crackling. Two of the Webslingers had not yet discon-
nected and were fried instantly, and moments later
the entire web began to shrivel and spark. The web
was designed to absorb energy output, but it couldn't
even begin to cope with what the planet-killer was
dealing it, and a few blazing seconds later the Tholian
web fell and burned away.

The Tholians, desperate now, opened fire, and the
Chekov joined them, launching photon torpedoes,
phasers, and a full antimatter spread. The planet-
killer fired back intermittently, picking off ships here
and there as if it were more of an exercise in marks-
manship than a serious offense. It didn't need to
mount one. The ships arrayed against it didn't stand a
chance.

The planet-killer then turned in leisurely fashion,
ignoring the attempts to slow it down, and started on
a direct course towards the Tholian homeworld.

It was at this point that the *Enterprise* showed up.

Yes, sang the Many. *You see they wanted to hurt us.
They are evil. They care for no one and nothing except
themselves. They deserve to die.*

Delcara felt her defenses weakening. It made so

much sense, really. She could intuit so much of the discordance that was part and parcel of the galaxy. There was so much chaos, so much evil. Not just the Borg, but everywhere. Yes. Yes, the Tholians had committed great harm. She sensed the truth of the telling. There had been raids. There had been attacks on neighboring starsystems. There had been extremely variable borders so that passing ships could be savaged on the flimsy excuse that Tholian space had been violated. Yes, there was the truth, clear now as light, guiding as a beacon, sending her toward the homeworld.

The planet-killer howled through space, closing. Not too far away, the great sun of the Tholian system crackled in space, uncaring of the fates of those planetary bodies that orbited it. Whether the second planet away—the Tholian homeworld—survived or was extinguished was of no interest. The star would go on for a million years, and that was all that mattered.

Tholian ships rose up to meet the threat and were smashed without hesitation. The planet-killer paused, ignoring the scraps of ships that floated past it, the crushed bodies of the Tholians whose life flames had been snuffed out. It ignored as well the frustrated attacks of the *Chekov,* which meant well. Delcara sensed that, and for that reason she would destroy the *Chekov* only as an absolute necessity.

Twenty seconds to being within range of the homeworld.

Eighteen seconds, seventeen, and it hung there, large and inviting. Its surface was hot, at least 200 degrees Fahrenheit, and it was about to get hotter. The intensity of the heat would serve the planet-killer well. Would put a fire in its belly.

Fifteen, thirteen seconds, and the planet-killer was closer and closer. Eleven seconds . . .

Nine . . .
And out of nowhere, there was the obstruction.

"Eight seconds until collision," Data said tone-lessly.

The planet-killer loomed larger and larger on the screen. Picard sat in his command chair, gaze riveted on the approaching instrument of doom.

When he had ordered an intercept course, everyone on the bridge had seen the madness of it. Picard was interposing his ship, and the lives of everyone aboard, between the Tholian homeworld and the oncoming planet-killer.

The Tholians were no friends of the Federation; indeed, they were more terrorists than anything else. They were notorious troublemakers. They had refused to aid in the allied defense mounted months ago at Wolf 359 against the Borg, and indeed had made it clear that they wouldn't have shed a tear if Earth and the entire Federation had been absorbed by the power of the Borg. In fact, the flagships of the Tholian fleet had been busy threatening the *Enterprise* before the planet-killer had blown them out of space.

Nevertheless, when Picard had issued the order that would very likely cost them their lives, it had been followed with utter confidence and discipline. Their lives and their dedication had been pledged to Picard, and they would fulfill that no matter what.

If only it weren't on behalf of the Tholians, Worf thought sourly.

"Seven," said Data, "six, five . . ."

Five seconds, and the planet-killer would either smash right through the *Enterprise,* or unleash its deadly beam to destroy the planet, and the *Enterprise* would be right in the way and cut to pieces, or the vast maw of the planet-killer, which was fast approaching them, might simply swallow them whole.

Of all the options under consideration, survival didn't seem to be among them.

Delcara saw, or sensed, or somehow knew, that the *Enterprise* blocked their path. The ship had been perfectly placed—there was no way to get at the planet without destroying the starship.

"Picard," she whispered.

He does this to challenge you, cried the Many. *He thinks you won't destroy him. He thinks he will triumph. Kill him. Obliterate him and take the world. The world is ours. We want the world. We hunger for the world.*

"But Picard risks his life to save them. That must say something for them," said Delcara desperately.

It says he is a fool. It says you give your love to a fool instead of us. We want the planet. It's ours. Give it to us. Give it. Give it!

The *Enterprise* hung there, glistening, white, a sacrifice.

Give it! cried the Many.

"Picard!" cried the One.

"Three," said Data.

The *Enterprise* did not budge.

The doomsday machine did not slow down.

On the bridge of the *Chekov,* the crew looked on in horror.

"My God, he's committing suicide," said Korsmo.

Shelby shook her head desperately. "He must have something. Some trick. Something."

301

"Fire phasers!" shouted Korsmo, but they were out of range. They were going to be too late.

"Two," said Data.

Picard gripped the arms of his chair firmly. Riker's back stiffened, his bearded chin jutting out defiantly. Troi was at peace. Worf was disappointed that they weren't firing, even though it was pointless. Data obliquely wondered if, should he survive the impact when the ship was smashed apart, would he then float in space, inseparable from other debris and ignored, but conscious and aware?

"One," said Data.

They were looking straight down the mouth of the planet-killer. The flames of hell danced deep within it, damned souls welcoming newcomers. The heat was overwhelming, the heat was everywhere . . .

The heat was gone.

"Son of a bitch," whispered Korsmo, staring in disbelief. "He's got to be the luckiest bastard in the cosmos."

"The planet-killer has veered off," Data said as calmly as if announcing a routine mid-course correction.

The engine of destruction was heading away from the *Enterprise,* faster and faster, as if anxious and desperate to put as much distance between itself and the starship as possible. And its course was taking it straight toward—

"The sun. The planet-killer is on a collision course with the Tholian sun," Data said.

The picture on the viewscreen immediately changed to accommodate the new direction. And there was the planet-killer, dwindling against the fiery face of the Tholian star. Its vastness was nothing compared to the giant sun that it was charging, looking as helpless against the white inferno as the Tholian ships had looked mere moments ago.

"The gravity of the star is pulling it in," said Data.

Slowly Picard got to his feet, unable to believe what he was seeing. "Delcara," he whispered.

In the Ten-Forward lounge, Guinan saw and whispered the same thing.

Smaller and smaller it became, and smaller still, and Picard imagined that he could hear screams in his mind, and one of the voices screaming was his. Tractor beams were useless. Everything was useless. She was going to die for some inexplicable, hideous reason, and there was nothing he could do.

A ship that could swallow planets whole looked pitiful and insignificant against the sun, and then it looked like nothing. It plunged, lemming-like, right into the heart of the star, into a furnace with the power and heat of a hundred million nuclear explosions, and vanished.

A silence fell upon the bridge, an awed and somewhat confused hush. Most of the bridge crew sensed that something more had happened here than they could understand.

Picard slowly sank into his command chair as if the air had been let out of him. Troi looked to him with grief and sympathy, but the captain said nothing. He just stared fixedly at the Tholian star, oblivious of all else.

"We are being hailed by the *Chekov*," Worf said, uncharacteristically subdued.

Picard didn't reply, but simply inclined his head slightly. Worf put it on audio, and Korsmo's voice came on with a brisk, "Picard? You okay?"

"All hands safe here, Captain," said Picard. Whatever he was feeling, he was internalizing it completely, but he sounded much older. "And yourselves?"

"We're all sound here. Damned lucky that monster ignored us."

"That monster," said Picard, "committed suicide rather than harm this ship. So do not—"

"Captain!" Worf said suddenly.

Picard and Korsmo spoke in unison. "Yes?"

"Sensors are detecting—"

"Oh my God," came Korsmo's voice.

And now Picard and the rest of the bridge crew saw it as well.

The planet-killer ripped free from the far side of the sun, undamaged, unslowed. It picked up speed with every passing second, glowing white hot and then cooling as it pulled away from the star, further and further into space, further and further from its pursuers, and within seconds it had leaped into warp space and was gone.

The two starships, and the remaining Tholian ships, sat there in space, as silent as the void that surrounded them. It was finally Korsmo who broke that silence, as his sarcastic voice sounded on the *Enterprise* bridge.

"Well, Picard," he asked, "any other bright ideas?"

GRAND FINALE

Chapter Eighteen

THE STAR HAD BEEN LEFT far behind, but the anger still remained. The Many were furious.

You tried to hurt us, they cried. *You tried to kill us!*

"No, my children, my loves," said Delcara, feeling very tired. "I knew that we would survive. I knew that we are great. I knew that our power and strength would enable us to survive even the raging heart of a star, for our heart rages far more."

You risked us rather than the Picard.

"Yes!" said Delcara, her fury brimming over. "Yes, and I would do so again. We are joined, Picard and I, in ways that I can neither explain nor understand. We shall always be together, although fate decrees that we must be apart. And I would not be the instrument of Picard's destruction. You must accept that."

We do not like it.

"You do not have to like it," she told the Many. "But accept it."

They were silent for a long moment. *Is our vendetta not important to you? Is our love not enough for you?* they asked. *We love you as he never can. He is mortal.*

He is meat and he will die and rot. We are forever. We can love you forever. The Picard cannot offer that.

"No," she said softly. "No, he cannot. Mortal love is so transient. If I have learned nothing else in my long life, I have learned that. I have lost so many. Children, mates. So many."

Not us, Delcara, said the Many. *Not us. Not ever.*

"Not ever," she said.

Shall we go faster, Delcara? We can go much faster, you know. Faster than even the ships of the Picard could follow. Our upward speed has not been measured. If you wish us to—

"Our present speed is satisfactory," she said. "We have all the time in the universe, my children. Let us savor the revenge and conserve our resources."

You do not wish to hurry, accused the Many, their voices becoming shrill once more, *because you do not wish to leave the Picard behind.*

"Perhaps," she sighed. "That may well be. If so, it is my desire, and you will honor it, my loved ones. You will honor it."

We will always do as you wish, Delcara, said the Many. But there was something in their voice that Delcara found disturbing. Something very unpleasant. An ugliness, an unquenchable thirst for revenge that even she felt was disquieting. And perhaps the most disquieting thing about it was that she saw the thirst, more and more clearly, in herself.

Deanna Troi sat across from Reannon Bonaventure in the latter's stark and functional quarters. She held the woman's hand in her own and stared deeply into her eyes, looking beyond those eyes, deep into the mind.

"Reannon?" she said softly. "I am beginning to get a sense of you. You are hiding, like a frightened child,

308

afraid to come out. Your soul is a terrified and vulnerable thing, virtually destroyed by the Borg. But you can rebuild it. With love and understanding, you can rebuild. It will take time, but you have that in abundance. It will take support, but you will have that in as great quantities. Come out to me. Reach out to my soul, Reannon. You see it there, calling to you."

Nothing.

There were footsteps just outside, and Geordi La Forge entered. He paused in the threshold and said, "Sorry, Counselor, I didn't know you were . . . I can come back later."

"No, it's all right, Geordi," she said, gesturing for him to enter. "Your presence can only be of benefit."

He sat down within arm's reach and shook his head. "Still can't believe that thing survived cutting right through a star. The radiation, the heat—it's just incredible."

"What's more incredible is that we're still in pursuit and trying to convince ourselves we can stop it," said Troi.

He looked up at her. "That sounds surprisingly fatalistic for you, Counselor."

"There's a fine line between fatalism and realism, Geordi."

"Hey, who would have thought that the Tholians would have let us depart from their space without any sort of further challenge? They still can't believe that the captain risked everything to save their home-world." He leaned forward towards Reannon. "Any progress?"

"There was that moment in the engineering room," said Troi, settling back and trying her best not to look discouraged. "That was a definite breakthrough. But now there's nothing. It's as if she's hiding."

"I can't say I blame her entirely," said Geordi.

"Nor can I. Obviously, she does not wish to face the reality of her memories of the Borg. So she has blocked out everything, rather than deal with it."

Geordi reached forward, took her hand and brought it up to his face. "This got a reaction out of her before," said Geordi. "She seemed interested in my VISOR. Maybe she will be again."

He brought her ice-cold hand up in front of his face, took the tips of her fingers, and ran them across his VISOR. When they reached the end he rubbed them back in the other direction, and all the time he kept saying, "Reannon? Reannon? I know you're in there. I know I can help you. Reannon?"

Slowly, ever so slowly, her gaze shifted to Geordi and actually seemed to focus on him for a moment.

"Geordi, she's reacting," said Deanna in a hushed voice, as if afraid that speaking out loud would somehow break the spell.

Reannon's fingers closed on the VISOR, and she yanked with all her strength. The VISOR flew off Geordi's face and the world immediately became blackness around him.

Reannon held the VISOR tightly, and again she started to make sounds, muttering incoherences. Out of a reflexive sense of panic to the darkness that had enveloped him, Geordi La Forge lunged forward, trying to get to the VISOR. He missed completely and fell heavily to the floor.

The ruckus immediately prompted the security guard outside to enter, phaser drawn. "Lieutenant!" he shouted, seeing Geordi on the floor, grasping about desperately.

"*No!*" cried out Deanna, leaping to her feet and raising her hands as if to ward off a phaser blast. "No, don't! It's all right. It's going to be all right!"

Reannon had turned away, moving quickly but in a

very tight circle. And she was trying to shove the VISOR onto her face. She got it on once but it slid off, and she grabbed at it while muttering incoherent, incomprehensible shrieks.

"What's happening!" called out Geordi. Troi was helping the engineer to his feet, and again the engineer said, "What's happening? What's going on? What's she doing?"

Reannon hesitated for a moment, looking around in confusion, and then, gripping the VISOR with one hand, she started clawing at her eyes with the other. Fortunately, it was the prosthetic hand that was holding the VISOR, because if she'd used that hand to attack her face, she might possibly have done serious damage to herself.

Troi reached forward and grabbed Reannon's wrist, all the time hushing her and whispering to her to calm down, that everything was going to be all right, that she was among friends. And finally the fit seemed to pass, and Reannon slipped back into the sullen, coma-like attitude that she had had before.

Without a word Troi handed the VISOR back to Geordi, who quickly replaced it on his face. As what passed for the world snapped into view once more, he sighed in relief. "Not damaged," he said. "That's a relief. What happened, Counselor?"

"I believe," said Deanna slowly, "that she was attempting to rip out her own eyes and replace them with a mechanical implement."

He hung his head. "Trying to re-create herself as a Borg. My God. That's what she was trying to do, isn't it."

"That is my guess," said Deanna. "And yet, she is of two minds. On the one hand, she tries to recapture her transformation into a Borg. On the other hand," and Deanna ran her fingers maternally through Reannon's hair, "she is repulsed by it and tries to deny what happened to her. She is a very tortured individual."

"But I was sure I was getting through to her," said Geordi fiercely. "I was so certain."

Troi looked at him curiously. "This is so important to you, Geordi. More so than I would have suspected. Beyond any of the explanations you gave before. Why? What is it about her that seems to have touched you so?"

He sat there, trying to find a way to put it into words, and ultimately was unable to. "I feel close to her, that's all. I admire the type of woman she is. Or was. The adventurer. Someone who is totally independent, willing to take on anything. I admire her and I respect her and—"

"Do you love her?"

La Forge looked slightly taken aback. "I . . . don't *think* so. I love the opportunity to help her, and I think about . . ." His voice trailed off a moment and then, softly, he admitted, "I think about her all the time." Then he drew himself up, squaring his shoulders, and said, "It's a challenge, that's all. A project. The same as any other challenging project. I want to help her to feel better. That's all."

"If you say so, Geordi," said Troi neutrally. He glanced at her face and wondered if she was smiling or not.

At that moment both Troi's and La Forge's communicators beeped. La Forge tapped his, as Troi did hers. Picard's voice came over both of them as he said, "I'm calling an immediate conference of all senior officers."

"What's happened, Captain?" Troi could instantly sense the controlled distress the captain was feeling.

"Reports from outlying starbases along the frontier," said Picard. "The Borg are on their way." He paused. "In force."

Picard signed off, and Geordi and Troi looked at each other. "They're obviously determined to destroy the planet-killer," said Geordi, "before it gets to Borg space."

"And in a battle between Delcara and the Borg . . . whose side would we take?" asked Troi.

Geordi chewed his lower lip and finally admitted, "That's going to be the big question, isn't it. The big, and maybe final, question."

Guinan walked slowly down the corridor, not even noticing the crewmembers who walked past her. That was extremely unusual for her, since on those rare occasions when she was noticed moving through the hallways of the *Enterprise*, she always had a kind word or a polite nod for anyone who passed her. Now, though, she was clearly preoccupied.

She stopped in front of a holodeck door and paused, as if considering her options. The ship was still on yellow alert, so no crew members were busy living out some sort of amusing fantasy through the *Enterprise* holo-technology. Guinan composed herself and walked in.

The yellow grids glimmered around her as she stood in the middle of the holodeck. She took a deep breath, clearing her thoughts, and then she put her fingers to her head.

"Delcara," she said softly, and again, "Delcara." And when she spoke, her voice went far beyond the confines of the holodeck, beyond the confines of normal space.

All was silence for quite some time, and then an image shimmered and appeared before her.

Guinan gasped when she saw her in spite of herself. Delcara's face was more lined than before, and now her hair was brittle and looked like it might even be falling out. When she stood it was with hunched back, as if she were carrying the weight of the world on her. And her very aura had changed. Once it had glimmered, white and pure, and now it was darksome and disturbing. Her eyebrows were heavier, her eyes seeming to be receding into her head. When she regarded Guinan, her entire face seemed constructed for exuding suspicion.

"What's happened to you?" whispered Guinan.

"Nothing," said Delcara. "Nothing, bond sister. You called me. I have come. What more can you wish from me than that?"

"Computer," Guinan said abruptly. "Access ship's log, stardate 44793.6. Re-create from visual records the woman named Delcara who appeared in holographic form. Physical form only. Do not animate."

Within an instant the computer had complied, and a perfect construct of Delcara stood before the two of them. She stood there quietly, unmoving, a mere shell. Yet there was a grace and quiet beauty still in evidence that had already faded from the being who had come to Guinan at her behest mere moments ago.

"Geordi tried this with his Borg friend," said Guinan. "A woman whose soul he is trying to recapture. I figured, if it's good enough for him . . ."

"A Borg friend?" Delcara looked at her skeptically. "Recapture a soul? That cannot happen, my bond sister. They have no souls. Nor does this," and she gazed in fascination at the body that stood before her, motionless. "This, however, does present interesting . . . opportunities."

She stepped forward, like a specter, and merged with the body.

The body staggered for a moment, as if getting its bearings, and then Delcara's heart shone through the eyes. She held up the hands and experimentally touched them to the face. "Intriguing," she said. She looked over to Guinan, who was standing there with quiet satisfaction, and held out her hands to her. "Bond sister, I feel as if I see you with new eyes. You are looking well."

"And you—" Guinan took her hands. "You look terrible."

"Blunt as ever," said Delcara. "Wrong as ever. You counseled forgiveness, Guinan. You counseled that I should live my life and not dwell on the past. But look at what I have achieved, sister. Look."

"Yes, let's look, shall we?" said Guinan sharply. "Don't you understand what's happening to you? Your obsession is destroying you. It's eating away at your soul. God only knows what it's done to your body. You won't let us see that."

"My body is in perfectly fine health," Delcara told her.

"Come aboard the *Enterprise*, Delcara," Guinan said urgently. "Leave the planet-killer behind. Come be with me. Come be with him. We are your future. Not that machine in which you hide."

"You do not understand, Guinan. They need me, and I need them."

"You only need them if you need vengeance. If you put vengeance aside, you need only love. And you don't need a machine that was built to destroy to provide you with that."

Delcara turned her back to her. "You don't understand."

"No, no, I've never understood," said Guinan. "Letting an obsession consume you in the way that it has is totally alien to me. I remember you as you were,

315

Delcara. There was a darkness in you, true, but you were willing to let in light. You were willing to love. You were willing to dream and hope of things other than destruction."

"We change, Guinan. Well, not you, of course," said Delcara with a touch of sarcasm. "You are the same, sweet-tempered, attentive individual you always were."

"I remember a time when that was important to you," Guinan replied. "Delcara, come back to us. To me."

"They need me," she began again.

Guinan squeezed Delcara's "hands" as tightly as she could. "They need. They need. But they don't give, bond sister. They take and take from you. But they don't give you the flesh and blood relationship that only other living beings can provide. The spirits of the dead possess you and destroy you. Leave them and return to us."

"I can't!" cried Delcara in exasperation. "What would you have of me, Guinan! What would you have!"

"Give up the vendetta . . ."

"I *can't!* Don't you see? That's all I am. That's all that's left of the woman you once knew. I don't know anything else, nor does anything else matter!"

"I don't believe that."

"Whether you believe it or not doesn't change it."

"Let us come to you," said Guinan desperately, urgently.

"Impossible."

"Not impossible. Let us into your vessel. See us like this," and she squeezed Delcara's "hand" firmly. "Let us address the many beings that you represent. Picard can be very persuasive."

"Picard," said Delcara with a faint whisper, and

then, her voice more firm, she said, "It's impossible, I said."

"That's not you speaking," said Guinan with surprising fierceness. "That's them."

"They are many. I am one."

"But you're the one that matters to me."

"All right," said Delcara, sounding extremely tired again. "All right, Guinan. I swear, you and your relentless nature. You would vex the gods of patience."

Guinan smiled. "At the very least, I'd give them something to think about."

"Time draws short, though," said Delcara darkly. "I sense more of the soulless ones on the horizons of space. There are three of them this time."

Guinan cast a glance in the direction that Delcara was pointing, as if she could see through a bulkhead. "Three."

"Yes. It will be a difficult battle. But I will prevail. That is the main reason that I agree to see Picard now, you see."

"On the eve of your great triumph?"

"No," she said simply, and sadly. "Because I anticipate that he will not face the Borg another time and live. And his departure will leave a great absence in me. How fortunate that I do not love him."

The holodeck-generated body arched her back slightly, and then slumped forward, its eyes vacant and wide, staring at nothing. Guinan nodded slowly and said, "How fortunate indeed."

Once again Picard had assembled his top officers in the briefing room, with Korsmo and Shelby in attendance as well.

It was a strategy conference, the type of which Picard had hoped he would never have to call again.

"The Borg," he said, "are on the way. The speed reported by Starbase 222 was somewhere above warp nine-point-nine."

Geordi whistled. "Incredible. The fastest that subspace radio goes is warp nine-point-nine-nine-nine, and that's with booster relays, which means that the Borg may be barely behind the radio transmission. You know, the laws of physics say it's impossible to reach warp ten, but if anyone can do it, I bet the Borg could. Not that I get any particular pleasure from that thought, mind you."

"What's even more incredible is that they ignored the starbase," observed Shelby.

"Obviously, they were in something of a hurry," said Riker. "And I think I know what they were in a hurry for."

He glanced out the viewing port. Ahead of them, space was warping around the speeding shape of the planet-killer, still on its head-on course to penetrate Borg space. Thus far the *Enterprise* and the *Chekov* were keeping pace, but it was not an easy task, and it required careful monitoring of the engines.

Riker shook his head in amazement. That it would take years to achieve her goal was clearly of no interest to her at all. As she had said, she had all the time in the universe.

It was time that the *Enterprise* did not share, which Data was just now pointing out. "If we can assume that the planet-killer is capable of surviving the next Borg attack, the next densely populated system will be that of the Gorn. Furthermore, beyond that she will inevitably—presuming she does not alter her course —enter a section of Romulan space."

"Just perfect," said Riker sarcastically.

"Why doesn't she just open fire on the Federation headquarters and be done with it?" demanded

Korsmo, sounding even more frustrated. "She's going to have the entire galaxy in pieces before she's through."

"I am aware of what she might and might not do, Captain," said Picard quietly.

"Well, she's not going to have the chance," said Korsmo. "I received a communiqué from Starfleet . . ."

"Yes, I know," Picard told him. "We received the same one."

Korsmo seemed surprised for a moment, but then shrugged. "Then you know."

Crusher looked confused, as did Troi and La Forge. "Well *I* don't know," said the doctor. "Someone care to let me in on it?"

"Starfleet is assembling a fleet to intercept her," said Korsmo with great satisfaction. "If the Borg don't get her, we definitely will."

There was silence in the briefing room for a moment. Picard cast a glance at Shelby, who was seated next to her captain but clearly wasn't sharing his enthusiasm. Nor did Riker look ecstatic. "Problem, Commander? Commanders?" said Picard.

Shelby looked at Riker. "It's Wolf 359 all over again."

"My thoughts exactly," said Riker.

"I do not like what you're implying at all," declared Korsmo. "Starfleet can no more let that woman carve her way through the galaxy than they could let the Borg assault us unanswered. For a galaxy to be at peace, that peace must be protected. Starfleet and the Federation aren't simply going to turn away when such a massive threat presents itself, whether it be the planet-killer or the Borg. And I will have you know, young officers," he added stiffly, "that Wolf 359 was heroism at its finest!"

"Wolf 359 was a massacre," said Riker. "I will never forget the look on Admiral Hanson's face when he told us of the fight he was going to give the Borg. He was like a war-horse put back into harness. You weren't there to see that, Captains. We saw it. A brave defender going off to be slaughtered. And we saw the graveyard of ships that were left behind in the Borg's wake."

"And that was against one Borg ship," Shelby said. "Now you're telling us that a fleet is being assembled—a fleet which can't possibly be as powerful as the one at Wolf, because most of the best ships were lost there—and it's going up against a foe that's more powerful."

Now Picard cleared his throat loudly and said, in a tone that was indicating that no further discussion on that topic was being tolerated, "It's of far more importance, I think, that we deal with the here and now. And the here and now would indicate that, sooner rather than later, depending upon their speed, we will be encountering three Borg ships. Mr. La Forge, what are our options?"

"We've developed ways to temporarily stall the Borg during an attack," said Geordi. "Fluctuating the phaser resonance frequencies tampers with their ability to adjust to our weapons. Also varying the nutonics slows down their ability to overcome our deflectors, although only for a matter of seconds."

"There was something else you did. Memoranda were circulated throughout Starfleet," said Korsmo, "and Shelby was telling me about it as well, with the deflector dish . . ."

Geordi's head bobbed up and down. "We discovered that the power nodules of the Borg were susceptible to phaser frequencies along the higher end of the band. It caused system-wide drops throughout the Borg ship when fired on them. Figuring that more is better, we generated a concentrated burst of energy using power from the warp engines, channeled through the deflector dish, to give us more punch than phasers or photon torpedoes could have provided. The problem was that since it took so much power, we couldn't maneuver at warp speed. Furthermore, it caused failure in the warp reactor core primary coolant system, and we came damned close to cracking the dilithium crystals."

"The result?" asked Korsmo.

Geordi shifted uncomfortably in his chair, and no one else around the table looked particularly at ease. "Nothing. The Borg shields absorbed it."

"That would be my doing," admitted Picard. "When the Borg 'recruited' me, they took all of our possible planned strategies from my mind."

"The other drawback is that it left us virtual sitting ducks," said Riker. "That kind of failure against one Borg ship is bad enough. Trying it again with two other ships to attack you while you're making yourself vulnerable attacking a third is even more risky."

"They can only prepare for what they knew we could do, up to the point where they abducted the captain," said Geordi. "But they don't know about things that we've come up with since."

"You have something in mind, Mr. La Forge?" asked Picard.

"Something that's worth a shot," said Geordi. "Wesley had been conducting experiments with creating warp bubbles."

"Oh God, don't remind me," said Beverly Crusher.

"But it may be something we can use," Geordi continued. "All the equations and records of the experiment are in the computer, and I've been looking them over from time to time when I had a spare few minutes. And I've been discussing possibilities with Data . . ."

"We have theorized," Data said, "that it would be possible to program into the computer a remix of matter and antimatter to duplicate, on a large scale, the warp bubble that Wesley created."

"In the main engines?" said Picard, looking somewhat taken aback.

"No, sir," said Data. "The mixture would be contained in the emergency antimatter generator on the lower engineering hull. However, upon command, the computer would then channel it through the warp field generators on the outboard nacelles. The warp bubble would interact with the subspace field of the Borg ship and encapsulate it in a shrinking universal field similar to the one which trapped Doctor Crusher. It would, for all intents and purposes, remove the affected ship from our space-time continuum."

"So we would have to maneuver close enough to the Borg vessel to, essentially, 'drop off' the warp bubble on their subspace field," said Picard.

"Yes, sir," confirmed Geordi. "And we would have to keep moving at impulse power to leave the discharge behind. We'd have maybe three seconds to get away—at impulse power—or risk being encompassed in the warp bubble along with the Borg ship."

"Sounds dicey," admitted Riker.

"How long would it take you to prepare the emergency antimatter generator?" asked Picard.

"Wesley did all the theoretical groundwork when he was first doing his experiments." Geordi shrugged. "This is just a straightforward application. Maybe half an hour."

"Make it so." Picard paused. "Captain Korsmo, I—"

But he didn't get to complete the sentence, as the briefing room communicator sounded. "Captain," came Chafin's voice, "the planet-killer is reducing speed."

"Are there Borg ships ahead?"

"No, sir."

"Maybe it's running out of gas," said Korsmo.

The briefing room doors opened and Guinan entered quickly. Korsmo looked up and sighed in exasperation, but kept his peace. Guinan, for her part, ignored him completely but instead went straight to Picard.

"She wants to see us."

"Wants to?" said Picard, not having to ask who Guinan meant by "she."

"Perhaps 'wants to' is too strong a term," allowed Guinan. "She will see us. That alone is a breakthrough."

"What *she* is that?" asked Korsmo. "The woman in the planet-killer?"

"Captain," Chafin's voice came, "it's dropping out of warp."

"Bring us alongside," said Picard, and stood. "Transporter room. Prepare for four to beam aboard the planet-killer. Doctor, Guinan, Mr. Data, with me."

"No, sir!" Riker said immediately, "that would be—"

"The only logical course of action," said Picard with quiet confidence. "This may be our only chance to ally the planet-killer solidly with Federation interests. If that can be accomplished, we need never worry about the threat of the Borg again. Mr. La Forge,

323

Counselor Troi, tell me of the Bonaventure woman. Could she be useful somehow in negotiating with Delcara?"

"You can't negotiate with her, Picard," Korsmo now said. "She's a terrorist! She does what she wants, where she wants. There can be no compromise with someone like that."

Picard simply stared at him icily, and then said very quietly, as if Korsmo had not even spoken, "I'm waiting for an answer to my question, Counselor."

"Using Reannon would not be advisable," said Troi. "She is at a very delicate stage in her recovery, and very unpredictable. She could do as much harm as good."

"I agree," said Geordi.

"Very well, then. She'll stay here." And seeing Riker's mouth about to open, Picard quickly interrupted with a curt, "There is nothing to discuss, Number One."

"Captain," Shelby now said, leaning forward, "this is not the time."

"Commander Shelby is right, sir. You can't be away from the *Enterprise* now. The Borg are coming."

Picard turned to Riker, and his first officer understood immediately from the look in Picard's face. This was more than determination on Picard's part to take the risk himself. This was a personal fulfillment of a lifelong quest on the part of his captain, and he came to the quiet realization that there was no way in hell he was going to be able to get in this man's way.

"You will have to give them my regrets," said Picard.

Chapter Nineteen

KORSMO STRODE ONTO the bridge of the *Chekov* and dropped into the command chair. Shelby followed a few steps behind him, looking far more composed and controlled.

"Against every common sense move," Korsmo said, more to himself than anything. But everyone on the bridge heard, and turned towards him with curiosity.

"Sir?" asked the man at ops.

Korsmo didn't look at anyone as he just shook his head and said, "There are certain people in the galaxy who go by the book, who always do the correct thing, and they lead satisfactory, but uninspiring, careers. And then there are the ones who do whatever the hell they feel like, and they get the attention and acclaim. Now, you want to tell me what you call that?"

There was silence on the bridge for a moment, and then Shelby said, simply and clearly, "I call that justice."

Korsmo fired her a look that wasn't filled with a great deal of affection. "Thank you for sharing that with us, Commander."

Shelby said nothing, just inclined her head slightly as if giving a tongue-in-cheek "You're welcome."

Korsmo looked at the screen, at the planet-killer that was now stationary in space. The *Enterprise* had drawn closer, and Korsmo said, "Hold our position here."

"Sir," said Hobson in surprise. "The planet-killer had been generating a field scrambler that had made transport aboard impossible. But sensors are detecting that a hole has just been created in the field. Should we—?"

"No," said Korsmo quietly. "Take no action. Hold us steady. You see, we weren't invited."

Guinan, Picard, Data, and Troi stepped up onto the transporter platform. Worf and Riker stood at the base, while O'Brien checked his readouts. "Transportation is now possible, sir," said O'Brien, not without some surprise. "And I'm reading a transporter beacon signal from within the planet-killer. Someone has someplace very specific they want me to send you."

"Then we shan't disappoint them," Picard said.

"Sir, I still recommend against this," said Riker firmly, though he did not think, at this point, that Picard was going to listen to him. In that he was correct.

"Recommendation noted, Number One."

Now Worf stepped forward and proffered a phaser. "Sir, you should have this with you."

"I don't think that will be necessary, Mr. Worf."

In a firm, even fierce voice, Worf said, "*I* do."

Picard was slightly surprised by the vehemence of his security head. He also understood it. It was a very difficult thing to ask a Klingon to stand by and permit a commanding officer to do something that he, Worf, felt was inappropriate. Klingons were driven by an immense sense of duty, and Worf was in tremendous conflict. On the one hand, he was obligated to obey the wishes of his captain. On the other hand, he felt duty-bound to protect his commanding officer from harm.

As much out of consideration for Worf's feelings as anything else, Picard took the phaser. "Thank you, Lieutenant," he said.

Worf gave a curt nod and stepped back, his arms folded across his broad chest.

Picard stepped back up onto the transporter platform and glanced at Guinan. "Your first time through a transporter?"

She shrugged. "First time for everything."

Picard nodded and then turned to O'Brien. "Energize," he said.

They shimmered and vanished off the transporter pads.

"Vaya con dios," murmured Riker.

Picard was staring at himself.

He took a step back and reflexively his hand went towards his phaser. Then he realized that the individual he was facing, who looked just like him, was doing the exact same thing. In less than a second upon first seeing his reflection he realized what it was, and he felt a bit sheepish. He retreated a step farther so that he could get a look around.

"Just as Geordi surmised," said Picard. "Crystal."

Picard, Troi, and Guinan stood in the middle of their surroundings, taking it all in. Troi and Picard were clearly amazed at what they saw. Guinan, for her part, merely stood impassively and looked around as if she had seen it all before.

All around them, for as far and as high as they could

see, they were surrounded by intricately designed structures from a material that looked for all the world like crystal.

The walls, vast sheets and pillars of crystal, reflected endlessly the images of the four *Enterprise* visitors. Picard reached out tentatively, after consulting with Data's tricorder readings, and placed his hand flat against one of the pillars. His reflection seemed to reach back at him. The pillar was warm to the touch, as if it were throbbing with life of its own.

"Incredible," he whispered.

From all around her, Troi sensed life. It was like nothing she had ever felt. The walls, the floors, the ceilings, wherever they might be—they were completely encompassed by emotions. She told this to Picard, and then added, "They seem—harnessed somehow."

"Imprisoned?" asked Picard.

"No. No, utilized, and willingly. As if . . . as if the ship is being driven by pure will power."

"It is being driven by more than that," said Data, consulting his tricorder once again. "These crystalline structures are actually power cells that harness all matter of energy: physical, kinetic, electromagnetic." He paused, checking further. The neutronium hull had made sensor readings extremely difficult, but now that they were within, he was absorbing the information as quickly as possible—which, for Data, was quite fast indeed. "My interior readings are confirming what Geordi was hypothesizing. The warp drive technology would seem to generate different fields from that of the *Enterprise.* There is a variant level in harmonic resonance that enables this vessel to warp the fabric of space with greater energy efficiency and speed." He turned towards Picard. "It is not dissimilar from Borg technology—indeed, it may even be more efficient."

"The Borg are always speaking of absorbing technology," murmured Picard. "The implication is that they develop precious little of their own."

"Of course they don't," said Guinan, staring at her reflection. She adjusted her hat. "Creation of new technology comes from imagination. You have to dream before you can do. Since the Borg have no imagination, they are limited in their capacity to invent."

"And it is possible that the Borg have realized that," Picard said slowly. "We wondered why their priorities appeared to have changed. Why they seemed interested not only in human technology, but also in interacting with humanity. Is it possible that they have come to realize the limits to their development, and want to tap into the human capacity for invention in order to expand themselves?"

"It could be a very intriguing hypothesis," said Data. "The centralized Borg mind may easily be capable of analyzing its own shortcomings. They may wish to harness the creative ability of the human mind. Intriguing. When you represented the Borg as Locutus, you referred to me as a primitive artificial organism, despite my own ability for invention."

"Obviously they have come to value the human ability to think, as it pertains to their attempts to improve themselves, while realizing the limits of mechanical life." He glanced at Data. "No offense."

"None taken," said Data calmly. "None is possible."

That was when Deanna Troi screamed.

Immediately the others were next to her, as Deanna was staring at a crystal wall. She was pointing in confusion and said, "My face . . . I saw my face and then it was . . . someone else's. Not just someone. A hundred someones, or a thousand . . ."

She seemed genuinely rattled, but calmed down when Guinan rested a hand on her shoulder. She shook her head to clear it and then said, "I'm sorry. I was startled."

"Very human of you," said Data consolingly.

"That was the Many."

They turned to see Delcara standing in front of them. Picard was taken aback, for he had not seen Delcara earlier in the holodeck, and she had deteriorated even further than when Guinan had last seen her. Troi gasped as well. Data merely aimed a tricorder at her.

Her hair was now a filthy white, and every visible inch of her skin was wrinkled. She was smiling, but it was with a death's-head rictus of a grin. Her eyebrows had actually converged, creating a single dark and foul line of hair across her face, casting her once-lovely eyes into permanent shadow. She was hag-like, stooped shouldered, the very structure of her face changing. Her brow hung forward, Neanderthal-like, and when she tilted her head slightly, contemplating them, she looked like a gargoyle.

And insanely, she appeared oblivious of her appearance. It was as if somewhere, somehow, deep within her, there was still the purity of spirit. An innocence, a naïveté that was simply unaware of what was happening to her. As if the heinous intentions pervading her had simply been layered onto her without touching the inner spark that once had been a simple, loving woman named Delcara. A woman who knew nothing of hatred and vengeance, but only love.

The woman whose inner beauty had once been

revealed, for only a moment, to a cadet named Jean-Luc.

Picard stepped forward and his hand passed through her. "Still a hologram, I see."

"Still a captain, I see," replied Delcara. "You were a leader of men even when I first saw you. How little things change."

"Delcara—" began Guinan.

But Delcara waved her off with a brief, angry gesture. "I brought you here because you refused to understand," and her voice was laced with barely controlled frenzy. "I brought you here to make you understand. I cannot go back to the way I was. There is nothing left for me. Come."

She turned away before they could say anything and strode down the corridor that seemed to stretch endlessly before them. Picard immediately fell into step behind her, as did the others. They were amazed at the silence around them. Within the *Enterprise,* there was always some sort of background noise. The steady humming of the powerful engines, the noise of servicing being performed on thousands of standard automatic computer systems—always something.

Not here, though. Within the heart of the planet-killer, all was silence. Even their boots made no noise, for the crystalline walls and floors seemed to absorb all the sounds.

They turned a labyrinthine corner and stopped.

Thus far they had been surrounded by towering pillars and, far above them, tubings and crossways that seemed to be channels for the pure power that coursed through the entire structure of the planet-killer. Now, however, they were faced with a single long, stretching corridor, lined with row upon row of odd slabs, each one freestanding, about seven feet high and positioned at roughly 45-degree angles to the wall. And at the end of the corridor was a single column that stretched upward, the top of it out of sight.

The hologram of Delcara walked toward it with measured steps, and then stopped. It turned and faced Picard and the others.

"Now do you understand?" she said.

Inside the crystalline column, held upright like a fly in amber, untouched by the corruption and beauty-destroying brush of vengeance-obsession, was the pure and unscathed body of Delcara.

On the bridge of the *Enterprise* Worf suddenly looked up. "Sir, long-range sensors are detecting three vessels approaching at warp seven, heading three-two-two Mark nine. At present speed, they will be here in seventeen minutes."

"Borg?" said Riker tonelessly.

"I believe so, sir."

"Alert the captain. Tell the landing party to be prepared to beam aboard."

"I am not able to raise them on the planet-killer, sir," said Worf after a moment, and anticipating Riker's next statement, he said, "and the field of the ship makes it impossible to lock onto their readings."

"So we can't beam them back if Delcara doesn't want us to," said Riker. "Terrific. Engineering," snapped Riker, "how long before you have that warp bubble formulation into the emergency generator?"

"About another fifteen minutes, Commander," came Geordi's voice.

"Sensors say that you're officially cutting it close, Mr. La Forge. The Borg will be here in seventeen minutes."

"If there's one thing I hate, it's spare time," said La Forge.

"There won't be much to hate here. Step on it."

"Yes, sir."

"Sir," said Worf with undisguised surprise, "we are receiving an incoming message from the Borg ships."

"Announcing the joy of their arrival, no doubt," said Riker. "Is the *Chekov* getting the same thing?"

"They indicate that they are, sir."

"Seems the Borg are having no trouble cutting through the subspace interference that thing out there generates," observed Riker. "On screen, Lieutenant."

The planet-killer vanished, and the last thing they expected to see appeared on their screen.

At first glance it was a Borg, but only at first glance. His head was shaped differently, the visible portion of his flesh and bone in the distinctive shape and size of—

"A Ferengi?" said Riker in surprise. "Is that a—?"

"It appears so," said Worf, no less astonished.

The Ferengi Borg paused a moment, as if allowing the humans to digest the full impact of his presence. Then he said, "I am . . . Vastator. Vastator of the Borg."

Riker started to identify himself but then he heard another voice over the channel. "This is Captain Morgan Korsmo of the starship *Chekov*." Riker promptly kept silent—technically, Korsmo was the ranking officer present and was the proper one to be in communication with the Borg. Not that Riker was especially thrilled about that idea.

"Vastator of the Borg," continued Korsmo, "you are in Federation space. I am ordering you, under my authority as a Starfleet captain, to return immediately to your own quadrant."

"Your orders are of no interest," said Vastator, and then, incredibly, his voiced acquired the silky subtlety of a Ferengi. "We are prepared, however, to deal."

Riker looked at Worf and mouthed the word, *Deal?*

"What sort of deal?" came Korsmo's voice.

"We have learned of the power of the weapon that you are presently near. It poses a threat not only to the Borg, but to yourselves. We will destroy the weapon, and you will not interfere. In exchange, we will not destroy you." It was bizarre to see the Ferengi speaking without the usual sneer.

"No deals," said Riker sharply.

He was astonished when he heard Korsmo's sharp rebuke of, "Commander, I am in charge here."

"The Federation does not deal with terrorists," said Riker. "You said so yourself, sir."

"This is not terrorism. This is negotiations with a threatened race."

"The Borg are not threatened, Captain," said Riker tightly. "By and large, they do the threatening."

"You need not decide now," said Vastator calmly. "You have sixteen minutes to choose. Ultimately, your choice will be of no relevance to us. Only to yourselves." With that, the Borg cut the communication.

The image of the Borg was immediately replaced by that of Korsmo, who looked angrily at Riker. "I don't appreciate your interference in those discussions, Commander."

"The *Enterprise* is not going to stand aside and let the Borg destroy Delcara's vessel."

"Oh no?" snapped Korsmo.

"No. That ship hurled itself into a sun rather than destroy us. I hardly think the Borg would be that considerate."

"And have you given thought, Commander," said

334

Korsmo icily, "as to what happens if Delcara does manage to destroy those Borg ships and continue unmolested. Within a week's time she will be intercepted by the fleet I warned you of. You yourself predicted major casualties for such a battle. The word 'massacre' was voiced, as I recall. If we have a chance of stopping her here, either by standing aside or even attacking her ourselves, we save the lives of countless members of Starfleet in a future battle. Are you willing to be responsible for their lives, Commander?"

"And what do you think the Borg will do if they destroy her," shot back Riker, trying his damnedest to keep his tone on the positive side of insubordination. "Turn around, head back home and leave us?"

"Perhaps. Perhaps they will continue into the heart of Federation space. And ships will assemble to meet them, and at least our two will be around to be part of that assemblage. We can't guarantee the same thing if we attack them here and now. And perhaps they can be negotiated with. This incorporation of a Ferengi would indicate a willingness to bargain on the part of the Borg."

"You can bargain with the devil, Captain Korsmo," shot back Riker, "but you always wind up on the wrong end of the deal."

"That, Commander, is your opinion. It is mine that when the Borg show up, we will not fire unless fired upon, and we will do nothing to defend the planet-killer. Furthermore, if the planet-killer is in dire straits, we will do what we can to aid in her destruction. Her existence poses too much of a threat. Furthermore, Commander," he went on before Riker could get a word out, "since I am the ranking officer present, you will follow my wishes as per Starfleet regulations. Is that clear, Commander?"

"Your wishes are very clear, Captain. But you're

forgetting one thing. Captain Picard and the away team are aboard the planet-killer."

There was a chilling pause. "I've forgotten nothing, Commander Riker. And Captain Picard was aboard the Borg ship, as Commander Shelby has told us on so many occasions, when you gave the order to fire on it. Picard's continued presence among us has more to do with Borg technology than with your concern about the ultimate safety of your captain. So don't get on your high horse with me, Mr. Riker. You've established that you know how to make the tough decisions. Now be so kind as to allow me the same courtesy. The bottom line is this: Starfleet's orders are clear. They want the planet-killer stopped. The Borg are going to stop them. Therefore, we will permit the Borg to do that. For all we know, it may be the first step to making peace with the Borg."

"Your interpretation of Starfleet orders—"

"Is the only one that counts, Commander," and he stressed the last word to underscore the rank difference. *"Chekov* out."

And with that final admonishment, the *Chekov* blinked out.

"Keep trying to raise Captain Picard," said Riker tonelessly. He stood and walked towards the viewscreen, as if he wished he could reach through and lift the away team right out of the planet-killer and deposit them safely aboard the *Enterprise* bridge.

And when he spoke next, it was with the tone of someone who was speaking to himself—but, for benefit of the crew. "I refuse to interpret orders in such a way," he said succinctly, "that it means standing aside and letting the most monstrous beings we've ever encountered destroy both our captain and the only weapon that has a hope of defeating them. And if that's what Starfleet does intend, they can come and explain it in person. In the meantime, that interpretation can go hang." *And you will too, Riker, unless you're damned lucky,* he added silently.

He turned to Worf. "Go to red alert. All hands to battle stations." He paused, as if for dramatic impact. "Tell the crew to prepare for one hell of a fight."

Chapter Twenty

"DELCARA?" WHISPERED PICARD.

He placed his hands against the crystalline encasement and felt, even more strongly than before, the warmth pulsing through. Inside the crystal she was naked, every line of her body as he remembered it from that night when he caught glimpses of it through her diaphanous clothing. Her eyes were closed, her hair long and cascading down about her shoulders.

Deanna Troi gasped once, her hands flying to her mouth, as if she wished she could take back her initial startled reaction. Guinan stood impassively, but it was clear from her demeanor that she was affected nonetheless. Only Data, of course, was utterly nonplussed. Instead, he held his tricorder before him and calmly studied the readings. "She is alive," he said.

"Of course I'm alive," said Delcara with annoyance, standing next to her body, apparently unaware of any difference between the appearances of, ostensibly, the same woman. "I am the life. I am the life of this entire ship. The pilot, with a powerful enough mind to use my body and soul as a physical channel for the wants and desires of the Many. Without such a pilot, they lack focus. They lack control. They're undisciplined, like a huge class of rowdy children. Don't you see?" she said in frustration. "They are the dead! The dead need the living if they are going to function! The dead cannot haunt themselves. They need—"

"A victim," said Guinan quietly. "You're a victim. A means to an end."

"A glorious end."

"Come out of there, Delcara," said Picard. "Come join us. It's not too late." He ran his hands across the crystal. "This barrier separates us. It needn't."

"Ohhh, Picard," sighed Delcara. "Dear Picard. Exquisite Picard. I am so tired of trying to explain the realities of the spirit when you are so obsessed with the unrealities of the flesh."

"I refuse to accept this!" thundered Picard. "I cannot simply turn my back on you and allow you to . . . *exist* . . . in this condition. Frozen between life and death, between heaven and hell. Spending an eternity in purgatory for sins that you did not commit."

"Oh, how you do overdramatize, sweet Picard," said Delcara. She smiled ruefully, and passed a ghostly hand across his face. "I have thought of you for so long. Wondered what would become of you. Wondered how far your drive would take you. It is truly a pity. Had we met in another life . . ."

"Perhaps we have," Picard said softly. "Perhaps ours are two old souls, striving to reach one another. This barrier is all that stands between us."

"The Borg stand between us. The unbalanced scales stand between us."

"No!" said Picard, and he drew himself up in righteous indignation. "No. Only this barrier. For this barrier is a creation of your own need for revenge. You can grow beyond that need, put aside your hatred and fury. Come out from your encasement. Return with us."

"It's not too late," whispered Guinan. "Bond sister, it's not. I know you believe it to be—"

"I believe what is true. I believe what I know. This is useless. Return to your ship. There is nothing for you here. Go." And when the away team didn't move, the holograph shouted "Go!" and then, even more loudly, *"Go!"*

And the holograph vanished.

And all around them the crystal walls came to life: Faces, hundreds, perhaps thousands, all contorted, all infuriated, all consumed by a passion that surpassed death, and they screamed in voices that echoed and re-echoed, through the corridors and into their minds, *"Go! Leave us! You are not wanted here! We are the Many! You are the few!"*

"No!" shouted Picard, his hands to his ears. Beside him, Deanna Troi was on the floor, her mind on the verge of shorting out from the empathic overload. Guinan staggered, putting up her hands in a defensive maneuver, and Data was at Troi's side, trying to aid but not knowing how. *"Stop it!"* Picard shouted again.

"You cannot have her! You have no claim to her!"

"I have claim!" shouted Picard. "I have as much claim as you! You have no idea what she has meant to me! I have held, in my mind's eye, the image of her throughout my career!" He could barely hear himself over the deafening roar of voices that were trying to shout him down. "Ever since that night at the Academy, I have seen her as a personification of what I was striving for! The living embodiment, whether imagined or not, of my greatest goal! She was the galaxy to me! She was the mystery of discovery, the calling of the unknown! I have truly loved no other woman in my life, *because the stars are my lover, and she is the stars!* By day I gaze out at the stars and see her image beckoning to me, calling me further and further. By night I lie in my cabin and dream of her. She is in my thoughts and my soul! There never has been anyone before or since who has captured all that I am. She is the stars! She is my life! Give her to me, damn you all! Damn you, you pathetic shades who know only hate and nothing of wonder. *Give her to me!"*

Picard allowed himself a brief flash of pride. He'd come a long way in the field of romantic extemporizing. He'd also come to realize that Delcara's madness was rejecting all manners of entreaties based on the rational and the sane. So instead he had turned to dramatic, ardent claptrap in hopes of breaking through the barriers and reaching her. It was overemotional, overwrought, and somewhat overdone. And it also had just enough of the truth in it to add genuine pain. Perhaps even more truth than he wanted to admit.

The Many screamed and howled in frustration, their anger and bodiless fury pounding against the structure that gave them both life and eternal damnation, and Picard would not back down, would not allow the hysterical wailing of the Many to wear him out.

And the image of Delcara stepped forward from the body that was imprisoned. The ugliness had fallen away from her, the physical manifestations of the usurping of the beauty within her erased as if by magic. The holographic representation was sobbing openly, and she reached towards Picard, her hand passing through him once more. Picard's grip flexed convulsively on the crystal entombment . . .

341

And within the crystal, the eyes of Delcara began to open.

And the planet-killer shook, as if with fury. Picard lost his grip and stumbled forward, cracking his forehead against the edge of the crystal column. He hit the floor and rolled onto his back, just in time to see the rest of the away team shimmering, their bodies enveloped in an odd effect that looked similar to the transporter, but different.

"What's happening!" he shouted.

The away team was gone.

Inside the crystal, Delcara's eyes had shut once more, and the holograph turned towards Picard, her face shining with excitement. "I have my own transporter capabilities, sweet Picard. You spoke such pretty words of love to me that I knew we must remain together. So I sent the other people back to the ship. Even Guinan, whom I will always love."

"But we can't stay here, Delcara, this vessel—"

"Is under attack, dear Picard." She smiled. "The Borg are here."

In her quarters, Reannon Bonaventure gazed out into space and saw the three huge Borg cubes dropping out of warp space and firing upon the massive vessel that hung nearby. Her breath caught, her eyes widened . . .

And she screamed a word.

"Borg!" she howled, a word torn from her innermost self.

The security guard who had been standing outside her door heard her and his eyes widened in shock. She hadn't uttered any comprehensible words until that moment. That he knew. He immediately pulled out his phaser, ready for trouble, because from her alert he fully expected that there would be a Borg soldier within, perhaps trying to capture her and return her to the Borg.

He darted into the quarters, and all he saw was the woman, standing in the middle of the room, and she was screaming over and over again, "Borg! Borg! *Borg!*", flapping her arms as if trying to take flight. But there was no sign of any attacker within, and the guard paused in his initial inclination to call for a security back-up.

"It's all right!" he started to say, but that was all he managed to get out before things weren't all right. Reannon moved with incredible speed and swung with all the strength in her mechanical arm. It connected with the security guard's face, breaking his jaw, and rendering him unconscious before he even hit the floor. Reannon grabbed the dropped phaser and bolted out the door.

She ran out into the corridor, looking around in confusion, and then ran to her right.

She darted down the corridor and saw a familiar symbol near one door. She knew she'd been in the room before, although she couldn't remember why or what it was. Everything was a fog to her with a few beams of light piercing through, and those lights were pulsing and black and evil. Living horror was eating away at her brain.

She ran in and stopped in her tracks.

She was in sickbay. The handful of Penzatti still recovering from their wounds (the rest having been moved to private quarters) looked up at her sullenly.

For a moment she didn't connect anything, and then her mind painted a picture for her. It was a picture of soulless, mechanized creatures that were living prisons, committing unspeakable and heartless acts throughout a cosmos. And she had been one of them, and she had murdered, and destroyed, and she had not cared, and she wanted that life back, a life that horrified her and soiled her, that was like a stench to her—

She staggered back and crashed into an equipment stand, knocking medical tools off it. She grabbed up one or two and stared at them, the part of her brain that was functioning, instantly intuiting the purpose of them.

From behind her she heard the confused shouting of voices—medical personnel. She scrambled to her feet and ran out the door just as Dr. Crusher and Dr. Selar entered from the opposite side of the sickbay. They didn't understand what had set the patients off, but a number of them were now shouting and crying out about the Borg. Things had happened so quickly that none of the medtechs had seen anything.

"They must sense somehow that we're encountering the Borg," said Crusher, who knew that the ships had just appeared mere kilometers away. Riker had alerted her, and she was preparing sickbay in dread anticipation of heavy casualties.

"That is a logical assumption," agreed Selar. And it was logical. It was also incorrect.

On the bridge all eyes were riveted to what was happening on the screen.

The three Borg ships, an awesome and terrifying sight in and of themselves, had opened fire on the planet-killer. They were not using half-measures. Instead all three were letting fly with everything they had. The powerful beam that had once carved up the *Enterprise* like a roast was now trebly powered as it ripped into the hull of Delcara's ship.

And then three shapes began to take form on the *Enterprise* bridge.

Worf immediately had his phaser out, and Riker was on his feet, both of them anticipating that Borg soldiers were about to appear. Then the light flashed away, and when it faded, everyone on the bridge was amazed to see Guinan, Troi, and Data standing there. Just as conspicuous as their presence was the captain's absence.

"Report, Mr. Data," said Riker, wasting no time at all.

Data looked around, not in surprise so much as interest in the surprising turn of events. "We discovered the living body of Delcara, sir, and were assaulted by the remains of the beings that created the planet-killer. Captain Picard stated an eloquent case for Delcara's release—"

"Which appears to have backfired," said Guinan. She shook her head. "If it's all the same to you, Commander, I'll return to Ten-Forward. I can't do anything here." Her gaze drifted to the image on the screen, saw the pounding that the planet-killer was sustaining. She turned to Riker and said quietly, "I assume that you can." With that, she departed the bridge.

Picard stumbled and went to one knee as the planet-killer shook around him.

"You see, lovely Picard," called Delcara. "You see the power of those you would have me turn my back on?"

"I ask you to turn your back on hatred!" said Picard.

"They don't understand such things. They only understand this."

The planet-killer fired back on the Borg ships. The anti-proton beam lashed out and force shields appeared around the cubes, absorbing the impact. They glowed from the intense battering they were forced to endure, but they also gave as much as they got, and cracks in the neutronium hull of the destroyer began to appear.

And the Many screamed in fury and fear, *"You are not focussed! You are not concentrating! What is wrong with you!"*

Picard covered his ears, but it was purely a reflex action. The true volume was inside his head, and he knew it wasn't even directed at him. The true target of the anger was Delcara, and he wondered how she could possibly withstand it.

"Nothing is wrong with me!" shouted Delcara.

"He has corrupted you! The Picard has corrupted you!"

"He has not corrupted me! He cannot! If anything, he has given me the purity of love!" she said desperately.

"This has nothing to do with love! This has to do with our vendetta, yours and ours! Now, attack them! Attack them with the anger and vengeance that drive you, as it drives us. Attack, or we are surely lost!"

Delcara turned away from Picard and spread her arms wide. Within the crystal, her body seemed to tremble for a moment.

"Damn you!" she cried out. "And *damn me!"*

"The Borg are ignoring us, sir," said Data, already seated back at ops and functioning as if nothing extraordinary had occurred to him. Troi, for her part, could barely speak, still overwhelmed by the mental assault they'd been subjected to on Delcara's vessel. Riker had wanted to send her to sickbay, but she had insisted on remaining at her post, even though she appeared pale and shaken. "They are concentrating their full power on the planet-killer."

"Damage sustained by the Borg?"

"Their power level has dropped an average of twenty-one-point-three percent. The planet-killer is draining their force shields. They are, however, inflicting considerable damage upon the planet-killer as well. If the Borg are able to re-energize their power nodes, as they have in the past with great speed, and continue their assault—"

"Then the captain dies, along with a weapon that the Borg actually fear and respect. Mr. Worf, target the closest Borg vessel." He sat down in the command chair, adjusting his jacket the way that Picard did, fully aware of what Korsmo's reaction would be when the *Enterprise* opened fire. "Full photon torpedo spread and phasers. Everything we've got including the kitchen sink. Fire."

No less aware was Worf, but he could not keep the satisfaction from his voice—the satisfaction of a Klingon who knew that battle was joined. "Firing," he said.

The *Enterprise* cut loose and their offensive array peppered one of the Borg ships, which was already suffering under the strain of resisting Delcara's blasts. But the Borg ship didn't dare turn its attention away from the planet-killer, for that's where the uni-mind of the Borg was concentrating its assault. So the *Enterprise* continued to barrage the ship, draining its power levels faster and faster.

"Commander, incoming hail from the *Chekov*," announced Worf.

"Tell him we're washing our hair," shot back Riker. "Continue fire, Mr. Worf," and he looked at the planet-killing vessel that was assailing the Borg ships with blast after blast. "The enemy of my enemy is my friend."

On the *Chekov,* Captain Korsmo was on his feet, his fists clenched in white-knuckled fury. "What in *hell* do they think they're playing at!"

"Power levels of the Borg ship currently under assault by the *Enterprise* are down fifty-nine percent," said Hobson. "Other Borg ships are sustaining damage. All are still attacking the planet-killer."

"That's what they're *supposed* to be doing! Get me Riker, now!"

"No response, sir."

"Damn it! Lock phasers on them!"

"On whom, sir?" asked the tactical officer.

"Enterprise!"

Shelby turned in her chair and looked at Korsmo in astonishment. "On the *Enterprise?"* There was no disguising the shock in her voice.

"I gave them a direct order, and they're disobeying. Mr. Davenport," he snapped at the tactical officer, "I said lock phasers! Half-strength, enough to shake them up and let them know we mean business!" The veins were distending on his throat.

"Phasers locked," said Davenport with deathly calm.

"Fire!" snapped Korsmo.

"Delcara, you cannot keep me here against my will," Picard was shouting over the din. "You must return me to my ship!"

"This was what you wanted! To be with me!" she said. "That's what you told me!"

"Not to be here! Imprisoned on this engine of destruction!"

"I can't leave them! And you mustn't stop me! The

348

battle is joined, and I'm your ship's only hope of salvation!"

He knew she was right. Even with the emergency procedures and strategies they'd developed, the odds were still long against the *Enterprise* remaining intact through a battle with even one Borg ship, much less three.

"Return me to my ship, then," he said again. "That is my place."

"Your place is with me. You said so!"

"Delcara! Concentrate on the here and now!" shouted the Many.

"Shut up!" howled Delcara, *"Shut up!"*

The ship trembled around them even more forcefully than before, and the scream of the Many was truly frightening, for they howled with something they had never expressed before. That no one thought they could express.

Pain.

"My God," said Riker. "Look at that. It's . . . bleeding."

And so it was, or so it appeared. On the surface of the planet-killer, bubbling out of a crack in its hull, was some sort of clear, thick ooze, a mile in length.

"Some sort of energy conversion plasma," said Data, quickly scanning the sensors. "Utilized for conducting energy throughout the body of the planet-killer."

"All weapons, on the Borg. Fire!"

"Sir!" said Worf. "The *Chekov* has opened fire on us!"

The phasers of the *Chekov* sped across the distance separating them from the *Enterprise* in the blink of an eye.

Davenport looked up from his station. And his voice was, once again, utterly neutral, as he said, "Missed."

Korsmo turned and faced him. *"Missed?"*

"Yes, sir."

"Fire again!"

The phasers lanced out.

"Oops. Missed again," said Davenport.

There was dead silence on the bridge. Korsmo saw the way that Davenport was looking at him, and turned to see Shelby regarding him in the exact same way.

And for a moment—just the briefest of moments— he saw himself the way they were seeing him. He saw all the rationalizations he'd been using, and all the reasons he'd followed that seemed like good reasons at the time. And he saw what might be behind those reasons. All of that, reflected in the eyes of Shelby and the rest of his bridge crew.

He knew he wasn't a bad man, or a bad officer. He knew that, in his heart. But he didn't see any of that in the way his people were looking at him. And after a long, soul-searching stare, he wasn't seeing it in himself either.

When he spoke again, it was with quiet irony. "Having trouble with targeting today, Mr. Davenport?"

"So it would seem, sir."

"Think you could target a Borg ship any better?"

A slow smile spread across Davenport's face, a smile matched by Shelby and the others. "It's a bigger target, sir."

"All right. The ship at"—and he glanced down briefly—"seventy Mark eighteen. As I recall, Commander Shelby, phaser beams at the higher end of the band are more effective."

"Yes sir," said Shelby proudly.

"I may forget myself on occasion, but I never forget facts," said Korsmo stiffly. "Mr. Davenport—blast them to hell when ready."

"Commander Riker," announced Worf, "the *Chekov* has begun firing on a Borg vessel."

Sure enough, there was the *Chekov,* darting towards another of the three Borg cubes, letting fly with everything it had.

At that moment the *Enterprise* shuddered.

"The Borg ship we were attacking has locked onto us with tractor beams," announced Worf. "Shields are failing."

Geordi had come up from engineering to the engineering station on the bridge, enabling him to react faster to what was happening. "Modulating nutations," he said.

"Shield failure continuing," said Worf. "Ninety . . . eighty . . ." It was a countdown toward death. "They have ceased firing on the planet-killer. Full concentration on us. "Shields at sixty . . . fifty . . ."

"Fire phasers, varying the harmonics. They've adjusted for the upper end. Try the lower."

"Phasers firing," announced Worf.

"Minor power disruption on the Borg," said Geordi. "They're still smarting from the planet-killer. Their power systems are down sixty-seven percent."

"Fire antimatter spread."

The *Enterprise* was giving it everything they had.

"Shields holding at fifty . . . dropping to forty," announced Worf.

"Nutonic variation failing," said Geordi, like a death knell. "Seconds at best."

And the Borg ship trembled as the anti-proton

beam of the planet-killer struck to the core. Sparks and power surges leaped throughout the ship.

"Tractor beam gone!" said Geordi.

"Full reverse!" shouted Riker. "Work on restoring shields! Give us some distance!"

The *Enterprise* hurtled away, and seconds later one more stab from the planet-killer blasted the Borg ship to pieces. It created a massive cloud of dust and rubble, and through it sailed the doomsday machine, triumphant, wounded, bleeding, and with the other two ships pursuing it.

"Sometimes," Riker said, "seconds are all we need."

They struck again and again at the gaping wound that had been carved in the hull of the destroyer. The *Chekov* concentrated fire on one of the remaining Borg ships, and seconds later, shields restored, the *Enterprise* dove towards the other unoccupied Borg ship.

The plan was unspoken and simple: attack the Borg ships and give the planet-killer enough leeway to destroy them with its superior firepower.

Riker prayed it would work. And he kept on praying right up until the moment when the planet-killer ceased firing.

"We hurt!" cried the Many. *"We hurt!"*

"I'm sorry!" Delcara screamed. "I'm sorry, my children. I should never have listened to him! He distracted me! I let myself think of things other than our purpose!"

"No, Delcara, listen—" said Picard, forgetting himself and reaching out. His hand passed right through her and rested against the crystal. "Listen to me—"

And then he heard it. The sound that was like an explosive, controlled popping. The sound he would never forget.

A Borg had appeared within the heart of Delcara's vessel.

Then he heard more. And more. God, how many? At least half a dozen.

They were coming towards him from just around the corner, and Picard's phaser was in his hand. A chill struck to his spine. They wanted to destroy Delcara. They might even want to recapture him. The thought of returning to that living nightmare called Locutus was almost more than he could stand, and when the first of the Borg appeared, he opened fire using the maximum stun setting.

The Borg staggered and fell over, and immediately a second was behind him. Picard squeezed off another shot and then quickly altered the frequency on the E-M band and fired again. A second Borg went down, and moments later, a third.

The holographic image of Delcara had vanished, as if afraid to oppose her greatest nightmare face to face. Picard charged forward, rolling forward and firing. A fourth Borg went down, but suddenly a fifth stepped into view. It targeted Picard with its gleaming mechanical eye and raised its huge metal arm. Electricity leaped out from the end, and Picard lunged to one side, barely out of the way.

The Borg stalked forward, the image of Picard now locked firmly into its mind. It stalked forward, firing again when it saw Picard dodge between two of the crystal slabs. From hiding, Picard fired again, and this time the protective shield of the Borg adapted to his phaser fire. The soldier was now ready for any phaser attack.

Picard flattened his back against one of the crystal slabs, his heart pounding so furiously he was certain the Borg could hear it.

The Borg stalked slowly forward, the uni-mind of the Borg exercising caution. Its tracking eye swept across the array of crystal slabs in front of it, trying to find the one called Picard. The image of the human was firmly in place . . .

And suddenly Picard was everywhere.

Every single slab had an image of Picard poised in it, ready to attack. Each one was distorted, furious, howling a challenge.

The Borg turned left and right, its arm moving to one side and then the other. Nothing but Picards.

It fired a burst of electricity to the right, electricity harmlessly ricocheting off a crystal slab, and Picard charged in from the left. But at the last second the Borg saw him coming and swung its mechanical arm. Picard caught a jolt of electricity that numbed his right arm, and he dropped the phaser. He fell to one knee and rolled to the side as the Borg came towards him, and then he lunged forward, slamming into the soldier in the midsection. The Borg had prepared for phaser attack but, insanely, not a physical attack. The Borg did not anticipate, only adapted. It was the single advantage the captain had. Picard and the Borg went down in a tangle of arms and legs and prosthetics.

The strength of the Borg was overwhelming as it tried to bring the end of its mechanical arm up towards Picard's face. It drew closer and closer, Picard shoving with his one functioning hand as hard as he could against the arm. It was a losing battle, one in which Picard had only seconds left.

And suddenly he released his grip on the mechanical arm altogether and slid forward the length of the

Borg soldier. Picard's hand lashed out and gripped the Borg's shoulder. The Borg brought his artificial arm directly into Picard's face and was about to blast enough electricity into the captain to render him unconscious and, possibly, dead.

Picard ripped away the circuitry on the Borg's shoulder, the circuitry that kept the soldier in communication with the Borg uni-mind. Like a marionette severed from its strings, the Borg's head lolled back instantly. Picard rolled to one side as the soldier immediately turned into a thin line of ash and vanished.

He felt a flash of triumph for perhaps a second. And that was when he heard the hideous whine of a phaser at a high setting—his phaser.

He scrambled to his feet and almost screamed.

It was a Ferengi, one that had been transformed into a Borg. And he was firing on the crystal chamber that held Delcara, using the phaser that Picard had dropped.

From the sound and intensity of the beam, Picard could tell that it was on setting 16. It was a setting so powerful that it could destroy a volume of metamorphic rock some 100 meters across. It was drilling full-bore into the crystal encasement, and whatever that casing was made out of, it wasn't going to be strong enough. That it was resisting as much as it was was nothing short of miraculous.

And Picard's voice and the voice of the Many were raised together, and they howled, *"Stop!"*

In front of the crystal, the holograph of Delcara sprang into existence, the phaser beam naturally passing right through her. She was holding up her hands, as if trying to ward off the pounding of the blast.

The Ferengi/Borg did not stop. In seconds the

crystal blackened and cracked, and the body of Delcara began to fry, the pure skin shrivelling, the beautiful hair burning like straw. The holograph screamed, a scream that would follow Picard to the end of his days, and vanished.

Picard was already in motion, charging towards the Ferengi, and the alien suddenly ceased fire, spun, and aimed the phaser straight at Picard. Whereas the crystal had momentarily resisted a setting-16 phaser blast, albeit it not especially well, Picard wouldn't survive for a second.

There was no way he could dodge it.

"No deals," said Vastator of Borg, and pushed the firing buttons.

Chapter Twenty-one

"THE PLANET-KILLER has ceased firing," announced Worf. "However, it is still moving. The Borg are now concentrating fire on it. Their power levels are beginning to increase."

"Mr. La Forge, get ready with that warp bubble. Mr. Chafin, bring us right down their throats at full impulse. Mr. Data, monitor engineering and computer release. The timing on this one is going to have to be computer-perfect, and I want you handling it."

"Yes sir," said Data.

"Emergency antimatter generator standing by, sir," said Geordi.

"Approaching Borg vessel, sir," said Chafin. The monstrous vessel loomed larger and larger. In the distance there were flares of the *Chekov* firing upon the other one.

"We will be in range in fifteen seconds," said Data. "Fourteen . . . thirteen . . ."

"Channeling emergency antimatter generator through main warp nacelles," said Geordi. "Preparing for release."

We're going to be looking right down their throats, thought Riker grimly.

Data was counting down. Riker could practically feel the surging of the engines, holding the explosive force of the warp field in place.

With the *Enterprise* not firing, the Borg ship was paying them no mind at all. Instead it was continuing to pound the planet-killer.

"Three . . . two . . . one . . ." Data said.

"Engaging warp engines!" La Forge called out.

And at that precise moment Reannon Bonaventure burst onto the bridge.

The warp engines of the *Enterprise* released the altered warp field and blasted forward. The warp bubble immediately integrated itself into the field surrounding the Borg vessel and contracted. Space twisted and snarled around it.

On the bridge everything happened with incredible speed. Worf saw Reannon and his eyes widened. Without hesitation he started towards her, and as smoothly as if this sort of thing happened every day, another officer leaped in to man tactical.

Geordi turned and spotted Reannon, and he froze, in shock.

Reannon swung her phaser up and Worf dropped to the ground to avoid the blast.

All of that happened in one second.

In the next, Reannon leaped forward toward Ops, where Data was preparing to blast the ship forward on impulse power, away from the rapidly spreading warp bubble. She screamed one word, the only word anyone would ever hear her say: *"Borg!",* and swung her prosthetic arm with all its strength.

She smashed in the side of Data's head.

The force of the blow was so powerful that it hurled Data from his chair and sent him flying into Chafin at conn. The crewman went down beneath the insensate form of the android officer.

Now there was no one at helm or navigation; the *Enterprise* had exactly one second to cut itself loose.

On the bridge of the *Chekov,* Hobson shouted an alarm as the ship abruptly shook. "Captain, some sort of tractor beam! We're losing shields!"

"Shift the nutonals," ordered Shelby.

Technically, *he* should have given the order, but Korsmo knew that Shelby was the expert and, furthermore, that she was right. "Do it!" he snapped.

"Ineffective!" said Davenport at tactical, unaware that the Borg ship they were facing had already learned to adapt because of the *Enterprise* pulling the same trick seconds ago on another Borg vessel. "Shields at eighty . . . sixty . . ."

"Fire phasers!"

"Shields gone."

The *Chekov* struck back at the Borg ship, which had momentarily diverted its attention from the moving planet-killer to dispense with the annoying gnat of a starship.

"Their power levels are at fifty percent but climbing," called out Davenport.

"Torpedoes and antimatter spread. Fire."

The *Chekov* attacked with everything, and the Borg ship absorbed it.

"Tractor beam gone," said Davenport.

The Borg laser beam lashed out, ripping across the unprotected hull of the *Chekov.* Bulkheads blew inward and crewmen by the dozens were immediately sucked out into the cold depths of space.

"Hull breach!" shouted Hobson. "Warp drive out! Structural damage on deck 36, sections 19 through 24."

The Borg struck again. This time the beam gutted engineering, moved up and sliced across the left nacelle. There was a massive explosion as the nacelle blew clean off. Hulls ruptured throughout the *Chekov*, and bulkheads on the lower decks collapsed.

Power went out all over the ship, the vessel barely limping forward. It was moving at a mere fraction of impulse power, and even that would be used up in minutes.

On the bridge everything was in smoking ruins. Everything had happened so quickly that they had barely had any time to react. It was as if the Borg had been humoring them all that time, making them think that they made a difference.

Davenport lay slumped over the tactical station, a huge gash in his forehead. Shelby was coughing, trying to pull herself up, her faced covered with grime. She spit out a tooth and licked the blood away from her mouth. "Captain," she whispered.

Korsmo was in his command chair, shaking his head. Blood was covering the right side of his face, and yet, in the semi-darkness of the battered and nearly dead bridge, there actually seemed to be grim amusement in his eyes. Slowly he turned towards Shelby and, through cracked and bleeding lips, said, "Picard *beat* these bastards?"

She nodded.

He shook his head. "Son of a gun." He didn't ask for a damage report. He knew what the damage was. And he saw only one response to it. "Shelby—you think a starship exploding against their hull would help stop them?"

She shrugged fatalistically. In a way, she still couldn't believe she'd survived her first encounter with the Borg. She inwardly believed she'd been living on borrowed time since then. Well . . . this was pay-back. "It couldn't hurt to try, Captain."

"Mr. Hobson appears unconscious. Take helm."

She did so, pushing Hobson's unmoving body aside. She wasn't especially gentle about it, but then, in a minute or so it wouldn't really matter.

The screen didn't have full power to it. The image was flickering, but they could still make out the cube of the Borg ship.

"The Borg ship is still functioning at less than full power," said Shelby, hoping she could trust the instrument readings. "It expended some energy firing at us. It's recharging."

"Then we'll charge first. Bridge to engineering. Come in, Parke."

There was a pause and then a voice that sounded on the verge of panic. "Bridge, Chief Engineer Parke is dead. They're . . . they're all dead. They're . . . this . . . this is Ensign Toomey, sir."

Korsmo nodded approvingly. "Pull yourself together, son. That's good. Ensign, I just saw our left nacelle go floating by, so I assume warp isn't very likely. Impulse?"

"I can give you half impulse sir, but not for very long."

"It'll be long enough. Get ready, son." He turned to Shelby. "Full ahead," he said quietly, aware that he was giving his last order.

"Captain," said Shelby, making sure her voice didn't catch in her throat. "It's been an honor serving with you."

"Yes." Korsmo smiled. "It has, hasn't it."

She shook her head and punched in the course. The ship staggered forward on a collision course with the Borg, on its final run.

And a massive object cut in front of them.

"What the *hell?!*" demanded Korsmo.

It dropped down, almost from nowhere, gleaming white against the scarred surface of the Borg cube and blocking the suicidal path of the *Chekov.*

Korsmo had a split-instant to make a decision. He made it. "Hard aport!" he shouted, and instantly Shelby cut hard to the left. The newcomer banked hard and neatly dove out of the *Chekov*'s way. It angled down and away from the Borg ship and suddenly a tractor beam had grabbed the *Chekov* firmly, taking it in tow.

It was a starship, and even through the battered viewscreen, Shelby was able to make out the registry number on the underside of the saucer section: NCC-2544. "It's the *Repulse!*" she said.

"The *Repulse?*" Korsmo couldn't believe it. "What's she doing here?"

"Saving our butts, Captain."

The *Repulse* swung around, releasing its tractor beam hold on the *Chekov,* and headed back towards the Borg ship.

"Open a channel. *Repulse!* That you, Taggert?"

"You've looked better, Korsmo," came the voice of Captain Ariel Taggert. "Sit back and watch the fireworks. Our engineer Argyle has got a knockout punch that Commander Shelby should find familiar. And our sensors say that the Borg ship won't have enough power to repel it for another ten seconds. Fortunately, we're ready in three . . . two . . . one . . . fire!"

Power churned around the deflector dish of the *Repulse,* and an instant later a massive charge of energy lashed out. It struck the Borg ship dead on, and huge pieces of the craft were blown away, faster than the monster could possibly repair.

Shelby's eyes widened. "That was Geordi's idea!

Powering an energy blast via the warp engines and pushing it through the main deflector dish! But they were prepared for it when we tried it!"

"They may be prepared this time," said Korsmo, "but they weren't ready. They may not have been expecting it from another ship, and they didn't have the power to counter it anyway."

The structure of the Borg ship actually seemed to crumble inward, power cells unable to cope with the sudden and total loss. The entire ship was held together by the collective strength of the Borg, and with no strength, there was no ship. As the *Repulse* kept up with the blast, second after long second, the Borg ship tried to rally, but it had no defenses to muster.

Shelby and Korsmo watched in helpless amazement as the *Repulse,* using the strategy that didn't work for the *Enterprise,* blasted the Borg ship. The vessel lost all cohesion and simply came apart, huge fragments tumbling away.

"Son of a bitch," said Shelby. "It would have worked. Riker will be pleased to know."

Riker leaped forward, under the swinging arm of Reannon, and hit the controls. The *Enterprise* surged gamely ahead, the impulse engines roaring.

The Borg ship's subspace field seemed to be twisting like a thing alive as the *Enterprise* ripped away. Geordi, fighting down his shock over the sudden and violent appearance of Reannon, quickly rerouted the navigation systems through the engineer station and pushed the impulse engines as far as they would go. He watched the monitors, sure that any second the overworked engines were going to blow the saucer section clear off the secondary hull.

It seemed as if the *Enterprise* actually stretched,

space warping back on itself around it, and then the mighty starship leaped free. Ahead of them, space was collapsing into a dazzling, spiralling whirlpool of light. The *Enterprise* vaulted towards it, the thick legs of impulse power picking up speed with every step.

Reannon swung her metal arm at Riker and he blocked it, slamming a fist forward into her stomach. She doubled over and, with a quick turn, Riker hurled her towards Worf. The Klingon snagged her and held her immobile with a hammerlock.

"Get her the hell out of here!" shouted Riker. As Worf obeyed, shoving her towards the turbolift and following her in, Riker continued, "Geordi, what's happening! Are we clear? You said we had only seconds!"

The light around them was blinding, blinding to everyone except Geordi, whose VISOR immediately made the brilliance bearable. And then the *Enterprise* ripped through the undulating fabric of space and out into the blessed peace of normalcy.

"Clear! We're clear!" Geordi crowed. "We made it!"

Riker noticed, on the screen, that another starship had shown up, and it was at that moment pounding the other Borg vessel with energy blasts that seemed devastating. It looked like the *Repulse*. He also noted, in a flash, the dire condition of the crippled *Chekov*. But first things had to be first. "Where's the Borg ship we dropped the warp bubble on? Did it work?"

The monitor switched to a rear view and there, rippling behind them, was a huge area of space that looked like a lake someone had just dropped a stone in.

It continued to ripple.

Then it flattened, seeming almost to turn sideways, as if something was struggling to get out.

"I don't believe it," said Riker. "I do not believe it."

The space where the Borg ship had been had now coalesced into a visible square, as if someone had simple cut a section out of the fabric of space with shears and walked away with it. The square took on form and substance, and then twisted on its axis and pushed out into a cube.

The Borg ship was back, and directly behind them. "I think we made them mad," said Geordi.

Chapter Twenty-two

VASTATOR OF THE BORG pushed the button of the large phaser that was pointed point-blank at Picard.

Nothing happened.

Picard, for his part, was already moving. He knew what the Ferengi did not: that after a type II personal phaser released a sustained blast at setting 16, there was an automatic cool-down period. Otherwise the weapon would overheat and, sooner or later, explode. That cool-down was precisely six seconds.

That was enough for Picard to cover the distance and ram his shoulder into Vastator. The Borg stumbled back, holding on to the phaser as tightly as he could, but Picard grabbed at it and managed to get a solid grip. They struggled, shoving against each other, and then Picard stumbled back, the phaser slipping out of his hands.

He dodged behind one of the upright crystal slabs, flattening against it.

"Picard," snarled the voice of the Ferengi. It was absolutely uncanny. There was a trace of the persistent obnoxious overtones of a Ferengi, but it was combined with the icy machine-like precision of the Borg. "Picard . . . let us deal."

The thing was stalking him. "What is there to deal about?" said Picard.

He heard the sudden whine of the phaser and the crystal that he was hiding behind started to superheat. He lunged for cover once more as the crystal exploded. He toyed with the idea of charging again but rejected it. The Borg was too far away, and might even be hiding behind another crystal. Six seconds was too short a time in which to charge a target when you didn't know exactly where it was.

The crystal slabs were maze-like, providing rudimentary shelter. He saw his face reflected in it. His face was screaming, as if the Many were personifying his personal agony. The agony of helplessness. Meters away, Delcara was dying. He knew that. And kilometers away, his ship was in the midst of battle, and he wasn't there.

What madness had possessed him? He had told himself that coming to the ship, coming directly to Delcara, he could persuade her to abandon the planet-killer. Once that was done, he had been certain the power could then be harnessed for the Federation. The ultimate defense against the Borg.

That was what he had believed. But was it the truth? Or had he been chasing a crazed dream of decades ago, a dream that was conjured up by a young, inexperienced teenager named Jean-Luc, and insanely pursued by an adult madman named Picard.

"Picard!" came the voice of the Ferengi Borg again, and again the phaser lashed out. This time, though, it was at the crystal slab to his right. The crystal sizzled and crumbled beneath the onslaught, and Picard put his arm up to shield his face as pieces flew right past him.

So the Ferengi didn't know exactly where he was. That was comforting. And the crystal blocks were so superdense that they didn't simply vanish, but instead put up a resistance and even maintained molecular cohesion in defeat.

He cast a glance in Delcara's direction, but his view was cut off. That was fortunate. He knew it would have been rather disheartening if he could have seen her.

Another crystal—further to his right—blew apart, accompanied by the whine of what had once been his phaser. The Borg was clearly starting to become impatient. "Picard," he said again.

"What do you want!" called out Picard, and then for good measure dropped back, scurrying crab-like to another crystal slab directly behind him.

"I am prepared to deal," said Vastator.

"Since when do the Borg deal?" demanded Picard. He didn't trust the Ferengi when they were normal Ferengi. He sure as hell didn't trust them when they'd been converted to walking cybernetic nightmares. "I would have assumed deals are irrelevant."

"You are a special case . . ." and then he paused and added with chilling familiarity, "Locutus."

Picard held his breath, waiting for the chill to pass through him. "Locutus is dead!" he called.

"Locutus is inoperative. Locutus can be restored."

"You'll have to kill me first!"

Vastator fired again at the slab behind which Picard had been hiding moments before. It blew apart especially violently and Picard thanked whatever gods were orchestrating this insanity that he was crouching behind a crystal slab for protection. A number of shards hurtled past him, looking unpleasantly sharp.

"I do not understand you," said Vastator. His voice sounded farther away, but Picard did not dare to stick his head out and check. Curiosity could kill the captain. "Your resistance is futile. We simply wish to make you a part of the New Order."

"The New Order!" Picard called back, wishing that he could shoot back with a phaser instead of with words. "The most disdained words in the English language. In the twentieth century they spoke of a New Order, and they were still mouthing such inanities when World War III began. So don't speak to me of the New Order of the Borg."

"Come now, Picard," said Vastator. His voice seemed to be moving once again, and Picard couldn't tell whether it was closer or further. "Do not forsake the Borg. Do not turn your back on us."

"Why? Because I'll end up with a knife in it?"

Another howl of the phaser, another crystal slab blown to bits.

And Picard suddenly gasped and looked down. A shard was sticking out of his right leg, blood trickling from the wound. Pain was creeping through the leg and he felt it starting to go numb.

He heard another phaser blast and it was striking the slab he was behind. As he lunged for another slab to his left, it suddenly clicked into his mind just what it was that the entire crystal set up was reminding him of: a cemetery. An array of closely set headstones, row upon row of the dead buried deep beneath the soil. It was not a pleasant realization.

He crawled on his belly, sucking in dust and coughing. He bit down on his lower lip, determined not to cry out, and gripped the shard that was sticking out of his right thigh. He pulled it out and internalized the agony that threatened to paralyze his entire body.

The vessel around him suddenly started to shake. Something was happening, something else. Something that seemed to suddenly provoke Vastator further. He fired three times, all around Picard, and the captain refused to give in, refused to sit still, refused to surrender, although every nerve ending was screaming for rest. His brain just wanted to shut down, tried to convince him that nothing mattered more than just resting for a few minutes, that's all, just a few minutes.

"We simply want to improve the quality of life for all species!" announced Vastator, saying words that had a haunting ring of familiarity to Picard.

"How do you intend to do that?" shouted back Picard.

"By improving the quality of the Borg, of course," said Vastator. "Then the improved Borg will assimilate all species, and there will be an end to war. An end to struggle."

"An end to imagination!"

"The Borg will assimilate that as well. Imagination assimilation has already begun, utilizing that which was taken from Locutus, and now from Vastator. The Borg continue to adapt and improve. That is why the Borg will triumph. Picard . . . I have endeavored to give you the opportunity to show yourself willingly. Such has not been your choice. So I shall force you." There was a brief pause and then the Borg said, "Show yourself or I will completely destroy the female."

"Leave her alone! You've killed her already!"

"There is a spark of life. But I will take it now, unless you show yourself."

Vastator stood still for a long moment, contemplating the foolishness of it all. "As you wish, Picard."

"Wait!"

And Picard stepped out into the middle of the pathway that led down to the crystal column in which Delcara was contained. Blood was pouring down his leg, and he had to lean with one hand against one of the remaining crystal slabs in order to remain standing.

"Picard," said Vastator. "You see? The Borg would not have acted thus before Locutus and, later, I were created. The Borg would not have conceived of such self-sacrifice. You value the life of one individual over another. Locutus and I have given the Borg new understanding. Locutus can again."

"Locutus," Picard repeated firmly, "is dead." His face was pale and he felt numbness spreading to his foot. He could barely move his toes. Walking seemed to involve commanding an inert slab of meat that was his right leg in name only.

"I mean you no harm, Picard," said Vastator. "If I had, you would be dead."

"Vastator," said Picard slowly, "who were you before?" He took another step forward.

Vastator was not concerned. Picard posed no threat. His leg was crippled and, besides, Vastator was holding a phaser. "Before is irrelevant."

"It's relevant to me," said Picard.

"I was called Daimon Turane of Ferengi. Daimon Turane is irrelevant. Ferengi are irrelevant. Only the Borg matter."

"Turane," said Picard slowly, with effort. He was now barely ten feet from the Borg. "I remember . . . what it was like when I was Locutus. I remember that there was a part of me, hidden away, that they couldn't touch. And that part was screaming for release, screaming even for death, rather than a continuation of that unnatural existence."

"You romanticize, Picard. Romance is irrelevant."

"It's not irrelevant, damn it!" Picard said, trying not to fall. Now he was eight feet away, and then seven. "This shell called Vastator is not you! It's some

371

representation, a re-creation. It's not really and truly you. Fight to be let out. Fight for release. On the *Enterprise,* we can help you, as I was helped."

"Depriving you of Locutus was not help," said Vastator. "It deprived you of your place in the New Order."

"There will be *no* New Order! Daimon Turane would understand that. Vastator can not. Vastator can't understand that humanity will fight and keep on fighting. Will never stop resisting, and will always find a way. Throughout our history there have been a series of conquerors, one after the other, and we have survived them all."

Vastator cocked his head slightly. "You require a better class of conqueror." He leveled the phaser at Picard's chest. "No further. Choose. Subject yourself to my wishes and the rule of the Borg, or die. There is no other choice."

"Fight them, Turane! Fight them—!"

"There is no Turane. There is only Vastator. Choose now."

"You won't kill me with that," said Picard with confidence.

"Is that your last, futile hope, Picard?" said Vastator. "Depending upon an appeal to a being who no longer exists, telling that phantom that it cannot bring itself to put an end to you? You believe that Vastator is inhibited by your petty morals from destroying you with this phaser?"

"Not at all," said Picard.

"What, then, do you mean, that I won't kill you?"

"I mean that a phaser at setting 16 has a capacity of only ten shots before being utterly depleted. You're out of power."

Vastator aimed and fired.

A phaser blast hit Picard dead center of the chest.

The captain staggered back, arms pinwheeling, and then he caught himself on the edge of one of the slabs. He felt a stiffness in his chest, and the wind had been knocked out of him. Vastator strode towards him and squeezed the button again. And this time, there was nothing.

"Maybe eleven shots," admitted Picard, "although the last one would be substantially depleted. A direct hit at setting sixteen and I'd be free-floating atoms by now. All you had left was one minor burst that would have rendered a hummingbird unconscious. Maybe."

Vastator tossed aside the phaser and came straight at Picard, leading with his mechanical appendage. A blue-tinged charge of electricity danced around the end of it.

Picard dropped to one knee as the deadly metal arm passed just over his head. At the same time, he yanked from hiding within his environmental jacket a shard of crystal, dark with blood and recently pulled from his own thigh. Vastator was carried forward by the weight of the arm and he overshot his mark. For a split second he was off-balance and vulnerable, and Picard took that moment. The captain swung his arm upward and drove the point of the crystal shard deep into Vastator's chest.

No blood came out. He might just as likely have hit some sort of circuitry. It didn't matter. It had the same effect. Vastator stumbled back, making strange, choking sounds, and he tried to bring his mechanical arm up to grab Picard once more. He didn't even come close. With a groan like a falling tree, Vastator tumbled forward and fell heavily to the floor.

Picard sagged, his energy depleted, and started to pull himself away from the collapsed form of the Borg. And then, to his horror, Vastator started to raise himself, as if doing a push-up. Then he flipped over onto his back, staring up at the ceiling, and his mouth moved, trying to form words. He gasped out in a low, hoarse voice, "Pi—card."

The captain did not answer at first, and then, trying to overcome the pain, he said, "Yes."

Vastator's mouth moved once more and no words emerged. But Picard believed—although he would never be positive—that the words formed on the lips of the Ferengi Borg were *Thank you*. Then the head of Vastator slumped to one side and didn't move.

Picard turned and saw, what seemed a mile away, the encasement of Delcara. Biting his bottom lip so hard that he was certain he would chew right through it, Picard hauled himself to his feet, clutching his right thigh with both hands as if he were trying to hold the leg on. He staggered down the aisle, feeling like some sort of crazy groom at a surreal wedding. His bride waited for him, near death, *'Til death did them part.*

The ground began to shake around him once more, and the last few steps were desperately hurried. He practically threw himself the rest of the way and landed against the crystal column. It was thicker than any of the slabs, which was why it had survived as much of the phaser pounding as it did. Not enough, though. Not nearly enough.

She was looking at him.

Not her holographic image—she herself. Her luminous eyes were open, staring down at him from a face that was a charred memory of what it had been. There was not an inch of her that hadn't been damaged. Her skin was broiled black, covered with cracks and rips, lifeblood oozing out. Once the crystal had been a symbol of purity, but now it was smoked and becoming smeared with the thick coagulation of vital fluids. Her long, lovely hair had been burned away, as had her eyebrows. Here and there her flesh and muscle had been so violently scorched that the bone beneath was visible, and that, too, was blackened and splintered. The lips that had once brushed against his forehead had been burned away, cracked and mutilated teeth visible in blackened gums.

She was a ghastly, flame-withered shell of her beautiful self. A single tear moved down her cheek, a crystalline tear, leaving a trail of glimmering hard wetness down her face.

Her ruined jaw moved, but the voice sounded in his head.

Oh my sweet Picard, she said. *Look what they've done to me.*

"The *Enterprise,*" said Picard urgently. His hands pressed against the crystal. There were cracks through it, but he still couldn't pry it away. He wanted to touch her. He wanted to cradle her burned and broken body in his arms and brush away her tears. "We can get you back to the *Enterprise.* We can save you there. We have to."

And if they can't, dear Picard? If they can't? Then I die, and none of it matters.

"They can! But we have to get back to them! My ship needs me! With you or without you, I—"

Your ship is safe, my love. In fact, it has helped me. It has given us the strength we need to do what must be done.

"What are you talking about—?"

And the planet-killer began to move.

Chapter Twenty-three

BOYAJIAN, THE SECURITY GUARD on the *Enterprise* who was standing outside the brig of Dantar of Penzatti, looked surprised when he saw Lieutenant Worf striding towards him, dragging the woman who had once been a part of the Borg. She was pulling at his grip, but only half-heartedly. With no patience at all, the Klingon stopped at the brig directly across the corridor and shoved her in. Then he activated the force field and turned to the guard. "Make sure she doesn't go anywhere."

"Yes sir," said Boyajian, not fully understanding what had happened. But he knew that look on the Klingon's face well enough to know that further questions would not be particularly welcome, much less answered. So he kept his peace as Worf turned and hurried back down the hallway.

The woman stood there for a moment, looking confused, and then she went to the bunk at the opposite side of the brig and lay down, her back to the corridor.

But Dantar had seen her brought in, and he began

to taunt her loudly. "Hey, Borg!" he shouted. "Remember me? The one whose family you destroyed!"

"Hey! Knock it off," snapped Boyajian.

Dantar ignored him. "Oh, but you probably wouldn't. I'm just one of many, and it's all the same to you, isn't it. Come in, massacre a few million living, breathing, loving beings, and then move on. All in a day's work for you."

Across the way, he could see her shoulders starting to shake, and the sounds of choked sobs. "Oh, am I upsetting you now?"

"Look, I'm warning you," Boyajian said, even angrier.

"Warn *her!*" shouted Dantar. "Warn her that I'll never forget. Nor will the rest of my people! Warn her that if she thinks she's ever going to go back to some sort of normal life, she can forget it. She has the blood of millions on her hands. Because she was one of them. One of the damned Borg. And no matter what she does, and no matter what she pretends she is doing, she'll never be able to erase that. It's too much. It cuts through everything! Do you hear me, Borg? Do you? Never forget! Never forget what you did! There's your warning! There's your life! Borg! Monster! Monster beyond imagination, doomed and damned forever and ever—"

The racking sobs grew louder and louder, and Boyajian pulled out his phaser and aimed it at Dantar. "I have never fired on an unarmed prisoner," he said angrily, "but so help me, I will this time. I'll put you to sleep until the beginning of the next century if you don't shut up!"

Dantar stared at him sullenly for a moment, as if trying to decide whether the guard was bluffing or not. Obviously he decided on the latter, for he retreated to the other side of the brig, contenting himself with the sobbing from across the corridor as the beginning of what he hoped would be a long and terrible penance that the bitch woman would suffer for what she had done. However long it was, it would not be enough.

He was disappointed when the sniffling eventually trailed off, and decided that soon he would have to provoke her once more. He hoped they didn't change her location anytime soon.

Worf made it back to the bridge in record time, but what he discovered there wasn't especially pleasing. The Borg ship had reappeared on the screen, and Geordi was just finishing saying something about making them mad. The Klingon immediately went to the tactical station, replacing the man who had substituted for him.

Chafin at conn had managed to lift the insensate Data off himself. Having no idea what to do with him, he propped the android back up in his place at ops. It was truly insane. If it weren't for the sizeable crease in the side of Data's head, you wouldn't know there was anything wrong with him as he sat at his post.

"Commander," said Worf, "energy readings of the remaining Borg vessel are at only twenty-seven percent of norm."

"It took a hell of a lot out of them," Geordi said.

At that moment the planet-killer swung towards the massive Borg craft, its great maw coming toward it. A beam of glorious blue light emerged from its maw and seized the Borg.

"It's a tractor beam!" said Geordi. "Delcara is trying to pull the Borg ship in!"

"Borg vessel is now at thirty-three percent of norm and climbing," reported Worf. "It is resisting the pull of the tractor beam."

"If it won't be pulled, maybe it'll be pushed," said Riker. "Mr. La Forge . . . status on deflectors."

"Fully charged and ready."

Riker's face was set. "Set tractor beams for repulse, rather than attract, and aim them straight at the Borg at full power."

"I can only keep that up for five-point-three minutes before risking power burnout," Geordi told him. "Also, with the tonnage of the Borg ship, we'll practically have to be touching them to have any effect."

"Activate tractor beams while bringing us gradually to within five thousand kilometers. Hopefully, with the combination of the planet-killer's and our tractor beams we'll have enough power. Engage."

"Here's hoping," murmured Geordi, and he carried out the command.

The *Enterprise* shuddered slightly as they approached the Borg ship, doing everything they could to push the ship towards the fate that was awaiting it.

"Why doesn't the planet-eater fire on it?" demanded Worf.

"The tractor beam probably takes up less energy than that anti-proton blaster," speculated Geordi. "Must be trying to conserve power."

The Borg struggled against the pull of the tractor beam, like a spider caught in a web.

"Commander, Borg is locking offensive weaponry on us!" Worf announced suddenly.

"Deflectors on full! Maintain tractor beam!" ordered Riker quickly.

Within an instant the shields were cloaking the *Enterprise* once more, just in time, as the Borg blast ricocheted off. The tractor continued to push.

And a second later the great starship was joined by another. The *Repulse* pulled alongside, and although she had depleted mightily her engine stores with the hammering she'd given the Borg before, she still had more than enough to provide additional tractor beam push.

Slowly, inexorably, the Borg ship fell towards the maw of the planet-killer. The flames from the massive doomsday weapon's conversion engines seemed to lick out hungrily towards the cube, as if it were a child eagerly balancing a tasty sugar cube on its tongue.

And at that moment the Borg ship's tractor beam lashed out.

"Sir!" called out Worf. "They've snagged the *Repulse!* They're dragging her in with them!"

"Photon torpedoes and phasers! Fire!"

The weaponry smashed down against the exterior of the Borg ship, blowing pieces into rubble, and still the cube stubbornly hung on to the starship. The *Repulse* struggled in its grasp, trying to pull away, its entire exterior trembling with the exertion.

"Reverse tractors!" said Riker. "Grab the *Repulse!* Pull her out of there!"

Instantly Geordi obeyed the command, and a moment later he had the *Repulse* firmly in the grasp of the *Enterprise* tractors.

Freed from the pounding of the starship tractor beams, the Borg ship started to surge forward . . .

But it was too late. It was too far into the maw of the doomsday machine, and the planet-killer's tractor beam dragged it all the way inside. The flames of the engine engulfed it, blasted it apart, and a massive explosion ripped from the heart of the machine, outward. The *Repulse,* with the aid of her impulse engines, the *Enterprise* tractor beam, and a healthy dollop of just damned good luck, rode the crest of the blast and hurtled out into space with only some bumps and bruises to show for the experience.

For a brief moment Geordi La Forge thought that was it for the planet-killer. He had studied up on the history of the previous one, once they'd realized what they were dealing with, and discovered that the exploding engines of a starship were enough to put it out of commission.

But his readings quickly told him a different story. This monster was considerably larger and more powerful, and it hungrily digested the raw power that the exploding Borg ship provided it. It feasted, thriving on it. The giant wounds on the surface seemed to be disappearing, and Geordi realized what was happening. The thing was repairing itself.

But it was slow, sluggish, and Geordi said as much to Riker. "Its power levels are rising, but it's not maneuvering the way it did before."

"Then what—?"

Riker didn't get to finish the sentence, because suddenly the planet-killer leaped forward.

"Planet-killer resuming heading, at warp seven!"

"Follow it, warp seven! Engage!"

The *Enterprise* took off after it, and the *Repulse,* warp engines exhausted after the assault on the Borg, was unable to follow. So instead they set about rescuing the remaining crew members of the unfortunate *Chekov.*

As the *Enterprise* hurtled along behind the planet-killer, Riker snapped, "Try and raise the captain."

"Nothing, sir," said Worf.

"We're still receiving interference with our transporter locks?"

"Yes sir. The vessel is still generating a scrambling field that makes locking on and transporting impossible."

"Damn," murmured Riker. "Bridge to transporter room."

"Transporter room," came O'Brien's voice.

"O'Brien, monitor that beast we're pursuing. If at any point the interference clears and you can lock onto the captain, beam him back immediately."

"But sir!" said O'Brien with alarm. "We can't beam him back while in warp unless we're matching the speed of the other vessel exactly. Otherwise his molecules'll wind up smeared all over the transporter deck!"

"I know that," said Riker coldly. "Leave that to us. Bridge out. Geordi, take the conn."

Geordi was momentarily surprised. He hadn't been at conn for quite some time, but he immediately understood what Riker wanted—the most experienced available hand in command of the ship's speed. Data, with his computer mind, would have been perfect. Unfortunately, Data wasn't even in shape to put his boots on at the moment. Geordi immediately took the position as Chafin slid aside, deferring to the chief engineer.

"Planet-killer moving at warp eight."

"Match it."

"Warp nine."

"Keep up with her, Mr. La Forge, or we'll lose him," said Riker.

"Warp nine, sir. With everything we've been through, we can maintain this speed for twenty minutes."

"If I'm not mistaken, Mr. La Forge, that will shortly be moot," said Riker grimly. And then, under his breath he murmured, "Come on, Captain. Get through to us."

Picard gripped the crystal encasement that was going to serve as Delcara's coffin. He looked up at her and could practically sense her life ebbing from her.

He knew what was happening, instinctively, as clearly as if he himself had decided on the course of action. She sensed that she was dying, even if she wasn't admitting it to herself. And driven by desperation, she was sending her vessel hurtling through space at whatever speed she could muster, trying to accomplish her insane dream.

He pounded in frustration on the crystal. "Delcara, stop! *Stop!*"

Her voice was barely a whisper in his head. *No, dear Jean-Luc. It's too late for that. I'm going to make it.*

"You won't!"

I will. I must. For them. For me.

"Delcara, you are dying. If you don't let me get you to the *Enterprise*, we cannot save you!"

Save me for what? Her voice was like a dying butterfly in his mind. *A lifetime of regret? A lifetime of frustration? A lifetime of a mission unfulfilled?*

"Enough of your mission!" shouted Picard. "Enough of your hatred and vendetta. Enough! You've let it consume you for far too long! Put an end to it!"

That, dear Picard, is what I'm trying to do. And you will be with me.

"Delcara—"

I will avenge the races. The Many. The Many I've lost. The Many who cry out. Every shattered dream, every word spoken in hatred, every life lost to senseless violence and cruelty, mine, all mine. So much to do. So much to do. Her voice sounded singsong within his head, as if she were a child speaking. *I never realized. I've been lazy. So much to do, and who knows what could happen. The Borg first. The Borg now. I do not feel like waiting anymore.*

"You don't feel like waiting because you're dying! Damn you! Come out! Come to me! You speak of love! Now act from love! Now! *Now!*"

And those eyes looked at him from deep within the ruined face.

Later. I promise. You and I, together, will do it all later.

"Warp . . . nine-point-two . . . nine-point-four . . ." Geordi was calling it off like a death knell. "I can't believe this."

The starfield hurtled past like multicolored strings. God forbid they hit a planet or even an asteroid at this speed. Ships could search for a thousand years and still not find all the pieces of the *Enterprise.*

"Warp nine-point-six!" called out Geordi. "Maximum rated speed! Danger of coolant overheating!"

The planet-killer showed no signs of slowing.

"She's at nine-point-seven! Nine-point-eight!"

"Catch up, Mr. La Forge," said Riker, with a voice so hard he could have driven nails with it.

The *Enterprise* roared forward, stress on every part of her hull.

No one spoke. They all knew what was happening and what was at stake. And their margin for error had been shredded to ten percent.

In the transporter room, O'Brien's fingers hovered over the controls, his eyes scanning for some sign, any sign, of life readings from the planet-killer. The scrambling was still in effect, his attempts to lock in continually thwarted. The nightmarish image of Captain Picard materializing in the platform in some hideously demolecularized state would not erase from his mind. He'd seen it happen once, and even now he woke up with cold shakes on occasion at night.

"Come on, Captain," he said. "A whisper. Something."

In a way that Picard could not explain, he sensed how fast they were going, and how much faster still they were going to go.

"You can't do this!" he shouted. "I know what you're trying to do! You're trying to exceed all known warp boundaries! You want to get to Borg space within minutes instead of years! You're hoping to cheat death! But you can only do that if you come with me!"

Cheat death and cheat myself. No, lovely Picard. You and I—

"No! Damn you! There is no you and I!" and he slammed his fist against the crystal. His hands were inches away from her, but they might as well have been miles. "You're insane! You're mad with vengeance! You won't listen to me! You won't listen to Guinan! You only listen to the voices that scream to pursue your obsession! I won't participate in it!"

You said you love me. Yet you only want me to come with you. You must come with me now, beautiful Picard. Wonderful Pi—

"You're mad! I thought there was hope for you!" and he turned away from her on his damaged leg. The agony spurred him on. "I thought there was something to be salvaged and loved! I wanted something that didn't exist anymore. That never existed! You were in my mind, and that's all you ever were! I reject you! Now and forever, I am no longer yours! I belong to myself, and I will have no part of you! None! *None!"*

And Delcara screamed.

"Warp nine-point-nine," said Geordi tonelessly.

"Increase speed to nine-point-nine," Riker told him, every word leaden.

"Engines will shut down automatically in two minutes," said Geordi even as he complied. Even under the best of circumstances, they could have sustained that speed for only ten minutes.

"Now or never, Captain," whispered Troi.

In Ten-Forward, Guinan watched out the window, and waited.

And knew.

Delcara screamed, and it seared into Picard's mind and soul, and he cried out a name.

A name. And a word, both the same.

And the name and word was *Vendetta,* spoken with hatred and fury and loathing. There was no trace of love.

And a voice cut through his mind and spoke four words in response. And the response was simple and eternal: *I thought you understood.*

And he disappeared in a haze of blue.

"Warp nine-point-nine-nine," said Geordi, pronouncing a death sentence.

At nearly 8000 times the speed of light, the doomsday machine, second and final draft, hurtled away. The *Enterprise's* engines powered down.

And then, in a burst of power that was unrecorded in the annals of Starfleet and physics, the doomsday machine, Mark two, leaped beyond all known speeds.

Alien warp technology of a like that had never been seen before, and never would again, smashed through the barriers of time and space, all driven by one overwhelming need.

It tore, unstoppably, and inevitably, towards the speed limit of the galaxy. Towards the unreachable. Toward warp ten.

And vanished.

Chapter Twenty-four

SWEET PICARD WAS GONE.

Delcara understood. Sometimes, for those you love, you have to let them go. None of it mattered anymore. He had his life, and she had hers.

The *Enterprise* was long gone now, unable to keep up. Delcara had reached and exceeded speeds that had been thought to be impossible. But nothing was impossible if the will and the drive and the need were strong enough.

Her life. Her vendetta. A journey of years would instead be a journey of minutes. She stood on the brink of accomplishing that which had driven her for so long. She would confront the Borg. She would defeat the Borg.

And after that, who knew? Perhaps she would return to Picard. Anything could happen. She was living proof of that. The universe was an infinity of maybes.

She held her breath. The pain was gone.

Just a few more minutes . . .

Chapter Twenty-five

SWEET PICARD WAS GONE.

Delcara understood. Sometimes, for those you love, you have to let them go. None of it mattered anymore. He had his life, and she had hers.

The *Enterprise* was long gone now, unable to keep up. Delcara had reached and exceeded speeds that had been thought to be impossible. But nothing was impossible if the will and the drive and the need were strong enough.

Her life. Her vendetta. A journey of years would instead be a journey of minutes. She stood on the brink of accomplishing that which had driven her for so long. She would confront the Borg. She would defeat the Borg.

And after that, who knew? Perhaps she would return to Picard. Anything could happen. She was living proof of that. The universe was an infinity of maybes.

She held her breath. The pain was gone.

Just a few more minutes . . .

Chapter Twenty-six

SWEET PICARD WAS GONE.

Delcara understood. Sometimes, for those you love, you have to let them go. None of it mattered anymore. He had his life, and she had hers.

The *Enterprise* was long gone now, unable to keep up. Delcara had reached and exceeded speeds that had been thought to be impossible. But nothing was impossible if the will and the drive and the need were strong enough.

Her life. Her vendetta. A journey of years would instead be a journey of minutes. She stood on the brink of accomplishing that which had driven her for so long. She would confront the Borg. She would defeat the Borg.

And after that, who knew? Perhaps she would return to Picard. Anything could happen. She was living proof of that. The universe was an infinity of maybes.

She held her breath. The pain was gone.

Just a few more minutes . . .

Chapter Twenty-seven

RIKER WATCHED IN APPROVAL as Picard slid off the biobed and tested the strength of his leg.

"You'll be limping for a couple of days," said Dr. Crusher. "So be sure to take it easy.

"Yes, Doctor."

"Oh, so he listens to you, does he?" said Katherine Pulaski, taking a few minutes to visit from the *Repulse,* which was cruising at warp one next to the *Enterprise,* en route to Starbase 42. The surviving crew members of the *Chekov* were all stable. In fact, Captain Korsmo was positively obnoxious, and she welcomed the opportunity to take a brief respite back aboard the *Enterprise.*

"Well, it's not easy," said Crusher. "He does have a tendency to have a mind of his own."

"That can so get in the way. By the way, Beverly, I heard about Wesley being accepted into the Academy. Congratulations." She shook her head. "So much to catch up in the half hour or so I can spare here. I hear Worf had a son? Data had a daughter?"

"Not with each other," said Riker dryly.

"Data as a father." She shook her head. "I don't

usually underestimate individuals I meet, but when I do, I don't do it in half measures."

"And how are you doing back on the *Repulse?*" asked Riker.

She shrugged and smiled. "You know me. The moment I got there, I just laid down the law, and everything was fine."

"I can just imagine," said Picard. "Doctor Crusher, now that you're done treating me, you might want to give O'Brien a sedative. He's still jumpy after his rather miraculous split second transport of me at warp nine-point-nine."

"He said the scrambling signal just stopped," said Riker. "The moment it did, he locked on and beamed you out. Closer than we like to call it."

At that moment Geordi entered, his arms folded. "Captain, I was hoping you had a moment to fill me in on what you saw when you were over in the planet-killer. I have a theory or two about what happened with—"

And at that moment the alarmed voice of security guard Boyajian called out through the sickbay inter-com, "Dr. Crusher! Emergency medical team to the brig! Immediately!"

Immediately Crusher bolted out, followed by Pulaski, Geordi, Riker, a limping Picard, and a medtech with a crash cart.

They weren't all able to fit into one turbolift, so the medical personnel took the first one that came, and seconds later Picard and his officers were on the other. He found himself automatically leaning on Riker's and Geordi's shoulders for additional support.

Seconds later they emerged on the lower deck, where the brig was situated. But before they saw anything, they heard something.

It was laughter. Loud, raucous laughter, coming from the area of the brig.

Dantar of Penzatti.

They got there and saw Dantar, leaning just inside the forcefield of the brig, laughing and pointing and laughing once again. Boyajian was shouting at him, furious, face almost purple.

Picard, Riker, and Geordi came forward and saw the disturbance was in the brig directly across from Dantar. Before they could get there, Boyajian was standing in front of them, addressing Picard. "I'm sorry, sir!" he kept saying, over and over. "I had no idea! She was just lying there so quietly, I thought she'd cried herself to sleep! I just left her alone! And then I saw the blood dripping down, and it was too late—"

"What?!"

Geordi pushed his way through, suddenly knowing and sensing with hideous certainty. He looked into the brig. Riker and Picard were just behind him and, when Riker saw, he put a steadying hand on Geordi's shoulder.

Crusher was passing a tricorder over Reannon's body, but it was merely a formality. She was shaking her head in dismay.

Reannon was lying still on the bunk, as a pool of blood collected beneath her. She had been half turned over now and Geordi could see her eyes staring out at nothing, just as they had for so long before. Now, though, there wasn't even life behind them—because of a long, perfect incision across her throat, dark and encrusted with blood.

Pulaski was removing something from the palm of Reannon's limp left hand. She held it up for Crusher to see.

"A scalpel?" said Crusher in astonishment, taking

393

it. She held up the laser device. "How in the hell did she get this? She must have sneaked it out of sickbay. Stuck it in her clothing."

"Worf didn't exactly have time to frisk her when he brought her here," said Riker regretfully. "But why—?"

And the word hung there.

Chapter Twenty-eight

AND AFTER THAT, who knew? Perhaps she would return to Picard. Anything could happen. She was living proof of that. The universe was an infinity of maybes.

She held her breath. The pain was gone.

Just a few more minutes . . .

Sweet Picard was gone.

Delcara understood. Sometimes, for those you love, you have to let them go. None of it mattered anymore. He had his life, and she had hers. . . .

Chapter Twenty-nine

"I FEEL HER. In here. And out there. Everywhere," she said.

In the Ten-Forward lounge, Guinan sat opposite Riker, Geordi, and Picard. The men had full glasses of synthehol in front of them.

"That's fine for you, Guinan, but it doesn't help us. Where is she?" said Riker. "Is she in Borg space? Is she dead? Is she——"

"There is an old paradox," said Guinan, "that says that if you are standing, say, a meter away from your destination, and then you travel only half that distance, and then half of that new distance, and half of that and so on . . . you'll never reach your destination. That you become infinitely closer, but never attain your goal."

Now Geordi spoke up, but he was very quiet and restrained. Usually in this type of conversation he was positively bubbly. "And there's another theory," he said, "that applies the same concept of becoming infinitely close to warp ten. The most you can reach is warp nine-point-nine-nine with an infinite number of nines repeating infinitely. And as you become infinitely closer to warp ten . . . subjective time slows down."

"I've heard of this," said Riker. "Time distorts infinitely around you as you get infinitely closer to warp ten."

"You wouldn't even know it was happening," said Geordi. "It's like, if the universe were shrinking and all units of measurement were shrinking proportionately. You have nothing to compare it to, and you don't realize that, for the rest of the universe, time is continuing normally. But for you there is no more normality. What is a second to us becomes eternity to someone who is trapped in an infinite time distortion. It's like the old line, 'The hurrieder I go, the behinder I get.'."

"But where is she?" demanded Picard. "I understand what you're saying, and I certainly know the theories, but . . . where *is* she? Is she trapped in warp space?"

"She's in warp space," said Guinan very quietly. "And subspace."

"What?"

"And she's here in Ten-Forward, and throughout the *Enterprise*," continued Guinan. "And throughout our galaxy, and throughout the cosmos. Don't you see? She's travelling eternally through time as the universe passes through her, for the universe keeps expanding. She's occupying all points of the universe simultaneously. To her, the stars will hurtle by, and she will look forward to endless tomorrows and an infinite stream of yesterdays. She'll continually pass through her own immediate past, and have no future. And she'll never know," she finished quietly. "I can't reach her. I can feel her here," and she touched her heart, "but that's all. And that's all that will ever be . . ." She looked down. "I don't think I wish to discuss it any further."

Guinan stood and walked away from the table. After a moment Riker did likewise, and headed for the bridge to keep an eye on things. Data was fully repaired from the brutal injury he'd taken, but he would be under close observation for the next twenty-four hours. Just to play it safe.

La Forge and Picard sat alone at the table, staring into their drinks.

"She always said she had all the time in the universe," said Picard slowly. "And now she does. And her vendetta, which ruled her life, will be her life. Forever. It will drive her on and on, and be the only thing in her existence, and she will never be able to accomplish it." He shook his head and, in one shot, drained his glass. "How disgustingly ironic."

Geordi didn't even look up, but asked, "What was she to you, Captain? If I may ask."

"She was . . ." He paused, trying to find words. "She was a concept. A symbol. The idea of her came to mean more to me than the actuality of her. What she represented was so pure, but the reality was far from that. In the end I tried to make her into what I envisioned her to be, and what she could never be. And yet, in a way, she is. Was. She was everything I could have asked for. Unreachable. Untouchable. Always out there, guiding me onward. I seek to touch the stars, Mr. La Forge. To brush my fingers across them, and search out the mysteries they hide. She was all of that. All of that, and more."

"You contradict yourself, Captain."

"Very well then, I contradict myself," replied Picard, the edges of his mouth crinkling slightly. "I am large. I contain multitudes."

"Shakespeare?"

"Whitman."

"Oh." He paused. "He could have been writing about Delcara."

"Yes," said Picard. "Yes, he could." He took another sip.

"I was the same way with Reannon," Geordi said after a moment. "I wanted to reach her. I wanted to do things on her behalf. And in the end, I never was able to."

"The woman was destroyed before you ever got to her, Geordi," said Picard softly. "Reannon Bonaventure died years ago. You also had an image you were striving for, that could never be achieved. Which simply proves that lieutenants and captains can both share a blindness for simple reality."

"Kind of a brutally hard knock against a quixotic view of life, isn't it," admitted Geordi. "The Borg are pretty damned big windmills to tilt with."

"But they are giants, Geordi," said Picard after a moment. "And in being caught up in the great turning arms of the Borg, we can be thrown down into the ground, or hurled upward to the stars. We all have our quests. And we do what we must, because it's expected. Because we need to. Because we want to. Because—"

"Because of Dulcinea," said Geordi, raising his glass.

Picard raised his in response. "To Dulcinea."

"To more giants," said Geordi. "And to more misadventures."

"More adventures, old friend," Picard gently corrected him, and smiled as they clinked glasses.

But the smile did not reach his eyes.

Chapter Thirty

THE UNIVERSE WAS an infinity of maybes.
She held her breath. The pain was gone.
Just a few more minutes . . .
Just a few more minutes . . .
Just a few more minutes . . .
Just a few more minutes . . .
Just a few more minutes . . .
Just a few more minutes . . .
Just a few more minutes . . .
Just a few more minutes . . .
Just a few more minutes..
Just a few more minutes.
Just a few more minutes
Just a few more minute
Just a few more minut
Just a few more minu
Just a few more min

STAR TREK:

THE FIRST 25 YEARS
by Gene Roddenberry
and Susan Sackett

"To Boldly go where no man has gone before..."

On September 8, 1966, those now-familiar words first introduced an entire generation of television viewers to STAR TREK.

Now, Gene Roddenberry, the creator/producer of this phenomenon has commemorated STAR TREK's landmark 25th Anniversary with the ultimate collector's item: STAR TREK: THE FIRST 25 YEARS

An oversized hardcover filled with both full-color and black-and-white photos, interviews and intimate glimpses behind-the-scenes, STAR TREK: THE FIRST 25 YEARS takes readers from the series inception to its network run, from cancellation to a new life through a growing network of dedicated fans, and to the incredible success of the STAR TREK motion pictures and STAR TREK: THE NEXT GENERATION.

**COMING IN HARDCOVER
FROM POCKET BOOKS IN SEPTEMBER**

POCKET
B O O K S

STAR TREK ®
THE NEXT GENERATION
Technical Manual
Mike Okuda and Rick Sternbach

The technical advisors to the smash TV hit series, STAR TREK: THE NEXT GENERATION, take readers into the incredible world they've creat ed for the show. Filled with blueprints, sketches and line drawings, this book explains the principles behind everything from the transporter to the holodeck—and takes an unprecedented look at the brand-new U.S.S. *Enterprise* NCC 1701-D.

Coming in July From Pocket Books

POCKET
B O O K S